The Waiting Time

NOVELS BY Eugenia Price

ST. SIMONS TRILOGY

Lighthouse
New Moon Rising
The Beloved Invader

FLORIDA TRILOGY

Don Juan McQueen
Maria
Margaret's Story

SAVANNAH QUARTET

Savannah
To See Your Face Again
Before the Darkness Falls
Stranger in Savannah

GEORGIA TRILOGY

Bright Captivity
Where Shadows Go
Beauty from Ashes

The Waiting Time

Eugenia Price

St. Martin's Paperbacks

This novel is a work of historical fiction. Names, characters, places, and incidents relating to nonhistorical figures are the products of the author's imagination. Any resemblance of such nonhistorical incidents, places, or figures to actual events, locales, or persons, living or dead, is purely coincidental.

Published by arrangement with Doubleday

THE WAITING TIME

Copyright © 1997 by Eugenia Price.

Library of Congress Catalog Card Number: 96-8250

ISBN: 0-312-96506-0

Printed in the United States of America

Doubleday hardcover edition / May 1997
St. Martin's Paperbacks edition / September 1998

St. Martin's Paperbacks are published by St. Martin's Press, 175 Fifth Avenue, New York, NY 10010.

10 9 8 7 6 5 4 3 2 1

For

SARAH BELL EDMOND

Prologue

September 1853

On the night of September 3, 1853, spirited Abigail Banes sat on the buggy seat beside the man she had just promised to marry and hugged herself with joy and anticipation. The well-shaped, aristocratic hands of her future husband, Eli Edward Allyn, were reining the horse in front of the Banes family's Mount Vernon Street house on Boston's Beacon Hill. Abby had been courted by Eli Edward Allyn for exactly one year today. On September 3, 1852, he had escorted her to their first dance in celebration of her birthday and, since that night, all of life had been transformed and would never, never be the same again.

She would always miss her beloved late father, Gerald Banes, but now and forever, she would have Eli and his coastal rice plantation in Georgia and no other young woman could ask for more. It worried Eli that he was so much older than she, but as his wife, Abby planned to be blissfully happy. Her enduring girlhood dream, heightened by the many romantic novels she'd read, was about to come true. She and Eli were getting married before the end of the year so he could start learning all about rice culture on his recently purchased plantation. And not only was he going to take her to the Georgia coast for a honeymoon, but they were going there to live together for always. Abby had so romanticized the area, she'd even thought of writing a novel about it herself—about life lived under spreading magnolia trees laden with ivory blossoms, where lovers could meander along flower-lined paths through lush gardens, tended, as would be her every wish, by smiling, singing, contented dusky-skinned slaves.

As though they were so close he could already read her thoughts, Eli once more began to ask his questions, all of which she'd answered a dozen times. "Are you absolutely sure, Abigail, that you won't be bothered as a Northerner to live among slaves?"

"How many times, dear sir, do I have to reassure you? I know some Bostonians feel strongly about the evil of slavery, but I also know my handsome husband's kind and generous heart. Eli, you simply are not capable of being a cruel slave owner! Besides, I just won't think about it. My blessed father didn't approve of slavery, but Mother assures me that it's quite possible to put it out of my mind and just be grateful to God for you. You know how that elegant woman respects and admires you, don't you? To my mother's normally critical eye, you can do no wrong. She'll be so pleased that we're going to be married. I'm sure it will make her feel she's done a superb job of raising me and she can now boast about God's goodness in giving her only daughter a well-to-do, handsome husband, the owner of a prosperous rice plantation." She was silent a minute. "Eli? You've never asked my exact age. Has Mother ever told you how old I am?"

"Why, yes, my dear, and that's another thing that worries me a little. I know you're twenty-four today and I had my forty-sixth birthday six months ago."

"I was afraid she'd told you her 'very tiny, righteous white lie' as she calls it."

"A lie, Abby?"

"I'm not actually twenty-four today. I'm *twenty-six*. But Mother insists on telling everyone I'm still twenty-four."

Eli didn't laugh often, but he laughed now. "Well, good, I say! That makes you only twenty years younger than I!"

"What difference could age possibly make? And I'm glad

you laughed when I told you about Mother's tiny, righteous lie."

"Never worry your lovely head about your mother and me," he said. "I think I rather understand the lady. When things aren't exactly as she wants them to be, she simply re-creates them."

"I—I love your laugh, Eli, but I also love you for seeing through Mother. She's really very sweet and good in her heart. But you're exactly right about her. My wonderful father used to whisper that now and then Mother rather enjoyed playing God. You've made me see that's when she's—*re-creating* as you say."

"Are you at all concerned that your mother will change her mind at the last minute and decide to move to Darien, Georgia, with us, Abby?"

"No!" She snapped out the word. "No, she wouldn't dream of moving to such a small town after a lifetime in Boston. Nearby Savannah maybe, but never Darien! Would she?"

"How would I possibly know that?"

"Because you know so much about everything. It truly amazes me that a man could be so gloriously handsome and attractive as you and still be so wise about all of life. Does being so wise make me seem young and foolish, Eli?"

He laughed again. "I'm not that wise, my sweet Abby, and you'll find out for yourself as soon as you see me, a Northern businessman all my life, trying to learn how to run anything so foreign as a coastal rice plantation. My lawyer has given up trying to change my mind, but he's convinced I'll fail as the master of a rice plantation—says it's much more difficult than growing cotton."

"Oh, I know. You told me what he said, but he's dead wrong. Your slaves will adore you, and since slaves come with the property you've bought, they must already know all about planting and shelling rice—or whatever you do with it."

She'd made him laugh again. "You plant it, my dear Abby, but I'm not so sure about the shelling part!"

"Oh, you will be. You're going to be sure about every-thing and don't you dare ask your other question again. It's all worn out. *I won't miss Boston social life.* I really don't like it nearly enough to suit Mother and I plan to be so happy living with you in our manor house that I'll probably forget there ever was such a thing as a theater performance or a concert once we're alone together. And I know that *someday* we'll have a splendid manor house, so you don't have to remind me again that we'll have to be content in a smaller house in Darien for a few years. We'll be together, I'll be Mrs. Eli Edward Allyn, and, for the first time, my life will lack absolutely nothing!"

Still holding the reins, he turned toward her on the buggy seat. "Abby, are you sure? Are you truly, truly sure? What if I fail? What if I'm just not cut out to operate a rice plantation? What if I grow old too fast in the trying? What if you don't find any friends you're at home with in that strange little town of Darien, Georgia?"

"Hush, Eli! Don't say another word. Just help me down out of this buggy and take me in the house so you can kiss me."

Part One

November 27, 1858—March 1859

Chapter 1

O n a chilly Saturday morning, November 27, 1858, as though he had nothing else whatever to do, no plantation calls to make, no office appointments or house calls, Darien, Georgia's prominent physician Dr. James Holmes settled comfortably into an armchair before a wood fire in the tastefully furnished, but modest parlor of the frame house where Abigail Allyn lived with her husband, Eli Edward. The fire's warmth felt good when it penetrated the bones and muscles of Holmes's body. As always in the bright, cultivated, cheerful company of pretty young Abby Allyn, he found no difficulty in shedding any guilt he might feel because he was a little overdue for attending his patients.

Abby Allyn had not sent for him. He was there because he wanted to be. He felt sure she was several years younger than his own beloved wife, Susan, who was now in her late thirties. But, like Susan, Abby was a healthy New England girl, warmhearted, filled with what to him was typical New England vitality, and often surprisingly complex. Also, as with Susan, she spoke freely and frequently did not hedge her true feelings with the niceties so often employed by Southern women of all ages.

"I wish you'd change your stubborn mind, dear Doctor, and allow me to ring for Rosa Moon to serve us something hot while we talk," Abby said. "You know you'll stay awhile."

With a grin, Holmes asked, "Am I that obvious? Is it so evident that I revel in your excellent company, Abby?"

"Of course, it is. It's always evident." She sighed so abruptly it didn't dawn on him to take the sigh seriously. Then her playful smile was gone and, not teasing at all, she blurted, "I needed to talk to someone today, Dr. Holmes. Rosa Moon lumbers around the house silent as a tomb. I long for another human being. You know Eli speaks only when he's forced to. Did you know I needed someone today? That I needed *you?*"

"Such a thought never crossed my mind, Abby. Are you not feeling well?"

"Physically, I guess I'm fine. That is, until my mind begins to play tricks on me. There are times when—when I actually feel panic inside. I don't let it show, I hope, even to Rosa Moon, but I don't know how to cope with panic, Doctor. You see, lately I've begun to be afraid of being alone. So afraid, I feel—real panic."

"Afraid, my dear girl? And why on earth should you be afraid? I hope you can confide in me. I'm not sure how I can help, but I'd like to. I'd like to help the same as though I were your father. At almost fifty-four, I'm old enough to be your father."

"My own father died at fifty-five, but—oh, Dr. Holmes, there have been times all this year when I've longed to have my father alive again. I get that feeling when I know I'm—utterly trapped. There. I've said it, and if you dare tell anyone but your wonderful, warm, caring wife what I said, I'll never trust a human being again!"

"This is certainly a rude question for a gentleman to ask of a lady, but exactly how old are you, Abby?"

"I was thirty-one in September. Only that's a secret too. My mother simply will not admit I'm not still in my twenties."

"I've never met your mother, but does appearing young matter so much to her that you have to falsify your age?

Abigail, do you know why you're telling an old sawbones like me such personal things?"

"Yes. Because if the Scriptures are true, I know you can help me."

"The Scriptures, my dear girl?"

"Doesn't it say somewhere in the New Testament that 'the kingdom is within'?" And doesn't that mean that when our hearts are troubled, our minds in turmoil, it can make us physically ill?"

Dumfounded by her fresh insight—fresh to him, anyway—Holmes studied her young, intelligent face. "I suppose you know you go on amazing me, don't you?"

"What I know is that you and your wife, Susan, visit me. You both talk to me, grant that I'm here to be reckoned with, that I like to laugh, make jokes, play games, give in to my feelings now and then. You *recognize* me."

"Surely your mother realizes some of these things about you."

"If she does, she seldom lets me know it. Oh, don't misunderstand, please. Mother always has done her best with me. For all I know she may still be heartbroken with grief over my father, but to show a sign of that would prove to her that she's not as spiritual as she insists people believe her to be."

"Abby, aren't we straying from the trouble in your own 'kingdom within'?"

She managed a half-smile. "I guess we are. I'm so in the habit of moving any conversation away from my own problems. Mother simply does not tolerate anything resembling self-pity. She even reminds me of that in her letters."

"Were you close to your father, my dear?"

"Oh, yes! He and I were partners in keeping the peace at our house up in Boston. We did or did not do whatever kept Mother on an even keel, always supporting each other, exchanging raised eyebrows, winks. When he died, I—I had no one to wink at or support me. Not—not until I met you right after I married Eli and came down here to live."

"My winks or raised eyebrows, I fear, give my sweet Susan anxiety on occasion, despite her being a rather talented winker herself. She vows, though, that she has a better idea of when a wink or a raised eyebrow is appropriate. I have no doubt she's right. Susan, I find, is generally right about most things and I count myself blessed that she does not gloat about it."

"Dr. Holmes, why does it seem so hard for some people—especially gentlemen of prestige and even a measure of success—to let their humor show? Or their deepest feelings. Are some people born without a shred of humor, no sense of play? I know that's a provocative question. It may even sound ridiculous since no two persons are alike, but I recognized your humor *and* your wisdom and compassion at exactly the same time Eli introduced us nearly five years ago. You're truly wise, but you also see the funny side of things and you're not afraid to laugh."

Still in his chair, Dr. Holmes bowed from the waist. "I doubt anyone could pay me a higher compliment, my girl. Would that it were as true as you make it sound. Were you, by any chance, demonstrating your own excellent sense of humor when you made such a flattering pronouncement?"

"I most certainly was not! It's just that I have a very direct question to ask and your answer probably is the only one to which I'd pay full attention."

"I only hope I can answer, Abigail," he said simply.

"Has anything ever broken your heart or caused you to feel—panic? You see so much suffering and pain and death as you make your rounds of sick people, how is it that you always—*always* appear to be—peaceful? Your humor so close to the surface?"

"Oh, my young friend, don't you realize that you strike me as always being peaceful too? And of good humor? I know the weather changes in all our 'kingdoms within,' but you've never greeted me without that infectious smile. Of course, I'm aware that most persons who send for me don't feel well, or think they don't, but you always act eager to enter into true pleasantry."

"I didn't ask you to diagnose me, Doctor. I asked you about your own 'kingdom within.' How is it that in the face of almost anything, you're *peaceful*? Don't you know you literally spread peace? Even faith?"

"My dear girl, everyone has a measure of faith. No one could function without it."

"Are you telling me you believe that everyone has faith in God?"

"Forgive me," Holmes said, almost sheepishly. "I didn't realize you were speaking of faith in God."

"What other kind is there?"

"Oh, for example, we all have faith in our ability to swallow the food we put into our mouths—faith that the food will make its way down through the esophagus into the stomach. Everyone expects the sun to come up in the morning because it went down the evening before. When I sat down in this chair, I had faith that it wouldn't collapse under me."

"Please don't make jokes with me now."

Holmes frowned, then tried to erase his frown, but her words—almost pleading as a small girl might plead—only deepened it. "Is there some definite trouble in your 'kingdom within,' Abby? Something you can talk about?"

"Do you honestly think I'd have brought any of this up today if I weren't—near panic?"

"You may want to dismiss me for saying this, but why on earth would you feel panic? You're married to one of the true pillars of our little community. Your husband, Eli, is certainly fine-looking. And I know he's what people call a good provider in spite of some struggling to learn a brand-new line of work. I also know his keenest delight is to give you everything your heart desires. In honor of you, he even named his plantation Abbyfield. He's devoted to you. Eli Edward Allyn hasn't noticed another woman in all the five years he's been married to you. He told me so himself."

She stared at him. "Eli told—*you*?"

"Yes."

"When?"

"When? Oh, I don't remember exactly when. Perhaps the day my horse threw a shoe and he kindly drove me in his buggy to an emergency call I had to make some two or three miles out of town. Yes. I'm sure that's when he told me, but he didn't need to. Everyone who knows him knows how deeply he loves his beautiful wife."

"Then everyone knows that except his wife, who admires and respects him, but most of the time feels trapped in—his deadly silence!"

"Abigail!"

"I'm sure that surprises you. Undoubtedly the man speaks somewhat freely when you happen to meet up with him somewhere. Here at home with me, he's as silent as a—tree stump!"

Stunned by what she'd just said, Holmes sat studying her now rather closed young face. "You—you don't know he loves you?"

She shrugged. "Oh, when we were first married, yes. In his way, I guess he still does. I only have to mention that I'd like to have something and he buys it. But his thoughtfulness just sinks into the thick, heavy silence of my days like a rock in water!"

"Do—do you want to tell me about it, Abby?" he asked in a quiet voice.

"What do you think I'm doing, Doctor? Forgive me if, as my mother used to remind me, I'm being sharp-tongued with you. You're the last person on earth I'd mean to hurt, but I do hurt people. I even hurt Rosa Moon this morning with my sharp tongue."

"Your fine, faithful, roly-poly Rosa Moon who bakes those delicious sugar cakes? What did you do to Rosa Moon? Did she say something to offend you? Did she sass you?"

Her laugh, which normally was all music, sounded almost bitter. "How I wish she had! I wish she'd sassed me or called me names—anything that sounded like a human response. Do you have the slightest idea what it's like sitting or standing at a window or pecking at the pianoforte day after day without a single word of real conversation unless you or your Susan or Laura Mabry happen to pay a call? I do everything but chain my callers to the chairs to keep them talking to me." Her voice rose, her words came faster, tumbling: "Eli and I sleep until exactly fifteen minutes past five every morning. Then, within five minutes after he finishes a mostly silent breakfast, my husband is off to tend his rice fields, his stock—anything and everything but me. I see him for dinner in the afternoon and then he's gone again. For the remainder of the day, until dark in summer and long after dark in winter, he comes dutifully home for the night, greets me with a perfunctory smile and a nod of his head, washes up, puts on a clean shirt, sits with me in almost dead silence through a few bites of supper, reads his agricultural magazines most of the evening, stands to his feet at eight-thirty sharp, and goes upstairs to bed—with or without me. It—it doesn't seem to matter. I flounder through all my days and most of my evenings in heavy, smothering, nearly unbroken silence. But it isn't silence with peace in it. It's silence with—nothing in it. And, Dr. Holmes, I do feel near panic sometimes. Oh, my proper mother has taught me even to panic in ladylike quiet, without uttering a word, but I do grow frantic. Sleep overtakes me finally, and when I wake up in the mornings, we eat breakfast together again and drink our coffee, exchanging brief, empty phrases about such important things as the fact that we get far thicker, richer cream for our coffee from old Mr. Smith than we ever got from our own cow."

Her outburst had literally picked up speed with every sentence, was galloping headlong as though she spurred some nearly wild, uncontrollable beast, all the while praying that the beast would fall dead from exhaustion.

Finally, Holmes saw her slump in her chair and lean her dark curly head back while big tears flowed—in silence.

"You see, Doctor? I don't even make a sound when I

cry. All of me is too much in the habit of doing everything—in silence."

For possibly a full minute or more, he sat waiting—also in silence. He could hear the silence they were making together and it caused him to feel somehow guilty. At last, he cleared his throat and murmured in a husky voice, "Is that about it, Abby? Is that about what you had to tell me?"

A knock at the front door seemed to startle her as though she'd just been roused from a nightmare. "Will Rosa Moon hear that knock, Abby?" he asked. "I'll be happy to see who it is. Try to compose yourself, my dear girl."

"I done hear it, Miss Abigail," Rosa Moon called as she shuffled along the narrow hall from the back of the house toward the front door. "Don't get up."

"Can't you at least greet Dr. Holmes, Rosa Moon?" Abby called in a cross voice.

"Try not to take it out on poor Rosa Moon," Holmes whispered. "She's not responsible for the silence."

"Oh, yes, she is. Partly anyway. The woman talks little more than Eli."

On his feet, Holmes, still whispering, said he must go and that he hoped her caller was someone Abby truly wanted to see.

"Aren't self-pitying people dull?" She tried to laugh. The sound was a little less bitter than before. "I'm sorry. Promise you won't tell your wife what a bad hostess I've been? I hope I haven't irritated you. Please come again soon. I do want an honest answer to the question I asked you."

In response, James Holmes simply nodded, patted her shoulder, and smiled. From the direction of the front hall, they heard Rosa Moon say, "Mornin', Miz Mabry. Miss Abigail, she gonna be glad it's you knockin' at our front door. I done made sugar cakes too. Jus' took 'em outa de pan."

"Did you hear that, Doctor? Not only does Rosa Moon

find her voice when your wife or Laura Mabry calls, she's baked your favorites, sugar cakes. Please stay. And do tell me I'm forgiven for my complaining. I promise not to do it again. I know how much really sick people need you."

Chapter 2

"I'm sorry Dr. Holmes felt he had to leave, Abby," pleasant, talkative Laura Mabry said as she took the chair Holmes had just vacated. "I do know how busy he is. In fact, my dear husband told me just before he left to take his boat down to Brunswick yesterday that he'd tried to get the good doctor to go with him to make his regular visit to Mr. James Hamilton Couper's plantation, but it seems Mr. Couper is taking no chances with his rigid schedule being interrupted and is sending one of his own boats for Dr. Holmes on Monday."

Ensconced in her own chair beside her pleasantly loquacious caller and close Darien friend, Abby sat smiling. She was so happy that Laura had come she felt perfectly content just listening to another human voice. Especially someone she knew did not take her for granted. Certainly Laura Mabry, whose husband, Woodford, was the U.S. port collector for both Darien and Brunswick, Georgia, could bring her up to date on all the latest news, not only of Darien but of most of the coast between Savannah and the Florida border at St. Marys. Smiling and, for the first time today, actually wanting to smile, Abby sat listening. Even though Laura Mabry was known for being a talker, it never *seemed* to Abby that she talked too much. Laura's valued friendship stood staunchly behind each word, so Abby only wanted to be with her.

Once she had determined from Abby that she wasn't ill, Laura continued, "You know Mr. James Hamilton Couper expects everyone around him to live by the clock as he does. I hear the elegant gentleman allots forty minutes for dinner—not one minute more, not one less. He even sets aside a special time each day for his poetry reading. I wonder sometimes how his much younger wife, Caroline Couper, keeps her delicious sense of humor. Of course, he's extremely good to her. An excellent provider. I'm certainly glad my Woodford isn't that organized. There are times, of course, when I wish he were a bit more punctual, more careful about small things. But, oh, I am happy as his wife. The fact that he's some twelve years older than I only adds to his manliness for me." Laura's own good laughter interrupted her monologue. "Will you listen to me? How do you stand me, Abby? I'm just always so glad to see you, I—I lose track of myself. You must wish sometimes that I didn't live within walking distance of your house."

"I wish you'd believe me when I tell you I literally sit here waiting for you to come and talk to me, Laura! Eli is so engrossed in growing his rice, he's too tired to remember I'm here at the end of his days. I even long for Rosa Moon to tell me something. Anything at all, just so she talks to me."

"Even though Woodford and I don't have slaves of our own, I do know that the colored aren't all alike, Abby. They have differing personalities too, and you've told me yourself many times that Rosa Moon is not only faithful and hardworking but an excellent cook." She sniffed the fragrant air. "Oh, I can smell the wonderful aroma of her sugar cakes all the way from her kitchen out back."

"Just be patient," Abby said. "I'm sure the poor thing will come trundling in soon with a tray no one else would dare try to balance. I do wish she'd listen to Dr. Holmes and lose some of her ample girth. She works hard from daylight till dark—in silence, of course—except when I force her to speak, but all that weight could make her ill and then what would I do?"

"Oh, your kind, generous husband would buy you another cook immediately. And speaking of buying people, have you heard the rumor that must be rampant all up and down the coast by now?"

Abby laughed a little. "Laura, you haven't been to visit me for a week. How *would* I have heard?"

"But Dr. Holmes just left here. Didn't he tell you there's a rumor of an illegal slave ship loaded with Africans somewhere in our waters? It's the talk of Darien. Frankly, I'm a little worried that my Woodford, as port collector, hasn't been concerned enough with the rumor. His is a truly responsible and important position, you know, and if such a ship loaded with illegally imported slaves should somehow sneak through his port, the dear man would never forgive himself. I first heard the rumor four or five days ago, but Woodford seems only to be taking it seriously as of yesterday. That's why he left so suddenly for Brunswick. I've tried to tell him, but I don't think he believes such a thing could really happen here. And I expect I simply talk so much he's found a way of going deaf in self-defense when he needs to."

"I certainly talked poor Dr. Holmes to the point where he must have turned a deaf ear on me too. He didn't say a word, though, about an illegal slave ship in our waters. I guess I didn't give him a chance. I was just so relieved to have someone sitting here listening to me, responding to me, I—Laura, when you see my husband somewhere in town without me present, does he talk to you?"

Laura laughed. "I guess I simply haven't noticed. I don't leave many empty spots in a conversation, you know. And it just struck me that maybe the reason Rosa Moon is so silent with you is the fact that her husband, Obadiah, your husband's handyman here and in his rice fields, just does not give her a chance. Like me, Obadiah runs off at the mouth without ceasing."

"But many days lately he's had to help out at the plantation doing work on my husband's precious banks and floodgates."

"Where would you be without those banks and flood-gates, Abby? Do you think you could have new draperies and slipcovers made without his rice crops to bring in such a good income?"

"Now you sound like my mother."

"You've told me many times how your mother affects you, but, Abby, my friend, you're involved in the business of living your own life—or you should be. I've never known a woman with more potential to be strong than you, so give yourself the kind of advice you keep expecting from your friends. Be yourself. Live your own life. Doesn't that idea appeal to you?"

Abby surprised herself by giving one of her quick, genuinely merry laughs. "Laura, you're the limit! If you'd started right out to defend my dear mother and attempt to set me straight about her, I'd never once have thought of laughing at myself."

"And were you laughing at yourself?"

"Yes. Because I'm suddenly—funny. I know I'm blessed. At least my husband doesn't act as though he's my master as well as Rosa Moon's. I know other women whose husbands boss them around the same as if they'd paid good money for them. Eli just—sits there. But in a kind of contentment known only to him. And from now on, I'm going to try to be thankful for that. Now tell me more about the rumor going around that there's an illegal slave ship in our waters. I've never had very strong feelings one way or another about slavery, but from a human standpoint the whole system seems bad enough that slave owners ought to at least stay within the law."

"Oh, I've heard all sorts of rumors in the last day or so. Some of them even claiming that the du Bignons of Jekyll Island are in on the scheme."

"What scheme? The du Bignons are such honorable people. I've been so occupied with my own silly problems, I'm completely in the dark about this. What does your husband say about the rumors? About the du Bignons? If there's an illegal ship nearby, wouldn't he know all about it?"

"That's what I keep asking him, only to be reminded that, as Georgians, we should be proud that so few attempts have been made to break the state or national laws against importing Africans. Woodford is a smart, hardworking port collector, but at times he's also too trusting, in my opinion. Eli's a slave owner. I wonder what he thinks about the rumors? He's surely heard them, hasn't he?"

"You know as well as I that, on the pretext of protecting me, he wouldn't have told me if he had. But I'm not going to fall into the trap of criticizing my husband again. What I need above all else is to—to count my blessings. To recapture my sense of humor. To be glad his only fault is that he ignores me much of the time."

"Abby, do you really believe that Eli ignores you?"

"If you asked Woodford the same normal husband-and-wife question three times in a row and received only silence in return, what would you think?"

Without answering her question, Laura asked, "Do you love Eli?"

"What?"

"A simple question. Do you feel you really love the man? I know how romantic you imagined life would be down here on the coast as mistress of a successful rice plantation. That you envisioned magnolia trees and smiling slaves to spoil you and a husband to grant your every wish. Well, you've tried it for a time now, Abby. Have you found that you really love Eli Edward Allyn for himself?"

In response, Abby just sat there studying the pattern in her parlor carpet, saying nothing.

"I heard you, Laura, but I just had an idea. You know your theory that my Rosa Moon doesn't speak unless it's demanded of her because her husband, Obadiah, talks her ears off at night when they're together? Well, Obadiah may be our one way to find out more about this illegal slave ship rumor!"

"As the port collector, my husband will surely get to the bottom of things, Abby. You shouldn't worry about it. Aside from your own well-controlled Northern scorn of slavery, none of it can harm you or Eli. I'm sure he's too honorable to be tied up in any way with breaking both state and national laws." For a moment, Abby felt Laura's dark eyes studying her. "You're dodging my question about loving Eli, aren't you?"

On a short, disgusted sigh, Abby said, "Yes."

"Why? You and I can tell each other anything. Don't you know whether or not you love your incredibly handsome Eli?" Another moment dragged by. "Abby?"

"I'm thinking. Give me time to think, Laura!"

"I know I talk too much, but you know I don't talk when I should be listening. I'm just a talker, not a gossip, Abby. You believe that, don't you?"

"Yes. I know I can trust you."

"But you don't know whether or not the five years of your married life have proven or disproven your love for this man?"

"I—I have a deep, deep affection for him. I'm truly grateful to him."

Laura stood to her feet. "I see. Well, I must go. I want to be home in case Woodford returns from Brunswick yet today. Why not try Obadiah, Abby? Heaven knows, he'll talk your arm off, but he does have a superb connection on his people's grapevine. I don't understand how that grapevine of theirs works so well, but it does. Obadiah probably knows far more than most white men about the truth of that illegal slave ship—if indeed it's in our waters. Remember how close he is to a few of the du Bignon people on Jekyll Island. Oh, and please don't scold Rosa Moon for not getting around to serving the sugar cakes. Tell her I'll try to come back later for them."

Chapter 3

*F*or nearly two hours after she investigated a loud crash in the kitchen shortly after Laura Mabry had gone home, Abby sat alone in her parlor trying to think. Instead of anything constructive, she mostly wondered. Not only why Rosa Moon insisted upon piling everything in her kitchen onto one already heavy silver tray, but how the woman had managed to let her entire plate of sugar cakes slide off the tray into a pan of soapy dishwater.

Abby didn't scold her. Spoiling her special sugar cakes had been punishment enough for the poor woman. But she was now thinking hard about her conversation with Laura, who she knew had been right. Little about life on what Abby once imagined would be a spacious, elegant Southern plantation had proven to be as she dreamed once she and Eli moved from Boston to Darien, Georgia. But the evening sky on the coast had enchanted her from the first moment she saw it. And, except on cloudy days, when late afternoon began to lay its bright streaks across the sky, Abby never failed to marvel at the unearthly beauty. Beauty that would come again today.

Eli had not yet come home for his big early afternoon dinner and she entertained a brief, puzzling thought as to why the always punctual man might be late, but mainly she drank in the clear, blue winter sky glory stretching above their pretty little town. That Eli was almost an hour late rather broke her monotony. The man was so dependable that the idea of something happening to him passed quickly through her mind and out. Rosa Moon lumbered in, grumbling only slightly that her dinner would be ruined, then shuffled out and back to her kitchen.

After a long, heavy sigh, Abby said aloud to herself, "She could have stayed a few minutes, I'd think. I know she finished with the ironing long ago. There's nothing for either of us to do now but wait." Strange to be in the same house together all day every day and feel minute to minute that for some unknown reason her servant was avoiding her company. Two women, even a mistress and a slave, should find much to talk about, but search her mind as she most surely had, Abigail Allyn could think of no reason why the enormous, but always willing house servant should go on avoiding conversation with her.

No one in town could question that Rosa Moon and her husband, Obadiah, were well treated by the Allyns. Eli saw to it that their cabin was kept in good repair. They ate from rather nice plates and bowls selected by Rosa Moon herself from Abby's own tableware. Heaven knew it took enough cloth for almost two average-sized dresses to cover Rosa Moon's girth, but she never lacked for new gingham or nice muslin for her dresses and aprons. And on a trip to Savannah last year, Abigail had bought two blue glass beaded bracelets and had them fastened together to fit Rosa Moon's wrist. Her eyes had actually shone when Abby gave her the bracelet, and proof of how much she loved the jewelry was still plain because she wore it even when she boiled laundry in her big wash pot out back. "Your mother once told me," Eli had said at dinner one day when Rosa Moon was out of the dining room, "that a German servant of hers in Boston stole one of her finest brooches. I wonder what she would think about your *giving* Rosa Moon her own jewelry."

"You know my mother," Abby said aloud again into the empty parlor, and felt some of the old guilt for the two same old reasons—reasons she'd known since girlhood.

The first: that it was as easy as ever to put the blame on her mother for almost everything that troubled Abby's life. The second: that each time she saw herself in a looking glass, she was reminded all over again that her own features were evidently as attractive as people said they were because she was Emily Banes's daughter.

Still wool-gathering, she remembered the rumor concerning an illegal slave ship and decided to ask Rosa Moon about Obadiah's odd, at times eerie way of connecting himself with the coloreds' grapevine. Before she reached the dining room, she heard a horse and buggy in the lane outside. Hurrying back to her parlor window, she gasped with surprise at what she saw, then she grabbed a heavy shawl from the hall tree and ran outside to watch Eli drive proudly up to the porch in a brand-new shiny black buggy.

There, doing the driving, was Eli, with skinny Obadiah sitting on the seat beside him. Master and handyman were bringing home a new buggy, trimmed with fancy gilt designs and sporting wheels with bright yellow spokes.

There was no doubt that Obadiah, who almost never stopped talking, and his master, who spoke much less freely, got along famously and seemed genuinely fond of each other. Nothing delighted Obadiah as much as to be right there on hand when Eli brought some new, unexpected present home to Abby. On these special occasions, Abby found that after she had exhausted her vocabulary of exclamations and thanks, Obadiah was absolutely essential. Eli seldom did more than just stand there and smile his pleasure, but Obadiah knew how to stretch and stretch a spiel of joy and merriment.

Anyone else, Abby thought as she stood on the front steps waving, would expect Obadiah to be driving the new buggy, his master beside him. Anyone, that is, who didn't know Eli Allyn's quirks. He was a Northerner turned slave owner living in the South. But to this day, so far as she'd been able to find out, he did not really approve of owning slaves. Still, since his rice plantation was so successful, he'd fallen rather quickly into the Southerner's rationalization that if one owned a rice or cotton plantation, one also owned slaves. And that was that.

And this was this—another day in Darien, Georgia, when Eli had come home with a surprise for her.

He didn't present the purchase merely as a new buggy for the two of them. To Eli, anytime he brought something home, it was for Abby alone. So Abby would thank him and thank him for the new buggy as though it was for her exclusive use and he'd never dream of riding with her even to church on Sundays in it.

For several minutes she walked round and round the buggy, admiring its design, exclaiming at the cheerfulness of its hand painted decoration and the bright yellow wheels.

"We got us a mighty fine new buggy here, Miss Abby," Obadiah said over and over, because nothing made him happier than the sound of his own voice. Because Obadiah knew that Eli wouldn't permit her to hug him until he'd washed up, the slender, narrow-shouldered servant vanished toward Rosa Moon's kitchen to prepare warm water and see to clean towels for his master.

Alone once more in her parlor while waiting for Eli to put on his clean shirt and for Rosa Moon to announce dinner, Abigail felt her heart reach toward the strikingly handsome, silent man who was her husband. Her kind, generous, odd, puzzling husband. They would share dinner in the dining room with Rosa Moon serving them and again Abby would wait while Eli and Obadiah hitched the horse to their old buggy and drove back to the plantation on Cathead Creek to finish what work Eli had planned for the remainder of the day. Her heart reached toward Eli's, but, as usual, she did not feel she truly touched his. All he'd thought of to say after her effusive praise of the new buggy was, "That's good, Abigail. It's good you like the new buggy."

That night, following his almost unvarying twice-a-week habit, when their light supper was finished, Eli started upstairs as usual at eight-thirty, but waited at the foot of the steep staircase for her to join him to climb the stair to their bedroom.

She went willingly and he made his deliberate, steady love to her. As always, she hoped that at the end there would be the closeness about which she'd dreamed all her young life. Instead, Eli went fast asleep.

Maybe at breakfast she would ask him if he knew of the rumor Laura Mabry spoke of earlier. A shipload of slaves smuggled ashore along their coast would cause a huge scandal all the way to Savannah, but if Eli remained his usual uncommunicative self, she'd have to bring it up. He wouldn't.

Communicating in words was just not her husband's way. And as he grew older, he seemed less and less aware of it.

The next day, Sunday, November 28, when Rosa Moon hoisted herself up the stairs with Abby's morning coffee and a piece of warm, freshly baked bread, Abby smiled at her and said, "Good morning."

"Mornin'. Mausa Eli, he done gone and take Ob'diah wif him," Rosa Moon said, and handed her mistress a cold cloth to "pry open dem eyes."

"I hope you didn't need Obadiah for anything special around the house today, Rosa Moon."

Jerking open the draperies to let in the bright winter sunshine, Rosa Moon said, "I don't need him here today no more'n usual. Kind of nice to have me some quiet. Ain't no wonder dat man so skinny. He talk off eber ounce ob fat dat tries to stick on his bones."

"Do you—do you miss him when he isn't around the house?" Abby asked.

Rosa Moon only shrugged her big shoulders. "No'm. I don' miss him so's you kin notice."

"Did he have anything special to tell you today? I mean, is there any kind of message on his grapevine you haven't told me about?"

"Seem to me like he jus' full ob nonsense talk. How he

wished he didn't have to go down to Jekyll Islan' today so's he can't git back to me for tonight."

"What?"

"Ain' I talkin' loud nuff? Ob'diah's frien', Polydone, he lib on Jekyll Islan'. Mausa Eli take Ob'diah down there today an' he git to talk a arm an' leg offa Polydone."

"I see. I suppose you meant Obadiah went with my husband to work at the rice plantation again, even if it is Sunday."

"Yes'm, but it tickled him good dat his mausa he want Ob'diah to help row dem down to Jekyll Islan' late dis mornin'."

"So that's why Master Eli told me not to expect him here at home tonight. I thought he just planned to spend the night at his overseer's house on Cathead Creek. He didn't mention Jekyll. Rosa Moon, if that man saved his money the way he saves words, we'd be the richest people in Darien!"

"Jus' to put yo' min' at res', Miss Abby, bof our husbands spend the night on Jekyll Islan' at the du Bignon place. Long wif Lonzo and Ed and Picken. Dey goin' too. To help row."

"Did Obadiah give you any idea of why they're going to spend the night at the du Bignon house on Jekyll?"

"Lordy, Miss Abby, I so glad to hear him hush up, I don' ax no questions to keep 'im goin' on. He talk mostly 'bout your new buggy an', to hear dat man tell it, the wheels is made ob gilsy gold!"

"I know he loves that buggy. And it is handsome. Rosa Moon?"

"Yes'm."

"Do you love Obadiah a lot?"

Abby had never seen the big woman turn so quickly, nor peer so intently right at her. "What you say, Miss Abby? I don't b'lieve I heard you right."

"Yes, you did. You and I see more of each other than I see of almost anyone and I've asked you a straightforward woman question. Are you in love with your husband?"

"Lord, have mercy! Sweet Jesus, have mercy!"

"That's just plain ridiculous. Anyway, when I ask you a question, don't I have a right to an answer?"

"Heaven look down on us, dey ain' no other white Southern woman eber gib a thought to whether or not two niggers loves each other!"

"But I'm not a Southerner! I'm a Bostonian."

"Call yo'sef whatever name you likes, ma'am, but I ain' neber heard tell ob such a thing."

"Rosa Moon, can't you even try to be friends with me? We've been together nearly five years. If you just try to be friends, you'd understand why I asked you if you and Obadiah love each other. Don't you ever wonder about your master and me?"

"No'm."

"Why not?"

" 'Cause he's my mausa, dat's why. I ain' got no right to wonder none 'bout such things."

"Then you have a lot more rights than you think you have!"

For what seemed to Abby a long time, Rosa Moon just stood like a big brown boulder in the middle of her bedroom floor and stared at the breakfast tray.

"What are you looking at?"

"Don' tell me I forgot to fetch yo' butter fo' dat good, warm bread!"

"You know you didn't forget. You buttered the bread down in your kitchen. And I do thank you. It's delicious."

As though the subject hadn't been shifted at all from Jekyll Island, Rosa Moon stunned her mistress by blurting, "I speck you knows dat Ob'diah's bes' frien', Polydone, done come here on one ob dem slabe ships from Africa when he was jus' a little boy 'bout ten or twelve year old."

"How would I know that? And what on earth caused you to tell me such a thing? Does that mean you and I are friends and that you might actually carry on a real conversation with me after all this time?"

Rosa Moon deliberately looked out the window. "No'm.

It don' mean dat. Least it don' seem to me like it do."

"Then why did you tell me about Polydone?"

"Ef you don' go ahead axin' me a pile of other questions, I like you to know Rosa Moon thinks a lot 'bout how lonesome you git, Miss Abby." And then the woman surprised Abby most of all by laughing her good, warm, low laugh.

She laughed so deep within herself for such a long time, Abby wondered if anything had ever made Rosa Moon's belly shake so merrily before. "I think you might tell me why you're laughing so hard. If you're wise enough and— *kind* enough to notice that I do get lonely, Rosa Moon, don't you think you should let me laugh too?"

"It jus' strike me funny dat ef Ob'diah's tongue be a whole foot long, Mausa Eli's tongue mus' measure no mor'n a inch!"

Abby tossed back the covers, jumped out of her bed, and threw both arms around Rosa Moon. Her arms didn't quite meet, but the more she hugged, the faster the thick, smothering cloud seemed to break from around her heart. Maybe, just maybe, the lonely waiting was over. The sun beamed into Abby's being and lifted the panic she'd tried so long and so earnestly to escape.

Rosa Moon was hugging her in return as though she'd been waiting too.

Chapter 4

By sunrise Sunday, November 28, Eli and four of his most trusted people, Obadiah, Lonzo, Picken, and Ed, were on their way from the Abbyfield dock on Cathead Creek into the Darien River and almost through General's Cut before Eli began to breathe a little easier. Heaven knew he trusted all four of the slaves selected to go with him. From the moment he realized the secret trip to Jekyll Island would be necessary because of Abbyfield's need for more field hands, Eli had been sure that he would take Obadiah. He and Obadiah were as close as master and slave could be, but he also felt secure with his choice of Lonzo, Picken, and Ed. All three were young men, strong and healthy, and he'd never caught one of them in a lie or trying to dodge their duties to him. He had committed himself to the purchase of at least two of the illegal Africans being transported to Jekyll Island in a yacht called the *Wanderer*. It was surely nearing its destination by now. And Eli hoped it was out of sight of anyone but John du Bignon, the only white man presently living on the island owned by his family.

So far, especially after a private talk at the Oglethorpe House in Brunswick last week with Henry du Bignon, the younger of the two brothers, Eli felt sure the carefully guarded conspiracy would work. In his mind, he had gone over and over the plans as told him by Henry du Bignon:

the *Wanderer* would actually reach the waters near Jekyll after dark because rough seas had delayed the arrival. And at the end of such a long sea voyage the supply of drinking water and food for the four hundred or so Africans packed tightly together on the *Wanderer*'s decks would be running dangerously short, so it would be important to unload them as soon as possible.

Eli had threatened Obadiah with a break in their special friendship if he indulged his mouth in the usual way. Keeping quiet, so natural to Eli, was just as unnatural to Obadiah, who vowed over and over that "if eber a man could trus' another man, if eber a mausa could trus' a slabe, you kin trus' me, Mausa Eli. Jus' ax my Rosa Moon. She be the firs' to tell you Ob'diah cut out his own tongue before he say one word you don' want him to say. Yes, sir, Mausa Eli, you likely knows already dat Ob'diah be the one ob the fo' men you pick dat keep his mouth shut tight! Ob'diah done got all he kin do workin' bof at yo' house in town an' at Abbyfield. If anybody knows we needs more hands, it be Ob'diah."

Grasping the boat's tiller, Eli smiled to himself, remembering that he had practically been forced to shout at Obadiah in order to get him to stop vowing his fidelity. Big talkers, of course, could not always be trusted. Not so with Obadiah. He trusted the man, and on this trust was built the foundation of their valued relationship. Not once had it occurred to Eli not to depend on Obadiah as much, he felt sure, as Abby must depend on Rosa Moon, even though she was so steadily silent.

The boat, all four slaves pulling steadily on the heavy wooden oars, had passed through General's Cut and, under Eli's orders, had moved out into the short stretch of the Butler River when the skies began to darken so suddenly Eli found himself rubbing his eyes on the chance that they were just having difficulty trying to focus on something in the distance. His vision did not clear, but, as always, Obadiah anticipated his problem and shouted, "Ain' yo' eyes,

Mausa Eli! We gittin' us a blow! Look at dem black clouds. An' we still got a fur piece to travel."

Eli wondered if Rosa Moon caught Abby's thoughts and heard her unspoken questions as did Obadiah. Wondered if the big woman felt she'd spoken her comforting words to her mistress while she'd only stayed quiet and left poor Abby puzzled by her silence. And then his fear of the coming storm brought shame. Eli's own shame. The puzzling, new kind of shame he'd only begun to experience for the past few days washed over him again as the red-brown waters of the Butler River washed over the evenly applied oars. Shame that he'd stayed so preoccupied, so busy struggling to learn how to test dikes, what to expect of the tidal flooding of his rice paddies, and figuring, always figuring how much profit there might be at the end of the year. Shame that he'd almost forgotten how he used to worry back in Boston before their wedding that Abby might miss the parties and dinners and concerts she'd attended since girlhood. He knew that in the busy, charming city of Boston, Abigail Banes, an only child, had lived like a princess compared to the way she lived now, no matter how hard Eli worked.

Abby. Her name caused him to tremble, not from the cold November wind off the roiling water, but because every thought of Abby still brought a sharp thrill, a feeling of deep hunger for the familiarity of her, the silkiness and fragrance of her body next to his.

Out here in the chill and danger of this stormy day, he felt the hunger more painfully. Eli had dreaded this day, November 28, 1858, because so big a part of him hated participating in it. And yet, here he was, listening to the wooden thunk of the oars in their locks, shouting an occasional order to four slaves whom he owned, headed for his part in an out-and-out conspiracy to buy more slaves illegally. Of the dark-skinned men in the boat with him, only Obadiah knew why they were going to Jekyll Island. He had told Obadiah because he was trustworthy. Even if Obadiah were somehow confronted with his master's act, he could talk so much and so fast people were inclined to believe they had heard the whole story. Obadiah even knew, in case of an emergency of any kind, in which pocket of Eli's valise to find not only the signed agreement to buy at least two of the hungry, exhausted passengers but also the money to pay for them.

"Miss Abigail, she know all 'bout dis?" Obadiah had asked just before they boarded the boat.

Eli had answered only, "No. She'd only worry."

When Obadiah laughed his almost whistling laugh, vowing he certainly did understand "why Miss Abby she git lonesome as Rosa Moon swear she do," Eli remembered the words he wished he'd said to Obadiah. With all his heart, he wished he'd made it plain to Obadiah so that he could tell Rosa Moon and she could tell Abby that from now on her husband meant to do better, meant to escort her to more social affairs in Darien, to laugh more, to talk to her more freely.

He hadn't told Obadiah any of that, and oddly, as the sky above them darkened with more dangerous angry clouds and especially when the wind—a hard coastal squall, as quick and dangerous as any ocean squall he'd ever seen—began to push the churning water up into swells, Eli felt an ominous chill.

In a desperate effort to keep his mind on steering the boat, on anything but the disaster threatening them, Eli forced himself to remember and take some real solace in the fact that earlier in the year he'd been fortunate enough to find a bright, well-spoken, good-natured, highly recommended young overseer for Abbyfield. Eli had not been pleased with the performance of his previous overseer and hoped that Thaddeus Greene's experience with rice growing would make it possible to give Abby a better, more satisfying life. That Thaddeus had been so praised by both Dr. Holmes and Woodford Mabry, collector of the Darien and Brunswick ports, had no small influence on Eli's choosing him to operate his beloved rice plantation on Cathead Creek. Cautious as always, Eli had given himself a full week to think it over, to investigate Thaddeus's past record in the rice markets, his dependability. He put aside the fact that Dr. Holmes assured him that Thad's extraordinarily attractive appearance—medium height, muscular body, light curly hair, and more charm than one man deserved—would almost guarantee that any future Mrs. Thaddeus Greene would be a more than acceptable lady. Eli did not want a married overseer right now. He wanted someone free to give the property and its crops full, uninterrupted attention. Still, young men as appealing as Thaddeus Greene were bound to marry someday and so he had simply put the matter to one side and hired him at eight hundred fifty dollars a year, in addition to all he could eat and the soundly repaired Abbyfield overseer's house to live in.

In spite of the glowing praise of Greene's worth, Eli did not yet trust him enough to let him know the real reason he was taking four slaves to row him to Jekyll Island. It was enough for him to know that Eli was going to Jekyll to visit his friends the du Bignons. Thaddeus appeared to be good with Negroes and had yet to show any intention of nosing into Eli's personal business affairs.

So far as Eli could tell, they must now be headed well out into Buttermilk Sound, although the fury of the wind and the water were bringing him almost to the point of confusion. He could not, would not, have sworn that he'd steered the men correctly out of the South Altamaha River, through which he thought they'd just passed. He had never seen men—black or white—work so doggedly or show greater courage than Obadiah, Lonzo, Picken, and Ed. Had he, Eli Edward Allyn, the same kind of fortitude? Even Thaddeus Greene, who had spent most of his life near Philadelphia, had known to warn Eli that the worst storms known along the southeastern coast often struck suddenly in the middle of Buttermilk Sound. Only now did Eli wonder how his overseer had known that.

One thing was certain. The wide, heavy plantation boat tossed so wildly, they must be battling the treacherous waters of Buttermilk Sound now. The water was too fierce, the wind too vicious to be any water but that of Buttermilk Sound, where he knew, even without Thad's warning, that boats both small and large that had left their docks in calm sunlight could be wrecked almost mysteriously as they fought their way through the rough waves.

Eli strained his eyes to gauge their proximity to land. Too far away from anything he could recognize as a landmark to order the men to do more than they were doing. And rather than take refuge from the storm, Eli felt a compelling urgency to continue heading south toward Jekyll to keep his secret appointment with the du Bignons. At least he hoped the boat was still heading south.

Heavy rain was pelting them now, and when a gust of wind like a strong, cold hand jerked off Eli's warm scarf and threw it to the bottom of the boat, he would have cursed had he been a profane man.

Since early November, Abby had insisted that he wear that scarf, and because she had knit it herself, he wore it—gladly. Now, icy wind cutting at his bare throat, he let go of the tiller and tried to grab his scarf. A sudden wave rocked the boat with such violence that he lost his balance and felt his ribs and shoulder strike the thick wooden hull of the boat as he fell over the side.

As he tried desperately to keep his head above the water, the wails he heard could be nothing else but faithful Obadiah screaming his name. Heavy, heaving waves kept closing over his head. He was thrashing about in the wet roar, the weight of it so heavy, he was sure his breastbone was being crushed.

All he could feel anymore was a strong hand gripping his foot—holding on until the weight of the angry, plunging water pulled off his boot.

Obadiah fought hard to jump into the water with his master, but the three other slaves, grunting and cursing, hauled their half-crazed friend back into the safety of the boat. Two of them held him there while the third tried to get control of the tiller. Obadiah went on screaming, "Mausa—

Mausa Eli—oh, my mausa, Mausa Eli . . ." The sound he made became a keening . . . as though his words were being drowned along with his master.

"Obadiah, shut yo' mouf! Stop dat yellin' like a ruttin' cat an' give us a chance to help some!"

Obadiah could hear himself, but he was powerless to stop screaming, even though the wild sound he made terrified him almost as much as the sight of his beloved master's long wet hair floating in the muddy water, the silver streaks of gray at his temples still showing. His screaming went on until Master Eli slid soundlessly from sight, fighting to the end against the hard, cruel sea.

The wind howled more loudly than Obadiah and joined with his cries to make a caterwauling duet of grief and impotence.

Chapter 5

The next morning, following the storm and a cold, miserable night spent on a sandy beach along the way, dawn had just begun to touch the sky with pale, rainy winter light when Lonzo felt certain that the line of trees he could make out ahead was Jekyll Island. He had been to Jekyll twice with Obadiah and remembered that the du Bignon dock was about halfway the length of the Island. The two younger men, Ed and Picken, plagued him to wake Obadiah to help steer, but nothing could make him do that to his exhausted, grief-heavy friend.

"Ob'diah he catch hisself a few winks an' we lets him sleep long as he can," Lonzo said, his low voice more of a rumble than ever from his own weariness. "Anyway, it look like I done steer us right. We near ready to dock our boat at the du Bignon landing."

"What you reckon make us think Obie he know what we gotta do nex' wif Mausa Eli gone?" Ed asked.

"He know 'cause Mausa Eli he done tell him," Lonzo snapped. "Dem two be close as any white man and any nigger in Gawgia. Jus' hold on. Help us git to shore, then we ax Ob'diah. He know it all. He tell us."

Obadiah woke up when they docked and thought you could have scraped Mr. John du Bignon's eyes outa his head when he told him his master, Eli Edward Allyn, had been drowned when a bad squall hit in Buttermilk Sound. The first thing that crossed du Bignon's mind, Obadiah knew, was that some way the four Negroes had pushed their master overboard. Curbing his lifelong habit of talking, Obadiah said nothing. He just stood on the Jekyll dock clutching Mausa Eli's valise in both arms while John du Bignon plied him with question after question.

Finally, pointing with two skinny forefingers to each of his own red, swollen eyes to prove how hard he'd been crying, Obadiah said, "You give me a li'l openin', sir, an' I tell you the whole story. I bein' fair to you, though, when I say I don't b'lieve you can afford to doubt my word a smidgeon. You knows Mausa Eli trus' me wif all his big heart. An' if you still thinks I be lyin' to ya, you won't once we takes care of our bi'ness deal."

John du Bignon stared at him. "Our business deal, Obadiah?"

"Yes, sir."

"What business deal?"

"Mausa Eli, he pick out me an' Ed an' Lonzo an' Picken to come wif him to bring at leas' two new slabes offa dat slabe boat an' I got his signed paper an' de money to close de deal once I picks out the slabes to take wif us back to Darien. I come all de way here after he drown so's I could do his bidness."

"Show me the agreement *and* the money."

"Firs' you tell me, please, sir, where is de slabes?"

"That's for me to know and for you to be told at the right time."

"But Mausa Eli he allus say money talks." Obadiah opened the small valise, reached with noticeable certainty into one special pocket, and took out a roll of banknotes. He didn't hand them over, though. "An' in the side pocket of this valise I got the secret paper my mausa sign 'long wif you."

Du Bignon smiled a little. "All right, Obadiah. I believe you. I should have anyway since I've known for nearly all the five years he lived down here that your master regarded you highly. And"—he gave Obadiah a definite bow of respect—"I—I do apologize and extend to you my deepest condolences upon the loss of your master. What will happen to his valuable rice acreage in Darien now?"

"We got to wait an' see, sir. But Mausa Eli he hire on a fine young gent'man, Mr. Thaddeus Greene, to be overseer. Doctah Holmes an' Mr. Port Collector Woodford Mabry dey say he a good planter. But I hab to tell you, sir, 'bout my bein' honored. Yes, sir. *Honored*."

"Oh? And who honored you, Obadiah?"

"Why, you did, sir. You sen' me condolence in my grief an' you honor me wif a *fine bow*. No white man eber bowed to Ob'diah befo' dis!"

"Oh, I see. Well, I do hope you'll feel free to call on me if I can do anything to help out in your grief and in the grief of Eli Allyn's widow. My word! The poor woman knows nothing of her dreadful loss, does she? Will you go straight back to Darien as soon as we handle the—uh—somewhat complex matter of unloading the Africans? They should be brought here to Jekyll anytime now."

"Yes, sir. I knows Mausa Eli he want dat I should do jus' dat. Go back to Darien. It—it be hard. Hard." Obadiah's voice broke and tears filled his dark eyes. "How I'm gonna tell Miss Abby we—we had to leabe his body dere in de—sound? You kin help me by tellin' me how I gonna do it, Mausa du Bignon. I done hol' on to his poor foot as long as I could, but"—still more tears flowed—"but—he boot it come right off in my han'!"

"Couldn't the other men with you help any?"

"Not an' keep rowin' in dat mean water, sir! You ain' neber been in no squall in Buttermilk Sound?"

"I don't believe I have. Bad, eh?"

"Satan hisself neber fight nobody no harder dan dat water fight!"

Neither man spoke for a few seconds, then du Bignon said, his voice warm, "You—you did your best, Obadiah. That's plain. You did your best."

Obadiah took a swipe at his eyes. "I—I done my bes' for

Mausa Eli all de time. I done my bes' to—keep dat roarin', pushin' water from taking him away." He hung his head. "I—I kep' his boot."

"You've still got Eli's boot?"

"Yes, sir. I aims to keep it long as I'm on dis ol' earth. Den I git Rosa Moon to—plant it right on top ob my grave."

"Few people knew or were as close to Eli Allyn as you, Obadiah. I think he's the one who honored you."

"Yes, sir. He sho' did honor me." A brave, quick grin lit the dark face. "I—I done mos' ob his talkin' for him, I reckon. Least, dat's what Mausa Eli say. He worry some dat Miss Abby neber gonna figure out how he could love her so much an' not talk no more to her den he did."

When du Bignon said nothing, Obadiah guessed he just didn't know what to say to a thing like that. Best to say nothing.

"You feel you oughta check the agreement I got here in Mausa Eli's valise, sir?"

"Why, yes, perhaps I should." The white man scanned the handwritten page, then asked, "Would you like me to read this to you, Obadiah?"

"Oh, yes, sir. Yes, sir!"

"I suppose it's proper for me to read it to you. He—he did intend that you pick out his slaves off the *Wanderer*."

"Do it say that?"

"Not in so many words, but—well, listen: 'I, the undersigned, do ask that I or my representative be permitted to select two strong young men from the *Wanderer*'s cargo to be paid for in cash by me or my representative and taken to live at my plantation, called Abbyfield, in Darien, Georgia, thereafter to be my property or the property of my estate. Signed, Eli Edward Allyn.' "

Obadiah, his eyes wide with wonder, even though he already knew the answer, asked, "Be—I Mausa Eli's rep-a-sentive?"

"For the—uh—transaction of this business matter, yes. Now, Obadiah, is there room in the plantation boat you came in to take two new laborers back to Darien with you?"

"Oh, yes, sir. Mausa Eli, he plan to do jus' that."

"And how well do you know Dr. James Holmes?"

"Purty good, sir. Doctah Holmes, he tends reg'lar to Mausa Eli's people at Abbyfield an' in town."

"Good. Holmes should be a big help to you with Mrs. Allyn when you break the tragic news to her."

"Oh, I ain' aimin' to do that. My Rosa Moon she tell her."

"I see. And will your wife agree to that? Won't you have to answer specific questions for the—grieving widow?"

"If Rosa Moon need me to help her, I'll be there, sir. As Mausa Eli's rep-a-sentive."

"The storm last night has the sky dark enough to help us bring the *Wanderer* a little closer to Jekyll before full daylight. And that's all I'm free to tell you, Obadiah. If you want to, you should be able to head back toward Darien within a few hours. I'm sending my big yawl out to help transfer the Africans." John du Bignon did not bow this time, but extended his hand and shook Obadiah's. "Needless to say, your esteemed master was not the only man who trusted you. I seem to also."

With Ed and Picken assigned to guard the plantation boat, Obadiah stood on shore with Lonzo and waited for more than two hours while over four hundred Africans were put ashore some two hundred yards off du Bignon's landing. They were taken from the most handsome yacht he or Lonzo had ever seen. Weeks, perhaps months had passed since the *Wanderer* had set sail from Africa with its huge, valuable load of illegal slaves. And in spite of his talent for talking, Obadiah could only think of one thing to talk about, and that was what must surely be the filthy, stinking condition of the interior of such a proud schooner. Of course, they both thought about the human misery aboard for all the long, cramped voyage, but nothing seemed to cause Lonzo as much pain as seeing that the hungry, thirsty, wretched, half-sick human cargo was made up mostly of boys from twelve to eighteen years of age. There were a few women and grown men, but the bulk of the cargo had been dragged as children from familiar surroundings and were now being sent only God knew where to a lifetime of slave labor.

But hardest of all for Obadiah was the dark thought of the long row back to Darien when he would have to sit where his master had sat to steer the boat. His friend Polydone, Mr. du Bignon's main slave, helped Obadiah in his unaccustomed and all-important role as Mausa Eli's representative. Obadiah was to select which two young Africans would be in the plantation boat for the trip home to Abbyfield. Polydone, who had also come to the United States as a boy years ago, could speak a little of the strange language the Africans spoke, so he was able to act as go-between for Obadiah and the two boys he chose. Once Polydone was no longer nearby, it would be up to Obadiah to figure out a way to talk to the new slaves.

Hard.

It was going to be hard, he thought, certainly for young Mr. Greene at Abbyfield, where the Africans would work. Then he put the thought out of his mind by remembering with a shudder that nothing would be as hard as waiting while Rosa Moon told Miss Abby that they were not even bringing home the dead body of her fine-looking husband.

Chapter 6

Early on Monday morning, November 29, after an almost sleepless night, Abby was up, dressed, and, without even a sip of coffee, hurrying along Madison Street toward the Darien waterfront, where Dr. Holmes's office was located. Her house was within easy walking distance, but there wasn't a minute to lose because she knew Dr. Holmes was leaving today to pay his monthly medical call at James Hamilton Couper's plantation near Brunswick.

Abby recognized the slight, energetic figure of her friend the doctor only seconds before she reached his door. A light valise in one hand and his medical bag in the other, he was hurrying to the boat waiting for him at the Darien wharf.

The instant Abby called his name, he turned and began to run toward her along the sandy street. "Someone 'up there' is looking after us, Abby, my girl," he called, pulling a folded newspaper from his coat pocket. "I was in the process of trying to convince myself that no harm would be done if I set sail for James Hamilton Couper's Hopeton Plantation without showing you this." As an afterthought: "Oh, good morning, my girl. I hope you're well today."

"I'm fine, I think, and good morning to you, Doctor. I'm so glad I found you because I'm worried about Eli. What on earth's in that newspaper?"

Dr. Holmes handed the paper to her. It was a copy of

the *Savannah Morning News* already folded to what he wanted Abby to see. "Read that," he said, pointing at an advertisement circled with a heavy pencil. "And do be quick, my girl. If I'm late, I could well give the always punctual Mr. Couper a heart seizure."

"It will save time if you just tell me what's here."

"You need to read this for yourself."

He hadn't ordered her to read aloud, but Abigail did:

" 'All persons are warned against landing on the Island of Jekyll for the purpose of gunning, cutting wood, removing wrecks, or in any way trespassing on said Island. Suits will be immediately commenced against anyone found on shore with guns in their possession. Captains of coastal vessels will pay particular attention. Signed, John du Bignon and Henry du Bignon, Jr.' "

"My dear friend, is it true that your esteemed husband took four of his people and dared to head for Jekyll Island yesterday?"

"I have to ask you, Doctor—how did you know that?"

"I am the port physician, Abby. Someone in Collector Woodford Mabry's office told me late yesterday that they were going."

"Did you know about this notice in the Savannah paper when you heard that Eli was going to Jekyll?"

"I did." He pointed to the date the notice was published. "It appeared nearly a week ago. You didn't see it?"

"Eli always reads the paper from the first word to the last. I sometimes don't even bother unless I'm looking for something special. Dr. Holmes," she said, dread evident in her voice, "he's taking some kind of risk, isn't he? I know you're rushed for time, but I have to know! I came hunting you to find out—something. Eli tells me nothing."

Holmes rubbed his square chin, then said, "If Eli read this notice and still headed for Jekyll, yes, he's at risk. Or he went in total confidence because he already knew of a secret plan in which the du Bignon brothers may be involved. The du Bignons are posting the island in order to keep everyone off—except those who may know the truth about the illegal slave ship rumors we've all heard for days. People are even saying the ship may be a large Northern-built yacht which can transport as many as five hundred Negroes, and that means a lot of money is the motivation."

"Someone's bringing slaves from Africa in a handsome yacht?"

"So the rumor goes. But if they are, the actual plans have been kept so secret that not once have I heard a breath of rumor about any local names. Eli may not be at risk. But if he knows of the scheme, if Eli is in on it, your husband and the du Bignons, my girl, could well be in trouble with both the state and national governments."

"But Eli's rice plantation is doing well. He can buy slaves in Savannah. We're not poor."

"At the moment, no. Still, so many slaves have been sold to Western states, rice planting could easily lose its profitability in Darien—unless someone finds a way, legal or not, to bring in more hands. Brace yourself, my young friend. My fears may be for nothing at all. On the other hand, the du Bignons are as honorable as Eli. Money can be hard— actually impossible—even for the best of men to resist."

All the way from the du Bignon landing to the welcome sight of the Abbyfield dock on Cathead Creek in Darien, Obadiah's feelings switched from pride that, as his dead master's representative, *he'd* been the one to select the two good young Africans to empty, pain-wracked grief that Mausa Eli was so abruptly gone. As he steered the big plantation boat toward home, he held on to the dead man's boot with one hand and gripped the tiller with the other. Once or twice the water was rough enough so that he needed both hands to steer, but during those times he held the cherished boot safely between his knees.

With the help of his friend Polydone, who spoke enough of their language to be understood, he first made sure that both new slaves could row, since Obadiah now had to take his master's place at the tiller for the trip back up to Darien. Neither boy could row the whole distance, he knew. Anybody would know from looking at their thin, half-starved bodies that they would not be worth much as workers until regular meals of good food had restored their unused, flabby, exhausted arms and legs and backs. Obadiah recoiled at the sight of their front teeth—white and strong-looking, but filed in the tribal way of signifying manhood, so that anyone familiar with the customs of the Congo would recognize them as imported slaves. Both, Obadiah felt sure, were terrified of what lay ahead for them in such a strange land where people must sound as peculiar to them as their odd prattle sounded to Obadiah. To make up for some of their fears, Obadiah did all he knew how to do in order to help them out a little. He smiled at them every time he caught their eyes and shouted, "Good!" It was the one English word Polydone had taught them. The smiles and that one word seemed to help. Polydone had convinced him that living with the other slaves at Abbyfield was a guarantee that both would learn some English—maybe not the right English, but Polydone promised they were good mimics and would get by all right.

What bothered Obadiah, beyond his own grief and his nervousness that he too had to learn how to talk to and understand them, was the moment he'd have to explain the two extra slaves to Mausa Thaddeus Greene, the overseer. It was not hard to understand that both of the boys must be so glad to be out of that filthy, cramped *Wanderer* that they would surely feel some kind of hope. Even with Mausa Eli gone, Obadiah scolded himself into believing that if these two young strangers felt hope, he could feel it too. And trading smiles did help.

Kindhearted as Mausa Eli had been, he didn't smile often, and Obadiah prayed he wasn't displeasing his master by using this way of making his own goodwill known. When they tied the boat at the Abbyfield dock in the twilight, the new Africans seemed especially to need Obadiah's smiles, and although he'd been born on a rice plantation as a Darien slave himself, somehow he understood that their fears and uncertainties would grow heavier as darkness came on.

Obadiah would have to spend the night at Abbyfield and was surprised that he felt relief rather than dread when he saw Mr. Thaddeus Greene striding briskly down the path toward the landing. The sandy-haired young man always seemed in a hurry, with energy enough to match his haste.

"Evening, Obadiah," Greene called, his hand out in greeting. "I'd almost given up seeing you tonight. It seems like it gets dark earlier than it did even last week, doesn't it?"

"Yes, sir. Winter's comin', Mausa Thaddeus. But we here, safe—'cept—'cept for Mausa Eli. We done los' Mausa Eli an' I don't know what I'm gonna do—wifout him. Mausa Eli, he—he los' his footin' an'—fell overboard in Buttermilk Sound. He dead, Mausa Thaddeus." Still grasping the empty shoe, he held it up for Greene to see. "I still got his poor boot. Come off in my han' while I was tryin' to pull him outa de water, but de water it win ober me."

"Good Lord, Obadiah! Do you mean to tell me Mr. Allyn—drowned? Was it during that quick, hard storm early yesterday?"

"Yes, sir. Dat when we lose him. I seen de water go ober his head—eben seen the silver where his hair gray on each side ob his face—an' I tried, oh, I tried so hard to—to—"

"I know," Thad Greene said, his voice thick and agitated. "No one doubts that you tried. No one will ever doubt it, I promise you! I'll see to it. I'll see to it, Obadiah."

Tears again streamed down the dark face, and Obadiah took a step toward the overseer, both hands out—one still holding the boot. "It be Miss Abby I cryin' for, sir! Mausa Eli, he love dat woman so much. Wif all his heart, he love Miss Abby!"

"God in heaven," Thaddeus whispered hoarsely. "I—I don't even know the woman. Mr. Allyn was going to introduce us one day soon. Did—did Miss Abby care a lot about the old fellow?"

"Old? Mausa Eli not be old. He be the finest-lookin' gent'man in McIntosh County! So good to Miss Abby. And I neber know why she not love him wif all her heart the way he love her."

"You forget I haven't been here very long, and with so much work to be done, I've only been in town a few times. Is Miss Abby about her late husband's age?"

"No. She 'bout twenty year younger than him. Dat worry Mausa Eli sometimes too. I reckon Miss Abby she be 'bout your age, Mausa Thaddeus."

"And you might as well get this straight right now, Obadiah. I'm not your master, so don't call me Mausa. Do you understand?"

"Yes, sir."

Thaddeus Greene laughed a little. "How about calling me Mr. Thad? My friends all call me Thad. You and I had better become friends, Obadiah. Don't you think I'm right?"

"Oh, yes, sir! You be right, Mr. Thad. Yes, sir!"

Not until after Lonzo had led the new boys toward their cabin space did Obadiah tell Mr. Thad about his part in the unlawful purchase on Mausa Eli's behalf. Surprisingly, the overseer smiled almost as though he'd known everything all along. "I wish you worked at Abbyfield all the time, Obadiah," he said. "I could use your wisdom here with all the men. You will come out often, won't you?" His smile widened. "Or I'll come to town when I get in trouble over something. Agreed?"

"Oh, yes, sir! I sure does, Mr. Thad. Yes, sir!"

Obadiah spent the night at Abbyfield because of fast-approaching darkness, and when he hitched Master Eli's buggy for his drive into town at dawn the next morning, his heart was heavier than ever. Riding along in his late master's buggy sharpened the missing. As Obadiah trotted the horse into town toward Miss Abby's house, his hands were holding the reins—the same reins his master's hands had held. Rosa Moon would be at the big house by now.

The sun was too high for her still to be doing any cleanup work in their cabin at the rear of the town property on Madison Street.

Obadiah tried his best to feel strong, at least in his spirit, but his step felt old, almost lame, as he made his way toward the rear gate that led to the back door of the house, the only entrance he had ever used to Mausa Eli's home. On the short brick walkway to Rosa Moon's detached kitchen, he stopped a minute and looked down at the still damp boot in his right hand.

Somehow it helped him to show people that boot. Obadiah, at least, had an idea that just holding on to the boot proved to folks, especially Mr. Thad, that he'd done everything possible to save the life of the best master a man ever had. No matter that almost everyone thought Eli Edward Allyn a strangely reserved human being. Obadiah knew better. He knew Mausa Eli as he was, maybe a little bashful—white folks would call it shy—but so hard-working that some of his lack of talk was due to the fact that the gent'man stayed just plain tired. Unless a man thrived on talking, as did Obadiah, talking for the sake of making sounds could wear a man out.

He'd tried to explain all this to Rosa Moon, but if she happened to have her ears shut to the sound of his voice that day, he knew she hadn't heard. Oh, she'd understand now. Nothing dumb about his Rosa Moon. And suddenly, he needed painfully to see her. There wasn't a dark-skinned woman in all of Darien as pretty as Rosa Moon in the face and her ample size only drew him to her. She was a soft, firm, brown pillow put on the earth by the Lord himself to comfort Obadiah. He needed her comfort today. And, Sweet Jesus, how Miss Abby would need it once Rosa Moon had told her that all Obadiah had been able to bring home of her husband was an empty, waterlogged boot.

Rosa Moon was in Miss Abby's kitchen just as Obadiah knew she'd be, stirrin' up what he hoped was a batch of pancakes. Even in the midst of the dread and the sorrow and the quick change in his whole life, he was as hungry as a man could be. Thinking back, he realized that too much had happened in the past two days for him to remember to eat much.

Rosa Moon did not know when to expect him, he knew, but to look at her round, pretty face, nobody would ever guess she didn't. When he whispered her name from her kitchen doorway, she turned slowly and wiggled her fingers at him in what a child might call a wave. Obadiah was always welcomed by the sight of Rosa Moon's wiggling fingers.

"I need a hug, Rosa Moon," he said softly.

"I'm makin' pancakes. Ain't that better?" Her smile was bright as a sunflower.

Obadiah knew she was busy, too busy for nonsense hugging, but he also knew she was happy to see him. Maybe almost as happy as he was to see her.

When he said nothing, she turned for the first time to look straight at him. "You sick, Ob'diah? You eat somepin' make you sick?" He went on standing there, just looking back at her, the boot in his hand.

The sunny smile now a frown of concern, Rosa Moon asked again, "You sick? You too quiet not to be sick! Lemme feel yo' forehead."

"He—he gone, Rosa Moon," Obadiah said, almost whispering.

"Who gone?"

"Mausa Eli." The boot held out to her, he murmured, "Dis be all I got lef' ob him."

"Where he go?" Her voice rose. "Where Mausa Eli go? What you doin' holdin' his boot in yo' han'?"

"He—he gone down in—de water. I done seen dat mean water comin' up ober he poor face. Mausa Eli, he drowned in Buttermilk Sound. I—I grab on to one boot, Rosa Moon. I held on to his foot in dat boot till—de boot come off in my han' when the undertow pull him away!"

"Ob'diah, you mean Mausa Eli he don' come home wif you?"

"How he come home wif me when he somewhere down in de deep water in Buttermilk Sound?"

"Lord God in heaven, she be—all by herself now! Miss Abby she way down here away from her mama all by herself," Rosa Moon wailed. "Lemme quick cook you up a stack ob pancakes, so's I kin go tell her. Ain' no way she know he—got drowned. Me an' Miss Abby we got to be frien's while you an' Mausa Eli be gone. Git the syrup off de shelf, Ob'diah—my batter's ready. I tend to your broken heart later. Fill your stomick up firs'."

"What you mean you an' Miss Abby frien's now?"

"We hugs!" Rosa Moon tossed the words over her big shoulder as she poured batter from a pitcher onto the hot iron spider, so that Obadiah thought he might faint from the sudden good smell filling the kitchen.

"Hurry, Rosa Moon. After what I been through, I'm like to starve to death."

She flipped the light, thick pancakes once and then, as on her own inner signal, a second time, and when she hurried out of the kitchen, Obadiah was already pouring cane syrup over the golden-brown stack.

Tears streaming down her fat brown cheeks, Rosa Moon pulled herself up the stairs by the handrailing and stood alone for a moment in the upstairs hall outside Miss Abby's bedroom, giving herself enough time to beg for God's help with what she had to do because there was no one else to do it for her. "Dis room be only Miss Abby's room now," she whispered. "From now on, Lord, it be only hers. Fill up de shadows wif light fo' her. Fill my mouf with the right words to tell her Mausa Eli ain't comin' home no more."

Chapter 7

M istress and servant had long had an agreement that there was no need for Rosa Moon to knock when she brought Abby's coffee each morning, but today she knocked—ever so softly.

"Rosa Moon?"

Opening the door and pulling back the draperies, Rosa Moon asked, "Who it be, Miss Abby, but Rosa Moon? An' Lord help us, I done forgot to bring yo' hot coffee!"

More awake than usual, Abby sat up in her bed smiling. "You—forgot? Then why on earth did you go to all the effort of climbing the stairs? Never mind. I'm fully awake. I can come down for my coffee and breakfast at the same time."

"You feelin' purty good today, Miss Abby? I hope you feels purty good 'cause Rosa Moon she done mess up a'ready by forgettin' yo' hot coffee. You sleep good?"

Abby laughed a little. "Why, yes. As well as anyone not accustomed to being alone in the room—in the bed. When do you expect Obadiah home today from that mysterious trip to Jekyll Island? I thought they might be back yesterday. Did he tell you before he left?"

"Dat man talk a lot, but not always what anybody want to hear."

"I suppose it's hard to predict with the tides and all the wind we've had. But if they made it through the hard storm that came up the day they left, I'm sure they're fine now. I feel uneasy about this trip, but they must be all right."

Rosa Moon could tell Miss Abby was peering at her hard, that curious look on her pretty face, so she wasn't at all surprised when her mistress asked, "Is something the matter, Rosa Moon? It's silly and spoiled of me to let you climb those steps every day with my breakfast coffee, so I don't mind that you forgot today, but forgetting isn't like you. And all those questions about how I slept, how I feel. Am I imagining that you're acting funny?"

"No'm, you ain't 'maginatin' it."

Her mistress was sitting on the side of the bed now, plainly needing a warm robe, but Rosa Moon seemed unable to do anything but just stand there on the floor, clearing her throat over and over.

"Are *you* feeling all right?" Abby wanted to know. "You aren't catching a cold, are you? I will if you don't hand me my robe."

Rosa Moon crossed the room for the soft woolen robe, held it while Miss Abby slipped her arms into it, still sitting on her bed. After clearing her throat once more, the big brown woman whispered, "He—he ain't comin' home— no more, Miss Abby."

"Obadiah's not coming home? What on earth do you mean?"

"Not Ob'diah. He done come. He down in my kitchen now stuffin' his face wif pancakes."

"Who's—who's not coming home again?" Miss Abby asked, her voice sounding like somebody else, somebody a lot older.

Rosa Moon had never been one to show tears when her heart hurt, but her brown cheeks were wet now and her own voice so quiet, she almost couldn't hear herself say, "He—ain', Miss Abby. Mausa Eli, he—he drownded in dat bad storm."

As though someone had jerked her to her feet, Miss Abby jumped up, dry eyes so wide open they looked about to pop out of her head. Miss Abby's face looked like Rosa

Moon had just slapped her. It looked like she was having a hard time believing that Rosa Moon would say a thing like that—like she couldn't quite let the words sink into her mind. Rosa Moon was standing so close to the bed, she'd only have to hold out her arms to catch her mistress in case she fainted, but Miss Abby didn't faint. She just stood there in her bare feet, weaving back and forth, her mouth partly open, but no words came.

"Ob'diah done all he could to save him, Miss Abby."

Standing as straight as a pine tree, she asked one question: "What have they done with his—body? Where is my husband's—body now?"

"Ob'diah, he held on to his boot till it done come off in his han'. All we got lef' ob Mausa Eli is—dat empty boot. Ob'diah hold on to it now—like some way it help bring Mausa Eli back."

Still standing straight and with what looked to Rosa Moon like pure pain in those big gray eyes of hers, Miss Abby said nothing. At last she turned her back and began to look out the bedroom window as though she might find him out there in the yard.

After another silence, Rosa Moon said, "I still rememberin' our good, hard hug the day dey lef' fo' Jekyll Islan'. You want I should hug you—agin, Miss Abby?"

Slowly, very slowly, the stricken woman began to turn around so that she faced her servant. Then she said, "Yes. Yes, I do. Will you please give me another hug, Rosa Moon?"

Chapter 8

*L*ater that same morning, Rosa Moon answered a
knock at the front door and felt comforted that it was
Dr. Holmes's wife, Miss Susan, and not her mistress's other
best friend, Miss Laura Mabry. Miss Abby's eyes normally
lit up when either woman came to call, but Rosa Moon
was glad, almost relieved, that the first caller this sorrowful
day was Miss Susan Holmes, because she was less inclined
to useless chatter than Miss Laura. And God knew Miss
Abby's heart was too broken, her life in too many pieces
today for anybody, even a good lady like Miss Laura Mabry,
to run on at the mouth.

Everything was different now, and all Rosa Moon could
think about was finding ways—big and little ways—to
shield her mistress through the talk-riddled days ahead with
Mausa Eli gone. She knew one thing that was plain: Miss
Abby was no longer the stranger she used to be. Oh, she
still had her Northern ways, still said her words different
from Southern-born white ladies, but thanks to Sweet Jesus, the wall between them was down. There was no longer
any need for Rosa Moon to fill her long work hours with
jobs that really did not need to be done. For the nearly
five years she'd worked at the Allyn house, she'd hunted
around for this to do and that to do to keep herself always
busy. It had looked like just keeping her mouth shut when
Miss Abby was around would always be the best way for

both of them to act for the rest of their lives. Good as Mausa Eli and Miss Abby was to her and Ob'diah, there still hadn't been nothing to talk about through the long, empty days and weeks and then months and years. That Miss Abby had felt lonesome too was plain as the nose on your face, but Rosa Moon had been afraid to reach out to her. But all that was changed now and even though she felt sharply the loss of her kind, generous master, Rosa Moon's life had a new purpose. It would no longer run on hour to hour just being filled with anything that would keep her busy. Her reason for getting out of bed in the mornings even had a name now. That name was Miss Abby.

After directing Miss Susan Holmes upstairs to her mistress's bedroom, where Miss Abby had remained after hearing the sorrowful news about Mausa Eli, Rosa Moon headed for her kitchen to prepare tea and biscuits to take upstairs to them. She hoped it wasn't too plain how glad she was that it had been Miss Susan at the door instead of Miss Laura Mabry. She knew Miss Susan could just sit with Miss Abby and let her know they were close without chattering on about nothing or, worse yet, without trying to force her to feel better when there was no way she could feel anything but a pain in her heart. There wasn't even a funeral to plan. Mausa Eli's fine, dignified body was just gone, bumping around somewhere in the waters of Buttermilk Sound.

Funerals were sad and folks cried and tried to comfort the poor widow, but funerals made a finish. Nothing took the place of a finish. There was no feeling like knowing a big, hard job was done. Sad as it might be, planning and attending his funeral would have left Miss Abby with something done. There wasn't even that for her. And Lord, how Darien tongues must be wagging today now that gossip around town had it that Mausa Eli Edward Allyn had drowned in a storm on his way to Jekyll Island, where a big slave ship was thought to have landed with a load of Africans for rich white men like Mausa Eli to buy illegally.

It wouldn't make a smidge of difference that nobody knew for sure whether Mausa Eli took part. The Darien tongues would keep right on wagging.

Susan Holmes pulled a small rocker up beside Abby's bed and whispered only that she was there with her and that no words were necessary.

For what seemed a long time, Susan sat with her friend in silence, loving her, trying to imagine how it would be if her own beloved James drowned on one of his many boat trips to area plantations as he made his medical rounds month after month in all kinds of weather. If James never came home again, the center would drop out of her life.

From habit, Susan guessed, Abby was lying now on what must have been her side of the bed. The sheets and covers on the far side were all but untouched. Empty. How empty that bed must seem to Abby!

"Even though he was mostly silent when he was home, I missed him when I thought he was only visiting on Jekyll Island," Abby said softly, not weeping.

"I—I know," Susan said, and felt like kicking herself. How could she possibly know? "Forgive me, Abby," she said, the words sounding as feeble and useless as they were. "How could I possibly know? I couldn't know how you—feel today. But I care. Oh, my friend, I do care so much. . . ."

After another long pause, Abby said, "I'm so sorry for you, Susan. What a dreadful thing to be forced to try to—comfort me. I wish you wouldn't even try anymore."

"All right," Susan whispered. "I won't. But I am here if you need me—for just anything. Unless you'd—rather be alone, I'll stay nearby."

"Fine." Abby was staring past the empty side of the bed out her bedroom window toward a giant oak tree outside the house. "It's—strange, Susan. It's—all so new, I find I—almost forget for minutes at a time. I find myself thinking he must have left the house early to go to his—precious Abbyfield. Is—is that terrible of me?"

"No, I'm sure it isn't. Everything's been such a—shock to you. If someone's been ill for a while and—and then dies, there's at least been some warning. You had none. My husband says the aftereffects of shock are rather like—an illness."

"Yes."

"Or—or the almost blank way one feels after a sudden impact."

Watching Abby's face, Susan saw that she was smiling slightly. "When I was a small girl, I had a glorious rope swing in a big maple tree in our backyard. I was swinging away on it one day when a half-dead branch broke and hit me right on the head. Father always said the first thing I wanted to know was why it didn't hurt more. Why I felt so—blank."

"My husband thinks any kind of blank feeling we have after sudden pain is a sign of God's mercy."

"He does?" Abby asked.

"He vows it's true."

"Sometime I'm going to pin him down until I get a direct answer to a question I asked him not long ago on one of his visits here. Before he got around to answering me, though, we were interrupted by Laura Mabry knocking on the front door. But maybe you can answer it even better than Dr. Holmes!"

For the first time since she walked into Abby's room, Susan thought she saw at least a fleeting glimpse of Abby's usual spirit—a flash of her always contagious energy. She was up on her elbow in the bed now, peering with interest at her friend. "I think I'll just ask you, Susan! Yes. If anyone knows, it would be you. Is Dr. Holmes always so peaceful?"

"Peaceful?"

"My question *can't* really surprise you, can it? You live with the dear man. Surely you know the way he seems to—spread serenity wherever he goes. Along with his delicious humor, there's always—peace. Was he just—born that way?"

"No."

"Then where did he find—the peace? Susan, I know that's a deeply personal question, but—do you ever feel unpeace in him? If anyone knows about that, you should."

"Abby, I can tell you that I often see how James handles some self-absorbed patient who has understandably irritated him, how sometimes he is simply too tired to make jokes, or even how he reacts when his colleagues in town push him too hard to run again for mayor or for the school board or councilman. But Abby, dear Abby, I don't feel free to answer your question about where he gets his peace of mind. That's a story he's never told to anyone around Darien except me. And I respect him so much, I—well, let me put it this way. There's no reason that I know of for him not to tell you but he deserves to tell you himself. The story is that important to him."

Abby looked straight at her. "Do you—do you think he'll tell me, since he hasn't told anyone else but you, Susan?"

"Yes, I do think so. He's due back in town sometime late tomorrow from Hopeton Plantation. You can be sure someone will have gotten word to him about Eli, and if he isn't knocking on your front door the minute he gets a chance, I'll be more surprised than you've—gone on surprising me today!"

"I've surprised you? How?"

"I don't know. I guess I expected to find you—devastated. I'm comfortable enough with you to confess that I fully expected to be drying your—tears."

Abby turned her head away again. "I understand that. I'm sure I am—more than a puzzle to you, Susan. But you'll just have to give me a little more time before I can even try to explain."

Chapter 9

There was little or nothing a woman could do about changing custom. As one after another of the prominent Darien ladies and gentlemen knocked at her front door the day after she knew Eli was gone forever, all Abby seemed able to think about was that once more she must work at adjusting to change.

Today, her first full day without Eli, her first day of seeking her own new identity as a widow, her first day without his counsel, his advice, his rocklike dependability in all the ways she liked—and didn't like—without his odd, silent ways around the house, she wanted only to be with her closest friends. With each knock at the door, she had hoped to hear Rosa Moon greeting Dr. Holmes, even though Susan Holmes had told her yesterday that he couldn't possibly be back in Darien until late afternoon. Each person who came—and each came bearing food—was made welcome, she hoped, and thanked God that Rosa Moon was there to see to serving them refreshments. Obadiah was even with her today to make sure there were enough chairs, to help carry heavy trays of pie and cake and ham and fried chicken and, of course, to bow and make incessant verbal pleasantries. As pleasant as he could be, at least, because Abby knew Obadiah's heart was truly broken.

What, Abby found herself wondering each time there

was a lull in the flow of visitors, was the real condition of her own heart? I know I'm the grieving widow, and although tears don't seem to come, even when I sense people are expecting me to cry, I do miss Eli. I keep wishing he were here to help me greet all these people, to tell me whether I'm conducting myself as I should. I need him, God knows, to give me some idea of how to carry on with Abbyfield, how to meet the pressures of the rice market, how to act as the owner of all those Abbyfield slaves.

And then she would almost choke with dread. She wouldn't be expected to do anything about plantation business until a decent time of mourning had passed. That realization relieved the anxiety some, but nothing, she knew, would help as much as Dr. Holmes walking into her house. This day, in a strange, but definite way, Dr. James Holmes, without even being there, had come to be her most needed friend. No one but the doctor could begin to take Eli's important place in her life. Except for James Holmes, she didn't trust anyone the way she'd trusted Eli.

Another knock at the front door jerked her out of such foolish thinking. It was foolish to allow herself to turn so completely, so suddenly to the busiest doctor in McIntosh County for help in her time of lostness. "We're so sorry, so sympathetic to your great loss," people kept saying one way and then another. Loss. Yes, Eli's death was almost as great a loss as had been the death of her father.

Even as she spoke the expected words to each person who came to share her grief, the difficult task of writing to her mother loomed. And with the dread of that, came the fresh dread that elegant, refined, self-righteous Emily Banes would insist upon coming right to Darien. She felt no guilt when the thought which should shame her, but didn't, crossed her mind. For most of Abby's life, her mother had struck her as *self-righteous*. She had even asked her father about it one day—the day she first learned its meaning: "Is Mama self-righteous, Papa?" she'd asked. To this hour, she only had to remember that question, close her eyes, and she could almost see the kind, tolerant smile on her father's face. His smile was also amused. That Abby, at age nine or so, had even learned the word "self-righteous" amused him. That they shared still another secret pleased him. As always, it pleased Abby too.

But she would write to her mother just as soon as she felt rested from the unexpected onslaught of sympathy and visitation.

"I feel so—unfinished, Rosa Moon," she told her servant after a light meal, unlike the heavy one Eli always wanted as his dinner. "Why is that? I know he's—gone. I know he'll never come through that door again. That he'll never sit in his dining chair at the head of this long table, but why do I feel so unfinished?"

Rosa Moon studied her face for a long time and then said, "Dis soun' too easy, I speck, Miss Abby, but you ain' got no fun'ral to help you finish up wif Mausa Eli. Fun'rals ain' fo' de dead. Dey's fo' dem lef' behind."

"Yes. I'm sure you're right. I do miss him, you know. Eli was a comforting presence for me. He could always untangle things. Even if he seldom told me in so many words just what he'd done about a problem, he took care of it. I miss that terribly. I—I need him to turn to now. I need to tell him you said I need a—funeral service." She stirred cream into her coffee. "Has Obadiah said anything to you about the overseer at Abbyfield? I knew, of course, when my husband took him on some time ago, but I know absolutely nothing about him. What does Obadiah think of him?"

"I speck he done run off at de mouf' 'bout Mr. Thaddeus Greene to me, but you knows I don' always listen when Ob'diah start in. It seem like he think a right smart of the young man. He be young as you, Ob'diah said. Got light hair the color of beach sand. Curly light hair. Full ob talk. Talked his way right into bein' Mausa Eli's overseer."

"Oh, no, he didn't! My husband was far too smart to let anyone talk him into anything. If he hired Mr. Thaddeus Greene, it was only because he believed he was the best man for the position."

"He a good rice planter."

"Who told you that?"

"Who you reckon? Ob'diah. You an' me only been talkin' a lot to each other lately. Up to lately, I don' hear nobody but Ob'diah. Mr. Thaddeus Greene, he come from de North. Place called Pennsylvania."

Abby smiled a little. "I think you know quite a lot about the overseer. You must listen more than you think when Obadiah talks."

"Yes'm. Can't hardly help it."

Then Abby caught the rattle of a buggy in the lane in front of her house and rushed to the window. "Rosa Moon! He's here. Dr. Holmes just drove up and I'm ever so thankful. It's—it's almost like having Eli again, because the doctor understands about wills and business and will know or find out for me what I'm to do next."

Rosa Moon started for the door, but Abby pulled her back. "Not yet. I think I owe you something, Rosa Moon."

"You don' owe me nothin', Miss Abby." She grinned. "I don' get no pay!"

Taking her cue from Rosa Moon's teasing smile, Abby smiled back at her. "I know that and never mind this minute that I think it's wrong that you don't, but before Dr. Holmes gets here, I want you to know and feel secure in the fact that whatever anyone suggests to me, I don't intend to leave Darien. It's—almost as though you and I have just found each other. You and Obadiah will be staying on here in your own cabin—as usual. Does that please you?"

"Yes'm. I ain' eben thought 'bout doin' nothin' else. Mausa Eli own Ob'diah an' me bof. An' dat mean we bof your property now." Suddenly she began to clench and unclench her pudgy fingers. "But, Lordy, Miss Abby, I gonna start prayin' you don' eber start thinkin' 'bout sellin' us!"

Rosa Moon looked the same to Dr. Holmes when she threw wide the front door of Abby's house on Madison Street, but the woman struck him as being highly nervous, even scared. She was doing her best to smile, but for the first time he noticed her doing something he'd never seen her do before. She was clenching and unclenching her fingers in a manner that indicated to him a condition akin to fear. One could never quite be sure about the meaning of some Negroes' odd habits and he had expected Rosa Moon to be sad, but could she be frightened too?

Abby was standing in the parlor when he walked in— both his hands out to grasp hers. For a long moment they stood there, clinging to each other's hands. Then Holmes murmured, "Abby, oh, Abby, my girl. I'm so sorry I wasn't here to learn the tragic news with you!"

"I know you are, Doctor. But I thank you for coming now. Now is when I need you. Any earlier and we wouldn't have had a chance to talk alone at all. People have been streaming almost constantly into my house—most bringing food. Rosa Moon says there's hardly any room left in the kitchen for more."

"Who told you about Eli, Abigail? Who brought the news to you that—Eli is gone?"

"The only person I needed right then—Rosa Moon. Obadiah was with him. He tried desperately to save him by clinging to Eli's boot—after he fell in the water. Rosa Moon says he still has the boot. Oh, Dr. Holmes, I was awfully slow realizing what a good friend I had all the time in Rosa Moon!"

"But you know it now, my dear girl. God's timing is never off. He knew how much you'd need her and I can't tell you how glad I am that the two of you have finally begun to talk to each other."

They took chairs near the fire and for a time neither spoke. Dr. Holmes had come at last. His being there calmed her.

When he did speak, his voice was quiet and unhurried. "I think I'd like to tell you that there's a real peace in this house today and that's a sure sign to me that you and God are in this sorrow and loss together, Abby. You may not be able to sense it yet, but there is peace here."

"So much has happened that it seems a far longer time, but it was only a few days ago that Laura Mabry's visit prevented your answering an important question for me. May I ask you now?"

"Oh, Abby, my friend, I want you to ask anything of me that might help you."

"I must tell you I asked my question of your Susan yesterday while you were still at Hopeton Plantation. She didn't answer because she felt so strongly that you deserved to tell me yourself. If you feel real peace in this house, I'm—well, I guess I'm relieved since my question has to do with peace. Are you always as peaceful as you seem, Doctor?"

Holmes literally jumped in his chair, started to speak, then fell silent, studying Abby.

"I've asked a terribly personal question, I know. But you do always give me the impression of a man totally at peace. Do you always feel that way? I'm sure polite Southern women don't ask such blunt questions, but I'm not that Southern yet."

When he still said nothing, Abby almost ordered, "Don't you go silent on me! Not today, of all days. I've counted so on your coming by to be with me, even if it's only for a few minutes. You see, I'm having real—trouble with my own emotions. I miss him so much and he just left me! How am I ever going to be rid of this disturbed feeling? Can't you help me? Won't you even try?"

"I want to, Abby, but how could you feel anything but disturbed so soon after losing the one man you've ever loved?"

Now it was Abby's turn to fall silent. She didn't stare at the doctor, but at the knot in the wide pine floorboard near Eli's chair.

"Abby, I know you longed for Eli to talk more to you, to be more overtly affectionate perhaps. To enter into the funny little word games many people play together—to tease, to joke more. But he just wasn't like that. Eli Edward Allyn was simply a very thoughtful man."

"Yes."

"What does that 'yes' mean?"

"I don't know. I only know you seem peaceful and I want to know if you really are. I wasn't. Even when Eli was still here, I didn't feel—peace. But isn't a widow supposed to feel—*something*?"

"You're still in shock, dear girl."

"Don't diagnose me! Help me. I don't need a doctor. I need a friend."

He leaned toward her, and in a voice he hoped sounded as gentle and understanding as he meant it to sound, began to talk to her as though she had not spoken sharply to him. "Abigail, I am about to tell you of the most glorious, yet heartbreaking time of my entire life. Undoubtedly, I will shed tears as I speak, but it is important that you know and believe that, except for my wife, I have never told another human being in the more than seven long years since the event. Oh, everyone in McIntosh County knew of the death of our lovely little daughter, Susan Florida, but only her mother knew or knows to this day of my unmistakable encounter with God that dark, agony-filled day when the child died."

"Susan told me how you loved her. I've never felt I should ask about your little girl. I know you adored her."

"Yes, oh, yes. But as for my touch from God that day, I can only say my own pride has kept me from sharing such a glorious thing through all these years. As my friend, I can tell you that I told no one because I must have been too proud to let it be known in the community where I was building a medical practice that years ago I was an agnostic. I believed that no one could know anything about God . . . about reality. I can still hear myself declare that God is unknowable!"

"When did you think that? When you were very young?"

"Yes, I was young. Agnosticism came upon me when I was a student at Yale College and continued through medical school at the University of Pennsylvania. I came back here then, began my practice, married Susan, and became the father of our firstborn son, Pierce Butler Holmes, and three other children, never giving a thought to thanking God for my good life, even though I did attend St. Andrew's Episcopal Church piously. Being a part of church life, I felt, aided my medical practice. Then, in the year 1851, our little daughter, Susan Florida, grew too ill for medical help. No one knew that better than her father. Most people in McIntosh County know of our tragedy, but to this day no one knows what happened to Dr. James Holmes except his wife, Susan, the equally heartbroken mother."

Tears were indeed flowing down his lightly bearded face when Abby asked, "What did happen to you, Doctor?"

"An encounter with God is the only way I know to express it. There I sat, clasping the already dead child in my arms, all but cursing the Lord for stealing her from me."

Abby stared at him. "You—cursed God?"

"Isn't that ridiculous? How does a person curse a God who doesn't exist? Who can't be known?"

"Ridiculous? Cursing God is merely ridiculous?"

"Yes, because thanks to the concentrated hours I spent talking to classmates both at Yale and in medical school, I considered myself a true agnostic. I bathed my spirit in Thomas Paine and Hume, while laughing at the Bible. To my intellectually astute, but spiritually dead mind, I held no belief at all in God for almost half my life! I made jokes about those who claimed any faith, especially the Reverend Abiel Holmes, once pastor of Midway Congregational Church and a relative of my own father. I should have made jokes, not at cousin Abiel, but at my empty, superficial self. Believing that God was unknowable, I failed to see that the joke was on me. I suppose that's why even such a kind God allowed my heart to shatter in order to make room for Himself." Flowing tears glistened on Holmes's graying chin whiskers as he spoke, but he pushed ahead as though he dared not stop, dared not give Abigail a chance to change the course of their conversation. "Hear me out, Abby, please, even though you do believe in God, hear me out. As a doctor, I knew my little Susan was dead, that there was nothing I could do for her. I also knew that I had made an idol of her, had permitted the innocent child to take the place of God in my life. I—I worshipped the little girl."

"Were you alone, Dr. Holmes? Were you alone with your—dear child?"

"Except for our saintly old nurse Angie, a name that surely came from the word 'angel.' To this arrogant, anguished agnostic, at that moment Angie *was* an angel of God. I will never, never forget what she said to me as I sat holding the lifeless little body. Your Rosa Moon knew Angie. I believe they were kin."

"What did your old Angie say to you that day?"

"First she draped a warm woolen shawl around my shoulders as though I were the child. I must have been shivering—the winter morning was icy cold, dreary. Then Angie held out her brown, work-worn hands and said, "Don't mourn, don't complain, my mausa. Our dear little Susan is now in the arms of the blessed Savior. He take care of her now, look after her every need. She can come no more to us here forever, but oh, Mausa, we can go to her. Yes, sir, *we can go to her!*"

"How—did you bear it?" Abby whispered. "How? I—I don't think, after five years with no children, that Eli and I would ever have been parents, but how did you bear that black moment?"

"I couldn't have told you then—it was all too new—but I can tell you now," he said, his voice firm. "*I* didn't bear it. God bore it for me."

"In the agony of such loss, do you expect me to believe that you began right then to—have your own faith?"

"I don't think I knew it, but yes. What you see in me as peace now, my young friend, began to take root that day. It has grown every day since, when I make way for it. It was in that heart-crushing moment when I took Angie's callused old hand and felt the quick, warm response of her fingers on mine that I believed what she said to be real . . . the source of peace was real." Looking straight into Abby's eyes, he added, "The peace still holds."

Several seconds passed in complete silence, but this, Abby realized, was the kind of silence in which she could find peace too. She sat motionless in her chair, almost snuggling in the welcome warmth of the new silence. She felt protected, almost cozy, hopeful, as Dr. Holmes must have felt when his faithful old Angie wrapped him in that warm woolen shawl as he sat holding the dead, cooling body of his little daughter.

Finally, Abby asked, "Where was your sweet wife, Susan, when you began to believe? Where was she when little Susan left you?"

"I had urged her to lie down in our bedroom. She hadn't slept in two nights, watching over the child."

"There's peace in this room now," Abby whispered. "I— I feel it too, Dr. Holmes. You won't have to try to explain again why you seem so peaceful. Is this the peace that passeth all understanding?"

"Do you understand it?" he asked.

"No. Do you?"

"No. I just count on it, because stormy days do keep coming for all of us, Abby. Such as these days are being— will be—for you until you've learned how to reach naturally for the great Comforter."

"I'll need your advice on so many things, Doctor. I have no idea what's in Eli's will. I'll need to see his lawyer, Mr. Bentley, for that, I guess. I'll be lost trying to do anything with Abbyfield. I know my husband retained a capable overseer, but I don't know him at all."

"You will, Abby. Thad Greene is a rather unusual young man, I'd think. A man to be trusted. Intelligent, for certain. And if his personal magnetism and energy are any indications, he's also most enterprising. He'll ride into town to see you, I'm sure, at the appropriate time. The fellow is a gentleman. And, you may be pleased to know, also a Northerner. I've made only a few visits to Abbyfield since he started, but he seems quite skillful at getting along with Eli's slaves."

"If he's a Northerner, I wonder how he learned so much about planting rice."

"I'm sure he'll explain all that to you too. I've never heard anyone say Thad Greene isn't a talker."

Chapter 10

*I*n a little over an hour, Dr. Holmes was gone, late already for a sick call he'd promised to make a mile or so north of Darien. Abby could have sat with him, could have listened to the peace and goodwill in his voice for hours. She could have gathered the solace of his very presence about her for far longer, but other people needed him too, and he had come to her first upon his return from Mr. Couper's plantation. Why did being selfish come so easily for her? she wondered as she sat alone in her parlor, turning over and over in her mind Dr. Holmes's story of the day God met him in the touch and the words of his old Angie. For an instant, she had considered begging him not to go, but somehow was stopped in the selfish act and now she was glad.

Abby was alone again, but this was a new kind of aloneness. She was not really lonely in it. Nor did she feel the deep, lasting kind of comfort about which the doctor had spoken. Instead there was what seemed, at least, to be a curiously healthy longing. A new faith? Perhaps. Something caused her to feel hope ahead.

"I will not feel guilty for having this hope," she said aloud in a firm voice. "I know it may not be appropriate in a woman widowed such a short time, but if I didn't have to write to Mother today, I'd feel almost the same kind of happy anticipation I felt just before I married Eli! I suppose that's sinful of me, because I do miss him. And yet so much of that empty boredom I felt when I finally realized life on a Southern plantation wasn't going to be as colorful and romantic as I dreamed, is just—gone! It *isn't* that I've been unhappy in this modest little house in town. Eli always did everything he promised to do for me and he was going to build a fine manor house someday nearer Abbyfield. He would have done it too, but what would change after he did? Would it have made him any younger? Any more interested in just talking to me in the evenings? Any more interested in the things that interested me? Any more sociable?"

"Who you talkin' to, Miss Abby?"

"Rosa Moon! I wish you wouldn't appear in a doorway and just stand there!"

"What you want me to do? How I know you in de parlor here all by yourself? You feelin' all right? Kin I do anything to help?"

"No, thank you. And I'm sorry I was sharp with you just now. You startled me. I—I was just sitting here talking to myself about Dr. Holmes's visit."

"You wasn't tellin' yourself 'bout Dr. Holmes. You was talkin' 'bout Mausa Eli. An' since you an' me's got to be easier wif each other, you don' need to mind dat I hear what you say. I done know a'ready dat Mausa Eli be too old for you."

"You what?"

"You hear what I say. An' Rosa Moon done turn all dat ober in her min' a lot since Mausa Eli he buy me an' Ob'diah an' brung you here."

"You did?"

"Yes'm. Five years kin bring a lot ob change to a man twenty-some years older dan you an' me."

"How old are you, Rosa Moon?"

"How old you think?"

"I guess I hadn't thought one way or another."

"All dis fat on my bones make me look older, but I ain't much older dan you, far as I know. Seems like I mus' be 'bout thirty-some. Never did know for sure."

"I'm thirty-one."

"Me too, give or take a year or so," Rosa Moon said, her new, friendly smile making Abby smile too.

"I like it that we're about the same age. Do you?"

"Yes'm. I likes it fine. Mausa Eli be in his fifties, Ob'diah claim. Dat ain' young."

"My wonderful father was fifty-five when he died. But he was still so full of laughter and saw the funny side of almost everything."

"De Lord, He don't hab no plaster molds for us. We all come out different ways."

"Yes."

"Your mama, she a religious lady?"

"Yes."

"She gonna be sorrowful 'bout Mausa Eli. But you lucky to hab a mama."

"Yes."

"You ain' feelin' up to so much blabbin'. You want I should bring you some good hot tea? Look like dis house be cold today."

"I don't need anything, thank you."

"I want you should know I misses Mausa Eli too. Look like he oughta walk right in from Abbyfiel'."

"Yes. And I've just decided I want to go look at the new buggy he was so proud of. Is that crazy?"

"No'm. It be cold to go to the stable, but it ain' crazy. I bring your heavy cloak, but don't stay too long an' ketch a chill."

Because she hoped to be alone with her thoughts and the new buggy for at least a few minutes, Abby hauled the mounting stool into place herself and climbed up to the tufted leather seat before Obadiah had a chance to find out that she was in the stable. It was possible that Rosa Moon had sent him on an errand. She hoped so. Abby liked Obadiah, but she wanted only to listen to her own heart now. The lost, half-guilty feelings she had about losing Eli were perplexing enough. Obadiah's steady talking would not have helped, no matter how well-intentioned.

She and Eli had taken only one quick ride around the yard in their fine, elegantly decorated buggy, *her* new buggy—before he left forever. As always, everything, even the new shingle roof he'd had put on the house last year, was to him a gift for Abby. No matter that the new roof would shelter Eli from a storm too.

But as with so many things he had done and even more that he had not done, it left her feeling alone. How she used to long to hear him say, "Look, Abby. This is *our* new dining-room furniture" or "This is *our* new hall carpet."

Now that he was gone, she found herself resenting his way of giving even more than ever. For the first two or three years of their married life, she honestly felt that she received from him in much the openhearted way in which he gave to her. Then it all changed. And it began to change when she admitted to herself at last that, without realizing it, she had allowed herself to become Eli's almost inanimate plaything!

Plaything? Playthings could be terribly important, she thought, her fingers moving slowly back and forth over the leather tufts of the driver's seat beside her. From habit, she had climbed into the passenger seat of the handsome buggy. That, after all, was where she would have sat because Eli didn't care for the idea of a lady driving her own buggy. At first, this quirk had only amused her. Then, when he had begun spending so many hours a day out at Abbyfield, often taking Obadiah or putting him to work at other tasks, it annoyed her when she wanted to shop or just go for a drive and no one was available to drive her. Their home was within walking distance of the business part of town, but a lady shopping on foot meant she couldn't buy more than one or two items unless she fancied looking like a dray horse struggling home with her arms full.

Sitting quietly in the buggy, Abby remembered one late afternoon some time ago when she had come to the disturbing decision that Abbyfield had taken her place in Eli's heart and mind. Or, at best, his wife and his beloved plantation had begun to occupy much the same place in his affections. When he wasn't poring over the Savannah newspaper, he was buried in one of his agricultural journals, especially if an issue happened to feature articles on rice field canals and their smaller drains, which were all dug with shovels and picks by the tough, callused hands of slaves. The extra dirt was hauled off by wheelbarrows pushed by other work-hardened hands. Each load of removed dirt was used to build what she finally learned from Eli were called banks. Banks that also made roads through the fields and held the canals in place.

Obadiah was not only the world's most useful handyman, he was also an expert builder, and after listening to Eli and Obadiah talk for two or three nights in a row from the front steps of her house, Abby finally persuaded Eli to explain to her that "trunks" were the floodgates at the ends of the rice canals, which was a relief since she had thought it ridiculous for Eli to order Obadiah to build an ordinary trunk when one could be bought so easily at a store. Her sincere, but foolish misconceptions amused Eli and his sketchy explanations annoyed her.

After a few moments in the passenger's seat, she scooted in a most unladylike way to the driver's side of the buggy and pretended to be holding reins. Then she startled herself with a question she had never before asked herself or anyone else: "Would I, a lady, really *want* to own a plantation myself?"

No well-built chair had ever seemed to suit her better than the driver's seat of what was truly now her own buggy, a handsome buggy with big, yellow-spoked wheels. Only extremely eccentric Boston ladies drove their own carriages, but a few did, especially when their husbands died and they could no longer afford to pay a driver's salary. Why shouldn't Abigail Banes Allyn of Darien, Georgia, drive her own buggy too?

"My husband is—dead," she whispered, and was stunned

by a heavy mixture of both sorrow and excitement.

"I don't like being buffeted by such contradictory feelings at once, Eli!" She wasn't whispering now. She was talking out loud. "How can I want to cry and laugh at the same minute, Eli? *Eli!* Don't just sit there. Answer me! I'm tired of not being answered. I'm tired to the marrow of my bones of—being alone!"

From behind her at the open stable door, she heard a man clear his throat. Then a respectful, but extremely pleasant man's voice said, "You're not alone, Mrs. Allyn. I'm here now."

Chapter 11

The look on her extraordinary face when Thaddeus Greene saw her turn quickly to stare at him with the most penetrating gray eyes he had ever seen was both startled and defiant—as though she were at once frightened and in full charge.

Standing beside the driver's seat of the elegant buggy looking up at her, cap in hand, Thaddeus said, "My name is Thaddeus Greene, Mrs. Allyn, and I've come to help you in any way I can. You and I will be conducting a lot of business together in the days to come, I'm sure, but for now, I'm just offering my services and my most sincere sympathy. I hope I haven't offended you by barging in like this without warning. In case you're wondering, I'm the overseer at Abbyfield."

"Yes," she said, looking down at him from her driver's seat. "I've heard about you, Mr. Greene."

"My name's Thaddeus. But my friends call me Thad. I hope you'll be my friend, Mrs. Allyn."

"Thank you." Her voice, he thought, wasn't exactly cool, just careful. "I believe even business dealings go better—between friends. I thought you'd come in from Abbyfield soon."

Thad smiled up at her. "You did? Why did you think that?"

"Oh, from what I've been told about you. My—my husband thought highly of you. I'm grateful for your condolences, but—everything's happened so fast I don't yet know which way to turn—even in my grief. I believe the correct thing for me to do first is to see my husband's lawyer."

"Of course. I'm not here on business. I did want you to know Obadiah can come for me anytime you need me— day or night. I thought knowing that might help a little. And to hear straight from me that everything is going well at Abbyfield. I feel sure the—the two new boys Mr. Allyn just bought are going to work out all right."

"Then, it is true, isn't it?"

"True, Mrs. Allyn?"

"That my husband bought illegal Africans in some kind of secret deal with the du Bignons. Darien is about to choke on the rumors. Do you know who else was involved in it?"

"I didn't even know about the transaction until Obadiah told me. Your husband said nothing to me about it, but through Polydone and his grapevine, Obadiah has learned that a man named Charles Lamar from Savannah is at least a part owner of the slave ship. The pieces, thanks to Obadiah, are gradually fitting together for me. I believe Lamar is on his way now, or will be in a short time, from Savannah to Jekyll Island. Polydone, du Bignon's head man, will know the details and then, by that famous slave grapevine, so will Obadiah."

"Well! Port Collector Mr. Woodford Mabry will surely have something to say about all this. It just isn't like him to have allowed an illegal ship to pass through the port in Brunswick. Wouldn't such a ship have to have faulty papers of some kind?"

Thad Greene's smile did not show surprise at her acumen, just admiration. "Most ladies in your social position wouldn't be so perceptive about such matters," he said.

"Mrs. Mabry is one of my closest friends here in Darien. Her husband holds the office of U.S. port collector for Darien as well as Brunswick. Laura Mabry and I talk often— and a lot."

Still holding his high-crowned cap in his hands, he said, "I trust I haven't interrupted too long. And dare I hope that one day, when you've had time to recover a little, you and I will be friends who talk with each other?"

She looked a bit perplexed, he thought, when she said, "Why, yes, Mr. Greene. In fact, once I've seen the lawyer, I imagine we'll need to talk quite a lot. And thank you for coming today."

He bowed. "It's—it's hard not being able to pay my respects to Mr. Allyn in some sort of memorial service. I'm sure that's difficult for you too." Thad held out his hand. As did she. "I must ride back to Abbyfield now. Shouldn't you go in the house and warm up? Your hand's cold. The day's cold."

"Yes. The day's very cold, Mr. Greene. Perhaps I would benefit from a good hard horseback ride too."

"There is an extra riding horse at the plantation named Fan. Should you ever decide to take a good hard gallop, I'd be honored to lead her into town for you. Mr. Allyn's own horse, Mister, is there too."

For an instant, as though she forgot herself, she smiled down at him. "The horse's name is—Mister?"

"Your husband thought him too elegant for a lesser name, I believe. I liked his dry humor."

For another instant—barely an instant—he realized he had taken her by surprise.

"His—humor?"

"Yes. He and I had some good laughs together every now and then."

"I'd like to hear more about that—sometime."

"I'd like to tell you. Don't forget. I'm as close as a short horseback ride for Obadiah—anytime you need me."

When Port Collector Woodford Mabry returned to Darien late on Wednesday, December 1, he felt for the first time the strong blast of the ugly rumors that had been blowing around town about the slave ship.

"How," people wondered aloud, "could an illegal slave

ship get clearance from Mabry's Brunswick office? How had such a thing been possible?"

Through common courtesy, no one asked Woodford directly, but he overheard the gist of the same question again and again. And even though he knew she didn't want to worry him, his talkative, lovable Laura told him about Eli Allyn's death and that she had been hearing even more rumors about a fancy schooner—and groups of strange slaves traveling up the rivers—and unfamiliar steamers making night runs among the coastal islands. Although Laura usually only hinted to him that he was too trusting, Woodford felt sure she was right to be suspicious this time. He realized with a combination of anger and sadness that it was possible he had been plainly misled by a captain named Corrie when Corrie brought the papers from the *Wanderer*, an elegant schooner, rather hastily to Mabry's Brunswick office for clearance the day before. Their conversation had been so pleasant, Captain Corrie so convincing, that Mabry now feared he'd compromised his own integrity and given false clearance. Corrie vowed the schooner had just returned from a pleasure voyage with some wealthy Northern gentlemen who wanted to visit at James Hamilton Couper's Hopeton Plantation before heading for Charleston, South Carolina. Not suspecting such a vessel to be involved in anything so sinister, Mabry didn't question Captain Corrie when he said the required St. Helena seal was missing because the U.S. Consul there had been away on leave.

When Laura finished one of her encouraging little talks about how reputable a port collector he'd always been and assured him that should a slipup have been made, she was certain U.S. Attorney Joseph Ganahl in Savannah would come to his rescue with the Federal authorities, Woodford looked grim.

"At least the clearance I gave the *Wanderer* doesn't permit them to proceed to Charleston until December 5. I have time to return to my Brunswick office first thing tomorrow and look at those clearance papers again. I have to check and recheck all the seals on them. I'm at the point where I don't believe anything Captain Corrie told me about the *Wanderer*'s magnificent adventures. But it isn't too late for me to cancel the clearance if things aren't as they should be. Oh, my dear wife, it's beyond me that reputable men such as the du Bignons, Lamar, even our late esteemed friend Eli Edward Allyn could even think of smuggling slaves into our country against both Federal and state laws! How do men do such things?"

"I have no idea, Woodford," she said. "Something like this should be proof enough to the 'moral Christian' gentlemen of the South that slavery is wrong, wrong, *wrong!* Just think—no, don't think! I've tried to pray for them, but I can't even allow myself to think of the suffering— the terror—of some four hundred Africans—human beings like us—forced to lie packed together in the hold of that stinking schooner!"

"It isn't stinking now," he said almost bitterly. "My men told me it's clean as a whistle, everything scrubbed and polished and ready for its gentleman owners to use again for their own lofty purposes! They must have removed the extra deck where the Africans slept. All vestiges of ever having been a slaver are gone."

"Do you think there's real trouble ahead for our beloved country, Woodford? You and I know in our hearts that the United States cannot endure as a divided nation, half slave, half free. What's going to happen to us?"

"I wish I knew. I wish I knew the answer to that, but I do know what I have to do right away. I have to get back to Brunswick and try to stop the *Wanderer* from any further adventures!"

While her husband was still in Brunswick trying to determine if the *Wanderer* had in fact transported illegal slaves to coastal Georgia, helpful Laura Mabry engaged a seamstress to make Abby's necessary widow's wardrobe. Custom required that Abby wear only black mourning clothes for at least a year, and because custom also restricted her ap-

pearing in public other than Sunday church, it was a relief
that her outfits could be few in number.

"I've always hated wearing black," she said when Laura
Mabry came with a few samples of black silky cotton and
velvet. The fabric was to be made up into no more than
two dress outfits, mainly because Abby despised wearing
the tight, tight corset required with hooped or crinoline-
stiffened skirts. Her new black dresses for wear around the
house would be suitable for receiving the callers who continued to come to express their sympathy and ask endless
questions. It distressed Abby that the ladies of Darien went
on trying to discover Eli's part, if any, in what was now
the full-blown scandal of the mysterious slave ship. And
Laura had explained that her husband feared he had been
misled into giving false clearance to the ship.

"You amaze me," Laura said as she was showing Abby a
sample of black cotton with a black overprint which relieved a little of the monotony of black, black, black. "I
don't know why you don't send for Thad Greene and ask
him right out what he knows by now of the exact connection Eli had with the du Bignons or that Mr. Charles Lamar, who is said to be part owner of the *Wanderer* and may
be involved too. I know Obadiah insists he's told Rosa
Moon all he knows about it and I know how closemouthed
Eli was. I also know, even though you insist you have no
strong feelings either way about slavery, that you are a
Northerner, Abby, and all this must embarrass you dreadfully. But isn't it better to know all there is to know?"

On an exasperated sigh, Abby said, "I don't know,
Laura! I honestly don't know how much more I want or
need to find out. If there's legal trouble ahead from the
Federal government, I'll face that when it comes. Legalities
are Mr. Bentley's problem. Not mine."

"Mr. Bentley represents Eli's interests at Abbyfield and
now those interests are yours. You're the owner of those
two new illegal Africans. Send for Thaddeus Greene! He
must know a lot more details by now. If the man wants to
help, let him."

"You don't think people will talk?"

"Of course they'll talk! But they're talking anyway and there's nothing wrong with your Abbyfield overseer calling on you—on business. Is there?"

"No," Abby answered, her voice vague. "I guess not."

"You said you liked the man. That he was most pleasant, as well as good-looking."

"You do talk too much, Laura," Abby said with a smile.

"I know I do, but I'm afraid you'll shrivel up and die just because you're a widow. You're not even thirty-two yet."

"Poor Eli's not even here to defend himself. Do you suppose in time the gossip will die down?"

"Of course it will die down eventually. Still Woodford says the whole rotten mess could drag on in the courts for years! But, even as quiet as little Darien is, something will turn up soon to give the wagging tongues a new direction." Laura held up a square of the sheer black crepe which was overprinted with vines and leaves. "Don't you like this, Abby? The pattern gives it a little life, I think."

"Widows aren't supposed to be lively. And I'm not!" She glanced briefly at the black crepe. "I like this all right, I guess. You're awfully good to take all this time with me on my mourning clothes, Laura, but I have to ask you something: Do you believe I truly miss my husband?"

"I know you do! I also know that as good and kind as he was, you weren't really in love with the man, so wouldn't it help if you and I could just talk honestly about your feelings when you need to, Abby?"

"I did love him!"

"But there are many, many kinds of love. All of it can be real love too, but one kind is simply different from the others. You told me one morning sometime last year that you finally admitted to yourself that you had fallen in love with the *idea* of living on the romantic coast of Georgia on a splendid plantation. That you were in love with the idea of being married to the man who could give it to you, but—not the man himself. A woman can love and a woman can also be *in* love. I'm in love with Woodford

Mabry. I have been since I was fourteen. Have you forgotten that you told me you loved Eli the way one would love a close friend?"

Quick tears filled Abby's eyes, and Laura went to her. "I'm sorry, Abby. That was cruel! I honestly didn't mean it to be, but that was a cruel thing I—forced you to remember." Then she stepped back and studied Abby's face. "Or was it cruel? Maybe the truth will help. You do remember you told me that, don't you?"

"I—I suppose I do. Yes. And I'm—I'm suddenly very tired from not sleeping. I respected, I almost revered Eli in many ways and I pray God he didn't suffer too long before he died. They do say drowning is a ghastly way to die. But right now, all I'm sure of is—is that I think you're right that the vine-leaf overprinting relieves the black a little. Yes. I'll have a church dress made of that material. Maybe some shirring or even ruffled trim to make it a bit prettier."

Beaming at her, Laura said as to a child, "That's my friend, Abby! That sounds more like you. Even your mourning clothes must be as pretty and fashionable as possible. In spite of all black, good style will lift your spirits."

"Laura, do you think I'm awfully slow becoming myself again?"

"Slow? My dear, no! Eli's only been dead a little over a week. I think you're brave and quick. Woodford at times thinks I'm too glib about giving God credit for intervening in our mortal trials, but I admire you so much for being as honest as you are. I'm sure God is giving you His very own courage!"

Tears gone, Abby smiled up at her. "You must be right. And have you ever noticed that God touches our spirits, our hearts, even our attitudes, through any number of ways? Sometimes it strikes me that He makes use of most surprising events—and people."

"People, Abby?"

"Yes. I think I'm about to tell you something I may be sorry I blabbed, Laura, even to you."

"You *can* trust me."

"I know. At least as much as anyone can know about another person, I trust you." She waited, then said, "Something began to happen in me a day or so after I lost Eli. The day Thaddeus Greene rode his horse in to give me his condolences and found me in the stable sitting alone in the handsome buggy dear Eli bought for me just before he went away. I suddenly longed to see the buggy, so I had gone alone to the stable and was just sitting there talking to Eli when I heard a man clear his throat and a man's voice address me."

"Thaddeus Greene?"

"Yes. There he was telling me quite simply that he was here now, that I was no longer alone."

"Oh, Abby!"

"What? Why are you giving me a look like that, Laura? We talked some but not a lot. Mostly about my need to see Mr. Fred Bentley, Eli's lawyer, who drew his will and can give me counsel concerning what to do next at Abbyfield. I've never even met Eli's Savannah factor! Mr. Greene *is* the overseer, you know. Such matters concern him too!"

"You're prattling. I'm perfectly aware that he's your overseer and also that it's winnowing time. What else is there to do at Abbyfield but get the good crop of rice Eli left you to the mill and the market?"

"But I don't even know what to do with a crop—good or bad! That's where I need a factor *and* Mr. Greene *and* Lawyer Bentley. And, Laura Mabry, you're standing there looking too wise and too eager to jump to conclusions when there aren't any. I'm thankful for Mr. Bentley because, kind as he is, Thaddeus Greene isn't much older than I am, if any. I—I need the advice of an older man."

"Abby, men in their thirties are old enough to run for the Congress of the United States. And Woodford says Thad Greene is an experienced rice expert."

"He's an overseer."

"An overseer with almost a decade of experience operating two of the most productive rice plantations around

Savannah! He's a jewel, Abby. I can tell you think so too. Why not admit it? I know you're confused, but Thaddeus Greene might well be good Eli's last marvelous gift to you. Does it clear your head a little even to think that way about it?"

Chapter 12

When Dr. James Holmes reached Abbyfield on a chilly morning in January of the new year, 1859, he was interested to find the overseer, Thad Greene, waiting to greet him. The doctor had been called to tend an emergency with one of the newly arrived Africans that Eli Allyn had surprised many people, Holmes among them, by buying illegally late last year. The subject of slavery was one Dr. Holmes tried earnestly to avoid since he had no strong feelings himself either way. But he was always gratified to see special concern among owners and overseers for the well-being of their slaves.

Of course, it was good business to keep them healthy and strong, able to labor and bring in the crops, but being Holmes, he cared that Negroes be as well and healthy as possible for their own good. Caring for them also helped his medical practice. Seeing Thad Greene first thing pleased Holmes for an even more important reason. He had a genuine concern and growing admiration for the young widow of Eli Allyn and somehow he believed that Greene's careful attention to every detail of operating the productive plantation she had inherited from her late husband was a perpetual gift to Abby.

Obadiah had told Holmes only last week, when the two met at Abby's home in Darien, that he had heard on his trusty grapevine that for some reason one of the illegal

Africans—a lad of barely twelve—was crying himself to sleep every night. It was possible that the boy simply had a bad case of homesickness, which could usually be treated by a big dose of kindness and good cheer, both of which Holmes had in abundance.

As they shook hands, Thad Greene thanked Dr. Holmes for coming so promptly and told him all he knew of the symptoms suffered by the African boy, Youngun, a name given to him by the other Abbyfield Negroes since he was plainly the younger brother of Oldun, the other new slave.

"He answers to the name Youngun now," Thad explained. "But I'm afraid he's so sick that soon he won't be able to answer to any name. You may have come just in time, Doctor."

"I hope so. I pray so. Does the boy seem to have a fever? Do you know if he's hot to the touch?"

"I was on my way out to the cabin where he and Oldun sleep when I saw your buggy coming this way. But Baldy, my driver, says he's burning up. Hurt his foot, I guess, but no one told me until today when Youngun couldn't stand up. The poor boy never did learn to wear shoes even in this chilly weather. I'm afraid he must have stepped on a rusty nail. Neither of the new ones seems to have any idea of cleanliness. I shouldn't have expected them to. Lord, I hope you're not too late to save him."

As Thad led the way, Holmes, hoping he didn't sound unfeeling about the sick boy, couldn't resist asking about the Abbyfield rice crop, which had been sold since Eli's death. "Did her factor get a good price on the market?"

"Fine, Doctor. And the crop was excellent. I plan to ride in to Darien tomorrow if your diagnosis on the boy isn't too bad. I wish I knew a way to lift Mrs. Allyn's spirits beyond telling her of our splendid crop results. Do you know how much she actually knows about planting and harvesting rice? Did she come out here to Abbyfield often with her husband?"

"Only once or twice that I know of. You must have caught on that Eli Edward Allyn was not prone to talk much. I doubt that he told her a lot. Not that he intended to keep anything from her. He was just a man of very few words. It would have seemed to Eli that he was troubling Abby if he talked about either problems or successes at the plantation. Burdening her mind with nonessentials."

Holmes waited. "Perhaps I shouldn't even mention this, but he—he was a strange fellow. Never seemed to get to know Abby as she really is. Unfortunately, the way he behaved toward her only served to accentuate the difference in their ages."

"I see. Well, we're almost there. The third cabin just down this lane is where you'll find the poor lad. Want me to go inside with you?"

"I'd prefer you did. If the boy's afflicted with gangrene, as I expect, I'll need help. There's only one thing to do and that is cut off his foot."

At the cabin door before he lifted the wooden latch, Thad whirled to face Holmes. "Doctor, you don't mean that!"

"I wish I didn't. But if he's got gangrene, there's no other way to save his life. I hate to say that. Hate even worse to do it. But if I have to, I'll need your help."

Inside the shadow-filled, gloomy cabin room, Dr. Holmes could see a fairly tall African stretched on a rumpled, lumpy straw mattress beside the inert, motionless, plainly dead body of a boy no more than ten or twelve years old, his fists still clenched in the death throes through which he had just passed. The tall lad Holmes thought must be Oldun, the only person Youngun really knew in this strange land, still lay beside the dead boy, holding on to him as though he could keep him from having to go away. As though his own life would be but half a life without his young brother.

Such a stench hung in the room, the doctor heard Thad cough.

"It was gangrene, I'm sure. Look at the size of that poor foot. If he managed to limp around until today, he must have done it in pure hell!" From habit, Holmes felt for a pulse. There was none. "Blessedly, he's all right now," he whispered to Thad. "I won't have to saw off his poor leg. And he's where he can run now. The lad's gone where he even understands everything that's being said to him." Looking up at Thad, Holmes surprised himself by asking, "Do you—believe life goes on, Thad?"

Despite the shadows and the gloom, he could see that all the color had drained from Thad's face, but he also saw a faint smile steal over his young, startlingly handsome features. "Do I—believe Youngun's—with God, Doctor? I— I think I do. Yes. Yes, I do believe that. I *have* to believe it."

As Holmes and Thad started to leave, Thad went back to where Oldun was still holding the wasted boy. When he laid his hand on Oldun's shoulder, Holmes knew he'd never forget the look on the African's face. Fully expecting to see hatred in Oldun's dark eyes, there were tears and a look of what could only be gratitude.

"Hello, now," Oldun whispered, as though he were expressing the gratitude from his heart. "Oh, hello now!"

Holmes stared at Thad. "Did he say—hello?"

"Yes, sir. I've heard that Africans are superb mimics. I know now that they are. It seems they can speak English words whose meaning they don't understand at all. I'd give almost anything to know what he thought he was saying, but oddly, unexplainably, he doesn't seem to hate either one of us."

"He has every reason to hate all white men," Holmes murmured.

"Yes."

"And along with you, Thad, I'd give almost anything to know what the lad—thought he was saying to us."

Back at the end of the lane where Holmes had hitched his horse and buggy, he and Thad stood for a time in silence. Then Holmes said, "Thad, I've just realized that I can't bring myself to tell Abby what just happened. She—was never known to give Eli any trouble about it, but the girl seems still to be forming her thinking on slavery. This may focus her thoughts. News of Youngun's death will break her heart. Is there really a chance you might be coming into Darien tomorrow?"

Instead of answering the doctor's question, Thad asked one of his own: "What did Mr. Allyn really think about owning slaves?"

"He—didn't really like it. He was a Bostonian too, you know."

Thad almost scoffed. "Just one of those Northerners who hated the principle of owning another human being almost as much as he loved the money those black hands and backs could earn for them, eh?"

"I—I'd rather not answer that."

"What about you, Doctor? What do you feel about slavery?"

"I'd—rather not answer that either."

"I guessed as much. And—honesty is a most admirable trait. At least, to me it is. I'll see you tomorrow if you happen to drop by Miss Abby's house just before noon. I'll want to be here with Oldun when they bury—Youngun. We'll do that first thing in the morning and then I'll ride into town to tell her what happened."

Chapter 13

Just before noon the next day, Thad Greene rode his late employer's horse Mister to Darien as soon as the laborers had returned from Youngun's burial to their early winter's work of preparing the harvested fields for spring planting. Thad was later than he intended on this mild January morning because he had given his driver, Baldy, a hand at assigning tasks. It gave him a sense of satisfaction that he now knew the Abbyfield workers well enough to be sure which men to assign to ditch and drain or to clean and mend floodgates— installing new ones where needed.

So far he had experienced few major problems in getting along with the Abbyfield slaves. He smiled at this thought as Mister took him at a brisk canter toward the modest Darien house where Abby, he hoped, would be glad or at least relieved to see him. His mind went to her to keep from thinking of the pathetic, wasted body of Youngun, so recently covered over with earth in the slave graveyard near the Allyn landing on Cathead Creek. His satisfaction over Abbyfield's work crew under his direction lessened sharply when he remembered that somehow he had failed to notice the worsening condition of poor Youngun's foot. The boy had suffered being jerked from his African home, endured the inevitable agonies, the filth and cramped muscles, the eventual hunger and thirst as the splendid schooner *Wanderer* brought him and his brother Oldun to live forever in the terrifying unknown conditions of a foreign land under an overseer whose only goal in life was to make a profit for the plantation owner who hired him.

Only Thad in all of McIntosh County knew what kind of overseer he really was. He was not even sure that the slaves themselves knew, because only Lonzo and Baldy had ever had anything resembling a serious talk with him. He had no intentions of letting anyone know exactly what he felt as a man about the whole institution of slavery. He suspected that Dr. James Holmes, who also kept his thoughts on the subject to himself, had no strong antipathy to the practice. After all, in the main, Holmes earned his living from plantation owners who retained him on contract, as had Eli Allyn, to take regular care of their slaves. For Holmes to disapprove of slavery would in no way be good business for him.

He goaded Mister to a quicker gallop. It was suddenly almost a necessity that he find out for himself what Abby truly thought.

Inside the town of Darien, he slowed his horse to an easy trot and headed toward Madison Street, his thoughts echoing the primitive songs sung with surprisingly intense feeling by the slaves gathered to bury Youngun, a stranger to most of them because he and Oldun had been at Abbyfield for such a short time. Thad's ideas on the whole subject of owning the very lives and deaths of other human beings were more in conflict than ever.

And then, above all those confusing thoughts, he felt a tingle of excitement because within minutes now he would be seeing Abigail Allyn. Despite his determination to be calm and comforting with her, as unemotional as possible when he told her of Youngun's wretched death, his heart was racing. At the moment of his first sight of her soon after Mr. Allyn's death, he had forced to one side the abrupt certainty that during that moment Thad Greene had looked upon the most remarkably beautiful face he'd ever seen. Beautiful? More than beautiful, as were other women in their early thirties, some of whom had given him every chance to come closer in all ways. He had waited.

Through more than a decade, he had gone on waiting for the one woman by whom he could bear to be captured. Captured? *Do I really want anyone to capture me?* At the instant of his very first look at Abigail some seven weeks ago, he knew he did. Thaddeus Greene, still at the peak of his youth and drive and energy, working as an overseer on a rice plantation simply because he knew he hadn't yet found his own vocation, welcomed the bondage of having been captured. Not by the work itself but by the almost bewitching attraction of Abby Allyn. By the vibrancy and beauty and restless intelligence hidden of necessity by the young, grieving widow toward whom he was riding now.

He had already waited so long.

How much longer would he have to wait before he would be free to allow his attraction for Abby to be known to her as well as the cultivated, but provincial citizens of Darien, Georgia?

Youngun would now never know the dizzying way a woman could entice an otherwise strong, self-sufficient man. Youngun, his once muscular, healthy body still a stranger in the earth piled over and around him, had been struck down before he even had time to accustom himself to a foreign land where both white and black voices spoke a scattering of unintelligible words. Where only his brother, Oldun, could express his devotion, his caring, his fear of saying goodbye. Oldun *had* looked so afraid beside his brother's grave.

On Madison Street now, Thad knew that in less than a minute the shape of Abby's house would be in plain view—and then *she* would be in plain view and he would be telling her about Youngun.

"Keep your mind right on Youngun," he said to himself. "You'll do much better learning what she's really like—letting her find out what you're like—if you stay away from anything personal." As he reined Mister in front of her house, he reminded himself once more that it would be important for him to know sooner or later her exact viewpoint on slavery. Just because she came from the North did not necessarily mean she even approved of the active abolitionists up there. Actually, as many Northerners as Southerners preferred not to rock the boat one way or the other.

With a few confidential words and a pat or two, he hitched his horse, turned toward the house, and was startled to see Abby in the yard. There she was—alone, radiant—in a warm red plush cloak, her dark hair loose, its curls tousled by the barely cool January breeze. In one hand, she carried a basket heaped with white narcissus blossoms and the startled look on her face when she saw him was that of a child caught stealing forbidden cookies.

"Good morning, Mrs. Allyn," he called pleasantly. "Or is it noon already? At any rate, I hope I haven't come at a bad time."

"You couldn't come at a bad time, Mr. Greene."

With a warm smile, he asked, "I couldn't? Are you sure?"

"What I meant to say is that no one could come at what to me would be a bad time these days. For a while, I was besieged with callers, most trying to pry into my business. They've stopped rather suddenly. I—I'm sure it's been three or four days since anyone's been here except Dr. Holmes's wife, my close friend Susan."

"Dr. Holmes didn't tell you I was coming by today?"

"He hasn't been here to tell me anything. I think even he's deserted me." She glanced briefly at her bright red cloak, ran a hand through her curls, then laughed. "I—I'll be wearing black for months to come. Today, I just felt like picking flowers in my scarlet sage cloak."

"Scarlet sage?"

"My husband always called this my scarlet sage cloak. He—he liked it." With a slightly defiant upward tilt of her chin, she added, "I like it too."

Holding out her basket of fragrant white blossoms, she said, "Smell, Mr. Greene. Aren't they dainty and sweet? Every year I'm startled, I swear, by their fragrance! The same with lilies of the valley. Don't you love the way they smell too?"

"Yes. Oh, yes, ma'am." There hadn't been a single flower anywhere when they'd buried Youngun this morning, but Thad's thoughts flew back to the dead boy, then to his brother Oldun, who must feel utterly alone now with no one to be close to, even to understand him when he spoke. No one to answer when he asked a question.

"The only other time you've been here, Mr. Greene, I remember we talked only for a few minutes out in our— my—stable, where I'd gone to look again at the new buggy my husband bought for me just before the accident in the storm. We shouldn't just stand out here in the yard this time. Please come in. My Rosa Moon will bring something to refresh you."

"Your lovely, fragrant flowers have already refreshed me, ma'am."

For an instant, their eyes met and Thad looked deep into Abby's beautiful gray eyes. He thought he caught just a hint of a smile, not formal, not informal. Real. The smile was fleeting, but he took it as a good sign. Probably only because I want so much to believe it a good sign, he thought, then said, "I'd be pleased to go inside for a few minutes if it isn't too much of an interruption, Mrs. Allyn. I have Abbyfield news for you and you'll need to know part of it anyway when you next see your lawyer."

As the two climbed the wooden steps to her front porch, she asked, "Do you find me disrespectful to be wearing this cloak when all widows are supposed to wear only black, Mr. Greene?"

"I don't find you disrespectful at all," he said easily, opening the front door for her. "The cloak is too becoming for anyone to think that, I'm sure."

On a slight laugh, while he took the cloak from her shoulders and hung it on the hall tree, she said, "Then you don't know Darien people very well yet. They're sticklers for proprieties, and even though I've been here a little more than five years, I'm still an outsider, a fact which necessitates their close scrutiny."

Thad hung his high-crowned cap and his coat on the tree beside her cloak and followed her into the parlor, where Obadiah had laid a perfect fire for such a mild winter day—not too big a blaze . . . just enough to give the room an inviting warmth. He seated her, then took the big chair across from her, wondering, hoping it had been the very chair used by Eli Allyn. Everything about sitting so near her in the same chair where her husband had sat struck him as exactly right. In a way he hadn't known since he left his childhood home in Philadelphia soon after the death of his parents, Thad felt at home. Felt himself to be where he belonged.

"Since you haven't seen Dr. Holmes, were you surprised when I rode up just now, Mrs. Allyn?" he asked.

"I was surprised indeed," she answered easily. "Pleasantly surprised, I must say. Dr. Holmes stays so busy. He and his wife, Susan, live out on the Ridge some three miles away and sometimes it's days between visits from either of them. Mrs. Holmes dotes on the good doctor, is well aware of his importance to our community, so his needs come first." He noticed her well-shaped, graceful hands as she rang a small brass bell, calling a servant. "I'll need to know, Mr. Greene, if you prefer hot coffee or hot tea. Rosa Moon will have something to go with either."

"Never learned really to like the taste of tea," he said. "I'll have coffee if I may, thank you."

"Rosa Moon is Obadiah's wife, by the way, and an excellent cook. In fact, right now—especially since my husband's death—she and I are becoming rather fast friends. I depend on her shamefully, I'm afraid. And, of course, this place, small as it is, simply wouldn't function at all without Obadiah. You're acquainted with Obadiah, I'm sure."

"Oh, yes, ma'am! Your husband and I said often that even though he's here in town working most of the time, in a very real way Obadiah is also a mainstay at Abbyfield. The man's a big talker, of course, but somehow he always manages to say something useful, and I know that he all but gave his own life trying to save Mr. Allyn in that storm."

"Yes."

"The last I heard, Obadiah vowed he means to keep Mr. Allyn's boot for always."

"Yes, I know. I don't know anyone who was as close to my husband as Obadiah."

Thad would have given almost anything to know all she had meant when she said that, but in response, he said only, "I—see."

The ensuing rather awkward moments were interrupted by heavy, shuffling footsteps in the short hall outside the parlor where they sat. And then Rosa Moon was filling the open doorway—a big woman, with mellow brown skin, a pretty face, and far too short in height to carry all that fat when she walked. His hostess seemed unusually pleased to see Rosa Moon and appeared sincerely happy to introduce her to Thad, calling the woman more important than a right hand.

Thad stood as though Rosa Moon had been white and bowed.

The ample woman's face, when Thad offered his gracious bow, made him think of the sun coming up on a clear winter morning.

"Mighty pleased to meetcha, Mr. Greene," Rosa Moon said, and gave him a smile that was far more than mere courtesy. He said nothing as Rosa Moon turned to Mrs. Allyn for her orders, but Thad knew as sure as gun was iron that at that moment he and Rosa Moon could become real allies. He would be able to count on her and he meant to do just that.

After Mrs. Allyn ordered a pot of coffee and freshly baked bread with butter and jelly, Rosa Moon left the parlor and Abigail turned to Thad. "I hope you're not in a hurry, Mr. Greene, because sometimes it takes Rosa Moon a while to serve. I'm sure she'll want to make fresh coffee. Wouldn't this be a good time for you to tell me what you feel I can understand about the crop you just harvested?"

Relieved to have an excuse to delay telling her about Youngun, Thad said, "My dear lady, we've gone a long way from harvesting by now."

"You know that I know almost nothing about growing rice, preparing it for market, or selling it, don't you? My lawyer did tell me my husband used an excellent Savannah factor named Joseph Habersham."

"From operating two Savannah River rice plantations, I know him to be one of the best. A fine gentleman too. Shall I give you a lesson in rice culture, ma'am?"

"If you have time, yes! I've always wanted to understand at least a little bit of what my husband did at Abbyfield."

"I have time," he said. "Plenty of time, if I'm not keeping you from something you'd planned."

"It's been so long since I've had a plan of any kind for anything, I doubt I could carry one out if I tried. I have all the time in the world, Mr. Greene."

"Good. Then I'll do my best to tell you briefly and simply."

"Simply by all means," she said, laughing.

"I'll begin with January of a new year. We need the first two months of the year, actually, to prepare the fields for a new planting. There's plowing, harrowing, hoeing, piling up and burning old trash and last year's stubble. We also clean ditches and drains, rebuild the banks where necessary, and mend the floodgates. Of course, new ones must be built where needed. Are you with me so far?"

"I'm certainly trying."

"From mid-March until early May, rice is planted intermittently. I don't need all the hands at this time, but those not planting rice always have plenty of work to do in other field labor. We do grow our own crops to eat, you know. Anyway, in the trenches, which have been cleaned out by now, workers sow seed rice—that's what we call rough rice, not milled rice. That means the inner husk is left on each grain. Then the floodgates are opened and water is let in the fields. This is called the first flooding or the 'sprout flow' and is left to stand from two to five days until the grain is pipped."

"Pipped? What in the world is pipped?"

They both laughed.

"The first showing of a sprout," he explained. "Anyway, it's at this time the gates are lowered to allow the fields to drain and dry. Then, when the seedling plants are plainly visible, the fields are again flooded. This irrigation is usually called the 'point' or 'stretch flow,' and that is left to stay on the plants two to five more days, at which time it is again drained off and the plants allowed to grow for about two weeks. It's during this two-week growing time that they're lightly hoed. It took me a while before I learned exactly who knows how to handle a hoe and who doesn't. I know now. Hoes are heavy, so it's not easy work in any way. The third irrigation, which we call the 'deep flow,' covers the rice plants completely for several more days, during which dead weeds and other trash floats to the surface to be raked off onto the banks. Water this time, by the way, kills any insects infecting the plants. We then drain off the water gradually to a level of six inches . . ." Thad broke off, studying her face. "Mrs. Allyn, I hope you'll excuse me for asking, but are you—really listening?"

"I'm not exactly sure, but I think you lost me about two floodings ago, Mr. Greene. Am I dreadfully ungrateful? I am interested, but it sounds—"

"It sounds boring in words all strung together like that?"

"I am being rude and I hope you'll forgive me. I know you tried."

Thad now had a good laugh. "I did try, but there's a much better way to educate you."

"Oh? How?"

"If you would like me to, I can give you a firsthand demonstration of every phase. Over the next few months, when it's a good time to observe the different processes, I'll ride into town and accompany you to Abbyfield in your new buggy. I'm sure Obadiah can hitch it for us. How does that sound to you?"

"Well, I—it sounds rather exciting, if you want the truth. I've always been terribly curious about all of it. But to keep people from talking, could I bring Dr. Holmes's wife, Susan, or Mrs. Woodford Mabry? At least on the first visit?"

"I think that could be arranged and I like the idea just fine."

Even her quick frown was lovely, he thought, as she asked, "Where on earth could that woman be? It simply can't take even Rosa Moon this long to brew a fresh pot of coffee and I know her bread's baked. I wanted you to have it while it's still nice and warm!"

She was reaching for her little brass bell at the same moment Rosa Moon heaved into view carrying an enormous tray with a silver filigreed basket and a big silver pot of steaming coffee. The size of the tray caused Thad to jump to his feet to help.

"Never min', sir. I kin do it jus' fine." Rosa Moon puffed out her words and skillfully managed the heavy tray.

"That woman could perform on a stage up North," Abby said, only half smiling. "I don't think I'll ever get accustomed to your near-spills with those overloaded trays, though, Rosa Moon. But we do thank you. The coffee smells delicious and so does that fresh bread."

The tray safely on a table, Rosa Moon wiped her forehead with her sleeve, then said, "Dat man, Ob'diah, hold me up. He jus' got to tell me all 'bout what he find at Abbyfield when I done send him out there to git me some more sweet taters fo' yo' dinner today, Miss Abby. An' you know how he go on an' on an' on."

Still standing, Thad asked, fearing the worst, "What did Obadiah find at Abbyfield, Rosa Moon? Nothing bad happened, did it? Nothing since I left this morning, I hope."

"It ain' my place to say," Rosa Moon answered in a loud whisper.

"What do you mean, Rosa Moon? What isn't your place to say about Abbyfield?"

"What Ob'diah jus' tol' me, Miss Abby. Look to me like

Mr. Thad you be the one to tell her. I ain' no overseer at no plantation! The bread's done buttered and I got me a wash to do," she said, heading again for her part of the house as Abby poured two cups of hot coffee.

"All right, Mr. Thad. Here's our refreshment. Now what am I supposed to hear about Abbyfield—straight from the gentleman who *is* my overseer?"

Chapter 14

f or at least a quarter of an hour, as they enjoyed Rosa Moon's warm bread and coffee, Abby listened as Thad started at the beginning and told her everything he could remember about the arrival of the two new African boys at Abbyfield. He explained again, as he had in their earlier meeting shortly after Eli's death, that Eli had told him nothing before his trip to Jekyll Island. And how in the weeks since then he had managed to learn more of the details surrounding the incident. He had learned from Obadiah how the boys had been brought from Jekyll Island to Abbyfield in Eli's boat by Obadiah and Lonzo. How, along with four hundred or so other illegal Africans, the two had been unloaded on Jekyll from the schooner *Wanderer*, which was now being called a slave ship. She said nothing as he talked and talked, but with every word Abby could feel him struggling to make the hard, ugly, cruel facts of the event as bearable as anyone could, considering all that happened. And into his whole narrative she tried to read the truth about Thad Greene, about what he was really like.

His voice was gentle, his words carefully chosen, his manner both courteous and sensitive. She not only listened, she watched every slight change of expression on his wonderful face. *Wonderful?* The word came to mind as he continued by telling her about Youngun's unexpected death the day before—sparing her only the hideous look of the dead tissue that once was Youngun's poor foot. Her heart swelled with a pain-filled sense of identification with the boy. She identified with his brother Oldun too, who until Dr. Holmes had pronounced Youngun dead, had lain beside the weakening body and held hard to the last familiar tie he had to their family life in the Congo.

So clear had Thad made everything, she even knew that both boys' front teeth had been filed—their African sign of having reached manhood. Her own teeth hurt at the pain both must have endured with the filing. Thad Greene knew how to reach her too deeply. For a time she resented his knowing. On only their second meeting, he had no right to know her so well! But he did and in his knowing she found the courage to admit to herself, despite the resentment, that it was good to be understood and known at last.

Thaddeus Greene understood her and knew her, but it was too soon for something like this to happen.

She had no idea how to live with real understanding from anyone. Oh, she was beginning to learn that Rosa Moon had known her mistress for a long time and seemed to understand her in a direct, respectful servant's way. But Thad was an educated man—a gentleman in every sense of the word. He was also a stranger. Perhaps she was not really puzzled by his uncanny knowing, but she had no idea how to respond, so soon after Eli's going away, to Thad's understanding . . . understanding that somehow angered her. And made her want to push along the days, weeks, months until it would be acceptable for her to let her real feelings show.

Thad was telling her now about the burial song sung by the Abbyfield people at Youngun's grave and how he had wondered if Oldun even realized that they were committing his brother's body to the earth with their singular ritual of coming together and singing around an open grave.

In her first words since he had begun to talk to her, Abby asked, "How did you know that, Mr. Greene? How did you know about their ritual of coming together that way?"

"Do you mean, since I'm from Pennsylvania, how did I know?"

"I—suppose, yes."

"Don't forget I was an overseer on two fairly large rice plantations outside Savannah. I'd been around slaves for eight years before Mr. Allyn hired me."

"I've never even heard a slave's burial song," Abby said, almost as though she felt embarrassed by it.

When Thad said nothing, she added, "I know I've probably missed a most elemental and vital side of life down here. Until lately, Rosa Moon was almost as silent as my reserved husband. Oh, I've heard that Obadiah sings all the time, but he's always busy outside or at Abbyfield. And Rosa Moon hums to herself in her kitchen, but the minute I appear, she stops."

"Did you know the slaves call their graveyard 'that ol' field'?"

"No! How would I know that? How do you know, Mr. Greene?"

"Well, from the first day I came South, I've been interested in knowing more about their African culture. Doesn't it fascinate you that they can adjust to our strange customs as they seem to do? At least, most of them."

"Yes! And I know I'm more than interested now. I must have been missing so much stuck away in this little house in town for five years. I—I wish I knew what they sang at Youngun's burial this morning."

With a respectful smile, he asked, "Would you really like to know what the Abbyfield people sang when we buried Youngun?"

"Yes. Oh, yes!"

"Oddly, the song they sang together is usually a solo dance."

"A dance?"

"I've learned—and I think it teaches us a lot more than mere cultural fact—that death to many Negroes is something to dance about!"

"Because their life with us is so hard?"

"I'll let you decide about that. I just know it's a dance and I'm told that over on Sapelo Island they call it Buzzard's Lope."

"And do you know why they call it by such a strange title?"

"You *are* interested, aren't you?"

"I don't suppose you can sing or hum any of it, can you? My husband always said their songs are impossible for whites to sing."

Thad laughed softly. "He was right about that, but if you like, I'll try. I've actually spent hours with my own broom handle beating on the floor of my cottage trying to get the hang of their rhythm." Thad picked up a knife from the big silver tray, held it by the blade, and began to beat a slow, strange rhythm with its handle on the table beside his chair. Then in a surprisingly tentative way—he had never seemed at all tentative about anything—he started to sing, the beat of the knife handle somehow integrated into the rhythm of his voice as he looked toward the ceiling and sang:

> "Throw me anywhere
> In that ol' field,
> Throw me anywhere,
> Lord,
> In that ol' field
> Throw me anywhere,
> Lord,
> In that ol' field
> Throw me anywhere,
> Lord,
> In that ol' field . . .

"And on it goes for as long as the spirit moves them to go on, I guess," Thad said. "This morning, I found myself wishing they'd never stop. I couldn't tell you if I tried, but somehow that strange, rhythmic song helped me as I stood there beside Youngun's open grave."

"Do—do you suppose it helped Oldun too?"

"I don't have any idea. Remember, I didn't even know whether Oldun knew they were singing a burial song. Everything in Georgia is as strange to Oldun—probably even stranger—than any African custom is to us."

For what seemed to Abby a long time, he sat there sipping what must now be lukewarm coffee. Finally, she said, "I find I'd like to know exactly what *you* think of the institution of slavery, Mr. Greene."

For another long moment, he looked at her, set down his cup, and asked, "What would you think of me if I said I thought it was all right?"

"Does it matter what I think?"

"Yes."

"I don't mean what I think of slavery," Abby said in an almost playful manner. "I mean what I think of you."

Giving her a quizzical look, Thad said, "What you think about everything matters a lot to me."

"I'm sorry," Abby said, her lovely voice serious again. "This somehow doesn't seem the time for playing word games, does it?"

"No, it doesn't. So I'll be honest with you about my opinion on slavery and trust you will be honest with me. I earn a fair living as overseer on your plantation, but I ask God's forgiveness every night for every task I assign. Especially when I know it would infuriate me if someone demanded that I endure such work."

"You—ask forgiveness?"

"Yes, ma'am. And the reason I do is because I know every time I order any kind of punishment for one of your slaves, I disobey God."

Abby flinched. "My slaves?"

"They're yours now, Mrs. Allyn. Your attorney, Mr. Bentley, sent for me to visit his office not long ago. Since your late husband left all that he owned to you, Mr. Bentley instructed me, as per his agreement with you, to take full charge of everything at Abbyfield. Among Mr. Allyn's most valuable properties were his slaves—your slaves now. You look surprised."

"I—I guess I am. I knew dear, generous Eli left everything to me, but somehow I hadn't dwelt on other human beings being included among his properties. You might as well know, Mr. Greene, that I don't think I approve of slavery." He said nothing. "You're silent. Why?"

"Don't you think it's a bit early—a bit too soon after your husband's death for us to discuss an issue as difficult as slavery?"

"That's thoughtful of you, but I fail to see the connection. Do you happen to know what Dr. Holmes truly feels about the practice of owning other human beings? Of owning their—daily lives, their evenings together, their nights and mornings?"

"I asked the old gentleman the same question yesterday."

"What did he say?"

"That he'd rather not talk about it."

"I see."

Thad took a large bite of Rosa Moon's tender, tasty bread, excused himself for speaking with his mouth full, and said he needed to head back to Abbyfield. "This is the day your people are given their weekly supplies of rice, cornmeal, salt meat, butter, and so on. I have the only keys to the storehouse and I'm a stickler for seeing that they don't stand in line a long time waiting for me." He stood up, his hand out to her. "When you see your friends Mrs. Mabry and Mrs. Holmes, please invite them to make the trip to Abbyfield with you sometime. I'd welcome either or both of them, and although I take ridiculous pride in my work as overseer, I'm rather looking forward to being a professor too for a change."

"I'll speak to them soon, and thank you so much for my first lesson in planting and flooding, hoeing and all the rest of it. Do you mind if I ask where you went to school, Mr. Greene?"

"I welcome all questions," he said at her front door.

"And I'm also ridiculous in my pride for having graduated from the University of Pennsylvania at age nineteen." His smile was an impish grin now. "Are you properly impressed, ma'am?" Quickly, he added, "Don't answer that. Let me leave you with this thought: Every minute with you has meant more to me than anything could mean to a man who lives alone and until lately has lived only for his work. Thank you."

Chapter 15

The following week, with both their husbands away from Darien, Susan Holmes and Laura Mabry went with Thad and Abby to Abbyfield for an inspection and Thad's first instruction in the art of rice culture. Laura, especially, seemed to enjoy the outing, but the day was so chilly they returned to Darien in time for Abby to have dinner at the Mabry home, which was within easy walking distance of her own.

Toward evening, the friends still lingered over coffee at Laura's dining-room table, where they had shared a tureen of her famous terrapin stew along with generous slabs of her equally well-known corn bread. "If you like my corn bread so much, Abby, why not take the remainder of the pan home with you? It's divine with buttermilk for a light supper," Laura said.

"Oh, I wouldn't dare do that! Rosa Moon would pout for a week, sure that I brought your corn bread home because it suited me better than hers."

"Is Rosa Moon like that? I've always heard that large people are usually even-tempered and good-natured."

"And she is most of the time. Especially since Eli went away. One day we just came to some sort of mysterious new understanding and I have no complaints. None whatever."

Laura laughed her easy, mellow laughter. "Just as I have

no complaints about *my* housekeeper. You should get to know her better, Abby. *Her* name is Laura Mabry and *she* comes cheap."

"You and your husband must have very strong feelings against owning people. Don't you get awfully tired having to do everything around your house? Cleaning, cooking—"

"Washing, ironing." Laura continued, "I don't mind, though. What would I do with my time otherwise? In fact, I rather like to iron. The results show right away. My dear Woodford never fails to thank me for every freshly ironed shirt. He even apologizes at times for wearing them and mussing them up." Laura laughed again, then broke off abruptly. "Speaking of my husband, I know I'd make a dreadful widow, Abby. I hope I don't upset you by bringing that up, but I'm all admiration for the way you're going on with your life alone."

"You don't upset me. And I do miss Eli. But, Laura, whether or not it was the difference in our ages or something else, we seemed to have so little in common. More and more I think I fell in love with the *idea* of living on a coastal plantation, and once dear Eli got here and learned how to plant rice, he fell in love with his work. And then there I sat, with nothing to do, living in a house in town— not even on the plantation itself. But what were you going to say about Woodford?"

"Just that he's away again on this dreadful *Wanderer* mess and who knows how long he'll be gone this time? You know, he was home only one day for Christmas because he had to return to Brunswick on the matter. I know his work is important but I don't sleep through a single night without him, and when I find a way to corner someone, as I've cornered you now, I talk even more than usual. Oh, Abby, how on earth do you get along all alone?"

"Would it help if you told me something about the trouble the poor man's having over the *Wanderer*? It won't be dark for another half hour. I'll be able to walk around to my house in that time."

"Did I ever get anything told in half an hour?"

"Of course, silly! And the last thing I heard was Obadiah's endless spiel about your husband's heroism in sending a letter to Mr. Joseph Ganahl, the U.S. Attorney in Savannah, telling him that he suspected the *Wanderer* of being a slave ship to which he had given clearance by mistake. And that on further inspection of the seals and activities of the *Wanderer*, he canceled the clearance, forcing the ship to remain in port in Brunswick. And in response to that all-important letter, didn't Ganahl promise to inform Washington, D.C., and write again to Woodford with instructions? Obadiah also says that once your husband learned that a tugboat from Savannah was en route to Brunswick to tow the big schooner back to Savannah, he clamped right down on the *Wanderer*'s captain, who, scared of what might happen to him, abandoned his vessel at once. In fact, he got out so fast that charts, letters, personal belongings, and his trunk were left aboard. Is that about what took place?"

"It is. And the intrigue goes on. So much intrigue, in fact, that I can't even remember it all. But the upshot of it is that, thanks to my Woodford's letter, three of the slave traders have been arrested. You know Woodford and I do not believe in slavery, Abby, but, as I see it, most of the men involved in this slave horror are Northerners! Northerners and their Savannah cohort, Lamar."

"And the du Bignons?"

"And the du Bignons."

"*And* my late husband."

"I'm afraid so, yes, but, Abby, Eli needed more slaves in order to take good care of you. The du Bignons had need too, I'm sure.

So the whole evil institution of slavery goes on making lawbreakers out of otherwise honorable men. It not only ruins the lives of the Negroes, it can also taint at least the reputations of their white masters."

"Eli only bought two young boys. And one of them hurt his foot and died of gangrene just last week. Mr. Greene told me all about it. I hope he rides back into town soon, so I can tell him some of what you've told me."

"Is that the only reason you hope Thad Greene comes back?"

"Don't start that again, Laura. Our half hour is up. I have to go home. Eli never wanted me out alone after dark. I find I still try to heed some of his warnings."

When Abby reached her house just at dark, Rosa Moon met her at the front door.

"You got time to let Ob'diah run his head some to you before I serves yo' a li'l supper, Miss Abby?"

"Why, yes. Is anything wrong?"

"No'm. Dat man jus' can't keep hisself from talkin' an' he swears he got somepin' important to tell you. He won't tell me nothin' 'bout it. Got to be you. I go git him. He's back in my kitchen, an' if he snitchin' the s'prise I done make for you, I tend to him good."

"Tell him I'm here, please, and that he can come right on in the parlor and talk to me."

Abby was looking out a window admiring the breathtakingly lovely camellias visible in the parlor lamplight when she heard Obadiah clear his throat.

"Oh, come in, Obadiah, and take a chair if you like."

"I thanks ya for the offer of a chair, ma'am," he said, twisting his thick knit cap as he talked, "but I do better to stand right here." Then he laughed. "Anyway, I talk more'n ever when I sits down. I speck my Rosa Moon she done tol' you that. An' what I got to tell you be to my mind so important that I wants to make it clear as I kin make it." He looked toward the door as though checking on any possible listeners.

"Obadiah, you know there's no one in this house with us except Rosa Moon."

"Oh, yes'm. I knows that. What I got to tell you is only for your ears, though, Miss Abby, so I jus' makin' sure." Obviously nervous, he laughed again. "Course, if you wants to tell her when I'm through, you're welcome to do it."

"Well, thank you," Abby said, smiling. "But what on earth could be so mysterious?"

"Oldun."

"Your news has to do with the other African boy at Abbyfield? He isn't sick too, is he?"

"No'm, he not sick, 'ceptin' heartsick since his brother Youngun he die from dat rusty nail in his foot. But Rosa Moon she just tell me you done been to see Miz Mabry today and I know dat woman she talk more'n I talks, so I wanted you to know the whole story. Her hero husband, Mr. Woodford Mabry, he still in Brumsick, so she might not know the whole story like I knows it. An' since Oldun he be your property now that Mausa Eli be gone, lemme bring you up on what all's happened. I'm sure Miz Mabry she tell you her husband he only come home for one day at Christmas las' month an' then skedaddled back to Brumsick. She be by herself now, ain't she?"

"Why, yes, she's still alone. Why?"

"Well, Ob'diah he can bring you up to the events ob almost today. Did Miz Mabry tell you that a man called Deputy LaRoche of Savannah send some mens called deputies out to hunt down an' arrest ebery African they could fin'?"

"No, she didn't tell me that!"

"See? Listen, I tell ya. Dese deputy mens and dey leader, Deputy Gordon, head straight for Jekyll Island to serve subpoenas on Mr. John an' Mr. Henry du Bignon fer bein' mix up in de *Wanderer* and then they suppose to look for the Africans. And I kin tell you that the young Africans are easy to spot 'cause they front teeth be file off almost pointed."

"I did know that. Mr. Thaddeus Greene told me. It makes the shivers go up my spine just to think of it!"

"Mr. Thad he be a fine fellow. Him an' me's got to be good friends. Mos' as close as Mausa Eli an' me. Anyway, these deputy mens and they leader slosh the length an' breadth ob swampy Jekyll Island, but dey only foun' one African boy and he got away! An' thanks to Mr. Mabry, de *Wanderer* itself be seized an' towed to Savannah, where it now be anchored down. But de main thing I got to tell you is that my frien' Polydone—he belong to the du Bignons—he sent word by the grapevine to me dat our fine frien' Mr. Thad he enter right in wif my hero, Mr. Mabry, an' he also enter in wif God."

"Mr. Greene entered in with God?" She stared at Obadiah. "You aren't telling me that Mr. Greene is—dead, are you?"

"Oh, no, no, no, no! I ain' sayin' nuffin' like dat. I jus' sayin' dat man be such a fine man 'cause he be on God's side in all dis slavery business." His bony brown hand flew to his mouth. "I say wrong? Lord hab mercy, Miss Abby, you knows Rosa Moon an' me's happy as clams here wif you!" Obadiah smiled ear to ear. "Did you eber wonder how anybody know how happy a clam be? Ain' dat a crazy thing I jus' said? Lord, hab mercy!"

"I have to admit I never gave much thought to the happiness of clams, Obadiah, but I do think I know what you mean by Mr. Thad being on God's side."

"You *does*, Miss Abby? Oh, thank you, Sweet Jesus!"

"I would like to know why you're so complimentary to Mr. Greene. Did he do something to help in this *Wanderer* trouble?"

"Not zactly, ma'am. But he do something to help Oldun. An' it's not jus' me, but ebery black man an' woman out at Abbyfield is partial to Oldun. Dey all go outa dey way to help de boy fin' comfort now."

"But Mr. Greene. What did he do to help?"

"He—tol' a white lie to de deputies from Savannah when dey ax him if he knew de whereabouts ob *any* Africans. He tell 'em he did *not* know nothin' 'bout nobody. See? I done tol' him how Oldun startin' to feel at home at Abbyfield. Polydone say dat eben back in de Congo he had it purty bad—specially after his own people stole him from his village an' sell him to a slabe trader. Mr. Thad he tell a white lie, but he done proteck Oldun. Oldun belong to you now, Miss Abby, an' no slabe nigger kin ax for better dan dat."

Chapter 16

During the remainder of January 1859 and into the month of February, Obadiah was sent to Abbyfield at least once a week to tell Thad that Miss Abby was ready for him to come for her. With infinite pains, she explained to everyone who might listen that as they drove in her buggy from Darien to the plantation, Mr. Greene gave her invaluable instruction concerning what he planned to show her that day about the complicated business of growing rice for market.

Each time Thad heard Obadiah's horse gallop up the lane to his overseer's house, he felt excited, as though he were being rewarded. To Thad's mind, there was no more welcome sight than that of the skinny black man astride his horse, because it meant that within an hour or so maybe he would be with her again.

True, for the first few visits she did not come alone, but brought either Susan Holmes or Laura Mabry or both. Thad liked the ladies, though, and felt sure that sooner or later they would tire of learning the art of rice culture, since their husbands were not planters. Actually, on their third visit with Abby, Laura and Susan chose to try their hands at working in Thad's straggling flower bed in the front yard of his cottage. This left him happily alone with Abby, who rode the gentle mare named Fan alongside him as he led the way on Mister, explaining as simply and colorfully as he could about the various winter procedures through which he directed Abby's slaves.

"You told me once, I'm sure," she said when they passed a gang of laborers hard at work with their shovels on a new section of diking, "but how much land do you assign for each person's task, Mr. Greene?"

"That depends. But in general, the standard daily assignment I make is a quarter of an acre per person. Just so you can visualize it, this measures out to about one hundred and five feet on a side."

"And does that include all types of work?"

"Yes, ma'am. The equivalent of this measurement is expected whether the work is planting, cultivating, harvesting, or preparing rice for market. We'll get to all that later on."

"And are women field hands expected to do the same amount of the same hard work as men?"

Thad laughed a little. "You really are becoming involved in all this, aren't you?"

"I like to think I simply care that none of—the people are made ill or too tired from overwork."

"Don't you mean none of *your* people?"

"Why are you so insistent upon calling them *my* people?"

"Because they are."

Now Abby laughed a little too. "Yes. And the truth is I'm trying to find out what *you* think of me for owning other human beings."

"I can tell you right now what I think of *you* if you won't think me too forward."

"That isn't what I want to know. I just want to know what you think about someone who becomes a slave owner—overnight—and doesn't know how to react!"

"I'm in the slavery business with you, Mrs. Allyn."

They reined their horses, but did not dismount.

"Do we *have* to play word games?" she wanted to know. "You told me once, Mr. Greene, how you felt about having to assign hard tasks to the slaves at Abbyfield."

"Since you remember that so clearly, do you also remember that I said I felt it was too soon after your husband's death for a discussion of any subject as potentially emotional as—slavery?"

"Yes."

"And do you know why that stopped me from telling you more?"

"Of course I don't know!"

"Well, I'll tell you. If you want to hear it."

"I do, Thad. I really do."

When he began to stare at her mischievously with his unbelievably blue eyes, she bit her lip, but said nothing.

"You heard yourself call me Thad, didn't you?"

Her sigh was short, harsh. "Yes! Yes, I heard myself and I'm sure I don't need to tell you I'm dreadfully—embarrassed."

"Sorry to hear that. I was just about to call you Miss Abigail."

"I wish you wouldn't, please. And I won't use your first name again either."

"I suppose there's no point in my asking why you don't want me to call you Miss Abigail when there's no one to hear us but our horses."

Nothing in her voice told him she was deliberately ignoring his question, but she did. "What about the women field hands? Or when the work demands strenuous labor? Too strenuous for younger men or older ones—or women?"

"I'm not an abusive overseer, Mrs. Allyn. I believe I said the size of the task varies. When the people are planting, the task of a full hand is from one to two acres, but when they're hoeing—hard work—the task is a half acre or less, depending on the density of the soil and the stubbornness of the weeds. When we're harvesting, the task is about three-quarters of an acre. When threshing with a flailing stick—hard, backbreaking work—I assign six hundred bundles of sheaves to each strong man and five hundred to each woman."

She sat her horse in silence for a time, frowning. Then

she said, "I—I do have so much to think through. So many things to untangle in my mind. I might as well tell you now that I'm considering a visit to Boston to try to discover my true feelings about—well, the real depth of my grief over my husband *and* my true feelings about owning slaves. I know what I believe about slave owners, but as silly as this may sound, I seem a stranger in these new circumstances and don't know clearly how I feel—about myself."

She might as well have struck Thad with her open hand. The mere thought of not seeing her at least once a week was such a blow that any kind of response left his mind. Words, which usually came so freely, failed him now. The only one he could find and manage to say was a question— a one-word question: "Boston? *Boston?*"

As though she missed the pain in his eyes, she said in a confidential, steady voice, in a tone she might use with Laura Mabry or Susan Holmes, "You see, I received a letter from my mother in Boston. She's a complex woman. I love and respect her, but allowing me to think for myself has always been next to impossible for her. She has one of her intuitions about me now, I'm sorry to say. And that means only one thing. If I don't visit her, she will board a steamer and come here. In so many words, she wrote: 'To see for myself the true state of my precious daughter's heart and mind.' I don't want her coming here now. This is one time and place in my thirty-one years that I fully intend to think—and decide for myself."

For an instant, Thad felt relieved. At least she had told him something altogether personal. But Boston? What he thought of saying was impertinent, but he suddenly heard himself ask, "Do you think going all the way to Boston— going to her of your own free will—can help? Can really help loosen the cord with which she's evidently tried to— hold on to you?"

She did not answer right away. Instead, she smoothed her mare's shiny neck with one hand. And then, unexpectedly, she smiled at him. "Are you sure you're only in your early thirties too, Mr. Greene? That was an extremely mature question."

"It was?"

"I thought so. What does early thirties mean? I suddenly want to know exactly how old you are."

"I'm flattered—and pleased that you do," he said simply. "I'll be thirty-three this year, which makes me old enough to advise you. And Mrs. Mabry told me a little about your relationship with your mother."

"And what do you advise, sir?"

"That you stay right here in Darien so we can go on with our cultivation lessons."

"Stop frowning. I wouldn't stay up North for long." She was teasing now. "And I can't be ready to leave until after we plant. So I won't miss but one 'flooding' at the most. I promise, sir, not to spoil a whole crop of rice, and a little time away just might make my life much, much better when I return." No longer teasing, she added, "Who knows, Mr. Greene? Life may be better for—everyone."

Chapter 17

O n a crisp late February afternoon, the air clear and less humid than usual, Dr. James Holmes and his wife, Susan, left their horse and buggy with Obadiah in front of Abby's Darien house on Madison Street. Both stepped along briskly, Holmes in high spirits because Obadiah's warm greeting had made him feel like royalty.

"You gonna feel better den eber, Doctah Holmes, once you sees the surprise my Rosa Moon she fix fo' yo' dinner," the jovial servant called as he trotted off toward the stable. "She done fix yo' fav'rite meal." The familiar, contagious laugh could still be heard as they climbed the steps to Abby's front porch.

"I can guess already," Holmes called after him, "but I wouldn't spoil her surprise for anything." To Susan he half whispered as he took her arm, "That man's spirit is absolutely indestructible."

"And so is your ability to act surprised. Do you realize it's been almost a year since Rosa Moon has prepared anything but her famous baked chicken for our dinners here?"

"I like the coloreds' childlike games," he said. "Even if my hair is turning a bit gray here and there." He didn't miss a beat when the door opened and Abby stood there smiling her warm welcome. "And I also like the amazing way that right before a man's eyes our hostess can cause a black gown to turn a gay color just by being so radiant!

Good day, my dear Abigail. Go ahead, ladies, and do your hugging. Then I think I'll get in on it too." He laughed, hugging Abby as though he hadn't seen her in a long, long time.

"Dr. Holmes—Susan! Come in, come in. I'm so, so glad to see you both and we've much to talk about! Isn't this a perfect February day in Darien?"

"It is indeed," the doctor said, hanging his hat on the hall tree. "And since I haven't been to Abbyfield in over two weeks now, I'm eager to learn all about how your planting lessons are coming along."

"Oh, Mr. Greene could explain much better than I." She turned to Susan, then back to Holmes. "I confess I'm learning more about rice culture every day. And the more I learn, the more fascinated I am with all of it."

Sensitive, perceptive Susan Holmes, who always conveyed far more than the mere words she spoke, said, "Oh, Abby, I'm happy to hear you say that. It must help when memories of Eli's love of Abbyfield come back to you these days."

"My dear friend, I'm sure it helps more than I even realize. I wasn't a bit fair with Eli. I only visited the plantation twice with him. That was his world. This was mine. I caused myself to feel shut out of his world and it wasn't Eli's fault. It was mine." She led the way to her parlor. "I understand so many things now."

Seated in the chair that had been Eli's and had now become Holmes's favorite, he said, "Don't blame yourself, Abby. You came to Darien from a totally different world. You left an exciting social life up in Boston. How would you possibly guess that such a thing as growing rice in coastal Georgia could be exciting? Could capture your interest as it obviously has."

"You couldn't have known," Susan said. "But you know now, and, as my husband always says, 'God's timing is never far off.' Your gray eyes simply light up when you talk about Abbyfield."

"And I doubt that either of us needs to tell you," Dr.

Holmes said, "that you have a jewel in that young overseer, Thad Greene. My wife tells me that Greene is still giving you regular lessons on preparing fields for planting, flooding, constructing banks, ditching. That you make more or less regular trips to Abbyfield these days. Thad isn't only expert at what he does, in my humble dogmatic opinion, he's delightful company."

Her only response was "Yes. He's very capable." But she didn't miss the double meaning of his words. Then, on an affectionate laugh, she added, "And I still love your humor, Doctor."

"Oh, Abby, my husband is such a tease," Susan said. "He thinks his phrase 'in my humble dogmatic opinion' is funny."

"Well, it is funny, Susan," he half scolded. "Just as Rosa Moon's surprising me with my favorite meal every time I'm invited for dinner strikes me funny. A good joke never grows old."

"And you never tire of acting surprised that she remembers baked stuffed chicken is your favorite," Abby said, then quickly put a finger to her lips and whispered, "I think I hear Rosa Moon coming along the hall from her kitchen. She's indulging you with a glass of wine before we eat. Eli was so proud of his muscadine arbor."

"And now you're proud of it," Holmes said.

"Yes. Oh, thank you, Rosa Moon. I thought I heard you and hoped you were bringing the doctor's favorite."

"Yes'm. Afternoon, Dr. James, Miz Holmes. I neber forgit to bring a little drop ob muskydine. Whets the appetite."

"As though I needed my appetite whetted when you're doing the cooking, Rosa Moon. Do I only imagine I can smell something unusually succulent all the way from your kitchen out back?"

"Now you ain' s'posed to go guessin', Doctor. You spoil my game agin an' you might not git no dinner."

"Our Phoebe bakes a delicious chicken," Susan said, "but Rosa Moon's still rates first with him." With an exaggerated sigh, Susan added, "I just hope no one ever tells Phoebe."

"I like Phoebe's baked chicken just fine," Holmes said, "but she stuffs her chicken with herb dressing and I happen to prefer Rosa Moon's oyster dressing."

"Hush, Doctor," Rosa Moon said with her low, easy chuckle. "A good sage dressin' be fine, specially if, like Phoebe, you ain' got no Ob'diah to git oysters for the stuffin'. An' it look to me like dis big bowl glass be the one I pick out for you, sir. You want it 'bout half full ob muskydine wine or less or more?"

"Half full will be excellent, Rosa Moon. And I do thank you."

Expertly, she measured his wine, then poured a splash for the ladies in two smaller glasses and gave them an approving look before she headed back toward her kitchen.

"I hope you don't mind having your wine in here," Abby said. "Rosa Moon does like to serve it this way so she can keep us out of the dining room until she feels it's exactly the right time to 'surprise' you with her baked chicken. Dr. Holmes, you're a dear to play her little games with her."

Half an hour later, Rosa Moon announced dinner and ushered everyone into the dining room before making her auspicious entrance bearing the temptingly browned bird with its oyster stuffing. Dr. Holmes carved, they all ate heartily, praised Rosa Moon, and at nearly four o'clock, when the sun began to lower a bit in the winter sky, everyone entered into that post-dessert time of pure relaxation.

"Just look at him," Susan said, nodding toward her husband. "If someone doesn't tell a joke or need a doctor in a hurry, he's going to fall asleep sitting upright in your dining-room chair, Abby."

"Susan," Dr. Holmes whispered. "Sh! Don't wake me up. We're all too happy, and if I'm truthful, it seems that the proper time to thank the Lord for such good food is after it's eaten and enjoyed, as I certainly enjoyed Rosa Moon's baked chicken, gravy, collard greens, spiced peaches, mashed potatoes, and"—he rubbed his somewhat rounded stomach—"that delicious pudding! We do thank Thee, Father!"

"I'm surprised you stayed awake long enough to pray, James," Susan said. "He lectures Rosa Moon, you know, about her weight and then sets such an example for her. Open your eyes, James. You do have to drive me back out to the Ridge, you know."

"I'll wake him up," Abby volunteered.

"Oh, Abby, dear friend, I doubt that even you could do that. I—I did eat far too much, true, and I must lecture myself any day now."

"You'll have to decide when to do that, Dr. Holmes." Abby smiled, then her voice and expression turned serious, almost insistent. "I'm going to break into your happy reverie because I need your advice. Not a lecture. Advice. My mind is partly made up. I just need a nudge from someone I respect and who—respects me."

Holmes sat up straight. "Do I owe you an apology for my self-indulgence, Abigail? I fear I'm a weak man and Rosa Moon knows exactly how to tap into that weakness. Nevertheless, I'm now alert and at your service."

"In the last day or so, ever since I received a letter from my mother in Boston, I've been toying with the idea of taking a trip up there. More than toying. I'm seriously considering it. I've told you both about my dear mother's sometimes overbearing 'spirituality.' She is now in the throes of one of her intuitions about me, and if I don't go to Boston so she can see for herself that her precious daughter is doing rather well, she'll come here to Darien. I fully intend to have her visit me, but—but I'm not quite ready for that yet. I've always had trouble standing up to her and every day now I can see myself growing a little stronger. At my strongest, though, I've never been a match for my beautiful mother. I want to be—a whole person when she comes here. I want to bear her inspection on my own territory. Be in charge of my life. At times, I'm almost convinced that there will come a day when I'm stronger than I've ever been in the past. When she and I can meet and be together as—equals."

"Did her letter upset you, Abby?" Susan asked.

"I believe our young friend asked for my advice, Susan," Holmes said gently.

"And I fully intend for you to advise her, James. But don't forget I'm a New England girl too. I understand what you're saying about thinking for yourself, Abby. And am I right to think your mother has rather taken the New Englander's faith in the power of individual freedom a bit far?"

Abby laughed halfheartedly. "Perhaps—yes. Yes, not perhaps. Mother gives God the credit, but even credit to Him comes *if* the Scriptures seem to coincide with her own thinking—her own way of interpreting them. Now, you must both forgive me. Please take my complaint mainly as a sign of how comfortable I am with you. I simply think a bit more time—even a few months—will make a big difference in me as a woman."

"You've made yourself perfectly clear, Abigail. Susan and I understand exactly what you're saying. In fact, an excellent solution may be coming to me at this very moment."

"What, James?" Susan asked a bit warily.

"The truth is I was planning to decide when my work would permit and then tell you as a pleasant surprise."

"What surprise, James?"

"You've been uncomplaining for more than a decade, my good Susan, and it's high time that I took you on a pleasure visit back to your native Boston and environs. And you know my cousin Oliver Wendell Holmes would welcome a visit from us. What do you think about taking our beloved Abby with us so she can visit her mother!"

He watched Susan's face light up. "James! Oh, James— really?"

"Really, Susan. I've thought often lately of our longtime friend Fanny Kemble Butler. In fact, I owe her a letter. You know we've had a standing invitation to visit her in Lenox, Massachusetts, ever since she found her house there, which she named The Perch. This should be a happy time to see her. According to Fanny's latest letter, her youngest daughter, also named Fanny, for her famous actress mother, will reach her majority soon and that frees her to spend all the time she chooses with her mother. So happiness will abound! And thanks to our Abby's need for advice today, we'll set the wheels in motion and plan to take Abby with us if she agrees! I'll write to Fanny at once to see if we can fit a visit into her busy theater schedule. She's much in demand up there now, you know, and perhaps best of all for her, she's totally independent financially."

"Oh, this is too good to be true," Abby said, clapping her hands like a child. "But isn't Fanny Kemble's former husband, Mr. Pierce Butler, one of your closest friends, Dr. Holmes?"

"He is indeed. We named our son for him. And I'll see my poor heartbroken friend early next week. I wouldn't dream of going North without telling Pierce. After all, when a man names his own firstborn son for a fellow, there's far more than a mere acquaintance involved. You ladies just leave all that to me."

"Your idea is wonderful, James," Susan said, "but won't you have to go to Savannah in order to see Pierce Butler? Isn't he holding an enormous slave auction there during the first week in March?"

"He is, my dear wife, and I am still under contract to him to attend the medical needs of his slaves at both Butler Island and Hampton Point on St. Simons Island. Do you think for a minute that I'd allow him to come down from Philadelphia and not see him? I know all the trouble he and Fanny had because she's so opinionated about owning slaves, but I understand it—from his side and from hers. I'm sure it sounds strange, Abby, for an issue like slavery to come between a man and wife to the tragic extent it came between Fanny Kemble and Pierce Butler. But you must take my word for the fact that both are excellent friends to us."

Abby had only listened. Now she asked, "Did I hear you correctly, Dr. Holmes? Did you call Pierce Butler a poor heartbroken fellow? Why, if he was the one who instigated the divorce, would he be heartbroken? I don't mean to pry, but my mother has a friend who knows Fanny Kemble rather well and she vows the woman was—perhaps still is—in love with her husband. I know it's none of my affair, but you must have a good reason for believing he's the heartbroken one."

"Abby, you're not prying! I'm sure it makes no sense to you, but no matter what his wife is said to have written about the cruelty of slave owners in her *Journal*—and thank God it's still unpublished—Pierce Butler cares about his people. Selling off over four hundred of them at auction simply breaks his heart! The fact that he's making the voyage down here to be on hand, to bid them goodbye, proves it. Slavery is an ugly subject. I believe it causes more trouble within some white families than we're led to think."

"I'd imagine it causes some trouble for the poor colored too," Susan jabbed. "Don't forget, James, you're in the presence of two former Bostonians."

Abby's look struck Holmes as being truly puzzled. "Does it cause trouble for the two of you?" she asked. "Since I'm being nosy, I might as well go all the way. You don't seem to disapprove of the institution at all, Doctor."

"I simply try never, never to put my foot into that bucket of hot tar, dear Abby. Susan and I have no trouble over the issue. After all, our income depends upon my medical contracts with coastal planters. Don't forget that. In a way, I'm as dependent upon slavery as are the planters themselves."

Abby smiled at him. "Don't worry, sir. We're not going to have trouble over it. I'm thinking it through these days, but I suppose I'd agree with Fanny Kemble. I know I'd certainly be honored to meet the great lady—but my own views aren't peace-threatening in any way. Thank you for being so honest about it. If you both really mean you'd like me to tag along, I'll be delighted." Her smile glowed. "And oh, how impressed my mother is going to be that I even stand a chance of meeting the great Fanny Kemble!"

Chapter 18

By the end of March, Abby was going out to Abby-field so regularly that Obadiah was driving her in order to give Mr. Thad more time for his overseer duties. Earlier in the year, she had made the three-and-a-half-mile trip to Abbyfield once a week, but lately she had been coming nearly every day. Today when they arrived her heart sank because Thad was nowhere to be seen as the buggy rounded the gentle curve in the sandy road and stopped before the overseer's cottage. Never before had Thad failed to be waiting for her, cap in hand, at the iron hitching post near his pine-straw path.

"Where you reckon dat man be today?" Obadiah asked, peering up and down the road.

"I—I can't imagine," she said. "Today was going to be a very important planting lesson for me. Something must have gone wrong at one of the fields. Yes. He's needed somewhere else or he'd be here waiting."

"Why this be a 'portant day, Miss Abby? An' stop frownin'. Mr. Thad he be fine. Some of the workers mus' hab make a bad mistake, so he had to go tend to it. Specially if this be a 'portant day for you. He always right here, waitin' for you. Yes, ma'am."

Poor Rosa Moon, Abby thought. It was no wonder at all that she used to fall silent. Her poor ears were battered by so much talk from this well-meaning, good man. "I know he's always here," Abby said, cutting her words short as she tended to do when she was afraid or annoyed or both. "This was going to be a big day for me not just because of my planting lesson but also because Mr. Greene promised I could help if they needed to do changing or repairs to the boots on any of the plantation mules and oxen. I didn't even know they wore leather boots!"

Obadiah's cackling laugh seemed out of place this time. "You joshin' me, Miss Abby. He don' promise you any such thing! Ain' no lady gonna let herself git all muddy an' her hands as dirty as hands git when a mule's boot need fixin'! Mr. Thad never let you do a thing like that."

"Mr. Thad lets me do anything that interests me," she snapped, as though proving her point with Obadiah was somehow vital. "That's one of the reasons I like to come here as often as possible. I rather like the woman I'm turning into, and if that's too hard for you to figure out, Rosa Moon can explain it sometime."

His face turned sad. "Lord hab mercy," he said softly. "I jus' thinkin' how much Mausa Eli woulda like habin' you carin' one way or t'other 'bout Abbyfield."

Don't let him do this to you, she told herself. Then, doing her best to hide the irritation such impertinence caused, she said, "I didn't know anything about rice culture in those days, Obadiah, and you know it. How could I care about something that took place out here where I was a complete stranger?"

"Yes'm."

"What does that mean? No, don't tell me. I'm too worried about Mr. Greene's not meeting us. Accidents do happen, you know. And he's always right here."

For weeks now Abby had been jumping down from the buggy with no help. It still puzzled Obadiah that any white lady would do such a thing, but he had heard the sound of hoofbeats too, so he wasn't surprised when his mistress suddenly jumped down to stand beside him waiting as Thad rode up.

"Can you forgive me, Miss Abigail?" Thad asked as he

dismounted and went to her. "Morning, Obadiah."

"Mornin', Mr. Thad. We bof gittin' mighty worried 'bout you not bein' here. I try to josh Miss Abby outa her worryin', but didn't do no good. She say dis be a 'portant day at Abbyfield for her."

"Well, she's right. That's why I was delayed. I was checking on Old Yellow, one of the plantation mules. He needs help with his dancing slippers and it occurred to me that Miss Abby is just the person to give him that help. In return, Old Yellow will supply the shoe repair lesson Miss Abby has been waiting for." Then, with a smile: "Good morning, Miss Abby."

The smile she couldn't resist brought on a kind of unwanted helplessness, but there it was. "Good morning, Mr. Greene. We're—probably a little early and shouldn't have worried about you."

"On the contrary," he said, his thick sandy hair appealingly tousled in a brisk March breeze.

Was his hair as thick and alive as it looked? she wondered, and scolded herself in what she meant to be an angry silence. The scolding did no good. As though not even one restraining rein quieted her, the thoughts she simply had to conquer went galloping off in their own direction and she could almost feel her hands holding his young, beautiful head, her fingers moving through the thick, healthy blond hair. She had always thought Eli's slightly long, thin graying hair becoming, making him look distinguished. But Thad's hair make him look much more than distinguished. He looked—glorious!

"Aren't you at all interested in the perfectly timed fact that Old Yellow needs your attention today, Miss Abigail? Right now? By noon, we'll be through the last piece of plowing and harrowing, but only if you're ready to attend to the mule's troubling slipper."

"You gonna let her git herself all muddy an' dirty foolin' with Old Yellow's hind hoofs? You gonna let her do that, Mr. Thad?"

Thad laughed. "I don't *let* her do anything she doesn't

want to do, Obadiah. The lady makes the decisions here. I'm just the overseer."

This time Obadiah's cackle lightened the moment. "You better be overseein' Miss Abby. See dat dem mean rear hoofs be pointed in the right dreckshun when Ol' Yellow come outa de mud!"

"I will. Don't worry, I will. And, Obadiah, you won't need to come back for Miss Abigail this afternoon. I cleaned up the old buggy yesterday. I'll bring her home. It just could take us longer for the shoe repair than we think."

"Yes, suh."

"Oh, there is one more thing you can do, Obadiah. I don't have Fan ready for Miss Abigail. Would you give her a hand up so she can mount my horse right behind me?"

"What?" Abby asked in a startled tone.

"I think you heard me, ma'am."

"*Yes, sir*," Obadiah said with glee.

Laughing because she couldn't help laughing when she was having a good time, Abby stepped lightly onto Obadiah's big hand and swung herself up onto Mister's broad back.

"Better put at least one arm around my waist," Thad called cheerfully. "We're going to fly! Old Yellow needs our loving care—right now!"

It had all happened so fast, Thad knew that Abby hadn't had time to make her adjustment to their being so close. Having her there, her lovely body against his back and shoulders, had started his own head whirling, his thoughts tumbling in all directions. She had changed today—just today—from her respectful black mourning dress to one of dark gray. That alone made him daring and he took hope.

Hope for what?

God knew he wasn't jealous of poor Eli Allyn or whatever thoughts of him might still be alive in her memory. To Thad Greene, Eli Allyn had been the giver of all good things. Not only had he given him the overseer's job at Abbyfield, but with it had come a dream fulfilled. From somewhere in his distant ancestry, Thad had inherited his surprising, almost irrational love of the land. But with that love of productive land he had almost a distaste for the heavy responsibility of being a financially successful owner. If an overseer did not produce a profitable crop of rice or cotton or corn or wheat, the full brunt of the failure did not fall on him, it fell on his employer, the land's owner, who dealt directly with his factor and the bank. Thad had the best of both worlds. He could supervise the tending of the Allyns' soil, reap the peculiar joy of watching crops sprout and grow, but avoid the problems money always brought. The most an overseer could lose was his job and another could always be found. Despite the years of his boyhood and early youth in Philadelphia, Thad loved the Southern weather and the salt creeks, the serpentine rivers and marshes. Free of the nagging responsibilities of other professions, the cultivation of rice was complicated and sufficiently difficult to challenge a mind bright enough to have graduated with honors from a fine Northeastern university.

And then had come Abby. The suddenly freed *widow* Abby.

And now she sat behind him, the warmth of her against his back, the pressure and sweetness of her arm clinging to his waist for dear life as he urged Mister to a faster gallop than was necessary. She had to cling to him or be bounced off the horse's big back. They galloped along the nearest bank beside a small strip of unplowed, unharrowed field where a helpless-looking field hand named Musky stood holding on to Old Yellow—both waiting for Thad and Abby to rescue them from the boggy mud.

Neither rider tried to speak until Thad slowed Mister to a brisk trot some fifty feet or so from where the wretched mule struggled to free one hind leg mired in the soft, sticky soil.

When Thad reined the horse, holding Abby's hand securely in his while she jumped to the ground, she gasped. "You don't just half mean the things you say, do you? I know I said I'd like to help fit a mule with his fancy leather boots, but I—I somehow—"

"You somehow didn't think I'd accept the offer?"

"I guess that's fairly close to what I thought."

He was standing very near her on the unstable, wet ground, still holding her hand. "I liked being close to you even for such a short gallop." His voice was quiet.

She replied only that she agreed the gallop did seem short and that as a girl she had loved riding. Then, withdrawing her hand gently: "I've heard, even read, that when she was quite young and first appearing on the American stage with her father, Fanny Kemble, the famous British actress, insisted that American women were out of shape and sickly because they lacked exercise. She rode horseback every day. I think I'd like to ride more than just when I go to look at the fields when I come for my lesson."

"Mister's a fine riding horse. I'm using him all the time now," Thad said, and patted the shiny brown animal with an affectionate hand. "But Fan is always here for you to ride anytime you want."

"Maybe when I come back from the North I can start riding more."

"Abby, are you leaving me?" he asked teasingly.

"Not leaving *you*. Merely going with the Holmeses for a visit to my mother and maybe I'll even get to meet Fanny Kemble. She's a fairly close friend of Dr. Holmes and still very much in demand to do her dramatic readings in Boston."

"Old Doc Bull's-eye does have high-toned friends North and South, doesn't he?"

"I don't think he cares to be called Bull's-eye," she said. "He got that nickname as a boy, but he's changed it now to Bullie. I don't think the old darling minds being called Dr. Bullie."

"I'm glad you wore heavier shoes today, Miss Abigail. We'll have to walk to where Old Yellow's bogged down. I also like it that your traditional black dress has become dark gray. On such a spring day, it actually looks . . ." He took her arm and began to lead her across the unplowed earth toward the Negro and the mule, held fast in the bog.

"What does my dark gray dress look to you—disrespectful?"

"No." He smiled down at her. "Cheerful!"

Neither spoke until they reached Musky, the field hand, and the stranded mule. Then it was the mule that broke the silence with a mighty, complaining "E-e-e-a-w-w!"

"He been doin' that," Musky explained. "He tired bein' stuck in de mud."

Before Thad could stop her, Abby was kneeling beside the mule's mud-mired back leg. "I hope you have more straw nearby," she said to Thad, almost as an order. "The straw padding someone put on the inside of his poor leg has slipped out and this hard leather boot has rubbed his skin off!" She held out her hand, fingers stained with the mule's blood.

"Oh, Miss Abby, it's risky business to touch a mule's sore leg like that! Run for a handful of straw, Musky. There should be some piled over against that bank." When the field hand ran off, Thad said, half laughing, "Luckily his hoofs were pointed in the other direction, ma'am, and that one was stuck in the mud. Otherwise, you might have been kicked good!"

"This is cruel," she scolded. "Poor Old Yellow."

"He must like you. He didn't complain once when you touched him with your hand."

"Be that as it may, it's cruel to let his boot bring the blood like this."

For a time Thad stood looking out over the fields at a gang of field hands bent above their heavy hoes. "It's cruel to them too," he said.

"You told me once, I think, how heavy their hoes are—just to pick one up."

"I've seen blood on their hands in spite of the heaviest calluses anybody ever had."

"You tell me a lot about yourself, Mr. Greene, even when you don't mean to."

"Musky's found his straw. He'll be back in a minute. When are you leaving Darien, Miss Abigail?"

"I'm not sure. Dr. Holmes has written to Miss Fanny Kemble. We should have a departure date within two or three weeks."

Now Thad was on his knees inspecting the injury to the mule's hind leg. She could see that the thatch of sandy hair curled a little on his neck.

"Could I ask you something?"

He stood up. "Anything."

"I'm so ignorant of everything to do with a plantation," she said, touching his arm. "But I do know it's best for you to replenish the straw under poor Old Yellow's boot. And while you do it, please teach me how. I want to learn. Teach me, Thad. I—I do want to learn about—so much."

Part Two

❧

April—May 1859

Chapter 19

I n early April, on the second night aboard the steamer moving her and the Holmeses toward Boston, Abby sat almost motionless at the tiny oak desk in her cramped, but neat stateroom. She was trying to imagine how she would sound, what she would say, and whether for the first time in her life she could stay composed through what, after more than five years, would surely be a difficult meeting with her mother.

"Oh, Mama," she said aloud, "how I wish I thought I could really pour out my heart to you this time!"

Her voice, muffled by the steady rush of water against the boat's hull, seemed anything but hopeful, and Abby felt more desperately alone than at any time since Eli had gone away forever. She still missed him in many ways, but she had felt alone most of their married life and what affected her most now, if she were truthful, was the fact that he would never come home again.

"Mama," she continued in the empty stateroom, "it isn't that I miss Eli himself so much, it's that I need desperately to learn how to *be myself* when I'm alone. I need to learn how to feel laughter inside again. But honestly, the only time I do is when I'm with—*him*. And I don't mean Eli. You don't need to remind me. I'm still wearing widow's weeds for Eli, and I know it's wrong of me to be longing to feel the kind of joy I've just barely sampled in the presence of another man."

Eli hadn't been dead even six months, and, feeling like an idiot, she sat on the hard berth in her stateroom longing to tell her mother that she thought she had fallen in love with another man.

Longing to tell her mother?

"Am I losing my mind?" she asked aloud again into the musty little room. "I've never spoken that freely to my mother in my entire life, and this is certainly not the time even to think of doing such a thing."

Deliberately, Abby turned her thoughts to Savannah, where a full month after Mr. Pierce Butler's horrendous slave sale at a Savannah racetrack, when some four hundred uprooted human beings were put on the auction block like cattle, people were still talking about the fact that Mr. Butler had actually attended. It was rumored that he showed what appeared to be genuine pity for the slaves as he doled out newly minted quarters at the rate of a dollar to each person. Most believed, or said they believed, Mr. Butler was personally attached to his slaves. Some, like Abby, wondered about his sincerity. But it was also rumored that Mr. Butler had looked crestfallen when the people being sold had cried and that they had called the rain-soaked hideous two days of the sale the "weeping time."

Abby, as she thought back on it now, felt that Savannah might just be a prophetic city. Prophetic of things to come. The newspapers there railed at the hypocrisy of Northern abolitionists and ran lengthy editorials in favor of secession from the Union. But a few people—but only a few—she heard, were more moderate and did not believe in slavery.

These days, the very thought of human bondage brought a kind of restlessness that made Abby search about for something else to dwell on. Thinking about slavery was as disconcerting and difficult as trying to imagine what it might be like to try to have a serious talk with her mother after five long years. She needed a good night's rest. Still, the thought of trying to sleep alone in the empty stateroom so repelled her she tried to remember what Thad had said about the ugly institution of slavery, his exact words. Instead, the words of perceptive, pragmatic Dr. Holmes on the subject came back to her, forcing her to face her own feelings about it. "You object to slavery, Abigail," he had once told her, "only in the *abstract*. I know you're from Boston, a hotbed of abolitionism, but you live quite well on the profits from slave labor down here in Darien, Georgia, so your antislavery convictions can't possibly run very deep." He chuckled. "You've adjusted well. I doubt that you lose much sleep over it."

How, even with Thad's skillful oversight, would her nearly four hundred acres of rice land have been prepared, planted, and harvested without slave labor? It couldn't have been, and, as though she were running down a steep hill, unable to stop, she allowed herself to think of *him*, then quickly began to try to picture the actual look of her rice fields, the seed rice which had been hand-flailed by her slaves. "Never use mill rice for planting," Thad had warned. "See that it is snugly in the ground in evenly laid-out rows twelve to fifteen inches apart and dug the total length of the field." She almost heard his lilting voice. Her seed, her fields. Orderly, well tended, profitable, but all nothing without Thad. And here she sat in the stateroom of a steamer plowing through the black waters, taking her farther and farther away from him. Taking her closer and closer to her fashionable, elegant mother. And, with luck, to a face-to-face meeting with the famous, much beloved *and* criticized Fanny Kemble.

That night at their shared dinner on the ship, Dr. Holmes declared, "Fanny Kemble is not only a great actress, she's indescribably lovely to look at. She's deeply spiritual, charming, funny—even playful. I disagree with her on her favorite subject, slavery, but I find her entirely delightful. She's cultured as only a lady reared and educated in Europe can be, but on the issue of slavery, she's a *monomaniac—*

abolitionist to the core. Her views cost her not only her wonderful husband, Pierce Butler; they also cost her the companionship of her two fetching daughters. The terms of the Butlers' divorce, you know, kept Fanny away from the girls until they both reached their majority. I understand her youngest will be twenty-one next month, so I imagine my friend, la Kemble, is glowing. You have a real treat in store, Abby."

"Don't get Abby's hopes too high, James," Susan Holmes said. "We aren't even sure Mrs. Kemble will still be in Boston."

"If she isn't, we'll find her, my dear. Don't forget our standing invitation to be her houseguests at The Perch, her cottage in Lenox." Holmes refilled their coffee cups from a large silver pot on the ship's table. "I'm as eager as a schoolboy at the prospect of my two lovely friends meeting face to face. One a rabid abolitionist, the other an abstract abolitionist. Just beware, dear Abby. Fanny Kemble is a most persuasive lady. Keep your pretty head firmly on your graceful shoulders—every minute."

"Is your mother an abolitionist, Abby?" Susan asked.

"Mother? Oh, who knows? She adored Eli and seemed to have no qualms whatever at my becoming the mistress of over a hundred slaves. I'm sure Dr. Holmes will decide she too is an abolitionist. In the abstract, of course."

Chapter 20

The steamer which brought the three Georgia travelers from Savannah to Boston Harbor on April 12 was met by a tall, dignified gentleman of fifty or so and, standing beside him, a slender, smartly dressed lady with graying hair. The gentleman was the doctor and author Oliver Wendell Holmes, the distinguished cousin of Dr. James Holmes. The lady was Abby's mother, Emily Banes. That the two had just met at the docking area would not have been easy to guess since both were so Brahmin in their manners that they would surely have been as formal and proper had they known one another well for years.

From the first moments of their embrace in the noisy, crowded public anteroom, Abby was relieved that her affection for her still lovely, well-spoken mother was genuine. She could feel it well up from deep within herself, along with fresh hope that her visit to Boston was going to be even more important than she'd dared dream. In what way it might be important, she had no idea, but for this moment it was good and safe to be near her mother's familiar scent of lilac, to feel her arms around her again. For the first time, Abby looked forward to being alone with the lady whose approval she had always yearned to experience. A lifetime seemed to pass in a matter of seconds. Introductions needed to be made, but surprisingly, all she wanted was to be transported this instant to the old, high-ceilinged, spacious rooms in her mother's Mount Vernon Street house.

The memory caused her to half stammer the introductions. But when Dr. James Holmes presented Abby to his relative, the now rather famous Oliver Wendell Holmes, she had no hesitation at all in telling the imposing gentleman of her admiration for his widely read series of essays *The Autocrat of the Breakfast-Table*.

"I'm honored," he said, bowing over her hand. "It's an entirely new experience to be published now in real book form."

"He's the intellectual of the family," Dr. Holmes joked, not teasing, simply enjoying himself.

"Of course, I've read every installment of the *Autocrat* in *The Atlantic Monthly*," Abby offered.

Mr. Holmes looked guardedly surprised. "You're a subscriber to *The Atlantic Monthly*, Mrs. Allyn?"

"Oh, yes, sir. My late husband subscribed for me the instant he learned that my favorite American poet, Mr. James Russell Lowell, was its editor."

"That's interesting, Mrs. Allyn," Holmes said. "Lowell would be so pleased to know you love his poetry that much and I'm sorry not to be able to introduce the two of you, but he's abroad for the summer."

"I say, Oliver," Dr. James Holmes broke in, "is my friend Fanny Kemble Butler anywhere in the vicinity of Boston right now? I haven't received a reply to my latest letter to her."

"Yes. But she doesn't go by the name Butler anymore, Cousin James," Holmes said. "She's still using Mrs. before her name for some odd reason, but she's Fanny Kemble again and I hear she's hugely enjoying her new life. It so happens she's reading Shakespeare at the Boston Museum this week. May I invite all of you to attend tomorrow evening as my guests?"

It was obvious to Abby that her mother was duly impressed to have met the much discussed Oliver Wendell Holmes and was elated to have been invited to accompany him to the theater. It's also no secret to anyone in our party this minute, Abby thought, amused, but for once not feeling critical of her mother's infatuation with society's best. It was just Mama's way. Accepting it under this unexpected circumstance was rather pleasant, compared to the old rebellions Abby had felt for most of her life. Why shouldn't her mother, whose own background and taste were flawless, feel more at home with her kind?

"I confess I'm delighted with your generous invitation," Abby said to Dr. Holmes's cousin. "And would I be impertinent if I asked how to address you? I know you as a fine writer—a real craftsman—but I also know you're a medical doctor. Don't you think it could get a bit confusing for a lady spending the evening with two Dr. Holmeses?"

"Just call me James or Dr. Bullie," her Darien friend interjected in a joking manner. "You can plainly see, Abigail, that there are high-toned gentlemen in my family, but you also know I'm the last person in Georgia to fancy himself as such. I take after my mother in that respect," he explained. "Father remained a noble Holmes, held himself to his dying day in highest esteem, always preferring the company of his own class. I even surprise my good, democratic Susan at times by the wide variety of those I choose to invite for meals at our house in Darien." He took Susan's arm. "You're almost accustomed to me by now, though, aren't you, Susan?"

"Indeed I am accustomed to you and I'm also quite cold, husband dear." To Emily Banes and the famous Holmes, she explained, "I'm also accustomed to our rather mild Georgia winters."

"Do forgive me, Cousin Susan," Oliver Holmes said, bowing. "Here we stand in the bitter Boston evening, Mrs. Banes, with no thought for our coastal Southern visitors. I have a carriage. May I drop you anywhere, Mrs. Banes, Mrs. Allyn? I assume you live on Beacon Hill."

Abby merely smiled when her old friend Dr. James Holmes said, "You assume correctly, Cousin. One only has to look at Mrs. Banes, mother of our dear friend Abigail, to know her front door opens only to Boston's finest. Oh, dear! Abby, kindly explain me to your good mother! If you don't, she'll begin to worry about the company you keep in Darien, Georgia."

"*Au contraire*, Dr. Holmes," Emily Banes said pleasantly. "You are much like Abby's late father—arms and heart open to the world regardless of standing or pedigree." On an unassuming laugh, she added, "I'm afraid the good Lord had to do much work in me, but over the years, I believe, He's made some progress. My daughter, Abigail, is truly like her father."

James Holmes bowed. "And I am like my mother—she and I both were the despair of my late father."

"Our conversation is erudite to say the least"—Oliver Holmes laughed—"but I for one can no longer tolerate causing Cousin Susan more suffering in this bitter spring cold. My carriage is only a few steps from here."

"So kind of you, sir," Abby's mother said, "but I have a driver waiting with my carriage too. Perhaps we should say good night and get your cousin's dear wife to a warm room. You live on Beacon Hill too, Dr. Oliver Holmes?"

"Charles Street, madam. It's been such a pleasure seeing all of you and tomorrow we'll make further plans for your stay in Boston. I'll send a note round to Fanny Kemble's hotel tonight. She'll want to know there are visitors in town from the garden spot on the coast of Georgia that so changed her life."

"Did his wife's writing actually cause Mr. Pierce Butler to end their marriage?" Abby asked as the group moved toward the carriage. "I find such a drastic measure hard to believe."

Oliver Wendell Holmes stood very tall in their group, an amused, but somehow understanding smile on his even-featured, handsome face. "I believe I'll leave that explanation to my cousin James, who still worships at the shrine of Mr. Pierce Butler, the slave owner. Or did he sell all his poor bondsmen to pay for his own foolish mountain of debt?"

"He——he did hold a large slave sale before we left Georgia," Abby offered. "I believe the remaining slaves on Butler Island belong to his brother's estate now."

Dr. James Holmes tried and failed to raise himself to his cousin's height. "We did not make that long voyage to start a war among friends, Oliver. Forgive my cousin, ladies," he said.

"There's no need to forgive him, Dr. Holmes," Mrs. Banes said. "You're perfectly free to idolize a slave owner if you like. As your cousin and I are free to decry them. Come, Abigail, we must say good night. It has been a pure delight—an honor to meet you, sir."

When they were seated side by side under a warm fur throw, her mother gave Abby a quick hug. "Now, Abby, my beloved daughter, we'll have the whole evening at home alone together!"

"I know," Abby said, feeling a touch of the old rebellion for the first time since meeting her mother again. "I fully intend for us to have a real talk, Mother. But I'd like to know why you cut down my fine friend Dr. James Holmes as you did.

"I didn't cut him down, Abigail!"

"Mama, you most certainly did and I hope—yes, I've even prayed—that you won't force me to think one way and talk to you another while I'm here with you. What did Dr. Holmes do to irritate you?"

"He did absolutely nothing, child! Except to admit that he approves of owning the very lives of other human beings."

"Because he thinks so highly of Mr. Pierce Butler?"

"Poor Fanny Kemble's former husband has the mind and black heart of a slave owner!"

"Mama! How do you know the color of Pierce Butler's heart?"

"A gentleman has to own slaves before he can put them on the block for sale, doesn't he? And, Abigail, we won't be talking at cross-purposes with each other if you understand at the outset that in the years past I've seen still more of God's light."

Abby's heart sank. It had surprised her to find herself *wanting* to feel close to her mother again and now the disappointment seemed almost too great. "Mama, please, Mama—don't preach! Don't you want us to—try to become real friends?"

Her mother's voice was gentler than Abby could remember its being—ever: "Abby, we're going to be friends because I'm going to speak only what I truly feel to you while you're here. Part of what I've come to realize is that I've been one way and spoken another to you for most of your life. I—I wish I could tell your father the same things I'm telling you. I must have confused him dreadfully and I'm sorry, sorry, sorry now. But at least I can be truly honest with you, child. Since I've been reading after the late Reverend Ellery Channing, I've become a sincere, determined—abolitionist."

"*What?*"

"Yes. I know you're a slave owner now, Abigail, but—your loving mother is an abolitionist—in mind and in heart. As is Fanny Kemble. I've gone to hear her glorious readings—often alone when I could find no one to go with me. But thanks to you and your Dr. James Holmes of Darien, I will now be able at last to meet the great lady. He won't like being the agent to my good fortune, probably, but oh, Abigail, it is more than good fortune. For me, now that I see so clearly, meeting her is a dream come true!"

Chapter 21

As Abby remembered well from her days at boarding school, there had been no stopping her mother when young Abby came home to Boston for a visit. Today, a bright, crisp April morning almost two decades later, nothing had changed. Certainly her mother had informed everyone of note ahead of time that her daughter would be in the city.

While mother and daughter were still having their breakfast coffee in the tastefully furnished Banes parlor, Abby broke a rare moment of silence to ask, "Mama, don't you want to spend some time with me—just the two of us?" Then she laughed. "Don't answer that. I know exactly what you'll say and I also know you think you've changed, but you haven't. And, honestly, I'm glad you haven't. If you'd allowed me to sleep late this morning, I know I couldn't have done it."

"What on earth do you mean, Abigail? It must be plain to you that I'm as excited as ever to have you home again. And I haven't planned much of anything. Just a few new friends of mine coming by for a cup of tea in an hour or so. Which, of course, is the reason I ordered such a small breakfast for you. You don't eat a heavy breakfast at your own home in Darien, do you?" When Abby's smile grew, her mother asked, "Now, what did I say that struck you as so funny?"

"Nothing you said," Abby replied pleasantly. "I was just picturing the look on your face if you ever saw the breakfast my Rosa Moon serves me every day. Especially since I've been riding so much with Mr. Greene around the plantation rice fields. Calm down and I'll give you my typical morning menu these days: two eggs, bacon or ham, biscuits, jelly, lots of fresh-churned butter, and maybe a sugar cake with my coffee."

"She serves you dessert with breakfast?"

"Sometimes. I always do my best to eat every crumb too. Especially since Rosa Moon and I have become such good friends, I wouldn't hurt her feelings for anything."

"What do you mean—good friends, Abigail?"

"I probably didn't mention it to you in a letter, but I was forced to find a way to live through almost unbroken silence and loneliness after Eli and I moved to Darien. He knew nothing about rice culture, and once he began to understand it some, he became so engrossed with it that he would sit in silence all evening contemplating his responsibilities as a plantation owner—with me sitting right in the same room. I now know that because of our Northern ways Rosa Moon didn't talk to me unless talk was necessary. And I—I was wretched."

"Well, how did you and this Rosa Moon person become friends?"

"We didn't until about the time Eli drowned."

"I see. But how does one have a real friendship with one's cook, Abigail?"

"My dear friend Dr. James Holmes would probably say something like 'any old port in a storm.' But that wouldn't be true with Rosa Moon. I know now that I couldn't have chosen a better, safer port."

Her mother set down her cup and saucer. "You've lost me, Abby. Must you speak in riddles?"

"I'm not speaking in riddles. Just a day or so before we got word that Eli had been drowned, I must have let it show how cut off, shut away, and downright lonely I'd been. At any rate, almost before I knew it, Rosa Moon and

I were hugging each other. From that moment, we've had a friendship more valuable to me than even I know, I'm sure."

"You go about—hugging your colored cook, Abigail?"

Abby laughed. "No, we just feel free to hug now. As real friends do, Mother." A smile on her face, Abby said, "I'm not being sarcastic this time. I know I have been with you in the past and I'm truly sorry. It won't happen again because I—long so for us to be friends too. But I thought you said last night that you'd become an *abolitionist* in your mind and in your heart."

"I—I did say that, my dear, and I meant it. You'll find out when my new friends come for tea with us a little later, but—despising the evil institution of slavery doesn't necessarily mean one goes about hugging the—Negro. One simply doesn't hug one's cook!"

"Rosa Moon is my friend! And even as skillful as she is in her kitchen, she does far more than cook for me. She's also my housekeeper. She sees to hot water for me in the mornings, launders and irons my clothes, mends them too. You know I never learned how to sew a stitch."

"You didn't need to learn. We've always had Thelma for that."

"Rosa Moon," Abby went on, "darned Eli's socks, kept buttons on his shirts. She's a marvelous cleaner. The woman doesn't stop from morning till night and never, never complains."

"Did she complain before you—became friends?"

"Not that I remember. She was just silent. As silent as a big rock. But I see now that she really felt strange with me. I certainly felt strange with her too."

"But you don't feel strange with her now?"

"No."

"Abigail, is it true they have a peculiar odor about them?"

"Negroes? Oh, the men and women who work under that Georgia sun in the rice fields and go home to cabins with no means of bathing but a pan of water may not smell like honeysuckle."

"I hear even Fanny Kemble declares they all have a peculiarly strong body odor."

"Not Rosa Moon. Not Obadiah either."

"Obadiah?"

"Her husband, my handyman around the house in town when he's not busy helping Mr. Greene at Abbyfield. Obadiah's a rather wonderful man, really. And he and I worked side by side just last week hanging my summer curtains Rosa Moon had just laundered, so I would have noticed any odor. Rosa Moon and Obadiah are fortunate. Unlike most slaves, they have a metal bathtub in their cabin. A gift from Eli. Every night, Rosa Moon washes Obadiah's back and he washes hers. Mrs. Fanny Kemble didn't happen to meet either of my house people!"

"I suppose dear, fastidious Eli gave them the tub out of self-defense."

"No. He got the tub because Rosa Moon asked for it. Obadiah wanted to buy it himself with money from the eggs his chickens lay, but Eli wouldn't hear of it."

"Oh, can they keep the money from things they sell themselves?"

"Most planters allow that, yes. But Eli wanted to buy it for them. He and Obadiah always had a special relationship. In fact, Obadiah all but worshipped Eli! And I'd trust Obadiah and like him if for no other reason than that he almost lost his own life trying to save Eli from drowning. He—he held on to Eli's foot until his boot came off. The man still has that boot, and Rosa Moon declares Obadiah's ordered her to have it used as a marker on his grave when he dies."

"Oh, my! They are primitive, aren't they?"

"Some of their customs are—different. But except for the color of their skin, I see no difference between colored and white deep down where it matters. There are dishonest, thieving colored just as there are whites. And, Mother, when one finds a Negro with real faith in God—it's truly *faith.* Rosa Moon talks to Jesus in her kitchen as though she could see him standing there beside her."

"Oh, dear!"

"To her, faith is simply having an idea of what God's nature is really like. As she says, 'The more I knows you, Miss Abby, the more I knows that you is right there backin' up everything you tells me. If you tells me you gonna be here in the house, you be here. Jesus say he won't eber leave us nor forsake us. He back that up hisself. So, the more I knows him, the more I trusts him.' Rosa Moon told me that one day when I went back to her kitchen to find out who was there conversing with her. It was during the time when I felt so alone, so shut off in my silent world, even from Rosa Moon, and I have to believe God prompted her to explain that to me. He was the only person who knew how isolated I felt."

"I see."

"I hope you do, Mama! Oh, I do hope you—understand. You see, as I started to tell you earlier, only a day or so before the terrifying morning when Rosa Moon told me that Eli was gone, I realized that to my surprise, to my total surprise, she had understood me for months and months, but felt so uncomfortable with me she just couldn't let me know. I long to be sure you also understand. I know we're different in a lot of ways, but people don't have to be alike to be friends."

"If you're so fond of this Rosa Moon person, why on earth don't you get someone to help her with all the work she now does alone?"

Abby laughed. "Because she'd be insulted!"

"There's one more thing I must ask you before my new abolitionist friends get here. Does—did—Eli permit his slaves to be whipped?"

"Absolutely not! And neither does my present fine overseer, Mr. Greene. He knows, because I've told him, that I don't really believe in owning other people."

"But you do own them, my dear." Her mother's voice broke and real tears filled her eyes. "As a true abolitionist,

Abby, it's important to me that you know how even the thought of a whipping affects me."

"But, Mother, I do know!"

"How could you? Abby, are you a secret abolitionist?"

"For heaven's sake, Mother, I don't have to be an abolitionist to know how brutal it is to lay a lash on anyone's bare skin!"

"Do you know that up here we call planters 'lords of the lash'?"

"Yes, I know. And to some of us in the South that makes all of you look—plain silly! Every slave owner does not mistreat his people."

"I'm sure you don't, Abigail." She cleared her throat, a habit Abby remembered as often preceding a righteous declaration. "But you're a Christian. You were reared as a Christian to believe that man or woman can obey only one master. The Bible says that 'if the Son shall make you free, you shall be free indeed.' And when any person's very life is owned by another person—another mere human being— that's sin. Not sin for the poor slave. Sin for the master. Did—did any of that truth torment gentle, good Eli?"

Abby thought for a moment, then stood up. "As I recall, you had no doubts about Eli's faith when I married him, Mother. You knew he would become a slave owner, but you almost revered the man."

"Eli was an honorable gentleman, from an excellent family. Two of his cousins still preach the Gospel in Connecticut."

"But you knew and certainly Eli knew when I married him and agreed to move to Darien, Georgia, that signing the purchase papers for his rice land there meant becoming a slave owner. How is it that you were so pleased to have me marry a man whose sin you cannot forgive now?"

Now her mother was also standing. "Oh, my precious Abigail, they've turned you into a—convinced slave owner! When someone becomes a Quaker, he or she is said to be a *convinced* Quaker." She rubbed her forehead. "Oh, dear God in heaven, they've turned her into a convinced

slave owner! Is this Mr. Greene, your overseer, the one
who did it? Lord, please don't allow this evil man to stain
my daughter's pure heart by his influence upon her thinking. Don't allow him to weaken her once strong faith!"

"I'm sure Jesus himself said we were not to pray on street
corners, Mother, where everyone can overhear us, but to
go into our closets and close the door!"

"Abby, what are you trying to do? Spoil our limited time
together on your first day here?"

"No, Mama. I guess I was just reverting to my girlhood
ways by proving to you that I know something about the
Scriptures too!" She moved toward her mother, looking
deep into her eyes. "Forgive me, please. It—it became a
habit, I guess, with the years. One I—hate now. And I'm
truly sorry." Her arms out, she added, "Mama, it's time for
us to have another hug—a good believable one. Don't you
think it is? We're not very practiced, but let's try—shall
we?"

"Yes, daughter. I say we do. I want only peace in this
house when my new dedicated abolitionist friends get here.
Naturally, they're all extremely sensitive to friction of any
kind. All gentle hearts."

"Naturally," Abby said, without a hint of sarcasm. "I
want only peace in this house too, Mama."

"Oh, I know you do, my dear. There is one more thing,
though."

Abby released her mother from the embrace. "Yes?"

"I would be most grateful if—if you just didn't mention
owning slaves. Is that asking too much?"

"I don't suppose it is, but I think it is a bit too much to
expect your friends not to know it already."

"Well, they don't!"

"And what am I to say if one of them asks a perfectly
plausible question about my life in Darien, Georgia? Such
as what daily life in a plantation household is like?"

"Do they need to know you own a plantation?"

"I suppose not. And I suppose you haven't told them."

"That's right. I haven't."

"I won't lie, Mama. So we'd better pray no one asks."

Chapter 22

"Sweet are the uses of adversity;
Which, like the toad, ugly and venomous,
Wears yet a precious jewel in his head;
And this our life, exempt from public haunt,
Finds tongues in trees, books in the running brooks,
Sermons in stones, and good in every thing."

When Fanny Kemble read the final line of that excerpt from *As You Like It*, which she had chosen as her encore at the close of her Shakespeare readings at the Boston Museum, she stood for a moment in the respectful silence before applause broke over the audience of some two hundred people. Abby waited a moment before joining the applause. The rich, vibrant voice of this amazing woman made her want to savor its sound and the last truth-filled phrase she had spoken.

Despite her so-called independence, Abby needed the reassurance that indeed there was "good in every thing."

Had there ever been a more purely spiritual experience? Could it be possible that Abby alone would carry away the truth that indeed God does make use of everything; that indeed "Sweet are the uses of adversity . . ."? Could it be that only Abby would carry away a new purpose in her own adversity, her own aloneness, her own struggle to return to some semblance of her once carefree self? She would try. God knew she meant to try to find, perhaps for the first time in all the years of her life, a place of comfort. A place with the freedom any woman needs in order to learn how to love again.

Thad. She spoke the name so clearly she half expected people to be looking at her instead of at the captivating woman making her graceful bows of gratitude to these applauding people, all of whom, Abby thought, were thanking her. All this was second nature to the nearly fifty-year-old actress, Fanny Kemble—world-famous, adored *and* despised, now grown a little thick in the waist and ruddy of cheek, but the whole of her proclaimed "beauty" as obvious as though her clear, musical voice were shouting the word.

Before her stirring finale, she had read a long passage from *Romeo and Juliet*, one from *As You Like It*, and had romped nimbly through a shorter excerpt from *A Midsummer Night's Dream*. Each would sound again and again in Abby's memory, but Mrs. Kemble's final words: ". . . tongues in trees, books in the running brooks, sermons in stones, and good in every thing" would stay with her always. And now, Fanny Kemble stepped to the apron of the stage and spoke extemporaneously as though talking privately to each person there with her in the spacious, ornate room.

"And I, Fanny Kemble, can assure you that even our illustrious leader, the Reverend William Ellery Channing, never preached a sermon in which there was more truth than in Mr. Shakespeare's words. As much, surely, but no more."

And if she said anything else, no one heard, because almost everyone in the audience was, like Abby's mother, a relatively new and equally radical abolitionist. The name Channing itself set the applause roaring again.

In Oliver Holmes's luxurious carriage en route from the Boston Museum to the Parker House, where he had invited Dr. James, Susan, Fanny Kemble, Abby's mother, and Abby for supper following the performance, Abby was seated between Mrs. Kemble and Dr. James. Dr. James Holmes could not have disagreed with anyone more than he disagreed with the Reverend Channing, but being Dr. Holmes and in possession of what could be the world's most pixie-like sense of humor, he seemed actually to enjoy a spark of controversy so long as the sparks did not catch fire and destroy anyone or anything. James Holmes had known Fanny Kemble since the late 1830s, when she and her former husband, Pierce Butler, had paid the now infamous visit to St. Simons Island which resulted in Fanny's downright inflammatory *Journal of a Residence on a Georgia Plantation*. The *Journal* was still unpublished, but Abby's mother had told her that there were Bostonians who prayed daily for its publication in the exalted cause of anti-slavery.

"Why isn't it already published?" Abby had asked her mother.

"Because Fanny Kemble is a real mother who loves her children and who refuses to risk their father's withholding anything from the two girls out of spite for their mother. The *Journal* is in one sense hostage to Pierce Butler's hateful beliefs in owning slaves. She wrote freely of their lives on Butler's two plantations in coastal Georgia. And he is, of course, furious with her."

"But his slaves have all been sold now. They went on the block before I left Georgia," Abby had reminded her mother.

"Which gives us all great hope that her important *Journal* may soon be published so that everyone can read her firsthand view of the evil in slavery."

Even if Fanny Kemble had not been holding the carriage passengers spellbound with one of her true funny stories about the time she played some joke on Dr. James Holmes during her long ago visit to coastal Georgia, Abby's thoughts would have kept her silent. Silent and listening— as entranced by the elegant lady beside her as though Fanny were some mythological enchantress.

* * *

Heads turned and hotel guests stared as the Holmes party made its way across the large, oak-paneled lobby of the Parker House toward the opulent dining room. Abby knew that people came from miles around to enjoy the excellent service and cuisine to be found there. But all eyes were on Mrs. Kemble.

Abby had never seen her own mother so impressed or so smitten with another human being. And, of course, because Fanny Kemble was there due to her longtime relationship with Abby's friend Dr. James Holmes, her mother's face was wreathed in smiles for her own daughter too.

"I regularly deny that I mind being middle-aged and I ignore my avoirdupois accordingly," Fanny Kemble laughed as Oliver Holmes seated her between his cousin, James, and Abby. "But I never deny myself an opportunity to sample these delightsome Parker House rolls." Turning to Dr. James, she asked, "Does it surprise you to learn that I heard their praises sung in a dining room in the South of France only last year, Dr. Holmes?"

"Nothing you have ever said has surprised me, dear lady," Holmes said. "You've succeeded in startling me a time or two, but looking back, I'm surprised at myself for ever being startled. Word of these delicious rolls has reached all the way to the backwaters of coastal Georgia. Why would I be surprised that you heard them praised in Europe?"

"What a relief to find your sense of humor still in such sprightly form, Dr. Holmes," Fanny said. "I doubt that I've ever conversed with anyone of such contrary opinions or done so with such sheer pleasure."

"I do my level best to keep it in play, m'lady. I'm grateful that you noticed."

"Oh, we should all be grateful—we *are* all grateful—for the truly elevating experience of listening to you this evening, Mrs. Kemble," Abby's mother said. "I vow I shall never, never forget this night as long as I live!"

Abby, who had said nothing since they were seated, studied the famous actress's expressive face. How did one ever know when such a woman, one who had spent so much of her life performing, truly meant anything she happened to say at a dinner table with a group of people, some of whom she scarcely knew? While Mrs. Kemble was a close acquaintance of Oliver Holmes, she had only that evening met Abby and her mother and hadn't seen Susan since her long-ago visit to Georgia. But without a doubt, Dr. James, her antiabolitionist adversary, probably knew her better than anyone else seated around the large circular table.

"How does it feel knowing that every minute in public all eyes are on you, Mrs. Kemble?" Abby asked.

"Well, I declare, Mrs. Allyn," Fanny said with a smile. "You *do* talk! I realize that, except for Susan, we're all chatterboxes, but I was honestly beginning to wonder about your inscrutable silence."

For a few seconds Abby just sat there feeling embarrassed. She knew full well that her blush showed, even in the softly candlelit dining room, because she had not worn her black widow's veil tonight. Leaving it behind at her mother's house was a small, secret sign of the new freedom that was beginning to take her over these days. During the performance and in the carriage she had felt almost as light and free as she had begun to feel in the last few weeks before leaving Darien. Almost as free and expectant as she always felt at the first sight of her own rice fields when she stood beside them with Thad before their day's lessons began.

"Forgive me if I spoke too impudently," Mrs. Kemble said, touching Abby's hand. "Your friend Dr. James Holmes can tell you I have a tendency to do that. Your black dinner gown is so elegant, so becoming, I'm sure I've been staring at you. You really should wear black often, my dear. And give thanks you're young enough to wear it!"

"My daughter's an excellent conversationalist as a rule," Abby's mother said. "I think she's simply still under the spell of your marvelous performance, Mrs. Kemble."

"And I wish with all my heart," Dr. James put in protectively, "that you'd convince her it's all right for her to wear another color now and then. So far from her home, who's going to gossip up here?"

"Mrs. Allyn is still wearing widow's black, Fanny," Oliver Holmes said, supplying the missing piece in the awkward dialogue. "I believe her husband has been dead only five or six months."

Fanny Kemble turned to Abby, her great, dark eyes seeming to search Abby's very soul. "I am more than sorry, my dear. No one thought to tell me. Not even one of the usually thoughtful Holmes cousins. But might it help you a bit if I could assure you there is another kind of separation far worse than death? If you think me brazen, I promise you I only mean to help by telling you there is a goodbye that's a far more painful event than—the clean, sharp, final pain of death. There is a kind that—never lets up. And gives one few, if any, cues as to how to find the exit. I'm talking about a failed marriage, of course. And I hope, at least, that you don't carry any false guilt about your husband's death. You see, I've found that when a marriage fails outright, one person, usually the wife, tends to assume false guilt."

"You didn't offend me, Mrs. Kemble," Abby said. "And when I've had more time to think about it, I'm sure I'll realize that you have probably helped more than you know."

In the momentary silence that followed, Abby's mother cleared her throat and said, "I'm a widow too, Mrs. Kemble. I'm also Abby's mother and heaven knows I've tried to help her. But mothers do tend to be taken for granted, you know." She looked at Abby. "Or—ignored." No one at the table could have missed Emily Banes's effort to look as noble as Abby knew she was feeling. "But," her mother went on, "no one is here to listen to my daughter or to me. We're all so eager for you to talk to us about our mutual efforts to follow the teachings of your close friend the late Dr. Ellery Channing. Do talk to us about him, please!"

As soon as they had all ordered, Fanny beamed her dazzling smile and began to reminisce about her friend Dr. William Ellery Channing:

"I have no choice but to smile when I remember my dear friend Dr. Channing. I'm sure most of you know he was a saint in his spirit and his mind. Truthfully, the man had an almost dwarflike body and was ill much of the time, but he had the heart of a spiritual giant. And without doubt, I became one of his devoted disciples."

"You're a Unitarian too now, aren't you, Mrs. Kemble?" Dr. James asked.

"I am indeed."

"My friend Fanny is her own kind of Unitarian, of course," Oliver laughed.

"I should hope, dear Oliver, that even at my age, I am still able to leave my own imprint on whatever I touch," she said with another smile. "But Dr. Channing's spirit was as strong and vibrant as his poor body was weak, and without doubt, he passed to me the satisfying comfort of his genuine religion. And, I must add, the not so satisfying comfort of his thinking on the evil of both slavery and war. If only the world had even one more pacifist as able and as convincing as he! Look at this country as it quakes because an ugly civil war seems inevitable. Nonsense! War gains nothing for either side and causes only sorrow and suffering. Peace could reign between North and South today if only the clearer heads in both sections of this land of opportunity would follow the reason of such a man as Dr. Channing!"

"I doubt that you'd find one dissenting voice at this table," Oliver Holmes said, "concerning the evils of war, but didn't you yourself find Dr. Channing's theories on how to end slavery rather unworkable, Fanny?"

"I should really have appreciated your *not* bringing that up, Oliver," she answered. "Still, I cling to the belief that one lifetime is not enough to give his theories about eventual emancipation a fair chance. Hatred dies slowly in the hearts of men and women. More to the point, I'm sure self-righteousness dies even more slowly. I sometimes believe, especially when I think back on my long-ago visit to coastal Georgia, that human nature would rather feel superior than—healthy! As long as there are those among white slave owners in the South who contend that men with white skin are somehow superior to those with dark skin, the evil will go on. Mankind falls easily into the role of master, when the truth is, nothing works unless the one Master, God Almighty, is acknowledged. With a few exceptions—and you are one of them, Dr. James Holmes—I found slave owners despicable because of their firm belief in the inferiority of the Negro. Oh, I think of a few others like you, such as dear old Mr. John Couper and his daughter, Anne Fraser, who allowed themselves truly to enjoy being friends with their people. In their hearts and, I believe in yours also, Dr. James Holmes, they were true democrats who did not feel superior to their black brothers and sisters. Who truly, with their hearts at least, did not believe in the vile institution—except as a way to make more money."

Abby looked quickly at Dr. James. His face turned crimson. Fanny Kemble, as usual, had struck a nerve, and for an instant, as a slave owner herself, Abby felt genuinely sorry for Dr. James. Sorry for him *and* for herself.

"Am I to gather from that remark, Mrs. Kemble, that although you were unable to rouse my anger over the subject all those years ago during your brief stay with us on the Georgia coast, you believe I despise slavery?"

"And don't you, Doctor?" Fanny asked, pinning him with her voice and her eyes as though with a long, sharp hatpin.

"To me, it is a matter of individual choice shaped by economic necessity," Dr. Holmes responded.

"In other words, Doctor, if a planter could make as large a profit without slave labor, overnight he would free them?"

Until now, her mother's insistence that slavery was against God's will had been merely another of Mama's dogmatic declarations. Now Abby felt guilty—somehow sinful. Was the magic in Fanny Kemble's voice potent enough to make Abby aware that her own heart had deceived her? Or had she been mentally and spiritually so lazy that for the years of their friendship she had accepted Dr. James Holmes's theory that she, Abby Allyn, was an abolitionist only in the *abstract*? That it really didn't matter one way or the other? Had thinking that way of herself been that comfortable, that comforting? She fingered the exquisite pattern in her black silk dinner gown and tried hard to believe that the bleeding black fingers she had seen gripping the heavy handles of the big hoes that loosened the soil in her own rice fields held no relation to her conscience.

"You know, my dear Fanny, that along with you, I'm a convinced abolitionist," Oliver said. "My good cousin Dr. James and I do not share anything resembling agreement on the subject. But you do admit, don't you, that your influential late friend Dr. Channing's so-called solution to the problem simply did not, could not, work? As I understand it, he allowed his almost childlike faith in the improbable goodness of man to twist his thinking."

"He did," Fanny put in quickly. "Indeed he did. I tried it, God knows, with my former husband, Mr. Butler. I tried it at his coastal residences during our visit there some twenty years ago. My efforts failed. I only angered my husband by allowing his wretchedly mistreated slave women to tell me of their miserable plight. Instead of causing him to decide gradually to better his people, which was my intent, he even ordered them whipped in my presence! Dear Dr. Channing honestly believed that there was divine spark enough in all people so that they could be convinced to reform themselves, to educate their slaves, to give them measured freedoms—to increase their freedoms as they progressed. He was wrong. Such a plan merely brought worse conditions to their lives since it did nothing to change the slave owners. I know now that despite my admiration of Dr. Channing's mind and his good heart, his solution was no solution at all. Slaves must be freed, must be emancipated by fiat—all at once. *Slave owners* have proven us right—those of us who saw with our own eyes, heard the cries with our own ears."

A heavy silence engulfed them, broken only by the muffled sounds of china and silverware in the heavily carpeted dining room of the Parker House.

Without understanding why, Abby again looked at her mother. Her patrician, aging features were as white as the table linen. Her mouth was open as though to speak, but no words came.

Finally, breaking the silence, Emily Banes's cultivated voice asked in an almost timorous tone, "What would Dr. Channing say about the war that seems to—be rushing toward us all? Is there no other way to solve the hideous slavery problem? I—hate war as much as Dr. Channing hated it. I'm afraid of—war. I'm terrified at the mere mention!"

The silence fell heavier than before—thick with dread. Seconds passed, as formally attired waiters moved almost soundlessly about the quiet room. Then Oliver Wendell Holmes said just above a whisper, "Once in Italy, I learned an old Italian proverb which comes to mind at this very moment: *'Silence was never written down.'* "

Abby looked across the table and saw tears on the face of her warmhearted, Northern-born Darien friend Susan Holmes.

Chapter 23

Two weeks later, Eula, one of her mother's house servants, brought Abby a hand-delivered letter—the elegant, beige envelope bearing the return address of the Parker House. Even though Emily Banes had trained her daughter from a small girl not to nose into other people's mail, it was evident that she hesitated slightly as she left the sunroom without a word as soon as Abby started to read the letter.

Eagerly, Abby devoured the single page, knowing, of course, that no one but the great Fanny Kemble would be writing to her from the Parker House.

Wednesday, 27 April 1859

My dear Mrs. Allyn,

I seem to be prompted by a Source higher than myself to send this and so I shall get right to the matter. Last night I had trouble sleeping for thinking what an all-important calling God may well have in mind for you. This concerns a subject far more important than mere woman-talk between two females who scarcely know each other. Since I must leave the day after tomorrow to keep stage engagements in Baltimore before a trip abroad, please notify me at once that you will come to my hotel for tea at 3:00 P.M.

on Thursday, 28 April. Let me know if you need trans-
portation and I shall gladly arrange it for you.

> Respectfully,
> Frances Anne Kemble

Abby's mother's new abolitionist friends must have had
a real and positive influence on her, because, to Abby's
complete surprise, when she shared the request with her
mother, she did not even hint that she was going to be at
all nosy about such a singular and unexpected invitation
and even offered to have her driver deliver Abby's reply.

Riding alone in her mother's carriage toward the Parker
House, Abby, so accustomed to the friendly, talkative Negroes in Darien, felt a little arrogant sitting up by herself
in such a splendid carriage exchanging only her destination
with Mama's old Irish driver, Danny O'Doul. Danny
seemed oblivious to her awkward feeling. Bostonians didn't
chat much at one another, although had Abby thought of
something to say, she knew he would be most pleasant.
She thought of nothing that needed to be said. Danny said
nothing to her, but gave her his almost toothless smile
when he helped her from the carriage at the Parker House
and agreed to return for her in an hour and a half.

On the carriage ride from Mount Vernon Street to the
hotel on the corner of Tremont and School streets, Abby
had read and reread Fanny's letter, but found no hint of
exactly where in the hotel they were to meet. She could,
of course, inquire at the registrar's desk for a message and
hope for the best.

There was no extra time for wondering, though, because
she had just set foot in the handsome hotel lobby when
sweeping toward her, smiling radiantly and dressed stylishly
in a dark green velvet suit, was Fanny Kemble, both hands
out in greeting.

"How good of you to come, Mrs. Allyn," Fanny said,
plainly having no trouble ignoring the stares and whispers
of other hotel guests. "I'm sure, as with so many who know

me, you think me a quite mad Englishwoman who acts on impulse, and I don't blame you a whit. I am English and I sometimes act quite mad, but I feel no qualms whatever at my impetuosity with you today. Our meeting is, oh, it is—or it can be—so important! Shall we have our tea in one of the small, private dining rooms where we won't be interrupted?"

"That sounds lovely," Abby said, mainly because there was nothing else to say with Fanny Kemble already leading the way.

"I do hope you'll forgive me for being brash, if indeed my impulsive invitation struck you that way."

"There's nothing whatever to forgive, Mrs. Kemble. I'm only grateful for this unexpected chance to see you again."

An attentive headwaiter escorted them to what appeared to be a small semiprivate room and seated them at one of the two small unoccupied tables as though they were both royalty.

"The order you placed will be ready in minutes, Mrs. Kemble," he said. "I want the tea to be as hot as I know the English demand it."

"Thank you," Fanny said, not quite brushing him off. Just almost. Then she turned to Abby across the small table. "I owe you an apology for my sudden invitation, which I hope did not spoil any plans you may have had with your lovely mother. I know now that you've been apart since your marriage some five or so years ago. So I do—"

"Mrs. Kemble," Abby interrupted, "you don't need to apologize for inviting me today. Can you just take my word for that? In fact, you have no idea how I welcomed your letter. And not merely because of your fame and brilliance on the stage."

Fanny almost fell back in her chair with relief. "Thank heaven for that! It usually takes such a long time to find out *why* people welcome seeing me. I believe you and I can have a rational talk together. Don't you agree? Don't you agree we're off to a good start?"

Abby laughed. "I do. I certainly do. Dr. James Holmes told me I'd find you easy to know."

"He's a sweet old wrongheaded slave owner, and I'm fond of him." She leaned toward Abby. "Mrs. Allyn, I think I'd like to call you Abby if you promise to call me Fanny."

"I promise."

"Just be totally honest with me and allow me to be totally honest with you. Otherwise, you'll leave the Parker House thinking me an old busybody."

"Now I am intrigued to know why you invited me."

"Did you think me peculiar when I said in my note to you that I felt prompted to see you by a Source higher than myself?"

"I confess I wondered a little at that. You see, my mother has always received guidance straight from God as to almost everything I should and should not do."

Fanny laughed easily. "We are going to have a marvelous time together. I love your humor."

"That was only partly humorous, I'm afraid."

Her smile suddenly gone, Fanny said intently, "I think one of the reasons I often startle people with my seeming impulsiveness is that they don't understand I often have immediate plans and obligations to be in another city at a specified time. I usually do. This time I'm headed, as I said, for Baltimore, where my younger daughter, whose name is also Fanny, is to meet me for our very first pleasure trip abroad together. Just the two of us. She will have reached her majority by then so will be free to spend as much time with me as she likes." A little frown line appeared between her luminous eyes. "You see, Abby, I wasn't so far out of line when I told you at dinner the other night that there are separations worse than—death. I know firsthand about the other kind. I had no business saying it in front of other people, but I do that at times. I'm afraid I'll lose the thought and what I said was worth saying. There is a clean, healthy, though painful, finality about physical death. One can eventually find a fresh start, I'm sure. Especially if one has your intellect. Your—kind of soul."

"My kind of—*soul?*"

"Yes. You strike me as a lovely, cultivated young woman whose soul has been kept behind bars for most of your life. I don't need to know why, but I'm sure I'm right. Perhaps you've spent your years trying to live up to your mother's image of you, trying to conform to what you know people expect of you, and, Abby, that never, never works. We all need to learn how to be *ourselves.* I must say," she went on with a slightly wicked laugh, "being myself was never hard for me. I'm rather like my own mother there. That delightful, sometimes moody, but altogether lovable lady adored nothing more than she adored fishing and not once did I ever hear her worry that today the fish may not bite. Always, she was sure they would. Pole and line in hand, she would stand and wait for that magic tug on her line even with rain pouring down on her."

"I can't imagine my mother risking ugly spots on her dress by trying to catch a fish in the rain," Abby said. "In fact, I can't imagine her not taking it for granted that someone else always did all the fishing. Please don't misunderstand, Mrs. Kemble—Fanny. I do love and respect my mother and admire her for having lived her own life with such grace even if my father and I did make it difficult at times. You see, I doubt that either of us really knew her."

"Perhaps your mother is a conformist by nature. Until lately, you know, the words 'conformist' and 'nonconformist' were both almost unheard of. But I suppose it's possible that being constantly aware of what others are thinking is natural to certain ladies. Certain gentlemen too, for that matter. Your mother may be truly being herself. I simply don't believe you have found—*you* yet. Would your mother be shocked at the things I'm saying about her? About you?"

"Oh, yes!"

"Then I'm sure she'd be shocked to know that I was so

unruly as a little girl in school in France that when warned one day that a student of hers was skipping about on the roof of the school building, Mme. Faudier, the headmistress, knew at once which child it was."

"Skipping on the roof by yourself?"

"*Oui.* And I fear that was one of my lesser crimes. But at once, upon hearing that a child was so misbehaving, Mme. Faudier said, '*Ah, ce ne peut-être que cette diable de Kemble!*'"

Abby felt she hadn't laughed so freely since the last time she'd shared a joke with Thad at Abbyfield. "Look at me," she said, "sitting here in widow's black, laughing like a— a silly mule!"

"A mule, Abby?"

"We—that is, I—have an old mule on my plantation down in Darien, Georgia, that laughs when my overseer's patience is tried with his stubbornness. We call him Old Yellow."

"You call your overseer—Old Yellow?"

"No. The mule, Fanny! He is such a washed-out color, he looks rather yellow."

"*Your* plantation?"

Fanny's skill at swinging from mood to mood was a somewhat disconcerting fascination to Abby. But maybe— just maybe—Fanny Kemble hadn't yet heard that she was the owner not only of a plantation in the South but of slaves too. The approval of this extraordinarily perceptive woman had become so important to Abby, she felt a stab of fear. Fear that was mingled with hope that Fanny Kemble might come to like her as a friend. No longer overwhelmed by her, Abby simply felt so drawn to the famous actress that her new regard for herself—what just might be her real self—was like a sudden cool breeze on a hot Southern day or the velvety warmth of a crackling fire when ice shrouds the bare branches of Boston trees in winter.

"In answer to your question about my home in the South," Abby said, her voice solemn. "I suppose I assumed, with some uneasiness, that you already knew. My good, generous late husband, a New Englander also, but a man who literally fell in love with coastal rice culture, left me his four-hundred-acre rice plantation, and—"

"And?"

"And over a hundred slaves. The rich rice land is worth nothing without them, you know."

"Oh, I've heard the dogma that the South, unlike the North of the United States, is economically dependent on slave labor. I've heard it over and over and over."

"Well, it really is, you know."

"But does that make the evil practice acceptable? Do you honestly believe that owning the very life and breath of another human being is pleasing to a God of love?" When Abby said nothing, Fanny repeated, "Do you, Abby?"

"I—I admit I probably haven't thought about it that deeply."

"You simply haven't thought about it or you haven't *allowed* yourself to think about how immoral, how scarring to the soul being a slave owner really is? Judging by your appearance, you live extremely well on the profits from your plantation."

"Yes. But in a very modest house in the somewhat provincial, though charming town of Darien. Abbyfield—my late husband named his beloved plantation for me—isn't the thing of beauty I dreamed it would be. But to my husband's eye, every rice plant was beautiful."

"And is every rice plant beautiful to you?"

Puzzled, Abby asked, "Is that really relevant, Fanny? Is the way my land appears to me your reason for inviting me today?"

"I deserved that impertinent question and I like you for being so straightforward with me. The answer is no. I asked you because I couldn't help asking. But I also long to see you free and unscarred by all this. I'm being as direct with you as I hope you will go on being with me. My former husband, Pierce Butler, was once a gentle, charming man. After all, I did fall in love with him. Felt drawn to him enough to want to spend the remainder of my life with him. But no matter what you've been told, when I married Pierce I did not know that the major portion of his income came from the bleeding hands and backs of slaves. I lived like a queen on that ugly income. Every new gown, every emerald, every diamond, every strand of pearls came from the blood and sweat of some hapless black slave who had no choice in the matter. It scarred my husband—made him even more wrongheaded than he was already—robbed him of the charm that once hid his wrongheadedness. Turned him into a grasping, cruel man. Oh, he was still handsome, still sophisticated, but so insensitive and selfish, he not only began divorce proceedings against me for hating slavery, he scarcely allowed me to see my two daughters during the all-important years when they were growing up. Pierce Butler became wholly concerned with material advantage, and I swear he didn't start out that way. Being a slave owner is not only a sin against the human beings one owns, it's a sin against one's self! It will enslave *you.* I want desperately to prevent that happening to you, dear Abby. I beg you in the name of the loving God we both follow to rid yourself of this wickedness."

Feeling as though she'd been struck in the face, Abby stared at this imposing, yet tender woman across the table from her. Finally, she whispered, "*How?* How would I do this? Eli left all his property to me! It's mine now, whether or not I want it."

"Sell the land—free the slaves."

"And how would I live?"

"If we take the first step toward obeying God, He takes two toward us by showing us His way to solve the problem. That's what's called faith, Abby. I'm not one tad dependent on Pierce Butler now. I haven't been since the day of our divorce."

"I don't happen to possess your fame and talent. I have no other means of earning an income. What on earth can a woman do to earn money?"

"Have you forgotten the lilies of the field?"

"Please don't quote Scripture at me!"

"You object to that?"

"No, not if there's no hint of self-righteousness in it."

"I defy you to say I feel self-righteous about any of this, Abby. I simply care."

Whether or not she was acting or speaking from a truthful, loving heart, Abby believed her. She wasn't sure she wanted to, but she did. And if Fanny Kemble had gone ahead and proposed a practical way to be free of every slave at Abbyfield, she would have jumped at the chance. But she made no such proposal. Said nothing more. Abby felt Fanny's firm, expressive hand on hers and grabbed it and held on as for dear life.

Fanny Kemble's arrow had gone straight to its mark. Her dear friend Dr. James Holmes could no longer call Abby an abolitionist "in the abstract." She would not permit the evil thing to come between her and Dr. Holmes, but one thing she knew: There was nothing abstract in her sudden desire to be relieved of Abbyfield and its people. Nor did her thoughts fly to Thad in the abstract. They flew to him as a man. The one man with whom she wanted to spend the remainder of her life.

Chapter 24

When the Banes family carriage stopped in front of the Mount Vernon Street town house, Abby's mother was nowhere in sight, but Abby knew perfectly well that she was inside watching for her. And why not? Abby thought, as she thanked Danny O'Doul for helping her down from the carriage. Why wouldn't Mother be waiting for me? I'm her only child and I've just had tea with one of the most famous women in the theater world. So why wouldn't she be curious to know what happened, to know why Fanny Kemble invited me to tea? And Mama must be lonely for companionship too. With Papa gone she has no one close she can talk to regularly. With a sigh, Abby realized that since she had come home, she and Mama had scarcely spoken of her father.

The steep front steps seemed steeper than ever as Abby mounted them, girding herself as always for whatever might lie ahead when she began to talk with her mother. An unexpected wave of loneliness for her father pushed at her and then receded so quickly it was much as though Papa had winked. She could almost hear his voice say, "Take it easy, Abby. You know how Mama is, but she loves us both."

Yes.

Oh, yes, Papa, she thought hard toward wherever her

beloved parent was at this moment, praying that somehow he heard her thought.

Using her own key to unlock the front door, she marveled that the time spent with Fanny Kemble had not upset her. Heaven knew it should have. This dynamic woman had all but ordered her to change her entire way of life! But nothing Mrs. Kemble had said seemed quite like an order. Everything she said was the clearest, most plausible challenge. Maybe the one challenge Abby had been waiting for.

Fanny Kemble hadn't ordered anything. She had simply dared Abby to be herself—her real self. And Abby had not been upset by it, not even scared. For a reason she hadn't yet had time to recognize, she had been invigorated by Fanny's every word. And, best of all, she had, in one instant, allowed herself the usually impossible joy of dwelling on Thad as a man! Every shred of the self-imposed conformity to custom for a new widow had melted. Even more amazing, she felt none of the old rebellion that had always propelled her and her mother to sometimes harsh misunderstandings. There seemed suddenly to be only the need to find a way to show Mama the easy kind of compassion she now felt toward her.

But was there a need to tell her mother about Thad? No. Not yet. Even showing Mama love had to be guided by sensitivity. Knowing *anything* about Thad beyond the fact that he was her excellent overseer at Abbyfield would be too much for her mother now. But to tell her she meant somehow to find a way to rid herself of the sin of owning slaves might even please her, thanks to Mama's newly found cause—abolitionism. That was just the way to unlock her mother's heart as surely as the big brass key had unlocked the front door.

Poor, innocent, sheltered Mama, she thought, as she hung her warm cape on the hall tree, expecting any minute to hear her mother call. Standing there in the entrance hall, Abby smiled, thinking of how her mother tried so hard to be self-contained, calm, a true, deeply spiritual

Brahmin by her own standards. Then came the realization that her mother too could have been struggling all these years to *be* someone she really didn't know how to be.

For a moment, Abby, alone in the front hall, fought back tears. This kind of sudden understanding of the parent who had seemed the cause of a lifetime of rebellion was unbearably painful.

I must tell Dr. Holmes about all of this, she thought, and hoped he would understand—not just pretend that he did. Even if he thought her peculiar for wanting to rid herself of dear Eli's dying gift to her, Dr. James Holmes would hold her in the same esteem as always and not allow her new, fresh hatred of slavery to come between them.

Abby felt strong, genuinely strong, but her voice cracked a little when she called upstairs to her mother as though she didn't suspect at all that the woman had been waiting on needles and pins for Abby to do just that.

"I'm up here, dear," Emily Banes called down. "Will you come up to my sitting room? Or shall I come down there?"

With an odd sense of excitement, Abby almost ran up the stairs, shouting louder than needed, "I'm coming, Mama! And I have so much to tell you!"

When she hurried to embrace her mother, Abby felt almost awkward, as though she was being too boisterous in the presence of such a cultivated lady. Then they both laughed.

"I probably am downright silly," Abby said. "But you couldn't have any idea how happy I am that we've just laughed together for no apparent reason."

"Sit down, dear," her mother said, gesturing, "and tell me all about tea with Mrs. Kemble! I've been teeming to hear about her every word to you."

Taking a small, graceful rocker near her mother's chair, Abby teased, "Don't tell me you've just been sitting here waiting all this time, Mrs. Banes!"

"Oh, of course not. I've had minutes of our last Society meeting to write up and that is not a minor assignment. But, of course, I'm the secretary this year."

"You wrote the minutes to—what, Mama?"

"Why, our newly formed Abolitionist Society, of course. Your mother is busy as a bee with such creative, important work to do."

"Just what do you do at these meetings?" Abby asked.

"Oh, you wouldn't be interested."

"But I am. I really am."

"Look at me, Abby. The Abolitionist Society's work is most important to me and I don't relish any smart remarks about it at all."

"Oh, Mama, I—I'm more than interested."

"Just since your tea with Mrs. Kemble?"

"Well, maybe that helped. Look, I know I've always or almost always had a smart remark about things that interest you. Forgive me. I was wrong."

"What?"

"Is it so impossible to believe I can admit to being wrong?"

"I suppose not impossible. Just—new. Strange."

"I'm trying so hard to—see down inside you, Mama!"

"You're—what, my dear?"

"Trying to—to understand you. As you are, not as I've always thought you were."

"And when did you begin to try to—understand me?"

"I've always meant to, I'm sure."

"I see. It's amazing how wrong a mother can be, isn't it?"

"Mama, I'm not saying you're wrong about anything! You and I are different. We're not alike. I mean, not exactly alike, just because we're mother and daughter."

"When you're showing such interest in me, when you're—kind and warm as you are now, Abby, you're very like your dear father."

"I am?"

"Yes. And I can pay you no higher compliment. I loved him so much. Oh, Abby, I loved him so, so much."

Involuntarily, Abby reached for her mother's hand and held it tight in her own. "Can you believe I wish with all my heart that I'd known how to comfort you even a little bit when we—lost Daddy?"

"You did comfort me, Abigail. You—tried. I suppose I was unable to be comforted, even by God. I know God tried to comfort me."

"He's 'the God of all comfort,' " Abby quoted.

Her mother's smile did not strike Abby as sorrowful when she said, "Oh, how interesting! You, who always frowned or scoffed when I quoted Scripture to you, have just quoted it to me!"

"I know. We are funny, aren't we?"

"Yes, I guess we are. What did Mrs. Kemble have to say to you?"

"Oh, we had a lovely tea and we just talked. She's certainly more than provocative. Have you ever had her speak or perform at your Abolitionist Society?"

"No, but we must try to do that. Thank you for the suggestion, Abby. The very next time I hear that she's giving an evening of her Shakespeare readings in Boston, I'll try to arrange that. It's a marvelous idea! I know your friend Dr. Holmes considers her a monomaniac on the subject of slavery. She'd be marvelous for our girls to hear."

"Dr. Holmes told you that Fanny Kemble's a monomaniac?"

"On the subject of slavery, yes. It's so strange that such an otherwise courteous, kind, charming gentleman as Dr. Holmes could possibly be one of those 'lords of the lash.' "

"Dr. Holmes is *not* a 'lord of the lash'! He's far from it. If ever a man treated his slaves well and with care, it's Dr. Holmes. I believe he owns only about three people to work in his home and to drive him occasionally on medical calls."

"I see," Emily Banes said almost absently. "Abigail?"

"Yes?"

"I find it awfully nice sitting here holding hands like this. Do you?"

"I was squeezing your hand a while ago," Abby laughed. "Do you remember when I used to hold your hand so tight when we crossed a busy Boston Street because I was afraid of galloping horses? You had to remind me not to squeeze too hard or the rings would cut your fingers."

"I didn't dream you remembered that, child!"

"Lately, I seem to be remembering lots of things. Good things. And finding new ways to make good memories for myself for later."

"I'm sure you've noticed that I've said almost nothing about how much you must miss kind, distinguished Mr. Eli Allyn. In fact, I've worried about it. I so longed to—to be with you when you lost him. I still long to comfort you, Abby, as a mother longs over her only child."

"I wouldn't know about that kind of longing, but I want you to know that you've been just right with me since Eli's death."

"Oh, I hope I have been. Abby, look at me. I don't see a single tear in your eyes. I still have to fight them back at times when your father's name is mentioned. Have you—cried all your tears?"

"I expect so. No, Mother. I find I can't be anything but truthful with you now. I don't ever want to be anything else. I—I tried to cry when Eli drowned, but I couldn't. And I know now I didn't love him in the same way you loved my father. I revered him, respected him, but I think I fell in love with the idea of life on the Georgia coast as reigning mistress of a fine plantation."

"Oh, Abigail!"

"I'm sure that shocks you. I vowed to myself I'd stop doing that, Mama. You see, I've always wanted to tell you the truth about everything, but I knew you'd be horrified, so lots of times, I—didn't."

"Abigail!"

Abby laughed a little. "Mama, I've always meant to thank you for having named me after the brainy wife of our second President. Did you know Abigail Adams has always been a heroine to me?"

"No, no, I—didn't know that. But I see that I—didn't know so much about my own daughter."

"Well, I do thank you for naming me Abigail. She was, I now know, a lady after my own heart. Did you know that when her husband, John Adams, was attending the Constitutional Convention in Philadelphia, she wrote and told him to remember when he helped frame that all-important document that there were *female* citizens in this country too?"

"Abby, where do you learn such things?"

"I read it somewhere. Fanny Kemble happened to mention it at tea today too. I was surprised she even knew about Mrs. Adams."

"Mrs. Kemble certainly must have been joking even to think that women might vote."

"I don't believe she was joking at all. She feels strongly that her own marriage failed because Pierce Butler did not consider her his equal."

"What?"

"She definitely does not think men should be allowed to think of themselves as the lord of the manor. That they have no right to overrule their wives when a decision needs to be made." Abby laughed a little. "Mama, dear Mama, don't look so distressed. I'm really not trying to shock you."

But her mother looked so startled, so stricken, that Abby honestly felt sorry for her—felt the compassion she'd so longed to feel toward the woman who seemed, at least, to have done her best to prove to both Abby and her father that she, Emily Banes, was indeed perfect. "Don't fret," Papa used to tell Abby. "How can a husband or a daughter be expected to please a woman who is perfect?" And then they'd both laugh. But Papa is gone and Mama is still here and I want to love her in the way she needs and the way I should. Sharing my own heart seems to be the best way, Abby thought, but it's hard.

Patting her mother's hand, Abby changed the subject. "I wish you could see the modest story-and-a-half house I live in, Mama. And the rice fields are three and a half miles away on a little body of water called Cathead Creek."

"Oh, I think that's a rather quaint, curious name."

"I agree," Abby said. "But there are no rolling green lawns and, except for Rosa Moon and Obadiah, I almost never saw a slave when Eli was alive. Oh, Mama, I'm not criticizing Eli. He was a good, good man. Generous to a fault and always kind to me. He just—didn't talk to me. He grunted or buried his nose in some rice culture journal. I wanted for nothing, except at least now and then to know the feeling other women say they have when they anticipate their husbands' coming home from work in the evenings. I found out soon after our marriage that I'd never experience a truly spontaneous feeling toward Eli. You see, twenty years do make a lot of difference. Although he was only in his fifties when he died, Eli seemed *old*."

"Oh, my poor dear!"

"No. I'm not your *poor* dear. Dare I tell you that almost daily I feel as though I'm becoming a new person?"

"Abigail, I'm your mother. Why wouldn't you dare tell me that?"

"For fear you might not like the new Abigail—*not* made in your image of what a daughter should be. The truth is, I don't really know her very well yet myself. But I intend to—soon."

"I suppose Mrs. Kemble filled your pretty head with all this kind of talk."

"She gave me a new interest in *myself*. I know that much."

"Has—has something special happened to you, Abigail?"

Abby looked straight into her mother's eyes. "Now you've rather startled me," she laughed. "Why did you ask such a question? Can you see a big change in me?"

"I don't think I know the answer to that." Her mother tried valiantly to laugh a little too. "Now, did you ever think you'd hear me say I didn't know the answer to anything?"

"Mama, are you really—teasing, the way Papa used to do?"

"I—I'm trying to, Abigail . . ." Her voice broke and tears began to flow. "You see? I—I still can't even talk to you about him and he's been gone such a long time!" Straightening her shoulders, Emily Banes added, "I know I'm—not a very—strong Christian. I've always been so—glib about my familiarity with God and His ways, His teachings. But we don't need to talk about me anymore, dear. You came home to glean comfort from your mother, not to discuss her spirituality or lack of it."

Jumping to her feet, Abby hugged her mother. "Mama, could we both be changing?"

"I don't know, Abigail! And you are perfectly aware that I do not like to be pinned down on—" She disengaged Abby's arms gently and looked up into her face. "It could be that we are both changing. It's hard, as your father used to say, to teach an old dog new tricks and your mother is no longer young. So, let me work out my spiritual problems and you work out yours. Is that suitable?"

Perhaps never before this minute had Abby really understood how hard, how wrenching it had always been for her mother to drop her own defenses. The look on Mama's face now is one of intense struggle, she thought. And I mustn't make it harder for her. She is changing. At least she's trying.

"I think I want you to realize, Abby, that joining the Boston Abolitionist Society has shown me so much about my own need to grow spiritually."

Abby sat back down in her rocker. "The—Abolitionist Society, Mama? How has that shown you anything new about yourself?"

"The truth is, Abigail, I read a pamphlet which has been in print, I think, for a decade or so, in which the author called groups such as our Abolitionist Society *moderates*. What he meant, I believe, is that we don't feel Northern states have the right to infringe on the rights of Southern states by forcing them to end slavery. He also declared that there are in the North also *ultra-abolitionists* and *fanatical abolitionists*. I much prefer being moderate. Don't you? We meet quietly, thoughtfully, and give God the full credit for our clear-sightedness about the ugly practice. It's wrong, dead wrong, but it's none of my business if someone disagrees with me. I just keep my peace and pray."

"Oh, Mama, do you mind that I admire you as a—growing woman?"

Her mother laughed and the laugh was sweet and it tinkled as Abby remembered it once did when she was a small girl. "Mind, Abby, I'm delighted and terribly curious to know just why you admire me now in particular. Did you expect me to condemn you because you're a slave owner, child?"

"I guess I hadn't let myself think that far. In fact, I hadn't given a thought to the possibility that you might—condemn me. You were terribly fond of Eli. Happy when I married him."

"I was indeed. Happy and proud that my only child had won the love and respect of such a refined, wellborn gentleman."

"Surely you knew then that if Eli fulfilled his dream of owning a productive plantation, he'd have to become a slave owner."

"That's what I meant a moment ago, Abby. I hadn't become even a *moderate* abolitionist in those days. All I could think about was how advantageous the marriage would be. Had I thought slavery was questionable, I would have warned you."

"Do you honestly think I'd have paid any attention to your warnings?"

"No. I know you wouldn't have, and before my new insights about certain aspects of my own ugly self-righteousness, I'm equally sure we couldn't have had this warm, wonderful talk."

She had startled Abby again. "Your self-righteousness, Mama? Did you—did you—"

"Did I know I was self-righteous all those years?" Her mother's voice was so calm and reasonable, Abby couldn't think of a single word of response.

"Are you sure you must go back down to Georgia at the end of next week, Abigail? Do you have to leave just when we're becoming so close and easy with each other?"

"Yes. But because I also feel we're—close now and easy with each other, I fully expect my *moderate* abolitionist mother to let me go in peace."

"She will," her mother said quietly. "You go when you must and I'll not badger you to take me with you or insist that you give me a date when you'll visit me again." Emily Banes reached for Abby's hand and laughed softly when she asked, "Do you think we both might be—going a little insane? Neither of us is acting much like her old familiar self."

Now Abby laughed too. "No. I think our real selves might just be emerging for the first time in both our lives! And if we are suddenly not quite right in our heads, who cares? I'm having a marvelous time with you, dear lady!"

Chapter 25

Every day of the week Abby's steamer was due to leave Boston, and head back to what had almost come to seem like the strange, foreign South to her, was better than the day before. The long, deep rift—she could now actually call it that—between her and her mother had narrowed, sometimes hourly.

If Thad were not waiting at the far end of this voyage, saying goodbye to Mama might be—for the first time since childhood—a moment to dread. But Thad was waiting and the eagerly hoped-for letter which Danny O'Doul had handed her as she and Mama climbed into the carriage kept her heart racing. Leaving Mama alone again would be far less painful because of it. On the outside of the still unopened letter, he had written in a clear, strong hand: "Do not read until aboard the steamer for Savannah."

"Aren't you at all concerned about the letter from your overseer, Abigail?" her mother asked as Danny started the team toward the pier. "Suppose something has gone wrong at Abbyfield."

"There's nothing I could do about it now anyway, Mother, so don't worry. I'm not a bit concerned." Was that a lie? Oh, well, it depends on the kind of concern, Abby thought, keeping her excitement to herself. She wasn't merely concerned. She was frantic with curiosity. She was so curious the minutes dragged by like hours as the carriage rolled along the familiar old Boston streets. Why, when he hadn't written once during her absence, had Thad written now and asked her to wait to open his letter until she was on board ship? Abby had seen his signature once or twice on receipts for various supplies brought by steamer to Abbyfield, but hadn't noticed the strong look of his hand until now. Despite the new, genuine closeness she felt toward her mother, the unopened letter tucked into her reticule seemed almost alive to her touch as she tried to appear casual—just another lady about to make a water journey—a lady who felt lyrical and tingly!

Abby had not written once to Thad during the time she and the Holmeses had been in Boston. He could have nothing planned for her return since he had no definite idea when that would be. Purposely she had not allowed herself to write. This visit was centered on Mama and the few seconds she did permit thoughts of him jerked her almost roughly away from Boston and the once dear, familiar rooms of the Banes house on Mount Vernon Street, away from the important, shining event the visit to Mama had brought about. The discipline of keeping her thoughts on one circumstance of her life at a time appeared to be working. Even if something had gone wrong at Abbyfield, she would have no idea how to deal with it. Thad, not Abby, supervised the work on the productive acres. She merely owned the land. The land and *the slaves*.

The slaves.

"I certainly don't mean to be insistent, Abigail," her mother was saying, "but since your time with Fanny Kemble, do you feel that you can live the rest of your life with the hideous burden of being a slave owner?"

Abby turned and smiled. "The way you say those words so flat and unadorned, I feel as though I should hang my head in shame, crawl up a very long flight of hard stone steps, and beg forgiveness for my sins."

"I suppose I am too blunt with it. I just feel so hopeful since you saw Mrs. Kemble. You've been like a different person. I don't love you one bit more, but oh, Abby, I *like* you so much better. And I feel so much freer with you now. Is it all a mystery to you too?"

"In a way, it is." She reached for her mother's hand. "Life *is* part mystery, though."

"Indeed it is."

"Do you suppose God knocked down the barrier between us, Mama?"

"Or—love. I once heard that the way to get rid of ice is not to hit it with a hammer, but to melt it."

"Get ready," Abby said impishly. "I'm about to quote more Scripture. So listen carefully. 'God is love.' "

Her mother's laugh was so lilting Abby could only wish with all her heart that her father could have heard it with his own ears.

"Your father would wink at you right now if he were here in this carriage with us, wouldn't he?"

"Mama! Did you know Papa and I used to—wink over your head?"

"Yes, my dear. I knew you winked when you both thought I wasn't looking." After a moment, Mama asked, "At the risk of ruffling your feathers the way I once did, I have to ask again, Abby, dear. Are you at least thinking of freeing your slaves as soon as you get back to Darien?"

"What?"

"I think you heard me."

"I did and I haven't the faintest idea how to answer you!"

"Do you mean it's against the law in the backward South to—free people created in the image of God?"

"No, Mother. I meant that I don't know, because the subject has never come up with anyone who could tell me about freeing slaves."

"Your late husband grew to be satisfied with things as they were?"

"Not once did the matter ever come up between us, so I can't tell you about that either. I'm sorry, but I do promise that I'll look into it as soon as I can. I'm sure Mr. Greene will know."

"And do you discuss your personal plans with a mere overseer?"

"Mr. Greene isn't the usual overseer! He's a gentleman. A graduate in business from the University of Pennsylvania."

"Then why on earth is he satisfied to work in a menial position where I would think he is generally rather looked down upon by other gentlemen?"

"We'll soon see Dr. James Holmes and Susan at the pier and I'm sure he can tell you far more about Mr. Greene than I. He's extremely impressed with his abilities."

"But you do have a lawyer, a Mr. Bentley, I believe, to handle business consultations with you, don't you?"

"Of course, Mama." Abby laughed. "We're really quite civilized in Darien, Georgia."

"Oh, dear!"

"Oh, dear—what?"

"It just occurred to me that you'll have to find out what to do with your slaves once you free them. Will that be a problem? How many do you own?"

"I believe something over a hundred. And yes, it's probably going to be one of those unsolvable problems Northern abolitionists never care to admit Southerners might ever have. How they'll eat and clothe themselves— even where they'll live—I have no idea. But I do know I won't turn them out without means to care for themselves."

"And I wouldn't want you to do that."

"Mother?"

"Yes, my dear? Quickly. We're almost at the pier."

"Are we comfortable enough with each other now so I can be plain with you and not have to worry on the way back home whether or not everything is still fine between us?"

"Why, yes!"

"Don't look so surprised. We'll be hundreds of miles apart soon and I have to know I can still touch you with my thoughts."

"I need to be sure of reaching you over all those miles too, Abby."

"Then promise me that you'll stop fretting and leave all the details—easy or difficult—of the slave question to Mr. Greene and to me. Will you promise that?"

"And your Mr. Bentley, of course. Oh, I do wish I knew more about this—rather sudden—Mr. Greene. But I promise, Abby. And I hope you'll promise to write often. I'll be so eager to know what Mr. Greene has to say about everything. Especially since he seems to stand so high in your regard."

After a pause, Abby said, "He does, Mama. Thad Greene stands very high in my regard."

Chapter 26

About nine o'clock in the morning on May 2, Abby stood at the ship's railing with the Holmeses and waved until they could no longer see Mama and Dr. James's cousin, Oliver Holmes, standing side by side on shore. Some relief came to Abby that the famous Oliver Wendell Holmes was with her mother, although she knew each would ride to separate destinations in their own carriages. It had never been easy to leave her mother. But this time, the almost unbelievable transformation in their understanding made saying goodbye even more difficult.

"Did I think I'd feel her aloneness less now that we're friends?" she asked Susan Holmes as they took deck chairs in the bright, unusually warm early May sunshine to wait for Dr. James to return with bowls of ice cream, still a treat to people who lived in small towns such as Darien, Georgia. "I shouldn't expect you to have an answer to something as personal as my new closeness to my mother, but you seem to have insights about so many things."

"I don't really think you want to talk about all that now, do you, Abby?"

"Why would you ask a question like that?"

"Because you're so fidgety—rather distracted. Your mother told me you were up late last night packing, so I know you're bound to be sleepy. It was lovely having breakfast with dear Oliver this morning, but James and I had to get up a little after five in order to be ready to meet all of you at the pier by eight. We shouldn't have allowed James to insist upon bringing us ice cream until we both had a little nap."

"But he was so eager."

"Of course he was, bless him. He loves ice cream that much!"

"Do you suppose he'd be too annoyed with me if I did excuse myself until time to go to dinner?"

"He'll act annoyed, but the truth is, he'll be delighted. Go on, Abby. He'll be back any minute now and if he has *too* much trouble eating your bowl of ice cream, I promise to help the poor darling."

Alone in her tiny stateroom, Abby sat for a time—a very short time—just holding Thad's still unopened letter. No matter how restful she tried to appear, she *had* fidgeted with dear Susan. She had not only fidgeted, she had lied to this fine, straightforward friend. Of course, it had been a white lie, without malice of any kind.

For the first time in her life, she startled herself by using the expression "white lie." Why did calling an out-and-out falsehood a "white" lie make it seem harmless? What would a "black" lie have meant? Was there even a remote connection between white and black lies in the context of what Eli had always said? "Slave owners, Abby, tend to believe that their Negroes—all of them—just lie by nature. They don't. They're not that different from us. We all lie now and then. At least we stretch the truth."

There was less and less pain when at odd times she still missed Eli. This time, she wished she could ask him to elaborate a little on white and black lies. But the unopened letter from Thad mattered most at this minute and her dizzying desire to read it was no one's business but her own. She was on board the steamer now, free to read it and read it and read it. Even if it contained nothing but detailed reports of the condition of the fields now that it was nearing time to plant, she would read and reread it because it was from Thad.

His hand—his strong, young hand with the silky, sand-colored hairs on his deft fingers—had written it, had held the pen that formed the letters in his firm, vital script.

Her breath came as rapidly as though she'd been running to keep up with him as they loped along beside a canal at Abbyfield on one of their inspection rides to check on needed repairs to things like the strong wooden floodgates. Her fingers trembled and for no apparent reason her eyes grew misty even though she felt an overwhelming happiness that she was finally alone to read Thad's letter.

The three full pages of his handwriting were so like him she could almost not believe what she was seeing:

26 April 1859
Abbyfield, Darien, Georgia

My dear Abigail,

I picture you sitting there reading, thinking: "He called me Abigail without my permission!"

I apologize and will get right to the purpose of this letter to you. Please know that each word I write is written with respect and near-reverence for the fact that you have honored me by making such a noble effort to learn about rice culture under my tutelage.

I miss you.

I also find that work which seemed so interesting in the days of old, when you were my pupil, has now turned as dull as the soil from which rough rice (never mill rice) sends forth its tiny green shoots.

By the end of next week, weather permitting, we will be well into the planting. If I do say so myself, I'm rather proud that work is on time. In fact, within a very few days, all will be ready for the "sprout flow" and I find myself hoping—praying—that the beautiful owner will have returned home in time to see the grain pipped.

I miss you.

We must think of some special celebration for our sighting together of the first sprouts of pale green.

It is my profound wish and hope that you realize my deep understanding of the predicament you are in because of the watchful eyes of a small community. You must, I know, continue to wear black, continue to call me Mr. Greene, since slips of the tongue come to us all. In no way am I attempting to take you by surprise in these lines so as to influence your response, but I fall asleep each night breathing a prayer that come harvest time, you, a vision of beauty in a dress of many colors, may find it impossible to remain aloof and proper any longer. Not one word needs to be said about anything in this letter when at last I see you again. I am broaching the subject by this means so as to make it easier for you to make my life complete by saying Yes to this *my proposal of marriage* when a respectful interval shall have passed.

The people are reasonably well, and Oldun can now speak a few more words of English in his inimitable way. Probably before this can reach you, the heavy wooden floodgates will be lowered to begin the "sprout flow."

I miss you.

Your next lesson will be to observe and help supervise the "stretch flow."

I've loved you since our first meeting. And wherever we are, whatever we do, it is my desire that we be together forever and ever.

Your true friend and overseer,
Thaddeus Greene

For maybe a full minute, Abby sat in the one small, straight armchair in the stateroom, clutching the letter in one hand, the fingers of her other hand pressed tightly against her forehead in a completely futile attempt to stop her head from going around. Reading the letter again to be sure she hadn't imagined it would do no good. She had read it carefully, word by word, and now the only thing she could think of doing was to call out: "Thad! You mustn't do this! It isn't time yet. You must not do this! It's too soon, Thad—it's far too soon!"

The playful, but loud knock on her door so startled her, she jumped to her feet, the pages of Thad's letter sliding across the floor.

"Abby? Surprise! I have a surprise for you, Miss Abigail."

She knew perfectly well who stood just outside her door, but for want of anything sensible to say, she called, "Who's there? Who is it?"

"It's I," the familiar, merry man's voice called back. "You'll be sorry if you don't open the door, my dear girl. I have a lovely surprise for you—and it's melting!"

Hurriedly, Abby gathered up the loose sheets of the letter, stuffed them into the top drawer of a small chest, and opened the door to Dr. James. He was beaming and holding out a huge bowl of ice cream.

"I thought it must be you, Doctor. I'm sorry not to have opened the door sooner, but I was—"

"You are not required to explain, dear Abby. I'm the one who should apologize." He handed her the bowl, its spoon sticking up at a cocky angle. "Someday I promise I'll learn to obey my wife, Susan, who did her level best to prevent my disturbing you. And I'm in more or less of a hurry. My bowl of ice cream is melting too out on deck under the bright spring sunshine. Enjoy yours and we'll see you at the captain's table for dinner."

"If there's room left for another bite," Abby called lamely as she closed the door, sank back down in her chair, and began to laugh. The almost merry angle of that spoon propped in her huge blob of ice cream was so like Dr. James's humor, there was simply nothing else to do but laugh. Laugh and begin to shovel down great spoonfuls of the icy-cold delicacy which should have relieved Abby's hot face—still flushed from the startling content of Thad's letter—but it did not.

"The sudden Mr. Greene," Mama had called him. The phrase, when her usually careful mother had used it, had struck Abby as odd for her at her stage in life. But Mama had been right. With absolutely no warning and with Abby hundreds of miles away on the high seas, the *sudden* Mr. Greene had proposed to her!

With every fiber of her being she wanted to feel irritated with him. She even wanted to feel angry that he had dared write what he had written from such an impossible distance when she had no way to reach toward him except in her memory of the way his sand-colored hair curled on the back of his neck; the way his smile invariably made her feel as though he had said a lot more than the words she'd heard.

More maddening still, his written words had left her unsure whether she felt irrepressible joy or downright fear of what lay ahead. Thad had helped her in so many ways, but could he possibly help now when he had allowed himself to become the cause of her unknowing?

Chapter 27

*I*n their stateroom a day and a half north of Savannah, where their steamer was to dock on May 9, James Holmes and his wife struggled to repack their belongings. "Isn't this infernal small trunk overstuffed, Susan? I've already broken my thumbnail trying to force the clasp shut."

"Well, physician, heal thine own thumb and give me five minutes to rearrange things in the tray of the trunk so you can fasten it without injury. Then I think we'd better get out of this stateroom and take a walk on deck until time to meet Abby for dinner."

"Will she be waiting for us at the captain's table again?"

"I'm sure she will. The dear man has invited us almost every day we've been at sea. I'm actually getting a little embarrassed before the neglected passengers."

"Can we help it that we're such excellent company?" he asked, picking at his wounded thumb.

"I think he's drawn to Abby," Susan said, refolding three shirts to make more room in the trunk. "We've only missed being invited to dine at his table twice on the entire voyage. One only has to notice she's wearing black every day to know Abby's a widow. I'm sure she's told him by now anyway, since it's been she who's seated at his right at every meal."

"Poor old Eli's been gone almost six months. How long does she have to wear her widow's weeds?"

"I thought you knew that custom dictates she wear black for about a year. And 'widow's weeds' is a disgusting thing to call her mourning clothes, James!"

"I didn't make it up. And, if you've noticed, I never use the expression in Abby's presence. Move over, dear, and let me see if you haven't made ample room for me to close the trunk now."

The clasp snapped shut and he applauded himself in triumph. "Come, dear, it's time to get your caged lion out of this tiny cell and out on deck in the sunshine of this happy homecoming May day."

"I do believe you're eager to get back to Darien, James," she said as her husband assisted her out the door of their stateroom. "That's a compliment to your wife whether you meant it that way or not. It pleases me that you'd rather be in our home on the Ridge than anywhere else. But you did seem to enjoy seeing Cousin Oliver again. He's a rather famous man now, especially since his essays that ran in Mr. James Lowell's *Atlantic Monthly* have been published in a real book. In fact, *The Autocrat of the Breakfast-Table* has made the Holmes family somewhat famous." Taking his arm, she smiled up at him. "I'm quite proud, dear James. Mrs. Kemble says your cousin Oliver Wendell Holmes is considered a brilliant man of letters both here and in England."

"Oh, Mrs. Kemble, my esteemed monomaniacal abolitionist friend. Tell me, Susan, what you think of her now that you're both a little older."

"I liked her—oh, more than liked. I found her one of the most compelling women I've ever met. The truth is, I'd have given almost anything if there'd been time for me to get to know her better. I knew she was an excellent actress, but she's a—superb human being as well."

"Susan Holmes, are you a secret abolitionist living right under my own Darien, Georgia, roof?"

"Sh!"

"Don't shush me, woman. I'm happily convinced that, like Abby, you're an abolitionist in the abstract. It's a habit with you both because of where you were born. 'Tis a Bostonian disease."

"I don't give you a moment's trouble over it, do I?"

"You never have and I commend you. I also know you live as well as do I on the income from my excellent medical practice, almost every dollar of which we collect from my friends the planters in our area, because they care enough about the welfare of their slaves to see to their health needs."

"I know, James. I know. Your practice wouldn't be half so good without slavery."

Her voice did not sound accusatory. She was merely stating a fact. Dr. James knew it, so he slipped an affectionate arm about her and smiled as she fell in step with him willingly while he reminded her that life could not possibly be better for them. "Our Darien Negroes are happy folk and, in the main, good and God-fearing people. The skies, beloved Susan, can only be peaceful and blue and filled with sunshine above Darien, Georgia."

The deck circled, their cheeks glowing, he asked in an intimate whisper, "You'd tell me, wouldn't you, Susan, if one of those Northern abolitionists such as my friend Fanny Kemble tried to frighten you about the danger of a slave insurrection anywhere near Darien?"

"I have heard almost nothing about such a thing since John Brown and his followers shot all those proslavery men out in Kansas some three years ago. What on earth made you think of such a thing?"

"No reason, my little lovebird. Ah! There's Abby just coming down the stairs from her own stateroom." He waved delightedly. "Good day, Abigail, our fine friend. Too bad you didn't join us sooner so your appetite could have been whetted by a brisk walk about the steamer's front porches!"

In the seconds before Abby joined them, Susan asked, "Do you think Abby seems rather—worried, James? Upset?"

"Oh, you're imagining things, Susan. It's bound to be a

little lonely traveling by herself except for meals and an occasional talk with us. Maybe she's especially missing Eli today. You must admit the girl seldom mentions him. Strong lady. Strong, brave lady."

"I agree she's all that, but I could almost guarantee you that she isn't missing Eli today. Your instincts are keen, husband dear, but I do sense her true feelings a bit more quickly."

"Now what on earth would make you say a thing like that?" Then: "Ah, good day, Miss Abigail! We were hoping to see you before your admirer, the captain, monopolized your every minute at table."

"I promise that won't happen today," Abby said, looking and sounding preoccupied. "I need to talk to the two of you and I hope the good captain won't be insulted if we ask him to seat the three of us alone."

As Abby hoped, the captain was gracious and didn't question Dr. James when he suggested another seating arrangement for dinner. And when they were seated with Abby between them, her friend lost no time in asking Abby if something was wrong, commenting that she looked a bit worried.

"Not really worried, Dr. James. Curious."

"Curious, Abby?" Susan asked.

"Yes. I need to know how one goes about freeing a hundred slaves in Georgia."

Dr. Holmes was able to swallow just in time to keep from spraying the table with scalding tea.

"Dr. Bullie!" Susan gasped. "Do be *careful*."

Holmes composed himself in time to make what he hoped was a small joke with Abby. "Susan only calls me Dr. Bullie, Abby," he said, wiping his mouth on a napkin, "when I've been a truly bad boy. It's a kind of gentle reprimand, in case you're wondering."

"Your question about freeing slaves has obviously taken my husband by complete surprise, Abby. Do forgive him. Good manners are generally one of his cardinal virtues.

You did take him—both of us—by surprise, you know."

"And also told us clearly, if not in so many words, that the influence of that enchantress Fanny Kemble has seeped deeply into your otherwise healthy system. You've caught her disease, Abby, and since I'm your physician, I prescribe a good book with no hint of antislavery foolishness in it and an immediate lesson at Abbyfield under the absorbing instruction of your splendid overseer."

"You're still being a bit Dr. Bullie–like, dear," Susan warned him.

"Perhaps. But Abby asked a shocking question and, shocking or not, she deserves an answer."

"And what is that answer?" Abby asked, not entering into his attempt at humor. "I really need to know exactly how one goes about freeing a hundred or so slaves. I don't mean selling them, I mean freeing them."

"I'm only your physician, Abby. You have a fine lawyer in Fred Bentley. You'll have to ask him. But off the top of my head, I'd say that to free that many Negroes would be a far worse fate for them than bondage to the most un-feeling master!"

"I didn't ask your opinion about doing it, Doctor. I need you to tell me *how* to go about it."

"I'm sure Mr. Bentley will also try to talk you out of such an impractical, impossible idea. And I beg you to tell me if Fanny Kemble was the one to put such an outlandish idea in your head."

"I suppose she helped, but something truly spiritual which took place while I was with my mother caused me to begin to see how wrong I've been to be complacent. How wrong Eli was, despite his fine qualities."

"Something you haven't told us, Abby?" Susan asked.

"Yes. If you'd known how hard Mama and I worked to become friends before I left Boston, you'd know without anyone telling you that something very cleansing and—and redemptive happened during my visit."

"But what in the name of heaven does it have to do with your wrecking the fruits of all Thad Greene's hard work at Abbyfield?" the doctor wanted to know.

"Dr. Bullie," Susan said in her firm, but gentle way, "I don't think we're being very responsive to Abby."

"Bentley is really the one to advise her, Susan, but I know from talks I've had with Woodford Mabry that any slave who suddenly finds himself free and tries to live his life in or near Darien is in for a really hard time. You know Mabry's a strong Union man and evidently, since his poor wife does all her own work, an abolitionist too. He, of all people, wouldn't misrepresent the ugly picture."

"What ugly picture?" Abby asked.

"The difficult road a free person of color travels—probably anywhere in the South."

"Explain that to me, please."

"Abby, you're really serious about this, aren't you?" he asked.

"Yes."

"Well then, I'll tell you what little I actually know as fact."

"Please."

"There was a law passed early in this century calling for a tax on all free persons of color. I'm sure Bentley can give you the details, Abby."

"If I could put in a word or two," Susan said, "it seems to me that the decision finally must be Abby's. If something happened between her and her mother while we were all in Boston, I'm sure she knows why and how it relates to owning slaves."

"But what possible way could the two be related?" Holmes asked.

"I realize I've told you only enough to make you annoyed with me," Abby said, looking at Dr. Holmes. "But if you could have any idea how Mother's thinking has been influenced by her contacts with the abolitionists who believe that slavery is wrong because it would break the heart of a loving God, you'd at least see her position—perhaps not understand it or, like me, even be able to explain it fully. But one thing is sure. The conviction I have that I must try, at least, to free my people is real. I'll go out to Ab-byfield as soon as we're back. It just could be that the only person who can help me in all this is my overseer."

With a look of honest surprise, Susan asked, "Your over-seer?"

"Yes."

"But the man earns his own living on the backs of slaves," Dr. Holmes protested. "I suppose the next surprising thing you're going to tell us is that Thad Greene is also an abolitionist!"

With a slight smile, Abby answered, "The truth is, Dr. Holmes, I only know a little about his opinions of slavery. But I mean to find out as soon as I can."

Chapter 28

By late in the afternoon of their scheduled arrival date, a light spring rain was falling—not enough rain to prevent the steamer's passengers from crowding the railing, but enough to dampen everything but the spirits of those glad to be returning from the North. Abby stood with the Holmeses, peering at knots of people on the busy, noisy Savannah wharf as though she expected someone to be there waiting for her. There would be no one.

Actually, there had been no planned return date. Abby's heart had set the departure time from Boston and, wonder of wonders, Mama had not complained once or tried to persuade her to stay longer. Even now, as she stood at the railing beside Susan Holmes, who was trying hard to see someone she recognized on shore, Abby thought again about the time with her mother and how it had been almost too good to believe.

And for at least the hundredth time, she was sure, she felt inside her reticule for Thad's letter. It was still there. But she knew there would be no special face to find in the crowd bunched together around stacks of cotton bales, barrels of salt meat and molasses, and crate after crate of merchandise of all kinds which had been shipped to the Savannah shops along Bay Street.

The carefully navigated trip from the sea up the Savannah River to the city had seemed slow and long to Abby.

So long, in fact, she decided she was worse than a silly schoolgirl. *My heart's pounding as though I had let him know, even asked him to meet me in Savannah.*

When Dr. Holmes reminded her that they would have to spend the night at a Savannah hotel, she had shamed herself out of a moment's rebellion because staying over would keep her away from Darien—and Abbyfield—still longer. But it would give her a chance, at least, to try for a brief talk with Miss Eliza Mackay the next morning if Susan Holmes thought it proper for her just to stop by the old Mackay house on East Broughton Street.

"Unless Miss Eliza is ill," Susan said when asked her opinion, "I know of no possible reason you won't be made welcome in her home. She's getting old, but not in her spirit or her mind. If I know my husband, he'll want to take a walk through Savannah's lovely old squares. We can walk to East Broughton with you."

"Oh, that won't be necessary, Susan. I—"

"I don't mean we'll stay to visit. Just make sure she's receiving. I know what's weighing on your mind, and if anyone can help, Miss Eliza Mackay can."

"He loves so to talk, Abby, that I forbid him to go in with you," Susan said the next day as the two ladies and Dr. Holmes stood at the Mackay front walk.

"Did you hear that, Abigail?" the doctor asked. "She *forbids* me."

"I'm sure she heard it, James," Susan said soothingly, "but you know perfectly well that our time is limited and Abby needs to be alone with Mrs. Mackay. You like the dear old lady so well you'll use up all Abby's talking time if you go inside with her."

"Cruel," he muttered. "The lady just might have a pearl of wisdom for me too. Who knows?"

"Don't mutter. And no one could talk you out of a pearl of wisdom faster than Miss Eliza herself. She never thinks of herself like that. That's why people believe her. It's the main reason she *can* often help. We'll be thinking of you,

Abby, and don't forget we only have a little over an hour until we must be ready to leave for Darien."

The door to the Mackay home was opened to Abby by an elderly, white-haired servant, her face beaming one of the most cheerful smiles ever. "How'd do, ma'am. Come right on in the house. It look some like mo' rain a-comin'."

"My name is Abigail Allyn from Darien. I've visited here before and I wonder if it would be an imposition if I asked to see Mrs. Mackay just for a few moments."

"I tell you, come on in. She be waitin' fo' you."

"How could she know I'm here?"

"Eyes too dim to read much in the paper, but she kin see out her parlor window. She seen you in the street with yo' friends an' she help me remember dat you come years befo' to visit us. Miss Eliza, she be happy to see you! I declare I think she feel better this morning than for a long time."

"Oh, I'm glad," Abby said, standing in the front hall with the servant. "Has she been ill lately?"

"Jus ol' age," the woman whispered. "She don' lak us to call it that, but she be ten years older than me. This way, Miz Allyn. She be ever so glad to see you."

"Company, Miss Eliza," the servant called to her mistress, seated in her favorite little rocker by the parlor window.

"Abigail Allyn! How glad I am to see you, my dear. Please take that chair and, Hannah, you'll bring us coffee and some of those delicious buns you gave me for my breakfast, please?"

"Oh, yes'm."

"That's my dear old Hannah, Miss Abigail. She loves to tell everyone she's ten years younger than I. The main thing, I'm sure, is that Hannah and I have been together since my marriage to Mr. Mackay more than fifty years ago and she and I tease some, but we're truly devoted. Hannah and I have been through a lot together."

"Has she always been so cheerful? Is she always happy around the house?"

"If you mean does she try to fool me in order to get me to favor her in some way, no," Miss Eliza said. "Hannah and I often speak of such behavior by—by—"

"Slaves?" Abby frowned. "I'm sorry. Perhaps you don't like calling them that. I've noticed since I moved down here from Boston that many don't. Many whites, that is, disapprove of calling their slaves anything but 'their—people.' "

"I'm aware of that, Miss Abigail."

"You've already been so kind to me by letting me barge into your home like this, but could you call me Abby?"

"I'd like that."

"So would I. My time with you is limited. I'm traveling with Dr. James Holmes and Susan, his wife. We must be back at the Pulaski House in an hour if we're to catch the little steamer to Darien on time. Somehow I feel if you'll call me Abby, I'll be able to speak more freely—more to the point."

"And I think it would help if you knew right off that while I am a born Southerner, I do somewhat see us as other folk see us—other people from other parts of the country. I also understand how often even old friends like Hannah and I fool each other—almost from habit." They both laughed.

Abby leaned toward her. "Coastal people know each other so well, perhaps you've heard that my husband, Eli, was drowned in a bad storm late last year. He was a kind, generous, fine man and I respected him, but I've realized since his death that as much as I thought I loved him when we married and moved to Darien, I didn't really love him the way you once told me you loved Mr. Mackay."

A faint, sad smile crossed Miss Eliza's gentle face. "I expect few women love that much, Abby."

"Forgive me. I don't know why I brought that up. But Eli, in his will, left me a hundred slaves and a four-hundred-acre rice plantation on Cathead Creek at Darien."

She squared her shoulders. "Miss Eliza, I'm a Bostonian—or I was—and I guess I've never truly believed slavery was right in the eyes of God."

There was a brief silence, then Miss Eliza said softly, "And I agree with you. When I grew old enough to begin to give it some real thought, I knew first that I did not believe in our government creating more slave states to the west and then I began to see that wherever slavery was a practice, it was wrong. I've lived my life with slaves. My dear husband, although he didn't know I was aware of it, did at least some dealing in slaves. There wasn't a kinder man in the whole United States, but he was a merchant and—" She smiled. "And a businessman."

"I understand."

"Oh, I hope you do. Because you would have held my Robert in such high regard. Everyone did who knew him. But what's your pressing problem now, Abby? I probably have no answer for it whatever, but if you bothered to visit me when your time is so short, I want to listen anyway."

As directly and in as few words as possible, Abby told her everything she had discovered about her reasons for marrying Eli and for seeming to overcome her grief in a shorter time than others expected of her. She found the telling easier and easier because Miss Eliza did seem to understand almost at once that Abby had indeed come to see herself as she really was when she married Eli—in love not with the older man but with the imagined romance of life on a coastal Georgia rice plantation. She fully expected Miss Eliza to have more trouble understanding her new, almost consuming desire to free every slave at Abbyfield, but the still pretty lady just listened in the quiet room. A smile lighted her aging face every so often as Abby talked, and one frail finger tapped the arm of her little rocker. When Abby began to speak of her own mother, the rebellion toward her she'd felt through the years, the transparent cloak of self-righteousness she'd believed her mother had worn, Eliza Mackay spoke for the first time since Abby began.

"We mothers can be totally deceived by ourselves, my dear girl. Giving birth isn't easy, rearing a child isn't easy. The general sentiment, I suppose, in most of the world, that mothers are somehow saintly simply because they're mothers can be truly seductive. Many of us believe that about ourselves because we want to. It feels good and noble and it can smother our children—boys or girls."

Abby was so at ease she plunged ahead by telling Miss Eliza how surprisingly her mother had changed since she became an active member of the Boston Abolitionist Society. "I'm convinced," Abby said, "that being with those women—women of her own class—who believe that slavery is wrong because it goes against a God of love has somehow given God His first opportunity to work His wonders deep inside my mother's heart. She not only prays for emancipation of all slaves, contributes to the cost of publishing their antislavery books and literature, but she's missed attending only one abolitionist meeting and that was when she had a dreadful cold last year. She's also fallen, as do so many people, under the spell of the most eloquent abolitionist of them all—Mrs. Fanny Kemble."

"Oh, yes," Eliza Mackay said. "I remember when she and her husband, Mr. Pierce Butler, spent a few months down here on his St. Simons and Butler Island plantations. I wanted so much to have the chance to know her. It didn't work out."

Abby peered intently at her. "You don't resent Fanny Kemble?"

"Resent her? I admire her greatly. Yes, my dear, I know that sounds strange coming from a slave-owning Southern woman who loves her secessionist, proslavery city of Savannah. I confess, though, that I seldom even try to read our newspapers these days. I don't see well, but I don't even mind that as much as I once did. To have the flame of hatred fanned daily can only make matters worse. Almost every editorial these days reads like a call to arms. I firmly believe in and love the Union. Emancipation must come— somehow. One thing I do know and that is that by some means the spread of slavery to the west as our great country moves that way must be stopped. I have no answer for those of us who, by inheritance or by whatever means, are still slave owners down here, but even without the right to vote, we women can do perhaps the most effective thing to help stop it."

"And what is that?" Abby asked eagerly.

"We can pray, my dear. We can pray that God's 'will be done on earth as it is in heaven.' "

Abby glanced at Mrs. Mackay's old clock on the mantel. "I must bring our wonderful, wonderful talk to an end and how I hate having to do it, but could you give me some idea of what you did about your slaves?"

"When we sold our Savannah River plantation, The Grange, our people went with it. I still pray for them daily. God knows exactly where they are and what their needs are. I still own Hannah and her helper, Emphie. And by the way, I wonder what's happened to the refreshments Hannah was going to serve?"

"I—thought better of doin' it, Miss Eliza," the rich, warm voice said from just outside the parlor door. "I couldn't help but hear how deep you both was in what sounded like a better sermon than I eber hear preached. I got your coffee and buns right here on the big tray, but it seemed like Hannah need to stay quiet."

"You did exactly the right thing, Hannah," Abby volunteered. "And I do thank you. I'm sure your buns are delicious, but I did come to talk with Mrs. Mackay. I'm so glad she has someone as smart and sensitive as you to care for her." Abby got to her feet.

"Do you have to go so soon, Abby?" Miss Eliza asked. "This big house feels awfully empty, especially on days like today, when my son, William, is resting his poor heart in his room upstairs and when my daughters are visiting friends. I'd love to have you stay."

"May I come back sometime? You've helped me so much, but I—I didn't get quite all my story told. I'm sure my overseer would be glad to bring me up from Darien sometime."

The encouraging old voice urged her to return anytime, and Hannah, her loaded tray on the hall table, went with her to the door.

"I hope you kin come back soon. She get lonesome."

"I'm sure I will, Hannah, and I'm sorry about your splendid buns and coffee. Could I ask you one thing?"

"Yes'm."

"Do you resent it that Mrs. Mackay still owns you?"

A big grin spread on Hannah's full face. "Lordy, no, ma'am! I'm thankful she do. If she didn't, where in the worl' would Hannah go? Me an' her, we owns each other."

Abby had prayed for Rosa Moon every night she'd been gone, but now, as she turned to wave goodbye to Hannah before beginning the walk to the Pulaski House on Bull and Bryan streets to sign out of her room, she felt a real pang of missing her own housekeeper. Her own slave. Abby had no trouble believing Hannah when she expressed her desire to stay with Miss Eliza because they owned each other, but how did Rosa Moon really feel? Did she feel genuine caring for Abby, or quiet resignation simply because, being black, she was going to belong to someone and Abby might be better than most?

Evidently Hannah had no husband. How did—how would Obadiah figure in the relationship between Abby and Rosa Moon when the time came to free them both?

What, she wondered, almost as naturally as though she'd been wondering about it most of her life, would Thad think of her plan to free her slaves? To free all of them? She had fully intended to ask Eliza Mackay if she, Abby, were allowing herself to think too soon, too often, about the way Thad's hair curled on the back of his neck, about his young, jaunty way of sitting a horse. Given the chance to confide her feelings for Thad to the understanding woman, she had not done it. No reason came to mind as she walked toward the hotel except that it had just seemed so good, so safe, holding all thoughts of him to herself. Anyway, at least another six months, maybe longer, would have to pass before she could expect people not to talk.

I've been waiting for him for more than thirty-one years, she thought. I can wait a little longer.

Chapter 29

When Dr. Holmes and Susan took Abby to her own house the next afternoon just as the sun was slipping down the western sky, she turned to them, taking a hand of each in hers, and said, "Thank you, blessed friends. How can I ever thank you enough for—for—"

"For what, Abby? You just helped make our trip to the North a happy memory for us," Susan said. "We should thank you. And we do."

"Oh, indeed we do thank you, Abigail," Dr. Holmes echoed, lifting Abby's hand to kiss it in his most gallant manner.

"I wonder if anyone ever had friends like you?" Abby asked. "How does it happen that you understand me so well? That you accept me in my present peculiar state as you seem to do? I am still half a spoiled young woman, you know. I'm ashamed to admit I hadn't even thought how I'd get from the Darien dock to my house. My parents, then Eli, always took care of such things, but I think I'll learn, don't you?" Before either of the Holmeses could answer, she heard herself thanking their driver, Peter, who had been there at the dock waiting for them in the doctor's carriage. "How did you know exactly when we'd get to Darien, Peter?" she asked.

"Doc Bullie, here, he write me a letter," Peter said

proudly. "All the way from Boston it come to me right here in Darien, Gawgia!"

"Well, does this mean you're responsible for teaching Peter to read, dear Doctor?" With the quick, merry laugh she knew Holmes loved, she added, "I was just sure it was against Georgia law to teach a—a servant to read."

"So it is," Holmes said. "But to this day I've heard of no one getting thrown in jail for such a crime, have you, Susan?"

"No, I have not and it's just as well," Susan said, not laughing. "It's a stupid, unfair law and I'm glad you had sense enough to break it." She turned to Abby on the carriage seat beside her. "You—you actually seem happy to be home, Abby. Are you, my dear?"

"Yes! Oh, yes, I am, Susan, so stop frowning and looking puzzled. My time with Mother meant a lot to me, but I'm the mistress of this little house and I'm ever so glad to see it again."

"Sure you won't feel lonely going inside all by yourself?" Dr. Holmes wanted to know as he reached for Abby's hand to help her to the ground. "Shall I drop by Rosa Moon's cabin and tell her you're home?"

"No need, Doctor, but thanks anyway. Don't you see who's rushing across the yard? She's already seen us. Rosa Moon!" she called. "I feel a little silly telling you when you're looking right at me, but I'm back. I'm home, Rosa Moon!"

"Yes'm, Miss Abby, I seen you drive up. First I thought it was Miss Laura Mabry making a visit in her new buggy. I be powerful glad it's you, though. Sure is good to have you back where you b'long."

Abby had already rushed toward Rosa Moon to hug her when she remembered that the Holmeses might think her strange for doing it. Besides, Rosa Moon stepped back a little to make sure Abby didn't do anything rash. They could hug later after Abby had said goodbye to the Holmeses and she and Rosa Moon were alone catching up on their talk. There was so much to tell her servant—her friend—

and telling Rosa Moon how she felt herself changing, what she planned to do, was, to Abby, all-important.

In Abby's bedroom upstairs in her Darien house, which seemed even smaller after the time spent at her mother's elegant old three-storied Boston home on Mount Vernon Street, she all but ordered Rosa Moon to stop puttering around with the unpacking.

"I know we came back much sooner than I'd thought, Rosa Moon, but I feel as though I need to talk to you for a whole day without interruption. Is Obadiah due back anytime soon?"

"Lord, who knows 'bout dat man? He done took that po' African boy back to his sleepin' quarter at Abbyfield once he heard the rumor on his grapevine be false."

"What rumor?"

"Polydone's rumor. Ob'diah's twisted-up grapevine tol' him dey was another depity man from Savannah in our waters huntin' Africans. He brung him here for safekeepin'."

"Obadiah had the wrong information?"

"Yes'm." Rosa Moon's stomach shook with her good laugh. "Musta been hard on Polydone to let Ob'diah find out he made a mistake. I declare, sometime I think Ob'diah dream up his grapevine messages."

"Was there really another deputy here from Savannah or was the whole story on the grapevine wrong?"

"De whole thing was wrong. But dat slave ship *Wanderer* trouble still be brewin' up in S'vannah. Even though Miss Mabry she done got her a new buggy all paid for with cash money from the reward her husband, Mr. Woodford Mabry, got for tellin' the Fed'ral mens 'bout dat illegal slave ship."

"Woodford Mabry got a reward for that? I thought it was his job as port collector to report such things."

"Lotta Savannah mens think he had no business gettin' de money, but it looks like Mr. Mabry done somepin' extra good. Anyway, back in March, I reckon even before you done leave for Boston, the *Wanderer* be sold at auction in

S'vannah, Ob'diah say for four whole thousand dollars, and it was decreed somewhere by somebody dat Mr. Mabry he due ober three thousand ob dat amount."

Delighted, Abby said, "Well, good for Woodford and good for Laura Mabry! She certainly needed a new buggy. What happened to the men who were really guilty of being mixed up in the *Wanderer* deal? The du Bignons, Mr. Lamar—those men?"

Rosa Moon shrugged her thick shoulders. "Nothin' yet. Dey say it gonna take a while to git through the courts."

"Who told Obadiah all this?"

"Ain' askin' him nothin' when I knows his answer already."

"What is his answer?"

With another shrug, Rosa Moon said, "Grapevine. Dat be Ob'diah's answer to everything." Looking straight at Abby while she shook the wrinkles out of one of her dresses before hanging it in the clothes press, Rosa Moon said, "You don' need to worry none that Ob'diah talk to anybody 'bout Mausa Eli's part in that bad business. He let 'em cut his tongue outa he mouth before he tell on Mausa Eli. Dat man ob mine still cry for him sometimes at night."

"He does?"

"Ain' nobody in de worl' as fine as Mausa Eli an' Polydone. If either one done wrong, Ob'diah swear the law they broke was wrong. Not Mausa Eli, nor Polydone."

"My husband would be honored."

"Ob'diah, he honor Mausa Eli till he die hisself." She held up a black skirt with a big spot in the front. "You want I should try to get dat spot out befo' we hangs it up?"

"Please. I'm sorry about it. But my mother's servant spilled cold cucumber soup on it one night. Do you think you can wash it out?"

"*Cucumber soup?* Never heard tell of it!"

"There isn't any grease in it. It's cold soup made with sour cream. I suppose the sour cream had some butterfat in it."

"*Cold soup?*"

"It's delicious on a warm evening. I grew up loving cucumber soup."

"Kin you tell me how to make you some?"

"I don't know. But I'm sure my mother can get me the recipe. I'll ask her when I write. Things are a little different up North, Rosa Moon. But there's a lot about it you'd like. Servants get paid up there, so they're employed—not owned. Would you like that?"

The dark-skinned woman turned slowly to look straight at Abby again. "What the niggers do wif the money dey gets paid?"

"Why, they buy food and clothing and pay rent for wherever they live, I guess."

Rosa Moon did some thinking before she asked, "You mama's housekeeper an' cook she got to buy her own clothes and food an' pay rent on her cabin too?"

"She has a cook and a housekeeper. My mother's house—our family home—is three stories high."

"Lawd have mercy!"

"So, one woman, an Irish lady, cooks, and a young German girl is her housekeeper now. I hadn't met her before, but she's very capable. Then there's old Danny, who drives Mama around Boston and takes care of her little back garden."

"He grow dem cucumbers for dat soup?"

Abby laughed. "No. It's just a flower garden. You didn't answer my question, Rosa Moon. Would you like it if I—if I began paying you a certain amount of money each month?"

"So's I got to go out an' buy my own yard goods an' victuals an' pay you rent for my cabin?"

"Well, I hadn't thought that far, I guess."

"Right off, I'd say I feel mighty sorry for dem folks dat work fo' your mama."

"Sorry for them? But they're free!"

"Ain' no store got no free grub to sell an' no free dress goods. Look how much goods I'd have to buy to make a dress to slide down ober my hips, Miss Abby!"

"You are one of a kind, Rosa Moon. What strange things you keep thinking of! Here I thought you'd be so happy with the idea that I'm thinking of freeing you and Obadiah and—and all the people out at Abbyfield!"

"Ob'diah, he hab to scour up nuff money to buy oil for our lamps too! Dat po' man even gotta buy lamps, I reckon!"

"Do not, do not jump to any conclusions now, please. And as a special favor to me, is it asking too much if I hope you can feel clear with your own self to wait until you and I have had a chance to talk a lot more before you tell Obadiah?"

"Miss Abby, I lay right down an' die 'fore I lie to Ob'diah, but I also got some sense 'bout de man. Effen I was to tell him you got a freein' bug in yo' bonnet, Poly-done down on Jekyll Island know all about it 'fore dark! Rosa Moon know when an' when not to talk. Count on that."

"I do count on it," Abby said, and gave her an affectionate pat on the shoulder. "You said you thought at first when I drove up with the Holmeses that it might be Laura Mabry. Did she tell you she had heard on *her* 'grapevine' that I was coming home today?"

"No'm. It jus' that she done come by the house here purty near ebery day the whole time you was gone. She be a nice lady. Has trouble bein' still at times, but she don' spread no bad things. An' she do think a lot of you, Miss Abby."

"Tell me one more thing and I'll let you finish the unpacking. Do you think I dare tell Laura Mabry what I have in mind about freeing all my—people?"

"Who-ee! Dat free stuff do make my head swim! It like a chile feel when she's tryin' to git up nerve to jump in the creek for the first time. That water look awful good, but oh, it scare me somepin' terrible!"

"I can tell it—scares you. But don't worry. I've just decided to tell no one but you right now. I do have one more truly important thing to ask you."

"Yes'm."

"Has—has Mr. Thad Greene been here while I've been gone?"

A deep smile seemed to begin at Rosa Moon's feet and move up and up until it engulfed her whole ample body with what Abby could only think looked like—joy.

"You gonna b'lieve what I tell you now?"

"Believe you? Why, you know I believe you."

"That man, he miss only one evenin' ridin' his horse in from Cathead Creek straight to dis house!"

"*What?*"

"You heard me. An' he eben splain why he didn't come dat one evening. Said he had a floodgate break dat need his lookin' after."

"But—but the other nights when he did come, what did he do after he got here? Did he come to talk to Obadiah about Abbyfield?"

"No'm. Look like he jus' come to—sit a spell wif you, Miss Abby."

"*With me?*"

"He one fine young fella. Me an' him we got to be friends. He splain that the first time he talk to you was in your buggy Mausa Eli got to s'prise you jus' before he—he pass. You kin say I'm foolin' you, but all but dat one night, Mr. Thad he ride up to yo' stable, git off his horse, an' climb up into the seat of your buggy. It weren't hitched to no horse. Not hitched at all. And he just laugh at hisself when he tol' me finally dat he come in to—to spend some valuable time wif—Miss Abby. Don' try to tell me you didn't know de man miss you eber minute you was gone!"

For an instant, Abby stood there, then all but collapsed smiling into a rocking chair. "Rosa Moon, Rosa Moon," she breathed. "Thank you! Oh, thank you! Soon I'll be thirty-two years old. But tell me what I ever did all those years without you?"

Rosa Moon looked so startled and shy, she might have been a roly-poly little girl twisting on the ball of one foot. "You joshin' me, Miss Abby."

"I am not."

In one quick motion, from the trunk she was unpacking, Rosa Moon jerked an almost cheerful-looking print dress—navy background but with tiny pink rosebuds and green leaves. "What dis? Wouldja just look at them pretty pink flowers? Miss Abby! You gonna wear this little spot ob color out in Darien where ever'body kin see you?"

"Do you suppose I dare? What do you think people would say?"

"That ain' for Rosa Moon to know. But I sure do think you oughta let me iron out some ob dem wrinkles so's you kin wear it tonight!"

"Now you're joshing me. You know I'll be having some supper all by myself later on."

"I don't know any such thing. It won't be good an' dark for more'n a hour. The days is gettin' a little longer all de time. He ain' miss but dat one day when de floodgate broke, an' Mr. Thad he deserve to see you in somepin' besides plain ol' black."

"Do you mean you think he'll be here—*this evening?*"

"Yes'm."

Out of her chair, Abby stooped to inspect herself in the looking glass over her dressing table. Almost frantically she pinched her cheeks, bit her lips, smoothed her eyebrows, and fluffed her hair. "But I'm not even freshened up. Why did you wait so long to warn me? What makes you think he'll ride in yet today? It really looks like rain outside."

Her smile almost impish, Rosa Moon hurried toward the door, the new print dress over her arm. "You don' need to pinch yo' cheeks. They already pink as dese roses," she said. "He be here. I done promise him my sugar cookies today. He like to take 'em back to Abbyfield to munch on of a evenin'. Mr. Thad he partial to my sugar cookies. I already leave a bucketful for him on the seat of yo' buggy."

"Do what you can with those packing wrinkles, please, while I try to freshen up a little. Oh, Rosa Moon, do you really think he'll be here anytime now? Scold me! Tell me to calm down and act like a—grown lady."

Abby could hear Rosa Moon's low, happy chuckle as plain as anything as she did her level best to hurry down the steep cottage stair toward her kitchen to heat her iron. "That woman's a smart minx," Abby muttered, brushing her hair as though she were putting out a fire. "Somehow I've got to be calm, contained. Aloof. I hope You know that, God. I'll need all the help there is!"

Rosa Moon was just hooking Abby into the rosebud dress when they both heard a horse gallop up and stop outside.

"There he is," Rosa Moon whispered.

"Oh, dear, I don't think I've ever been as nervous as I am right now, Rosa Moon! And I don't know why. I simply need to talk with my—overseer. He probably has so much to explain about Abbyfield and—things like that. I'm sure the rice must be nearly planted by now. I think Mr. Thad said planting went on intermittently through May. And I suppose the workers not occupied with the actual planting have been doing other field work."

"Yes'm."

"What do you mean, 'Yes'm'?"

"What I eber mean? Take a deep bref so's you kin simmer down an' I kin git this top hook fasten."

"Oh, dear, do you suppose I gained weight while I was in Boston?"

"Hush, Miss Abby, an' draw in. There! Now, you does look mighty purty. It be so good to see you in a little touch ob color. You better git on out to the stable. Mr. Thad be there, I know. I hopes he like my cookies!"

"Do you really think I should just—go on out there with no real reason?"

"If I eber seen a woman wif a special reason, I sees her when I look at you, Miss Abby. Now, git!" Rosa Moon's deep chuckle sent Abby flying out the bedroom door and toward the stair. In her strong way, she was sending Abby straight to Thad.

*   *   *

Her slippered feet moved soundlessly along the pine-straw path that led from the house to the stable, where she fully expected her world to be turned upside down forever.

Her eyes fell first on the back of his head. The air was damp and his sandy hair was curlier than she'd remembered in her most vivid, most disturbing thoughts of him while she was in Boston, on the steamer coming South, and especially on the tiny steamboat from Savannah to Darien. With all her heart she wanted to stand there and stand there—looking, looking—trying to believe that she could actually speak to him again, hear his lighthearted voice speak to her. She had waited so long. Soundlessly, she said, "I have waited so long, Thad. So long. . . ."

Abby could tell that something on the buggy seat had his attention and then she heard him laugh.

"Good, trustworthy Rosa Moon," he said aloud. "She didn't forget. Here's my bucket of sugar cookies. How could one man be so lucky? One day—some day—Abby will come back to me, but in the meantime I have a whole bucket of Rosa Moon's sugar cookies!"

He laughed again, and although she stood motionless on the spot outside the open stable door from where she'd first glimpsed him, he turned as though she'd called his name.

For what seemed an endless span of time, they looked at each other. Then, in one graceful, unbroken leap, he was beside her on the pine-straw path.

Neither spoke.

After another seemingly endless moment, without taking even one more step toward her, he held out his open hand.

Abby felt a wild, young surge of joy so vibrant, so filled with energy and life, she could have sworn the earth shifted a little beneath them. Still, without a word, he waited, his hand out to her.

She reached for it and found it warm, protective, and strong and knew that for as long as she could find that hand when she reached for it, she would be at home with herself in her new upside-down world.

Chapter 30

Side by side on the buggy seat in the empty stable, Abby and Thad sat smiling and munching sugar cookies.

"We don't talk much, do we?" Thad asked.

"Do we need to?"

"No. But I could have told you that even before you came back to me."

"Are you always so smart?" she asked, determined to keep her voice calm.

"Almost all the time, ma'am," he said, popping half a cookie into her mouth so that she couldn't have commented if she'd tried.

"Didn't your mother teach you not to talk with your mouth full, Miss Abby? And aren't Rosa Moon's cookies delicious?"

She chewed as fast as she could, swallowed hard, then said, "Yes, yes, they are, but I think it's high time you told me about the planting. Is it finished or not? After all, that seed rice went into land I own."

"And no man ever had a more beautiful employer, which makes me feel so special, I just may be forced to give you another cookie."

"No! Do you want me to get fat?"

"I know I want you."

"Mr. Greene!"

"Didn't you receive the letter I sent to your mother's address in Boston?"

"Yes. I received it. And I'm sure you know that custom—one that's held by all persons of our class—forbids me to stop wearing black for at least a year in memory of my late husband, to say nothing of speaking of—of—"

"Romance with me? I promise you, Abby, that if you'll just do me the honor of acknowledging that letter and agree to marry me someday, I won't say another word about it. I swear to you, I won't."

"I—I do find you excellent company, Thad."

"I'm making a little progress. You called me Thad."

"I know I did!"

"Will you marry me someday? Not an hour before custom allows, but very soon after? And I'm only your overseer. How is it that you believe we're in the same class?"

"I don't even like that word."

"Class?"

"Yes. And, besides, you know that you're as educated and cultivated as anyone in coastal Georgia."

"Well, getting back to your question about the planting. By this time tomorrow, your seed rice will all be planted. Or almost all of it. Your hands all worked extremely well and fast during your absence. I suppose you've forgotten all you learned from our rice lessons."

"Try me."

"What comes next—after the planting is completed?"

"I want to know first if all our people are well. You were careful not to overtask the women carrying babies, weren't you?"

"You can see for yourself, ma'am, when you come out to Abbyfield first thing tomorrow. You are coming for another lesson, aren't you?"

"After I make short calls on Laura Mabry and Susan Holmes."

"But you've already spent so much time with Mrs. Holmes lately, I might be jealous if you don't come straight to Abbyfield after seeing only Mrs. Mabry."

She smiled. "I've never thought of you as being jealous."

"Are you stalling? You still haven't answered my question about planting. What comes next now that the planting is in its final stage?"

"I'll have to ask you a question before I can answer that. I know planting is done intermittently, but have you lowered the floodgates so the sprout flow has stood the proper time on the planted rows?"

"What is the proper time, ma'am?"

"Two to five days."

"I've heard professor friends of mine declare that extremely bright pupils are often harder to cope with than the slow ones."

"Am I bright?"

"Bright enough to give all the light I'll ever need. I do love you, Abby."

"Are you always so impetuous? How could you possibly be sure that you love me, Thad? We scarcely know each other."

"I feel as though I've known you all my life."

"Well, you haven't."

He waited a moment, then asked, "How did you know you loved Eli Allyn when he asked you to marry him?"

"I didn't know. Thad, can't we just be good, loyal friends for a time? I do so need someone to listen to me, to talk to me. Is it asking too much to hope you'll allow whatever is between us to—grow? You should know all living things need growing time."

"Abby, have you always had quick answers for everyone to every question?"

"I was just wondering the same thing about you," she said.

"Why did you frown when you admitted that?"

"I guess because thinking is hard work. What are we, Thad? Are we already best friends born out of due time? Did we somehow spring from the same beginnings? I don't think it's quite safe that I feel at home with you so quickly. That I feel so—comfortable when we talk. As though I'm not your—employer. I don't think we make very much sense, do you?"

"No. But do we have to make sense, Abby? Can't we just be as delirious with joy to be together again as we both want to be? Aren't you delirious with joy to be with me again?"

"I don't know!"

"Then be my pupil for the moment. How long did you say the sprout flow water is allowed to stand on the fields?"

"Two to five days, I think. Until the rice grains have pipped."

"Do you still think pipped is a funny word?"

"Yes and I remember that it means when the rice seeds begin to open so that the little sprouts show on each seed. And are they greenish white?"

"You knew that instinctively, didn't you?"

"Perhaps."

"Then you should know about us."

She gave him a look halfway between amazement and plain old irritation. "That's a silly thing to say!"

"It's anything but silly. You asked a while ago if we somehow sprang from the same beginnings. Isn't rice— rice? Wouldn't all seed rice send out the same or similar kind of pips? Abby, rather than being confused about us, I feel all things are clearing up so fast my head swims!"

"Don't leap ahead of me so fast!"

"You forget how much time I had alone to think while you were away. You must have stayed on a big-city social whirl. I was back here in this blessed silence—letting great truths dawn on me."

"You're making fun."

"Far from it, young lady."

"I'm only a year younger than you."

"Did you like being married to a man enough your senior so that you could take his word as gospel truth on just about everything? Do you wish I were older than you—a lot older?"

"In case you haven't noticed," she said, keeping her

voice very steady, "we *aren't* married, so what does my age or yours have to do with it?"

"May I offer you another of my cookies, ma'am?"

"No, thank you. But you have made me realize how rude I've been. I don't usually entertain callers in my stable. Would you like to come inside and have some coffee with your next cookie?"

"I'd like that more than I could possibly find words to tell you, Miss Abby, but I think I have a better idea. A far more workable idea. I have rather pushed you to know your mind before anyone in your position could possibly know it. A better idea, I'm sure, is for me to mount my horse and ride back to Abbyfield alone. You need time to allow your thoughts to catch up with mine. You need some blessed silence all your own. Tell me goodbye if you think my idea is a good one, but please add that you'll have Obadiah bring you to Abbyfield first thing tomorrow—after you call on Laura Mabry."

Abby laughed as she held out her hand to him. "Goodbye, Mr. Greene. I do need some time to think. I'll be at Abbyfield before noon tomorrow. I want very much to watch the sprout flow begin to drain away from those lovely fields."

Abby was up early the next morning, bathed, dressed, and having her breakfast of eggs, biscuits, and bacon—fried crisp and crunchy by Rosa Moon, who still didn't understand how her mistress could prefer all that good, bubbly bacon fat drained away or why she refused butter on her hot biscuit.

"You're still puzzled by my tastes, aren't you, Rosa Moon? After all this time, I'd think you'd be accustomed to my Yankee quirks."

"Makin' a samidge outa dat dried-up bacon in one ob my biscuits with no butter on it. Course, it's your bidness, Miss Abby."

"Yes, it is. And your biscuits are so light and fluffy, they don't need butter. Anyway, I don't want to put on any more weight. I must have gained at least five pounds in Boston."

"How you know dat?"

"I can just tell."

"Lord have mercy." Rosa Moon laughed. "Best to be so big you can't tell when a pound slips on or off. They's worse things. I'd hate to be skinny like Ob'diah. He hate me to be dat skinny too. Might could cut him to ribbons of a night!"

"You're feeling chipper and happy today, aren't you?"

"Yes'm. It be good to hab you home agin. Hm-*hm*. After all dem years ob seein' you grump an' look lost an' lonesome round de house, Rosa Moon like yo' smile more'n eber."

"Well, thank you! I guess—I guess I'm awfully happy to be back home too."

Refilling Abby's cup, the beaming woman said, "An' ain' *he* one happy gent'man havin' you back? You knows I was mighty respeckful ob Mausa Eli—and I reckon eberybody in Darien know how much Ob'diah thought ob dat man, but—" Leaning close to Abby as though they weren't alone in the room, she whispered, "Truf is, Rosa Moon be more partial to Mr. Thad den any man in McIntosh County. Could be in the whole state ob Gawgia! Course, Ob'diah come first."

"Speaking of Obadiah, where is he? Shouldn't he be out back by now hitching the buggy to take me to Abbyfield?"

"He likely still out in our cabin rubbin' oil in Mausa Eli's boot."

She might just as well have struck Abby. Her joy in this day was not related to poor Eli, so why did Rosa Moon keep bringing him up? "Are you trying to make me feel guilty, Rosa Moon?"

"Sweet Jesus, no, Miss Abby! Dat be de las' thing on my min'!"

"Well, I just wanted to be sure. I know I don't say much about him, but I do miss Eli. But I am still alive. And I have to find new reasons to—be glad I am."

"Yes'm."

"Now, don't look so crustled One minute you're—"

"I'm—what?"

"I don't know!"

"Well, Rosa Moon know." Abby could have smacked her own cheek for allowing the round-faced, grinning woman to tease her like this. "Rosa Moon see right through you to the other side, Miss Abby. Besides, you gotta find a way to see through yo' own self now dat you's changin' so fast. You like what you see too. Just wait."

"You are teasing me, aren't you?" Abby asked.

"No'm! I ain' teasin'. You done change some eber day, it seem to me, an'—Miss Abby, be this a good time to ax you is you still got it in yo' mind to—make me go free?"

"Rosa Moon! Are you worried about that?"

"Yes'm. It look like you an' me jus' gittin' to—to know one another an' you goes ahead an' starts talkin' 'bout sendin' me off."

"Come here where I can be sure you're looking right at me. If such a thing turns out to be possible, don't you think I'd hold up my end of our friendship too? Do you actually think I'd—just send you away? The whole idea just might be one of my dreams, you know. I now realize I have never believed slavery was God's way for His children to live. Owners or slaves. Going back to my home at the North brought all that back to me. My mother attending abolitionist meetings and being with other women who also hate slavery has somehow seemed to make a new woman of her. She and I get along better than ever in my entire life. You must believe that should such a thing be within the law down here—or even possible—and I don't know yet—nothing bad will come of it. Owning other human beings is hard on owners too. They don't know it or won't admit it most of the time, but it is. Freeing you so we could be friends just because you and I want to be together can't possibly be bad."

"No'm."

"Trust me to find a way that's good for you and Obadiah—and for me. Can you do that?"

"You gonna tell Mr. Thad 'bout this?"

"Yes, I'm sure I will. Maybe not today, but soon. Does that make you feel better?"

"Yes'm. It do. It make me feel some better."

Part Three

June 1859—January 1860

Chapter 31

The hot, steamy final weeks of May, then June, followed each other in the typical parade of bright sunshine, darkened almost every afternoon by thunder clouds, lightning, and brief hard rainstorms. Day after day, Abby was driven out to Abbyfield in her buggy—Eli's final gift to her—by faithful Obadiah, who watched over her almost to the point of suffocation.

"One of these mornings," Thad told Abby in June, "the sun isn't going to be shining when we all wake up and what then? Will Obadiah refuse to bring you here to Abbyfield in the rain for fear you'll melt?"

"Don't be irritated with Obadiah, Thad," she said. "That man is taking good care of me because he thinks he's pleasing the two people he's loved more than any on earth—Rosa Moon and my late husband." She smiled. "Why, each time a speck of anything gets on my buggy, he shines it so hard I fully expect to find the paint disappearing off it someday."

"Any ideas about how I might find a way to win some of his loyalty for myself? There are still times when he makes me feel almost like an intruder."

"Funny, but almost daily when he's driving me back to town he tells me how proud Eli would be of the fine fields this year."

"If he thinks the place looks good, he certainly keeps it

a secret from me. Just before we opened the floodgates for the tide to begin the stretch flow, I thought sure he'd compliment me on the good condition of almost every gate on the place."

"But he didn't?"

"He complimented Baldy, my driver, instead." Grinning, Thad added, "Maybe that's the same thing. Even though I had my thirty-third birthday last week, I probably still like to be bragged on. I'm sure Obadiah's intentions toward me are as pure as the driven snow."

"Do you ever miss snow down here on the coast, Thad?"

"Yes, I miss it. Why?"

"I have a 'why' for you. Why didn't you tell me you were having a birthday?"

"I figured you'd find out soon enough. What do you think of those fine, sturdy seedling plants, my dear Abby? If Obadiah never pays me a compliment, I thrive on yours. Can't you think of something splendid to say about the new plants? We'll be lowering the gates to flood them again—their second irrigation—as the textbooks would say. We experienced rice planters call it the point flow or the stretch flow."

"Why?"

He shrugged. "Haven't the slightest idea. I just know it works. We let the water stand on the plants from two to five more days, drain it off again, and let the plants grow about two weeks."

"What do the people do while the plants are busy growing? For that matter, what do you do?"

"Always something, Little One. The people give the plants a light hoeing during that growing time."

"Did you call me Little One?"

"I expect so." He was standing beside her in an open field—close beside her—his arms aching to hold her despite the heat. Her face never looked hot and flushed, just roseate and full of light. "I think of you as Little One when I'm alone. I guess it just slipped out. You have to admit, though, I've kept my promise even though you didn't keep yours."

"What promise?"

"I said if you'd just tell me you'll marry me someday, I will never mention it again. I haven't, but you haven't told me you'd marry me. Is that fair?"

"Oh, Thad, I don't know what's fair!"

He took only one step toward her. "It is hard to tell about us, isn't it, Abby?"

"And it's also hard to tell what you really mean about asking me to marry you!"

"What?"

"We haven't really discussed it properly, you know."

"I know."

Playfully, but sincerely, she said, "You must already know I love you."

"Oh, Little One, thank you!" Without another word, he reached both hands toward the sky, then turned the most impressive handspring Abby had ever seen.

"Thad!" Laughter overcame her and together they stood on the sandy ground, Abby applauding and Thad bowing his appreciation.

"I had no idea you would be so impressed with my handspring ability." Looking deep into her eyes, he said, "But never mind the handspring, tell me your intentions toward me. Will you promise to marry me, Abby? Just say yes or no."

As though her heart itself beat out the words, she whispered, "Yes, oh, yes! Someday—someday. Just help me while I wait. Do you have enough—strength for—both of us? Can you, will you help me get through the—waiting time?"

They had not touched. Not once, because in all directions across the rice field where they stood, they could see at least fifteen or twenty men and women at work. "I refuse to take the chance of putting you on their grapevine, Little One. But I'm really—holding you this minute. And I'll do everything I can to be strong for us both."

"The waiting time seems—endless," she whispered just as a flock of red-winged blackbirds soared overhead, calling their wild cheer into the sky.

It was thundering and the wind had risen, the feel of rain in it, when Obadiah drew the buggy up in front of Laura Mabry's house and helped Abby to the ground. The predictable afternoon storm was moving toward Darien as surely as Abby had been moved toward Thad. But as she stood waiting for Laura to answer the knock, her thoughts flashed like the lightning stabbing the summer sky—not to Thad himself, but to the people working in the field earlier today, some laughing at Thad's childish handspring, all in bondage and laboring because Abby Banes Allyn owned them as her property.

Except to Rosa Moon, Abby had not spoken a word about the fate of these enslaved human beings since her awkward discussion with the Holmeses on the return trip from the North, but her mood—even her dreams alone in her bed at night—invariably included the burden of them as though that burden was chained to a limb over her head—in danger of crushing the new spirit, the chance for happiness she had just found. Why? Why would they— how could they—possibly crush her new joy when, as far as she knew, each man, woman, and child showed nothing but loyalty and obedience to her every wish? To Thad's every order and instruction.

With all her being, she longed to be able to discuss this with her mother. For the first time in Abby's life, she was comfortable and without dread in their friendship but Mama was too far away. If she could speak freely to anyone in McIntosh County about her own dislike of slavery, it was Laura Mabry. Laura and her husband, Woodford, owned no people. Oddly, Abby felt as close to Dr. Holmes as to the Mabrys and he did own a few slaves, but he certainly looked on the evil practice with the same acceptance and economic pragmatism as did most other Georgians. She felt truly grateful that at least she knew enough about human values and God's kind of inclusive love to avoid resenting those who disagreed with her. The burden of being a slave owner was heavy enough. She needed to give and to receive all the love she could muster.

Where in the world could Laura be? Abby could see the Mabry buggy through the stable door.

She knocked again more loudly this time and heard Laura call, "Who is it?" from her backyard.

"It's Abby, Laura. Have I come at a bad time?"

"No," Laura said, rounding the house. "I was out back hanging Woodford's shirts on the line."

Growing up in a family with funds to hire servants for all their needs, Abby, now owning slaves, never failed to be surprised when she realized that Laura actually washed and ironed those shirts. True, she sent bed linens and tablecloths and towels down the road to a free person of color named Sallie Burke, but Woodford liked the way Laura ironed his shirts, so Laura ironed them, along with her own day dresses and other clothes.

Laura looked anything but bored or tired as, arm in arm, they went inside. Her face was radiant and, as always, she declared that doing a few shirts for her beloved Woodford was only pleasure. "And now that my wonderful husband has been given that reward for his splendid work in capturing the slave ship *Wanderer*, we can certainly afford to pay Sallie her weekly two dollars. Come in, Abby. I'm so glad to see you. I had a marvelous dream about you last night, and if you hadn't dropped by, I'd have come to you first thing this afternoon. Has something good happened for you? Don't try to pretend. Tell me. Let's sit in my parlor. I've kept the curtains drawn against that sizzling morning sun."

They took chairs, and immediately when Laura settled herself, she jumped up to bring them a glass of cold lemonade.

"How on earth did people stand it down here before we were able to get ice from the North, Abby?"

Laura was almost always full of talk, but never with a

single touch of malice, so Abby rather enjoyed listening to her leaps from topic to topic. "Now, Abby, what's happened? I know something splendid has happened in your life and I must be right or you wouldn't have had Obadiah bring you here straight from Abbyfield."

"How are you so sure I came straight from Abbyfield?"

"I know your habits just as you know mine. Now, start talking."

"I—I don't know quite how to begin."

"You see? I knew it! And I'm absolutely bursting at the seams with curiosity."

"Well, could I begin with a question?"

"If you think I can wait that long. You know how I go on once I start to answer a question. But what?"

"Do you think I could ever learn to—iron shirts and day dresses?"

"There's nothing to it, Abby! And you know I can teach you anything about ironing you don't already know."

"I don't know anything about it!"

"Oh, that's right. But wait a minute, just wait a minute. Who, might I ask, would need you to iron his shirts? Abby! Abigail Banes Allyn, my dream was right, wasn't it? I knew it. I knew it. Thad asked you to marry him, didn't he?"

"Now, you wait a minute, Laura. Who said anything about Thad?"

"My dream!"

"You dreamed Thad proposed to me?"

"Well, not exactly. I dreamed I saw you—more or less as though you were standing on a high rocky cliff with the wind blowing through your hair, the sun lighting your face and—oh, Abby, you were so beautiful in my dream that it had to be because Thad proposed to you and you accepted! It just couldn't have been anything else. Nothing else in all the wide world could make a woman happy enough to be as beautiful as you were in that dream—high on that craggy cliff—rather like the rocky shore in Maine as I remember it when we used to go as a family to the coast on holidays. You were radiant! Radiant, Abby, and your cheeks were as pink as roses in full bloom and—"

Abby gasped. "Hush, Laura! For heaven's sake, hush! I need to ask another question of you."

"What? What? *What?*" Laura demanded, her own excitement so high Abby had trouble not laughing.

"I can trust you as my friend, can't I? The way I always have? I know you even tease yourself for talking so much, but I'd stake my life on the fact if you told me you'd keep a secret you would keep it. Is that still true? And don't flare up because I asked. This secret could be dangerous."

"Dangerous? How could anything with so much beauty in it possibly be dangerous?"

"Forget your dream, Laura, please."

"Did Thad Greene propose to you or not?"

"That has nothing to do with the possible danger of what I mean to confide in you. And I'd really appreciate it if you'd let me tell you in the sequence I choose." Abby grinned. "I hope that didn't sound fussy. I didn't mean it that way. It's just a very difficult, almost frightening thing I have to tell you and I think you would really prefer *not* to make it harder for me."

Laura pretended to lock her lips, then throw away the key.

"Thank you. Yes, Laura, Thad has proposed to me. More than once, in fact. And again—this morning. We were both standing outside at Abbyfield—not alone. Any direction we looked, there were knots of my people working away. Some laughed when Thad turned a handspring— that's what he did when I said I loved him."

"I knew it! I knew it! Oh, Abigail, my beloved friend, put down your lemonade so I can give you a big, happy hug."

Abby hugged her in return, even clung to her. "I do love him, Laura, and now you have not only my reputation in town in your hands, but in a minute you'll have what I fear may turn out to be a far bigger scandal. If not really a scandal, at least trouble."

"I've been hoping, even praying when I remember to,

that you and Thad would be honest enough with each other to admit your love. But because it won't be a year until fall since Eli died, I *can* see trouble for you, but what else could possibly be wrong? What else could even come close to being a scandal?"

"Laura, ever since I spent those good days with Mother, I've known something that could very well ruin me down here in the South. It's as though the whole subject had been lying dormant in me for the years I was married to Eli—before I married him, in fact. I never really thought slave owners admirable people, but somewhere along the line a romantic notion that I could be happy in the novelists' concept of life on a Southern plantation took me over. I'm ashamed of that now, but being ashamed doesn't help. The only thing that can help is for me to free my slaves—all of them!"

Laura gasped. "Abby!"

"I know what a shock that is. I suppose his slaves are a large part of what dear Eli left me, but I can't face being a slave owner. I can't face it one more day without some idea of how to go about freeing myself along with them!"

"But, Abby, what do you want *me* to do?"

"I don't know. I only know you're the only friend I have in town who will really understand that I could never, never be persuaded to go on like this in what would amount to a foreign country! I can't even bring myself to discuss it with Thad yet. Oh, Laura, seeing things as they really are has brought all manner of problems tumbling down on me. I—I know you and Woodford would be Unionists if, as Thad says, worse comes to worst and there's real trouble between North and South. Laura, if it secedes, the South would be a—a foreign country, and I love the country I was born into! Most of all, I hate being a slave owner! Sometimes I feel more bound than they seem to be!"

Chapter 32

About the middle of the growing season, Thad had begun to study Abby's every expression more closely. Something had changed. He could not have put it into words, but the childlike pride and excitement she'd shown before her visit to Boston no longer seemed spontaneous. When she smiled and attempted to answer one of his tutorial questions about the name of the irrigation which should be done next, it was obvious that she was working hard to hide concern, even worry, over something else. But what? The crop was most promising and, as closely as any overseer could manage, the workers and the results of their labors were right on time. Abby still laughed when he bragged on his progress, but the sparkle didn't seem as childlike in her expressive eyes—the searching gray eyes that had haunted him since their first meeting.

Eyes that haunted but never tried to fool or mislead him. Something was heavy on her mind, but all she seemed to be trying to do was keep him from worrying. She had made no effort to explain. He simply knew her well enough by now to trust her honesty with him. Before the Boston trip, his diatribes about the nature and reason for each flooding of the fields had held her interest the way talk of fashion or a new recipe interested most women. Maybe the waiting time stretching ahead for them was proving intolerable. He certainly felt that way. Abby could not marry him until after at least a year of widowhood without causing talk in Darien. And Darien was where they lived.

At night, alone in his bed, he could bear the pain of needing her beside him if he could see that somehow he was helping her literally find her way from one life into another where *he* could be the one to care for her. He knew people sympathized with Abby over the loss of the fatherly Eli Allyn, but even the much praised Eli had thought Thad's skillful oversight worthy of his prized plantation. His education had equipped him for a career in business, but until he met Abby he had been almost peaceful—shunning the heavy responsibility of having his own business. He loved working outside and, with housing and food provided, he did well enough financially on an overseer's salary. The position, though looked down upon by most, had suited him fine until he'd found Abby—and especially since he now knew that she loved him with the same intensity he had for her. Still, as long as he could sense her recently troubled thoughts and because he was well practiced in keeping his own thoughts to himself, he would not burden her with questions about what she really thought of his job as overseer.

This eased Thad's own leap into what to him was an equally strange world of assuming full responsibility for her happiness. Laura Mabry had helped him begin to see why Abby's life could eventually be fuller with Thad in it than it had ever been before. Laura, who almost never stopped talking, had blessed him forever because she'd vowed to him while Abby was in Boston that: "Patience is your key, Thad. That poor girl sat in a chair for over five years knowing Eli would see to her every material need, but waiting all alone for someone to love who wasn't old, whose imagination had wings young and strong enough to take her on whatever flight he might think up! You're that man, Thad, and even you are going to be surprised by how good it all is once the wait is over."

How long had Laura known that Abby loved him?

No matter. Abby did love him and Laura Mabry could

be trusted to protect Abby, her friend, and to help him too. Remembering her words helped on a quiet morning as he stood waiting for Obadiah to bring her.

"I've never waited well at all," Thad said almost as soon as he'd helped Abby down from the buggy and Obadiah had driven off to handle some chores for Rosa Moon while he waited to take her home again for dinner in her own empty dining room in town.

"I don't wait well either," she said. "At best it's waiting with very little grace in it. Was I awfully late getting here today?"

"You always seem late to me."

"I met Dr. Holmes—Dr. Bullie, as Obadiah always calls him—on the road out here. He'd just made a call on old Miss Hoop. What a truly kind man Dr. Holmes is! How many busy doctors would take the time or have the patience to stop just because he worries about an elderly woman who's a little peculiar in the head? He vows he's afraid something dreadful could happen to her because that old servant who lives behind her crumbling mansion is more unbalanced than she is."

"Uncle Elmer? Uncle Elmer always struck me as being convinced he's on this earth just to look after his mistress. You know he'd mount that ancient horse of his and hunt until he found Dr. Holmes if he thought Miss Hoop was the least bit ill."

"Oh, my imagination runs way beyond that," Abby said. "I imagine that half the time Elmer pretends his mistress is sick and bothers Dr. Holmes just so they can have company. He never cleans her yard or dusts her house. I could write my name on that old dining-room table. It's a shame too. She owns one of the handsomest tables I've ever seen. At least it was the last time I was able to see around the piles of newspapers and old clothes piled on it."

"Did Dr. Bullie have any nuggets of wisdom not related to his good works on behalf of old Miss Hoop?"

"I don't think that was very nice of you."

"Did you think I was making fun of old Bullie? Not on

your life, Little One. I'm the good doctor's greatest admirer."

"Well, just don't ever belittle him—or his good deeds.
We may need him someday as much as half of Darien has
needed him in the years past."

"Are we skirting the edges of a small quarrel, Abby?"

She reached toward him, then drew back her hand. "No.
No, Thad. That's the last thing we need. I—I guess I'm
just jumpy. The slower the days drag by, the jumpier I get.
I'm sorry." She tried to smile but couldn't. "Dr. Holmes
thinks the whole country is waiting."

"For war?"

"Oh, he didn't use the horrible word exactly, but—
Thad, if it does happen to come true—if the South breaks
away from the Union, what will *we* do—two Northerners
stuck down here?"

Intending only to calm her, he laughed softly. "What
will we do? Why, we'll just run away."

"Run away? Right in the middle of the long flow? Or is
it the deep flow?" she asked, trying nobly to laugh with
him.

"Well, we experienced rice planters—I mean truly experienced rice planters such as the two of us—call it either
one. Long flow or deep flow. Which do you prefer, Little
One?"

"I like deep. Long is too much like—*waiting*. Please tell
me again what happens in the deep flow."

"Well, it's the last irrigation until the lay-by flow."

"Oh, I know what that means. At least, I think I can
guess."

"Guess."

"The lay-by flow means the harvest flow. The last one
just before harvest time. Thad?"

"What, Little One?"

"Harvest time—will come, won't it?"

"Yes. Late in August."

"Is harvest over in September?"

"That depends on how well our hands work. You're going to be impressed when you watch harvest," he said.

"I'm always impressed by everything you do."

"For once that isn't what I meant. I was talking about the laborers. It's a treat to watch them use those rice hooks, Abby."

"A treat? Why?"

"Because they're so skillful at it. Especially the women. Did you know women make far better harvesters of rice than men?"

"Why do you suppose that is?"

"Wait and see. Women just have a knack for it."

"I have a feeling that's all you're going to tell me."

"I can't let you ruin my lesson plan. That's one reason you've been such a bright pupil. You've allowed me to set our tempo. And not once have you reminded me that I'm merely your employee."

"You're not *merely* my anything! Thad, do you suppose people talk because I come out here every day? Do you think they really believe I never go inside your house? Are you as certain as I am that Obadiah doesn't gossip about us? He's such a talker!"

"Forget Obadiah. He's harmless and so devoted to the memory of your late husband, he'd never think of gossiping about you. He, of all people, probably knew exactly how much Eli Allyn loved you."

"Sometimes you say the strangest things."

"No man can go through what I'm enduring these days without acting a touch peculiar now and then."

Standing side by side under the bright sun in the middle of a treeless rice field was not exactly the place to speak of the pain their love was bringing to them both.

"Thad, this is one of the times I don't think I can do this!"

He stepped back and felt the pain in her begin to bond with the pain in him and felt tears sting his eyes. He stood there clenching and unclenching his fists. Then he forced a laugh. "I think we're both a little crazy, Abby, for always standing out here like this. What possible harm could it do for you to sit in what shade there is on my little front porch and share a glass of lemonade? I make excellent lemonade, ma'am."

She did not laugh, but stood looking at his young, boyishly handsome face, her fingers aching to touch his thick, sun-bleached eyebrows, the clump of damp curls at the back of his neck.

"Thad, I—cherish you."

"Oh, I cherish you too!"

"And I'm also terribly thirsty."

"The lemonade is already made. I made it fresh this morning—just in case. Come on."

"Can you promise me we won't take one step inside your house? I'm too weak to promise you that—but please?"

To help her over the rough ground toward the pine-straw path that led to his house, Thad took her hand.

"We're holding hands now," she breathed. "If we only knew where to go, we could run away this minute!"

He was almost running, clutching her hand for dear life. "Let's pretend we're—on our way," he said, his breathing hard and uneven. "There's nothing wrong with pretending, is there? Then we can pretend to be surprised when we—finally get there."

While Abby was out at Abbyfield for each of the several days of the deep flow, when water was allowed to stand on the fields before being drained away again, they were triumphant in their vow *not* to set foot together inside the overseer's house. Most days shared humor saved them from what would surely be risky conduct had they been out of the sight of every worker in the rice fields. Once a near-argument about the work assigned to the women saved them, kept them safely on the small porch sitting side by side in Thad's homemade swing.

"I think you make the women work too hard," she said out of the blue.

"Where did you get such an idea?" he demanded, his voice stern. "Women are slaves too, you know, and the work they're doing with those long sticks and rakes out there isn't quite as hard as hoeing. But the dead weeds and other trash that float to the surface of the water during this flooding time have to be gotten out in plenty of time for drainage. Otherwise, weeds go on sprouting. Why on earth should I give the women free time and order only men to do the hard work?"

"Because such unfeeling treatment is what caused Fanny Kemble and Mr. Butler to divorce! The women used to troop into her house on St. Simons Island with their complaints, all of which had to do with the way Pierce Butler insisted upon playing God in his slave women's lives by keeping them working whether they felt like it or not. Some even too soon after a new baby was born. I won't have my people treated that way!"

"You won't have a profit when the rice goes to market if I'm forced to begin to coddle them!"

"But it isn't fair. It's wrong, wrong, wrong. Even owning slaves is sinful in God's eyes and I won't have mine mistreated!"

"But you've got them, Little One. As long as you own those people and this land, they have to keep working."

"But do they have to have a driver walking on dry land beside the trenches threatening them with a long whip?"

"That's the custom. We're not free to embrace or kiss each other until a certain length of time has passed after your husband's death. That's another custom. The South is crammed to the brim with relentless customs—all the way from drivers with whips in their hands to widows in black clothing from head to foot."

"Widows wear black in the North too!"

As usual, Thad finally found the one way out of their tight places. He laughed. And behind the relative safety of the thick vine growing across the corner of the porch, Abby dared to do something she would never have dared do while standing beside him in an open field. Out of frustration, she hit him on his hard biceps.

Then she laughed too. "Thad, how could two adults ever

find themselves in such a ridiculous predicament? I want so much to be close to you, I even like hitting you on the arm with my fist!"

"If you didn't want me that much, I might run away by myself," he whispered, grinning even while he rubbed his arm where she had hit him. "Will you hit me again, Abby? Only with some warning so I can tighten my muscle first? You hurt!"

"I'm sorry," she whispered, touching his arm. And that was all he needed to break his vow to her. Too much time had passed, too many days and weeks and months without even touching each other beyond holding hands when they ran across a stubbly rice field.

Neither bothered to look beyond the porch railing for possible prying eyes. Both were too close to the edge of the high cliff of their passion. They had leaned too far when she touched his arm. Only a sudden loud explosion and one agonized cry kept his mouth from hers.

Abby jumped to her feet as quickly as Thad, but she was so weakened by desire that she fell against him and might have crumpled to the porch floor had he not shouted, "Abby, in the name of God, stand up! That was a gunshot!"

Chapter 33

Holding hands, their hearts pounding with fear and passion and dread, Abby and Thad ran down the front steps and across the yard toward where they felt sure the gunshot had gone off.

"Who could be shooting so close to the house?" Thad gasped. "Could someone right here hate enough to shoot a fellow human being, Abby?"

"Maybe it's not that, Thad. Maybe it was an accident. Or maybe a horse or a mule broke a leg and had to be shot. Do you think the blast came from that toolshed?"

"It sounded that way. Can't you run any faster, Abby? I'm not going to run ahead and leave you. I'm not going to do that!"

"I'll be all right. Please go."

Still he clung to her hand, pulling her along over clods and around piles of trash raked off the flooded fields. "I have a few bad-tempered hands, but none bad enough to kill. Abby, what are we going to do if someone is—dead?"

"We'll just—be together," she answered.

"Listen! I hear a buggy!" Thad said, his voice so full of alarm, Abby felt weaker than the kind of weakness a mere run could bring on.

"It's—my God in heaven, Abby, it's Obadiah flying toward town in your buggy!" Then he shouted, "Obadiah, come back here! Do you hear me, Obadiah?"

"He can't hear you! Thad! He's gone. Please calm down and don't try to stop me from going inside the toolshed with you, because it's our toolshed now and I'm going in too!"

They raced into the shed to find Thad's driver, Baldy, kneeling beside the prostrate form of a young slave, so covered with blood from his waist up, he was unrecognizable. But he was alive. Both arms reached toward his bleeding head, and Baldy slid closer in order to hear the weak, almost soundless guttural whisper: "I—steal Miss's—prop'ty. Tell her—so—sad . . ." The bloody head raised ever so slightly from the ground. "So sorry . . ."

"Sweet Jesus," Baldy breathed. "It be Oldun! Sweet Jesus, don' let po' Oldun—die on us! Not Oldun, Lord! Not—good Oldun." And as though he believed himself to be alone, Baldy broke into sobs.

Abby's instinct sent her to Baldy's aid. Without thinking what anyone might say, she knelt, lifted the driver's woolly head, and began to soothe him. "There, Baldy, no! Try to stop crying and tell us—what happened, please! Somehow it's going—to be all right. Somehow, Baldy, it's—all going to be all right. You'll see."

"I'll send for Dr. Holmes," Thad said, trying to sound in charge.

"Oh, no, sir." Baldy kept trying to talk between sobs. "Ob'diah, he done—gone—fo' de doctah. He done—drove off fo' Doctah Bullie! He kep' sayin' him an' Doctah Bullie was good frien's. Dat Doctah Bullie he come—quick."

"He'll come, Baldy," Abby said, "if he's in his office and not on a call somewhere. Dr. Bullie will—be here—if he can be." She made a choking sound. "But look, Thad! Look at those blank eyes. He's dead! Oldun's already dead. No pulse . . . no pulse!"

Between sobs, Baldy moaned, "Lawd, I pray it ain' too late for no doctah . . . I prays, Lord! I prays . . ." Suddenly, realizing that it was his mistress trying to soothe him, Baldy jumped to his feet, bowing, trembling, stifling his sobs. "Scuse me, ma'am. Oh, please do scuse ol' Baldy. He done let dis po' black boy break he heart so bad he didn't think fiot to let you put yo' clean white han's on my sweaty head!"

Thad, who had stood silently staring down at the sprawled, lifeless form, marveled at Abby's touching concern for Baldy and realized that he loved her with a new kind of respect and reverence.

"What happened to—cause this ugly tragedy, Baldy?" Thad demanded.

"Let him stop crying first, Thad. Please!"

Baldy wiped his eyes on his shirtsleeve and said in a shaky voice, "Oldun, he done—shoot hisself!"

Thad sounded near tears too. "What? How can you—know that, Baldy?"

"I done went for my shotgun to git me a rabbit or a squirrel an'—de gun be gone! Den I hear de shot . . . Lawd hab mercy, de boy be layin' dere—bleedin' when I git here! Tryin' to tell me why."

"I know he hadn't learned much English, Baldy," Abby said, "but could you understand anything he was trying to say to you when you found him?"

"Yes'm. I could make out he thinkin' 'bout you, Miss Abigail. He done try to say how sorry he be that the las' ob Mausa Eli's Africans be—gone when Oldun die. Said he knowed he—stole your property when he done—shoot hisself! He might not talk good English, but dat boy he hab a Christian heart! He want you—should forgive him for gittin' too lonesome . . ."

No longer making an effort to hide anything from Baldy, Abby buried her face in Thad's chest. "Thad, did you hear what I heard? He was asking my forgiveness because he—stole his own life—*my property*!"

"Yes, Abby, I heard. But we'll have to sort all this out. I beg you not to take any of it—personally. Above all, don't blame yourself even in the smallest way."

"I know you mean well, but I have every right—even though it's all dead wrong—I still have every legal right to get to the bottom of this and I want to know what kind of mistreatment caused Oldun to do a thing like this!"

"Oldun did nothing to cause you to use your whip, did he, Baldy?"

"Oh, no, sir! Dat boy work as hard as anybody in any fiel', anywhere. You know you done tol' me to use my whip only when I had to."

The unmistakable rattle of the buggy returning stopped their useless, helpless talk. Thad ran out to meet Dr. Holmes, even though everyone knew it was too late for a doctor to do anything but try to calm them down.

"Don't try to explain anything," Dr. Holmes said. "Obadiah's already told me, but I'll take a quick look for myself."

"Dr. Holmes," Abby said, her voice flat with grief and shock, "Oldun tried to—Oldun killed himself. He borrowed Baldy's gun and shot himself in the head." Tears, the first she'd shed, coursed down her cheeks. "He—the boy tried to ask *my forgiveness* just before he—died!"

Holmes, bending over the still, still body, stared up at her. "He asked your forgiveness, Abby?"

She nodded her head. "For—what he called—stealing *my property!*"

"He was your property, Abby," Holmes said softly.

"Dear God in heaven, do you think I don't know that?" She was almost shouting now. "I'll hate myself until I draw my own last breath because he was right—he *was* my property."

"You know my regard for Eli, Abby," Holmes said, evidently missing her point entirely, "but Eli bought Oldun and his brother, Youngun. You shouldn't hate yourself for that or—"

"But I do hate myself for it. I hate myself for growing tired of my mother's domination of my life and allowing Eli to think I loved him enough to be happy at a place where one class of human beings dare claim to own the very lives of another, more helpless class of human beings. Why wouldn't I hate myself?"

"But you didn't buy Youngun and Oldun," Holmes said. "Eli bought them—with both eyes open to what he was doing. *You* didn't buy them. There's nothing I can do for this lad. He's in God's hands, so stop grieving, Baldy. If you believe in God, you already know that one day you'll see Oldun and Youngun again. We're all blameless in God's eyes for what happened—especially you, Baldy, who treated Oldun well."

His dark face twisted, stricken with grief and horror, Baldy said only, "Yes, sir."

Chapter 34

*I*t be almost like buryin' Mausa Eli," Obadiah said in a reverent voice as he drove his mistress home after the burial. "It purty near break my heart all ober agin, Miss Abby. Po' Mausa Eli, he neber got a chance to see what a good worker Oldun turn into. He neber eben got a chance to see Youngun or Oldun. Lord, dat gent'man neber got a chance fo' nothin'. He sho' didn't hab no chance in dat mean water."

She knew there was no need even to answer Obadiah, who would go right on talking whether she answered or not. The thought even crossed her mind that the faithful slave might interpret her silence in a way that would comfort him. Obadiah had all but worshiped Eli, and now and then, since he'd been gone, Abby thought she detected displeasure in Obadiah because she, Eli's widow, showed no more open signs of grief than she had.

Losing Eli had been, was still, rather like losing a fine, handsome-looking, extremely comfortable easy chair. One she'd been proud of owning—a place to find far more than mere physical comfort. Eli had given her security in all ways, but he had also given her nearly unrelieved boredom. She now realized that toward the end her boredom had been so complete, she was still learning how to enjoy laughing again. Certainly, until Thad, she had forgotten there was such a thing as excitement. The kind of spontaneous excitement which she'd always had to pretend with Eli in order to please him, or worse, to keep herself from feeling sorry for him.

"I hopes you got a appetite, Miss Abby," Obadiah was saying. "You know it upset Rosa Moon when you pick at what she cook."

A flood of relief swept over Abby. Until that moment, she hadn't thought what genuine comfort she would be getting from Rosa Moon when the two of them were alone in the dining room while Rosa Moon served Abby's dinner. She realized to an even greater degree than ever before that there was probably no one else anywhere in the world who understood her as did Rosa Moon. No one else on whom she could totally depend—not even Thad. Dr. Holmes filled his own wise and valued niche in her world, Laura Mabry and Susan Holmes theirs, but no one was Rosa Moon but Rosa Moon. She was never too busy to listen, and she knew how to go right on with her work while Abby talked to her.

True, Rosa Moon had seemed almost frightened when Abby had even mentioned freeing her and Obadiah, but some time had passed and she fully expected her servant to have thought it through. She fully expected Rosa Moon to see Abby's side of the matter by now. Oldun's suicide had left no doubt whatever in Abby's mind about freeing her slaves—all of them. And it was no one's decision to make now but her own.

The thought brought her abruptly upright on the tufted buggy seat. Thad! Wasn't it Thad's decision to make too? Hadn't she told him they would be married when the time was right? When the cruel, suffocating waiting time was over at last?

"You fidgetin' on dat nice padded seat, Miss Abby?" Obadiah asked.

"What, Obadiah?"

"You jump almos' straight up in that fine padded seat in dis good buggy Mausa Eli git fo' you. Somepin' wrong?"

"No! I'm just thinking, Obadiah. I guess I still can't accept the fact—the ugly fact that life on a plantation I own could be so hard that a strong young man would be forced to—to kill himself because he couldn't bear the strangeness even one more day!"

Obadiah said nothing. Silence from this talkative man puzzled her. Finally, she asked, "You know why he did it, don't you?"

"You done answer your own question, Miss Abby, when you called the po' boy young. He be so young he didn't git time to learn that unless a man's skin's pale as yours, he got to fin' a way to fit hisself to life, 'cause life sho' ain' gonna fit itself to no dark-skinned man."

Even though she had vowed to herself that she would say nothing yet about freeing her slaves to anyone except Rosa Moon and Laura, she blurted, "But that kind of life isn't fair! Skin is only—skin! What difference does its color make?"

The second long silence from Obadiah made her anxious.

Finally, he said, "De white preacher at yo' church he say God put a curse on niggers. Somepin' 'bout de curse ob ham." Obadiah saved her *and* the ghastly awkward moment by laughing. "Look to me like ham be too good to eat to put no curse on a man or a woman." He chuckled again. The humorous chuckle which had always made Abby laugh too. Not this time. "*Hm-hm,*" he went on. "Ain't nothin' in dis wide worl' as good to eat as Rosa Moon's biscuits an' ham! No, ma'am. I b'lieves all dat preacher say 'bout God lovin' us all the same, but I don't speck dey's many niggers b'lieves nothin' 'bout no curse ob ham!"

Rescuing Abby as always, Rosa Moon's voice came back to her, saying, "Dat man Ob'diah jus' got to feel important! I knows how to cut him down to size, but he do like to feel puffed up."

Abby searched about in her troubled mind for a way to follow Rosa Moon's suggestion. "I'd like to go on talking a long time, Obadiah, but I need to ask you something important. At least, it's very important to me. And I'd value your opinion. I should have asked Mr. Thad about it, but—but our morning was so tragic and sad and—anyway, I can ask you just as well."

"Oh, yes, ma'am, Miss Abby! You sho' kin ax me anything!"

"You know, I'm sure, that Mr. Thad and the people have just about finished raking off the dead weeds and other trash that floated to the top of the water during the deep flow."

"Oh, yes'm. Dat water's standin' right now. Got the rice plants all the way under it. Helps kill the bugs dat might git on de plants too, habin' dat water on 'em like dat."

"I think I remember Mr. Thad telling me that when he was teaching me about the deep flow. I'd like you to remind me about how long it takes to drain off the deep flow. I have a reason."

"Yes'm. It got to be drained off slow an' gradual. Not fast. An' it got to be drained off to a level with about six inches of water lef' on de fiel's. Dat water stand on the plants—oh, 'bout two to three weeks, then it be drain off all the way. Den de hard work begin."

"What do you mean by hard work? It all looks hard to me."

"Yes'm. But—" He grinned. "Dat be de curse ob de ham again, I reckon. What I'm sayin' is that during the several weeks or so dat the fiel's stays dry before harvest flow, de groun' git two hard hoein's. An' hab you eber tried to lif' one ob dem hoes, Miss Abby?"

"I—I did just once. They weigh a ton each."

"You makin' a joke, I reckon, but dey's heavy all right. No doubt about that. I tell you a secret. Ob'diah done use all his manhood through all de time he be married to Rosa Moon to see dat we is mainly house people. House slaves works hard, but field slaves . . . ain' nothin' worse than seein' a woman usin' one ob dem heavy hoes durin' dat double heavy hoein' time. It be right pitiful. Dey hands bleeds a lot an' dey backs hurt. Look like some ob 'em 'bout to have a hard time tryin' to stan' upright in de fiel's."

Obadiah reined the horse in front of Abby's house in town and helped her down the high buggy step.

"Thank you, Obadiah. I'm sure Rosa Moon will have your dinner ready in the kitchen. But—could I ask one more question?"

His shoulders very straight, Obadiah answered, "Ain' nuffin' I likes better den allus havin' the right answer, Miss Abby. Leastways, dat's what Rosa Moon claim. What your question?"

"This will stay between us, I promise, but I'd like to know your opinion of Mr. Thad Greene. Will you tell me?"

"Oh, yes, ma'am. He be a fine-lookin' gent'man, an' when he gits a li'l older, he might could purty near match Mausa Eli Edward Allyn."

Rosa Moon was waiting when Abby let herself in the front door, the big woman just standing there in the hall, hands on ample hips. "Look like dat man ob mine jus' can't find a place to stop talkin'!"

"Don't blame Obadiah," Abby said. "I was the one who kept our conversation going. I asked him a pointed question."

"Ain' nothin' he like better. An' you oughta *know* better, Miss Abby."

"I swear to you, this time he didn't say—quite enough. Could I ask you the same question?"

"Yes'm. But yo' dinner be ready to serve an' I don' want my ham an' biscuits to git cold. Dis be one ob de bes' hams we's had in a long time."

"Obadiah will be happy to find your ham and biscuits for his dinner, believe me," Abby said. "He gave me quite a sermon about the wonders of ham on the way into town from Abbyfield just now."

"What you question, ma'am?"

"It's about Mr. Thad. Does that surprise you?"

"Not quite sure when it was, but I wasn't just borned yesterday! Course I ain't surprised."

"I know you *like* Mr. Thad, but I need to know what

you think about him deep down and if you understand the way I feel about him."

Rosa Moon had one sly smile that usually endeared her to anyone who saw it. She flashed it on Abby now. "What you think? Me an' Mr. Thad, we frien's! An' no matter what Ob'diah say 'bout him, you take Rosa Moon's word for it. Mr. Thad not only the best-lookin' gent'man in McIntosh County, he be a good man. He be the kin' ob man dat strikes a woman in de *heart*."

With no warning, right while Rosa Moon stood talking to her, Abby began to cry.

A bit timidly at first, then tossing caution to the winds, Rosa Moon threw her big arms around her mistress. "Miss Abby, Sweet Jesus, Miss Abby, you got it bad for Mr. Thad Greene, ain't you?"

"Oh, I'm sure I have, but—I think I'm—crying mostly because of—because of what happened at Abbyfield this morning. Rosa Moon, Oldun, one of the two brothers Eli bought illegally off the slave ship, is dead!"

"He done ketch a 'Merican disease he didn't know how to cure?"

"No, no! He—shot himself in the head—with Baldy's shotgun!"

"Lawd, have mercy on he soul an' lay yo' comfortin' han' on my Miss Abby's heart. An' Lawd in heaben, don't let her blame herself for what dat boy done!"

"But, Rosa Moon, he must have been so—miserable! His life on *my* plantation must have—been so—horrible it drove him to—to—take his own life. How can I *not* blame myself? I—I know now that I've always hated the—evil system, but—Oldun smiled so often and seemed to be getting accustomed to—"

Smoothing Abby's back with her warm brown hand, Rosa Moon said, "Ain' nobody gits used to bein'—homesick. De boy jus' got *too*—homesick."

"But if he'd been left alone to stay in his own country, he wouldn't be—dead now!"

"I vow to myself a long time ago I wasn't gonna fall in

de trap ob hatin' white people—none of 'em. Dey's good white folks dat owns slabes. Mausa Eli, eben though he wasn't de man to fit into your heart, was a good man anyway. Ain't no use tryin' to make any of it sensible. It ain't. He the man dat paid his money to buy bof them nigger boys from de Congo. Leastways dey's bof outa their misery now. They bof be all right now. An' you be all right too, Miss Abby. You an' Mr. Thad find a way to—get through this waitin' time. Mark my word. It gonna be ober an' done wif someday."

Abby stepped back to look straight into Rosa Moon's compassionate face. "It will be, won't it? This—ghastly waiting will end, won't it? And it is all right if I confide in you some of—how hard it is for me to—wait?"

"Rosa Moon be sad if you keep still 'bout it wif her. It don' make no sense sometimes, but I—didn't marry up wif Ob'diah 'cause somebody else wanted me to besides him. I know I'm too smart to say this, but I love dat—blabbermouth man. An' you come someday to see dat Ob'diah wake up an' fin' out dat he jus' as partial to Mr. Thad as he was to Mausa Eli."

"I don't think he knows quite how to be with Thad. And I think it's because he knows that I—love Thad Greene in a way I never loved poor Eli. I tried to—love him, Rosa Moon! You watched me, didn't you? You saw me trying."

"I saw an' I knowed for a long time that you was fightin' a losin' battle. Don't forget, you married Mausa Eli by followin' yo' *head*. Like me wif dat talkative Ob'diah, you done come to love Mr. Thad by followin' yo' *heart*! Jus' keep followin' it, Miss Abby, an' one day you find dis hard time behind you, wif Mr. Thad and Rosa Moon standin' right beside you—watchin' you grow up to be a strong, fine lady."

"I hope you're right, but there's something that puzzles me. You and I are very nearly the same age. How is it that you're so much wiser than I am?"

"I reckon wisdom come from hoein' hard an' fast—hard

nuff so's your fingers bleeds. Jus' happened I got to hoein' a little ahead of you. All the hard things you can't figure out right now is part ob your hoein' time. But eben hoein' time stops. When it come to an end, you look aroun' one day an' see the strong, fine lady you done grow up to be."

"Thank you, Rosa Moon. You've given me—hope."

"You ain' growin' up to be nothin', though, unless you eats. An' I ain' 'bout to let my biscuits burn. Lemme hang up yo' hat. You go wash up. Rosa Moon serve yo' dinner."

Chapter 35

Through the early fall of 1859, Abby went every day to watch the work at Abbyfield, but her interest had changed so drastically it was hard for Thad to keep believing that she was there for the sake of learning how the fields progressed month to month from one flooding to another.

"Are you pleased with the way your crop is developing?" Thad asked about mid-September when Obadiah drove her to the plantation for her daily visit. "I think we'll almost double your profit from last year. I hope you're happy about that. I know Mr. Allyn would be."

She gave him a puzzled look, a tiny frown creasing her forehead. Why had he suddenly brought Eli into their talk? Deciding not to pursue it, she asked, "Aren't we almost at the end of the harvest flow—the lay-by flow? I'm so glad the deep flow is behind us. I couldn't have stood one more day of watching all that hard hoeing going on. I dreamed at night about poor bleeding hands."

"I hate that part too," Thad said with unexpected feeling.

"Do you really, Thad?"

"Yes. Does that surprise you?"

"No. I guess it doesn't. It's just that often you seem detached about—things. I know we've avoided talking about it much, but I have to know how you really feel about owning slaves. And it's only fair to tell you something I've decided to do because I have a strong feeling that deep down you hate slavery as much as I now know I do."

"You hate it more since your trip to Boston, don't you? I think they turned you into an outright abolitionist. That's a dangerous thing to be down here, Little One. Your mother's influence? Or Mrs. Fanny Kemble's?"

"Maybe I just began on my own to face how evil it really is. I can think for myself, you know. Thad, I've needed to have this talk with you ever since I came back, but I honestly think I was afraid to bring it up."

A big flock of bobolinks, ricebirds, the Negroes called them, swooped down into the field beside where they stood and Thad grabbed a broken tree branch from the ground and began to wave it at them. "A visitation from ricebirds can ruin a whole field in an hour or so," he said, flailing the air with the leafy branch.

"You're not scaring them at all," she said.

"Where in blazes are my bird minders?" he wanted to know.

"Your what?"

"I thought I told Baldy to keep a handful of bird minders near every field today. Bird minders are people too old for hard work and children just learning. I should have brought my new clapper along so I could scare them away myself."

"Do bobolinks really destroy the rice?"

"Yes, Abby. When they flock down on their way north in the spring, they eat the new sprouts and then they have another feast on their way back south about this time every year. Bird minding should be one kind of work you approve of. The young ones are excited when I begin to assign them as minders. Especially when they earn their first wooden clapper."

"I'm sure clappers are important," she said, "but I have something far more important to talk about while we're out here in the fields alone."

"But why should we be uncomfortable? Why not share my fine porch swing, Little One?"

Her voice when she answered was almost curt. "No! I mean, I—dare not do that, Thad. I want to tell you what

I've decided here, where you can't—touch me. Where I can think and find words for what I have to say."

"Abby! Is something wrong?"

"Some days when I wake up in the morning, it seems as though everything is wrong! Will you just listen to what I'm going to tell you and then help me find a way to make it right again?"

"Nothing's wrong between us, is it, Abby?"

"No. Unless you say it is after I've told you."

"Well, in the name of heaven, tell me! First, tell me you're still going to marry me. You are, aren't you?"

"Of course I am, if you still want me after I've told you that I've made up my mind to free *all my slaves*. I sometimes think I'm in far worse bondage than they are and I can't live with myself any longer as a slaveholder. Help me, please! Help me find a way to set them all free."

For a long, tense moment, he just stood there staring at her perplexed, troubled face. Try as she would, Abby could not even guess what he might be thinking. Maybe he wasn't even putting one sensible thought after the other. In one sentence, she had not only taken away his work, she had made them both liable for the ugliest kind of gossip, even retribution from the good folk of Darien, Georgia. Of McIntosh County for that matter.

"Thad! Please don't—look that way! I love you as much as you love me, but—even our marriage won't stand a chance with both of us torn up inside. And we will be as slave owners."

Still he said nothing.

"I know you're a strong man," she said, almost whispering. "But I didn't know you could be downright—cruel!"

"You should have agreed to share my fine porch swing," he said, and turned his back.

"I knew I'd—surprise you with my decision, but I certainly didn't think you'd turn your back on me."

"The porch swing, Abby?"

"No," she breathed. "Today I think we should be inside away from any chance of being overheard. I must really mean to free the slaves or I'd back right down this minute.

I can't, Thad. I can't back down. I—have to do it."

Without another word, he took her arm and led her across the now muddy field toward his house. Unable to bear such a long silence from him, she tried to get him to talk to her. "You know perfectly well why I've never even been inside your house before now."

"You've always been welcome, Abby."

"I know. But I've been scared. I'm still scared to be alone inside with you."

Still holding her arm, Thad kept walking.

"At least I'll get a chance to find out if you really trust me," he said, his emotions seemingly well under control, a fact that almost angered Abby. The sun, which had been bright when Obadiah first helped her down from the buggy half an hour ago, had slid behind an autumn cloud. Her gray dress looked almost black. She hated it.

Finally, they were climbing the three shallow steps that led up to his porch and Thad stood holding open the front door for her. Inside his neat tiny parlor, the shadows made it dark, but she could see well enough to notice, even in her near-panic at the way he was acting, that the room, while plainly and simply furnished with only one armchair, was neat as a pin and even bright sunshine would not have shown a fleck of dust. It had never occurred to her to wonder what kind of house Thad kept, how it was furnished, its neatness or lack of it.

"You can see," he said, "that I don't entertain. Sorry I have only one reasonably comfortable chair. The furnishings are as I found them when your husband first hired me. Please take the chair, Abby. I'll sit here on what I laughingly call my bed."

"Don't you have a bedroom?" she asked.

"There is one upstairs. But the ceiling slants, so I'm not comfortable standing up in it except right in the middle under the roof gable. I do fine down here on this cot. It's too hot upstairs in the summer anyway."

"Who keeps house for you? Everything is so neat and clean. One of the women, I suppose."

"No. I'm not accustomed to house servants. If it's clean, I take full credit."

"I don't like your being cold and polite to me. Especially since I so want you to kiss me!"

"I'm not fond of having been hit over the head with a two-by-four first thing in the morning either."

"Thad, before we have a real argument, just tell me one thing, please?"

He only looked at her, listening.

"I already know you hurt to kiss me too, but I have to have an answer: Do you approve of slavery? Do you really believe God approves of it? Do you think there is any circumstance when one human being owning every right to another human being is—civilized?"

"Civilized?"

"Yes. Men own animals, but can they really own human beings and keep their own characters unstained? Their own souls—safe in God's hands?"

He paced the length of the tiny room two or three times, then stopped before her and said, "I just wish you'd given me a little warning, because the truth is, Abby, I'm having a battle over this question myself. I don't own anyone, but I certainly contribute to ownership in my way, and when the owner, by a quirk of fate, is the beautiful, tender-hearted, strong woman I love, each new day comes rolling down on me faster and faster like a big boulder down a mountain. I'm scared. I thought I could make it come out right for myself at least. I now know I can't and I certainly can't be any good to you."

"Thad, try to make more sense, please! You certainly haven't acted a bit scared. You don't seem scared now. You just seem—"

"What, Abby?" He reached for her, and as she rushed into his arms, he held her gently and said over and over again, "What, Abby? What do I seem like to you, my dearest Abby? Weak? Confused? Lost? I can't be lost this close to you, can I? Abby, help me!"

She reached to touch the curls on the nape of his neck,

her fingers exploring, caressing. Her whole self needed this man who filled her with so much pain and joy. Still standing together in the middle of his tiny, neat parlor, they clung together like two children, both afraid, in a sense guileless, seeming to hope for the best.

"Don't feel scared or weak—or confused, Thad. I need you to be sure and strong. No! Forget I said that. Be exactly the way you are. And tell me if you're as—surprised as I am that in each other's arms for the first time, there seems to be only—gentleness in this room. I—love you with far more than—my body, Thad."

"You're too good to be true, Little One. How do you make it possible for me to—be exactly the way I feel? Do you know I've never been this way with anyone before? Have you? Abby, have you?"

"No, of course I haven't. Do you feel almost giddy and innocent? Almost as though we've both found a passionate playmate forever?"

"I feel so much I can't begin to think of words to tell you, Abby. I've dreamed of our passion but this reverence is a mystery, a joy so overwhelming . . ."

"Oh, Thad, is this enough to hold us when we face what might be—real trouble? Can this tenderness hold us both through the waiting time? I'm *going* to free my slaves, you know. And that could bring us dreadful trouble."

"Little One, can't we just—make this moment last a little while longer? We both need to think a long time—love a long time. We need to keep holding each other like this so neither of us can forget what we now know we really have."

A golden bright-dark hour or an eternity passed, Thad and Abby both too overwhelmed to be sure it had not been a deeply shared dream.

Thad was almost shocked to remember what they had been discussing before. "Dearest Abby. Yes! *Yes.* Whatever comes, we can face together now. You must have a good long talk with your lawyer before you make a single move toward anything so drastic as trying to free a hundred slaves in coastal Georgia! Can't you sometimes *feel* the hatred and fear in the very air itself? I've gotten so I don't like going into town these days. Do you and your women friends know the men are actually talking secession from the Union?"

"We're not dumb, Thad. And there has to be a way. If you don't feel free to try to help me, I'll find it myself. *If I can be sure of one thing.*"

He held her closer. "That I love you with all my heart?"

"And that you also need to be free of slavery. That you don't want me to have to live in the bondage of being a slave owner any more than you'd want to try it."

"Rest your dear heart, Little One, on that subject. I know I'm aiding and abetting the ugly system by the very work I enjoy doing, but my political disagreement with slavery has somehow also turned into what must be a personal hatred of it. One of these days, that personal hatred will cause me to do something that affects my work. And that will hurt you. So, let your heart rest. I'm with you, Abby. I'm sure there won't be an easy way out of it, but if there's a way at all, I'm right here—agreeing with you and loving you at least as much as I want to sleep beside you at night and wake up with you every morning for the remainder of my life."

She reached to pull his head down closer. "Is this really true? Are you real?"

"Yes, Abby. And I'd give anything in this world if I could promise you your new decision can be worked out."

"Forget that for a minute. I want a little time to realize that I've found someone who actually *talks to me*, who lets me look—inside. Whose hair curls on his neck the way yours does. Would you think I'm crazy if I said I'd like us to take at least a month or two before we start—rocking the boat? I need a little time to believe the way you've been with me this morning. But don't get any ideas that I might change my mind. *I do not want to be a slave owner any more than I want to live without you.*"

He laughed softly. "I believe you and there's nothing I'd like better than a little time for us just to be—us."

Chapter 36

The weeks passed into October and Abby did her best to keep her troubled thoughts off her growing guilt and distaste for her position in life as owner—mistress— of the dark-skinned folk who made up the work crew at Abbyfield. Most of the time, she found herself not including Rosa Moon or Obadiah in these thoughts because both were more like part of her personal life, her family. She knew she could pay them a modest salary and keep them with her. Still, each time she thought of them as family, she shuddered because she literally despised the condescending way most women sounded when they deigned to describe their house slaves as "part of our family."

Thad laughed at this, reminding her that what mattered was the welfare of all the people—Rosa Moon, Obadiah, everyone at Abbyfield—not the patronizing, class-conscious, carelessly chosen words some Darien women used to describe their slaves.

"Your people all know how fortunate they are to belong to you," he said over and over any time the subject came up between them. She came to expect, almost to dread it when he invariably added, "I thought we were just going to be *us* for a month or so before we made any decisions. Waiting a while to give things time to settle was your idea, Abby."

"I know it was, but I don't like being reminded of it.

Oh, Thad, forgive me. You don't deserve that tone of voice from me. But every day that goes by makes me wonder more than I wondered the day before why I don't make an appointment with Lawyer Bentley and find out legally exactly where I am in all this. I—I think I must be afraid our beautiful idyll might be ruined. Or worse yet, that it might come to an end."

"Abby, my dearest Abby, how could it come to an end? There isn't any end to the way I love you."

"How long do you suppose I have to wait until you and I can be married?" she asked. "Do you think a year and a half would be long enough for the Darien tongues to run down? I don't think I care, Thad. Part of me doesn't give a fig what people say. But they'll blame you, and I have your feelings to think about too."

"You've taken full care of my feelings this minute," he said, his expressive face beaming. "That you're impatient to marry me is—well, Little One, it's almost enough for me."

"But if I free my slaves, that means I'll have to sell Abbyfield and that will be robbing you of your livelihood—the work you seem to love."

"Abby, listen to me. It's you I love, more than my work. I've needed to grow up for a long time and the adult in me keeps saying this is the time—now. I'm educated for a totally different kind of work. Don't let me dodge the responsibility of it any longer. Would you like to live in Savannah, Georgia?"

"What?"

"I haven't told you much about any of this, but I've been mulling it over in my mind. I graduated from a fine university with a degree in business. Two or three years ago, while I was working as overseer for a Savannah River plantation owner, I got to know his factor and I may have fooled myself, but I felt he liked me and enjoyed our brief talks as much as I did. I've been thinking about seeing him the next time I could get away long enough to spend a night in Savannah. There just might be a place for me in his business. He's a wealthy gentleman who holds his own factoring business as well as a large interest in his family's shipping company in Philadelphia."

"Who is this wealthy Savannah gentleman?"

"His name's Mark Browning. His office is on Commerce Row, and he lives in a fine house on Reynolds Square."

"Mark Browning? I know who he is, Thad! He's been like a son to my wonderful friend Miss Eliza Mackay, since the first day he came to Savannah as a young man many years ago. Miss Eliza thinks the sun rises and sets on him, so he has to be a fine, honorable man. Do you really think you'd—like to work for him?"

He laughed. "The point is, would he like to have me?"

"But you've told me so often that one of the things you like best about being an overseer is that it's almost like working for yourself. You do the planning, handle the marketing, give the workers their instructions—"

"And you're wondering if I can take instructions from someone else, is that it?"

"You took them from Eli. If the two of you ever had any problems with that, he certainly never mentioned it to me. Of course, he seldom mentioned anything, so I suppose that means very little."

"You forget that for the first three years or so you and Mr. Allyn lived in Darien his crops all but failed. My predecessor as overseer must not have been as expert as he led your husband to think."

"Thad, is that the truth? Do you know Eli never mentioned the possibility of a crop failure to me?"

"I gather he wasn't exactly talkative, or didn't want to worry you. Fortunately he had inherited money, so he was able to cover his own losses. The man must have been altogether honorable. He left you no debts and lawyer Bentley has never even intimated to me that there's anything resembling a shortage of funds now. He authorizes everything I need at Abbyfield."

*   *   *

Abby said goodbye as usual to Thad that day when Obadiah drove up for her in the buggy. She intended to arouse no suspicions that she had decided to go visit Lawyer Fred Bentley's office in Darien without delay, and she succeeded. Their goodbye was as it always was with Obadiah present— warm, friendly, with Abby's final word that she would see Thad again in the morning. Today, though, it was suddenly imperative that she talk to Mr. Bentley about more than the legalities of freeing slaves. Obadiah chattered away during the drive toward Darien and, as she requested, took her without a question to Bentley's law office on the waterfront in the tiny, but active business section of the town.

"I won't be more than half an hour," she told Obadiah as he helped her from the buggy. "If I find he's in his office, I'll wave to you from his upstairs window."

"Yes'm. He have it wide open to catch some ob this good breeze today. Take yo' time, Miss Abby. I be down here waitin'."

Lawyer Fred Bentley was his usual gallant self as he led Abby through the small waiting room into his private office, where he seated her in an attractive red-and-white-striped Queen Anne chair.

"To what do I owe this unexpected and pleasant surprise visit, Miss Abigail?" he asked, taking his high-backed desk chair behind the wide polished desk.

"I need advice as usual, but I must tell you how pleased I am to find you here and really free to talk to me. I promise I won't keep you long. Obadiah is waiting for me."

"Are you comfortable in that chair, Miss Abby?"

"Perfectly comfortable. I'm curious about something, though. Are you always so solicitous of all your clients who come here?"

Bentley laughed. "Oh, no, I assure you I'm not. You see, all my clients aren't of the—shall we say—caliber—to bring out my charm as you inevitably do."

This tall, dark-haired, rather stately gentleman had a way about him that to Abby was pure Southern. He could charm the paper off the wall *if* he chose and was born with the gift of causing almost everyone to hope he wasn't as gallant with anyone else. "I don't mean to sound flippant, sir," she said with a smile, "but it's a good thing you're so convincing or you'd have your bevy of clients fighting among themselves."

"And why, dear lady, would you say a thing like that?"

"We all think, fleetingly at least, that each of us is your favorite client."

"Surely you aren't accusing me of insincerity!"

"Positively not," she said, her voice suddenly almost solemn. "You see, if my late husband believed someone to have a sterling character, to be truthful, then I believed it too. He thought highly of you, Mr. Bentley."

"Eli would be extremely proud of the way you seem to have adjusted to life without him."

"I hope he would. And it's true, I guess. I've adjusted quite well for a woman who seldom had to make a decision for herself and would have felt put upon if she'd been forced to. I have made a decision now, though. A firm, unshakable one and I pray you can help me carry it out."

"Do you want to talk about it now?"

"That's why I'm here. Not for advice about the decision, though. That's already settled."

"I understand."

"How could you? I haven't told you yet what it is." She laughed. "I'm so glad you *do* understand that I never feel as flippant as I sometimes sound. You see, I'm here for advice about something far from flippant. You and I have only talked around the edges of the subject since Eli's been gone, but I want to free all my slaves, Mr. Bentley, and I simply need your advice on how to go about doing it. Is it against Georgia state law to free one's slaves?"

For once, poised, urbane Fred Bentley's eyebrows shot up in total surprise. Then, as though to give the impression of a calm he obviously did not have, he leaned back in his chair to study her.

"Surely you know whether or not it's against the law," she said.

"Yes, oh, yes indeed, I know. I—I'm just wondering how to go about telling you."

"It seems a simple yes or no would do."

"It does seem that way, but in this case I'm afraid that won't be enough. As your lawyer, I need to explain a few things. Actually, I'll need to explain several things."

"You know best about that, except I don't want any explanations of why I shouldn't free my slaves. I have to! I no longer have a choice."

"Legally they're still your property, Miss Abby. Why don't you still have a choice?"

"Not if I obey God."

Careful not to show his surprise too plainly, Bentley said, "You came to me for spiritual advice?"

"No. For legal advice. How do I go about freeing them?"

"Perhaps I need to ask you a few questions first. Where would your people go after you set them free? Do you realize that if any of them are forced by circumstances to stay in Darien, there are taxes and fees to be paid? This would amount to many thousands of dollars for the one hundred people you own. Way back in 1818, there was an ordinance passed calling for all free persons of color—Negroes, mulattoes—to pay an annual tax if their previous living quarters had been in or near Darien. Men aged fifteen to fifty paid ten dollars, women five."

"But how would a Negro do that?"

"I don't know. But that isn't all. Anyone considered a newcomer to Darien, even if newly freed by his owner, must pay a special newcomer's fee of fifty dollars within ten days of arriving in town!"

"That sounds outrageous!" Abby gasped.

"Maybe so," Bentley continued, "but if either this newcomer's fee or the annual tax is not paid on time, the Negro is imprisoned and put on the block for sale to pay for the delinquent charges."

"It's ridiculous for free persons of color to be forced to

pay just for living near their old home. I need you to tell me if I can afford to pay the fee for each person I free until they all get on their feet financially."

"Your tender heart is concerned about how your people will fare even in freedom, isn't it?" he asked.

"Never mind about my tender heart. I need some practical, down-to-earth answers."

"I understand, but human nature, Miss Abby, tends to lump certain persons—white, colored, free, enslaved—into groups. Each group is thought to act exactly the same under the same or similar circumstances. Whites don't. Coloreds don't. They don't even think the same. Their needs and wants are different."

"I love to hear you philosophize, Mr. Bentley, but I am in a place in my life where I need practical help. I need you to give me step one, two, three—definite, workable steps—in order to free all my slaves."

"I understand."

"There you go again."

He gave her a quizzical look. "What am I doing, Miss Abby?"

"Using your obviously favorite word when you want to keep things on an even keel. When you want to avoid the danger of causing misunderstanding, you simply say, 'I understand.' I truly hope you do, but I need advice. So, will you please explain step one?"

"You won't like my explanation, but I'll try. Step one may just be your need to realize, to admit, that your hundred or so slaves are *not* all alike. As with any hundred persons, they differ. Some can take heavy responsibilities, others need to be told everything to do. Some yearn for freedom, others are so accustomed to having decisions made for them, so accustomed to being fed and clothed and housed, they'd be scared children with your gift of freedom."

"You're saying a lot more than it seems, aren't you?"

"I'm saying that if you get into the business of actually telling those people they have to go, that they have to find ways to feed, house, and clothe themselves for the remainder of their lives without your help, your funds, you'll find dozens of them not only unwilling to leave but unable to."

"Do you really ever take time to imagine what it must be like not to own yourself, sir?"

"Yes. I not only try to imagine what it must be like not to own my own rights, but I have seen here in coastal Georgia the downright panic among some slaves who have had to be sold or set free because their owners died or suffered financial losses. True, some owners who draw their wills so that certain slaves are freed when the owner dies specify that the freed slave be looked after, but those cases are few and far between. But a hundred people? You are asking an impossible thing, Miss Abby. I've never even heard of such a request. The only way you can sever relations between yourself and your human property would be to sell them outright to another planter."

Abby stared at him. "I thought you understood. I think I really thought you would at least *try* to understand. Can't I free them and give them funds to travel North to free states?"

"What would they do once they got to Massachusetts or Pennsylvania or New York? The cold, icy weather up there would, for one thing, make them miserable if not ill. Free states are more and more industrialized states. Your people are, in the main, field hands. How would they earn a living?"

Abby sat there in silence for what seemed to her a discourteously long time—the ugly truth gradually dawning on her—the cruel reality of it. Miss Eliza Mackay had told her during their visit together at her home in Savannah that there were more plantation owners than most people suspected who also hated the evil system, but who were caught like animals in traps by the impossibility of freeing themselves of the burden of slavery. As surely as their slaves were in bondage to them, Miss Eliza had declared, they were also in bondage to their slaves unless they were heartless enough to sell them to the highest bidder no matter how that person might treat them.

Finally, she said softly, "Thank you for giving me all this time. I—I'm sure you're right, but I'm equally sure that it's God's will for me to free myself and my people. It would give me some measure of relief, Mr. Bentley, if you'd just promise me you'll give it a lot of thought. I have come to love coastal Georgia—except for the hideous scar of slavery. I don't want to leave. Everything isn't peace and quiet in the North either. There are those up there so satisfied with the status quo that abolitionists like my mother and Mrs. Kemble are treated with unbelievable rudeness at times. I'm not afraid of that, but I'd prefer to remain down here as a citizen of the United States. Do you think that will be possible—ever again for me? For anyone? *This could all lead to war!*"

"Hideous trouble may be ahead, Miss Abby, but I cannot read the future. I do understand your feelings in all this, even though I find it more desirable to live and let live as I've done all my life. Slavery is the South's economic heartbeat. I admit I enjoy my good life too much to make enemies of my neighbors or cause myself more trouble than day-to-day living causes us all wherever we are. I will promise to give it more thought, but you're asking the impossible, my friend. Didn't you learn how to adjust your thinking by watching Eli through the years he was with us? Eli Edward Allyn was a Northerner in all ways when he first decided to adopt our gracious Southern life. Can't you just try to do that too?"

"I don't think so. No, I can't. Not any longer. It's a matter of conscience with me all the way."

"I understand."

He walked her to his office door.

Abby gave him her best smile. "I'm sure you mean with all your heart to—understand, sir, and I thank you for that, at least."

Chapter 37

On October 19, 1859, Obadiah brought Abby's copy of the *Savannah Morning News* as usual for Rosa Moon to give to her. A headline above a short editorial caught Abby's eye at once:

BLOODY ATTACK BY JOHN BROWN IN VIRGINIA

Few details are known at this time, but it is reported that the rabid abolitionist John Brown, known as "Old Brown of Osawatomie," has raised a band of followers and taken over the U.S. Arsenal at Harper's Ferry, Virginia. Their number is not now known, but joining Old Brown in his dastardly deed is a band of slaves expected to spill blood and cause widespread damage and trouble.

For the next two days, the *Morning News* contained a few more, often garbled details of the event, which, despite the distance to Virginia, had people throughout McIntosh County shuddering with fear of slave uprisings there. For a reason even she did not fully understand, Abby did not discuss Old Brown with anyone, not even Thad. For reasons of his own, Thad had not mentioned Brown to her either. Neither, she was sure, doubted that the other knew.

The almost daily information was simply too confusing to discuss, even with someone she trusted as she trusted Thad. They agreed in their hatred of slavery, but the very subject could, without extreme caution, change the course of their own future together. Both wanted her slaves freed. Neither had any idea of how to go about it.

Settled alone in her small parlor to read the *Savannah Morning News* on Friday, October 21, Abby found a more detailed account of what really had happened in the Virginia mountains under the erratic leadership of Old Brown. As she read, Abby found herself praying that few Negroes had dared answer John Brown's call to join him and his followers in any act that might spill blood. She hated fighting and killing as much as she hated human bondage.

The big black headline leaped at her off the page:

MORE DETAILS OF TERRIBLE INSURRECTION AT HARPER'S FERRY

Direct, further information has it that the murderous John Brown, known throughout the South as "Old Brown of Osawatomie," led a bloody attack at Harper's Ferry, Virginia, on Sunday, October 16. He is already infamous as the man who three years earlier, with his followers and some of his own sons, murdered five proslavery men in Kansas for no reason except that he, John Brown, is a demonic abolitionist with a killing passion to free slaves, who are the legal, personal property of their owners. Now he has organized his followers so that they were successful in capturing the U.S. Arsenal at Harper's Ferry, where his plan was reported to lead to multiple slave insurrections. The entire town of Harper's Ferry was captured and every inhabitant made Old Brown's prisoner.

However, the latest report informs that in spite of Brown's urgent call that went out to black slaves, not one has joined him.

It is widely known that Brown and his men are "blatant freedom shriekers," hate-filled abolitionists who are even called dangerous by some at the North who fear Brown's insane plans and violent actions. Brown's murderous conduct is almost surely known to be inspired by abolitionist leaders, among them the leaders of the Republican Party, in which Abraham Lincoln is prominently mentioned as a candidate for nomination as President of the United States. May the God of our fathers save this country from such a dire fate!

Abby did not finish reading the disturbing, lengthy piece. She could feel her blood pound, her own strong abolitionist feelings well up, then shrink back when she remembered that there were indeed many in the North who also considered John Brown a madman and that Brown claimed that his motives were inspired by God Himself. She began to shake all over almost as though she were suddenly ill. That anyone could think that an honorable man like Abraham Lincoln of Illinois was behind such bloody behavior as John Brown's was more than she could absorb. Lincoln, when mentioned at all, was maligned in the Savannah papers, of course, but her mother had sent clippings containing his enlightened, wise arguments made during the now well-known Lincoln–Douglas debates last year. Since then, Abby had felt drawn to Lincoln. Never so strongly as at this minute, though, and soon she knew she would have to share her deep convictions about him with Thad.

She felt suddenly almost untrue to Thad for having kept her feelings to herself so long.

Over the next few days, depending upon how much time she stayed at Abbyfield on each daily visit, she and Thad finally talked at length, not only about Old Brown but also about what might happen in the country should Lincoln be elected in November of 1860—next year.

"Your mother's right," Thad said one morning near the end of October, "when she declares that Lincoln says very little about slavery in practical terms. I wish he'd say more."

"But tell me again that you agree with me that he's our only hope of ever being free ourselves of this—guilt," Abby begged. "I feel just plain guilty every morning when I first wake up. I know I didn't buy the people I own, but I do own them now and I think I'm just beginning, for the first time in my life, to understand what people mean when they speak and write and sing about the greatness of our country. How much I'd hate seeing it torn apart."

They were standing beside the boat landing on the bank of one of the canals that marked off the rice fields into squares. No one loitered or worked within hearing distance. He smiled down at her. "Do you want to try to explain what you mean by what you just said, Little One?"

"I'm not sure I can explain. But it has to do with Old Brown on another of his violent rampages as much as it has to do with my growing hatred of slavery. When things are so wrong—one causing the other—someone should be on hand to find a way to help. If our government, our Constitution, is so great, there should be, there *must* be, help for us somewhere in Washington."

He grinned a little. "Who down here in the South would agree with that? Most Southerners want more power given to the states, not Washington. Not the Federal government. They always expect the worst from Washington. It's called believing in 'states' rights.' "

"Oh, Thad, I know what it's called! And I know I must sound silly and womanlike to you, but I think what I really mean is that I never gave enough thought before to how important it is that we all remain together—that we not be divided. That the South *not* secede. That we grow together as one, strong, powerful nation."

"You should write political speeches, my love."

"Don't tease. I'm serious. When a wagon is mired down on a muddy road, a team of horses can pull it out of the mud far easier than just one horse trying to do it alone."

"I meant what I said. You could write dandy political speeches. You should be writing them for Abraham Lincoln if we're blessed enough to have him run for President."

When Abby reached home that day, she found a letter from her mother on her parlor table and smiled at herself for feeling so glad to see it. For most of the years of her life, she had almost dreaded seeing the elegant wax seal and writing paper that was her mother's pride and joy. One of Mama's main interests in life had been training her only child in acceptable proprieties—dresses that showed genuine good taste, hours spent practicing her pianoforte for the ladylike perfection Abby knew she'd never achieve, nor really want. And an elegant script—along with a high quality of paper and a perfect wax seal—was of the utmost importance to Mama, who seemed never to have realized that something vital and tender was missing from her daughter's life.

A letter from home held only anticipation these days, hope that there had been no more ugly criticism of her mother for having become active in the Boston Abolitionist Society. Abby expected criticism should people outside of her close and trusted friends Laura Mabry and Susan Holmes find out about Abby's Northern sympathies. But it was worse somehow for Mama to be gossiped about in the North, where plantation owners, even the goodhearted, honorable men who did their best to be kind to their people, were called "lords of the lash."

From the moment Abby had read of John Brown's violence in Virginia, she had longed to know everything her mother thought about him. Had she joined the Northern intellectuals—Emerson, Thoreau, Hawthorne, William Henry Channing, and the others who, in Abby's opinion, had gone overboard in their praise of Brown? What were the ladies in her Abolitionist Society thinking? Saying? Did Mama still think so highly of Lincoln?

Abby broke the dark red sealing wax and began to read:

Boston, Massachusetts
20 October 1859

My dearest Abigail,

I will go straight to the urgent point of this letter since I am due at an Abolitionist Society meeting soon and must bathe and dress. Our papers carry stories that alarm me, not for the reasons they would alarm Southern "lords of the lash," but for your sake. I fear you will be gossiped about or worse once John Brown's activities at Harper's Ferry, Virginia, become known. Be very, very sure that you can trust those among your friends who know that you have been newly awakened to what you must have believed all your life. That you told me that you still mean to free your slaves is a great source of pride to me, but I hope you will move with extreme caution.

I will keep you aware of any new developments up here, but for now, it is common knowledge that, without doubt, our country is in great trouble, North and South, unless wonderful, wise Mr. Lincoln becomes President. John Brown claims that he himself is an instrument of God. Surely, Brown's cause is just, but his methods are barbaric, some say insane. Mr. Abraham Lincoln is our only real hope. He is no antislavery radical, heaven knows, but how right he is to quote the Bible when he declares that "a house divided against itself cannot stand." Keep your excellent resolve about freeing your slaves, but act with wise caution and move more slowly than your sensitive heart prompts, I beg you.

I send you my love,
Your mother, Emily Banes

When Abby finished reading the letter, she looked up to find Rosa Moon standing in the parlor doorway. "For heaven's sake, Rosa Moon, you startled me! I do wish you'd say something and not just stand there watching my every move."

"I hope you feel all right, Miss Abby," the big woman said. "You sure is jumpy these days. You not still got that freein' notion ticklin' the back ob your min', has you?"

"Yes, I have, but it has nothing to do with either you or Obadiah. I've already decided to free you both when—if ever—I can find a way to do it in this provincial town. But I will also pay you both a salary. Does that put your mind at ease?"

"What kind ob town you call this?"

"Provincial. It is. Charming, but stuffy and full of wagging tongues."

"It be full ob tongues, I know. Ob'diah's grapevine done tol' him dat white folks got wind ob what a gent'man named Brown done up in Virginia an' now we's all in danger! I'm scared, Miss Abby!"

"Why on earth should you be scared?"

"Don' need no reason. Just need to hab dark skin, Ob'diah say." Changing the subject abruptly, Rosa Moon said, "Yo' dinner be ready to serve, Miss Abby. I speck my sweet taters done bake too long already. You eat now, please, ma'am?"

"Rosa Moon, can you forgive me? Since I started reading those newspaper accounts about John Brown, I've been so worried that I've been cross with you. And now this letter from my mother has me even more concerned. I'm so sorry. When you just said 'please, ma'am,' you brought me to my senses."

Rosa Moon's pretty face broke into a big smile. "Dat be good?"

"It taught me a lesson, yes. You take such good care of me and I go around preaching about freeing people but using a cross tone of voice with the one person I know would *never* fail me."

"Dat be right, ma'am. Rosa Moon be your rock." She laughed so that her big stomach moved under her housedress. "Ain' no lady in Darien, Gawgia, got a bigger, more solid rock den you!"

With a warm smile, Abby said, "I know that, Rosa Moon. I do know that. But before we go to the dining room, I need to know something else."

"Yes'm."

"If Obadiah heard about John Brown's capture of Harper's Ferry, why didn't he tell me?"

"You knows why, Miss Abby."

"I don't know! Sometimes I'm—dumb about these things."

"Ob'diah didn't tell you 'cause he got dark skin too. He don' feel free. I tell you 'cause you an' me be frien's now. Ain' nothin' dat man wouldn't do for you, but bein' frien's is a li'l somepin' more. Now, you gonna eat yo' dinner or not?"

Chapter 38

As Obadiah was driving her to Abbyfield the next time, he was almost irritatingly less talkative. Everyone, including Abby, expected him to chatter incessantly about something, so silence from the tall, lean man was disturbing. She trusted Rosa Moon with all her heart and, until the odd silence from Obadiah, had never once wondered if Rosa Moon or Obadiah was really trustworthy.

"Obadiah," she said as the buggy neared the Abbyfield drive, "is anything wrong? I can't believe you're so quiet. Are you worried about something?"

"You knows of any reason why I needs to worry, Miss Abby?"

"Why, no! How would I know about your private thoughts? I respect your personal life fully. Rosa Moon's too. Why do you ask a strange question like that?"

Obadiah forced his familiar cackly laugh in an effort to make her think he was fine. That might fool her but not Rosa Moon, who once had told Abby, "Dat man's better than a open book to me. I couldn't read no open book, but I kin read Ob'diah ever' time."

"Ain't nothin' worryin' me, Miss Abby," Obadiah said as he reined the horse at the end of Thad's front path. "You don't know ob nothin' dat Ob'diah oughta be worried 'bout, does ya?"

"Nothing at all Just ask Rosa Moon. She knows me through and through."

He laughed again. "I don' need to ax her. Dat woman tell me eber'thing I needs to know, den some. An' she ain' tol' me nothin'. So I reckon eber'thing be fine wif us all." He looked around him. "I ain' seen hide nor hair ob Lonzo or Baldy. Don' see Mr. Thad neither. Wonder where dey is."

"Isn't that Lonzo running this way across the south field?"

"You's right as rain, Miss Abby." Then he yelled, "Lonzo!"

When Lonzo came running up, Abby asked, "Are you here alone, Lonzo? Where's Mr. Thad?"

"Oh, dat man, he get a headful ob new ideas by de minute. He done ride into Darien right after first light today to get him a roll ob balin' wire. He got de notion dat he kin use it some way to hold the stacks of sheaves just right once they be tied up an' piled on top ob each other to dry. He goin' to stop to see the mill gent'man too. We movin' right along wif dis fine crop, Miss Abby."

She couldn't help noticing the look on Lonzo's face. He had worked so hard to plant, grow, and harvest someone else's rice crop, a far more intricate job than the cultivation of cotton or any garden vegetable. Could it be pride she saw on Lonzo's regular, dark features?

"Mr. Thad, he say to tell you to go right on in de house, dat he ride back as fast as the wind."

Standing in his tiny, neat parlor, Abby pictured Thad galloping as fast as the wind, his hat tucked under the saddlebags, so that the breeze tousled his sand-colored curls. Her heart wanted to stop, to hold the moment, the picture, the one warm, safe, happy reality in her life these days. Thad himself.

Mama makes me happy now too, thank heaven, she thought, and wished she hadn't forgotten to bring her mother's letter to show Thad. Well, I can tell him that

Mama's on his side in one way, even though I haven't told her we're engaged. She also wants me not to do anything too fast, too rash. *Caution, Abby, caution.*

When she heard his horse galloping toward the house, she ran to the front porch, down the steps, along the pine-straw path, and had to restrain herself to keep from throwing both arms around him.

"Oh, Abby, Abby," he said, careful to stand at least a foot away from her after his graceful leap from his horse to the ground where she stood, her face flushed, she knew, her eyes kissing him, kissing him. "What a wonderful welcoming committee," he whispered, still standing near, too near, because a dozen or more field hands were stacking sheaves not a hundred yards away. "At least, the people are not within hearing distance. I love you, Abby. I love you."

"This is the first time in months you haven't been here waiting for me when Obadiah drove the buggy up to your house. I missed you. I love you too, Thad. I love you—so much. And there's a lot to talk about."

"I secured our crop delivery at the mill today. It's easy to be delayed by the rush to the rice mill once harvest is about over. Other plantations are letting their sheaves dry now too. But we'll be received first. I saw to that."

"Oh, see to me, Thad! Always see to me."

"I will, but there is one condition."

"What?"

"That we go straight into my parlor this minute. I might die if I can't hold you instantly."

Once inside his cottage, the kiss was slow, tender, full of both passion and gentleness. "Whatever we have to talk about," he breathed, "can wait for one more kiss. It has to wait, Abby . . . it has to wait!"

Finally, she heard her own voice begging that they go out to the porch swing. "It's—it's safer out there, Thad," she gasped. "Please! I can't stop kissing you in here, so please make me go outside where the people can see us if they happen to look this way."

He released her immediately, but in a gentle way that gave no hint of annoyance, only tenderness. Then with one arm still around her waist, he led her to the door and tactfully allowed her to pass through it onto the porch alone, just in case one or two of the people had slipped toward the house out of curiosity. After he seated her in the swing, he even went so far as to pull up the one wooden rocker on the porch and sit down in it himself.

"Are you better out here?" he asked. "I want you to know that letting you go wasn't easy for me."

"Dearest Thad, I know it wasn't. How could moving away from each other ever be easy for either of us? Don't worry about me. I'm all right, I guess." She tried to laugh. "I'm as all right as I can be. I'll be better after I've told you what I did without letting you know I was going to do it."

He didn't ask what she'd done. He just gave her an expectant look.

"I've been to talk to Mr. Bentley."

"About freeing your slaves, Abby?"

"Yes. As usual, he said he understood, but he didn't. At least he had no answer for me except to try his best to talk me out of even trying to do it."

She began to try to remember her conversation with Fred Bentley, to share with Thad every objection he raised, but the more she talked, the harder she tried to make her case for freeing the people, the more frightened she became. "You—you agree with him, don't you, Thad?"

"My dear Abby, I haven't said a word."

"I know. That's the trouble."

"I—I guess I've begun to think of all you'll face once we tried it, even if there was a workable way."

"What if I find out there's enough money left to send them North to freedom or to pay their fees in Darien should they remain in Georgia?"

"Enough money?"

"I—I guess I was so nervous when I spoke with Mr. Bentley, I don't believe I asked outright. But there would be if we sold the land itself, wouldn't there?"

"Why sell good fertile rice land without the hands to work it?"

"You're siding with Lawyer Bentley, aren't you?" she asked.

"No. I don't have a right to be on anyone's side except to keep you reminded that I love you with all my heart."

"Have you seen the latest edition of the *Savannah Morning News*?" she wanted to know.

"Not yet. Is Old Brown in more trouble up in Virginia?"

"I keep thinking of what they might do to him. He did a—fearful thing, didn't he? I wish I could talk to Mrs. Fanny Kemble right now. Just for a minute. She always knows exactly what she thinks and makes no bones about saying it. I'd love to know what she thinks about John Brown taking over a Federal arsenal and inviting Virginia slaves to kill their masters in their beds. I know she understands why he did it, but she hates violence. I know what they think of him down here, but I'd give almost anything to know what Mrs. Kemble has to say."

Thad thought a minute, then said, "People who are otherwise perfectly sane can go overboard even in a good cause. I guess the man's entire adult life has been driven by his desire to free slaves. Even if it means committing a crime against the Federal government or more outright murder as he did back in Kansas in 1856."

"Thad, are you saying you think John Brown's gone insane over the whole idea of setting men and women and children free?"

"He calls himself an instrument of God! That puzzles me, frankly. I always thought God brought a kind of balance to a person's life."

"I think God does do that. I guess there must be something wrong with Brown's mind. Maybe he drove himself too hard. Maybe he tried to do it all too fast."

She could feel Thad weighing his words. "Could there

be a lesson in all this for us Abby? Could we be trying to push things along too fast? Should we continue delaying serious talk about freeing your slaves until at least early next year? By the time the Christmas holidays are over, there may be more news of Lincoln's chances at the Republican nominating convention. That man could offer hope at least."

"And maybe enough time will have passed since Eli drowned," she said in a soft, soft voice—almost a whisper. "Laura Mabry says she's almost certain people won't criticize me too much if we get married sometime early next year. It's—it's early November now, Thad. We've already waited almost a year. We can wait a little longer, can't we? Can't we?"

"We already belong to each other, Abby, dearest."

"I know. I also know you don't need an impetuous, idealistic wife! Oh, is even God good enough to let me become *your* wife?"

Chapter 39

O ne afternoon just before Christmas, Rosa Moon answered a knock at Abby's front door and, within seconds, it was plain from her delighted greeting that their caller was Dr. James Holmes.

Abby, too, was pleased and relieved to hear Holmes's booming "Merry Christmas, one and all!"

"Merry Christmas to you, dear Dr. Bullie," Abby called from her parlor, where she'd been hard at work creating a holiday wreath for her front door. "Please come in if you can find your way around all the cedar mess on the floor."

"My dear Abby, I like your kind of mess! And I like the start you've made on that beautiful big wreath too. I was wondering, though, don't you need some color tucked in it here and there?"

"I most certainly do, but I don't have any red berries to cut anywhere in my yard. Not even any cassina berries. I really need some red, don't I?" she asked, studying the wreath.

"And you shall have it, my dear friend." He smiled his impish smile and called to Rosa Moon. "Bring it in now, please, Rosa Moon. The moment is just right."

In came Rosa Moon, her arms laden with wild holly branches, bright with berries and glossy green leaves. "Looky here, Miss Abby," she said as though she'd just cut the greenery herself. "Just looky here!"

"My youngest son, James Edward, cut these just for you," Holmes said. "I'm not only pleased he found trees loaded with berries, I'm pleased with myself for arriving at just the right moment!" He directed Rosa Moon to lay the offering down and began to fish around in his coat pocket. "Ah! Here it is. Another offering from my good wife, Susan! Enough red ribbon for a big bow to top it all off."

"What would I do without my friends?" Abby asked, beaming at her welcome caller. "You've come with the very spirit of Father Christmas himself. Thank you, thank you. Rosa Moon and I promise to have a glorious wreath on our door to greet you on your very next visit, don't we, Rosa Moon?"

"Oh, yes, ma'am! Ain' nobody eber come to dis house more deservin'."

"Can you stay long enough to have a cup of coffee and a piece of the best gingerbread Rosa Moon has ever made?"

"I can indeed," the affable doctor said, moving the fresh greenery with his foot and taking a chair near the one he knew Abby liked best. "I didn't bring the spirit of Father Christmas, Abby. The spirit is here of its own accord. My, my, what a difference from last year, eh? You've made a remarkable recovery from your tragic loss of Eli, my dear girl. I not only commend you, I'm downright proud of you. He'd been gone such a short time when last Christmas came round. Eli would be proud of you too."

"I hope he's proud."

"Why wouldn't he be?"

"I don't know. No special reason, I guess, but I just hope Eli would agree with what I've decided to do at Abbyfield."

"What are you going to do at Abbyfield, dear girl? I knew Eli so well, I'm sure I might have some idea about whether or not he'd approve."

"Could I ask you a question first?"

"Fire away."

"Do you think Abraham Lincoln of Illinois stands a chance to become President of the United States?"

"My good friend, Abigail, you take me by surprise."

"I know most people around here, except for the Mabrys, don't even like to hear his name mentioned, but you're different."

"How am I different?"

"You're one of the few people I know who can disagree in peace. You call Mrs. Fanny Kemble a monomaniac where the subject of slavery is concerned, but you never sound cross about it. You obviously like the lady very much."

"I not only like her, I find her amusing and quite charming. She has such a strong mind, she actually seems to think like a man."

Abby laughed. "And is that supposed to be a compliment to her?"

"Well, yes, I suppose it is. I meant it as a compliment."

"I'm sure you did."

"Good. But what in the name of heaven does Mrs. Kemble have to do with Abraham Lincoln, that rail-splitting populist from the far prairies? Except, of course, were she an American citizen, I'm sure, as radical as she is, she would probably think him a superb choice and be praying for his nomination at the Republican convention next May." He rubbed his forehead. "Aha! You're trying to trick me into something, aren't you?"

"I swear I'm not, Doctor. I am asking simply what you, my friend, Dr. Bullie, think of Lincoln."

"I have no opinion of the man one way or the other," he spluttered. "Well, not a very clear one anyway. Never thought him worthy of my careful study, always necessary for a true evaluation."

"Do you consider him an abolitionist or, as the saying goes, an ultimate extinctionist?"

He peered over his spectacles at Abby, an eyebrow cocked suspiciously. "I sense a tiny, very sharp arrow being slipped into your bow, my dear girl. Those intellectually penetrating questions sound almost exactly like something Mrs. Fanny Kemble would ask. How do *you* think of Mr.

Lincoln? As merely another abolitionist or as an ultimate extinctionist?"

"I—I admire his thought. With so little to read beyond the bias in the Savannah newspaper, how would I know what I believe him to be? Along with my own mother, I believe him to be exactly right when he quotes Jesus by saying 'a house divided against itself cannot stand.' "

He sighed. "Slavery again."

"Yes, slavery and my decision to free my slaves at Abbyfield!"

At that tense moment, they heard Rosa Moon coming along the hall toward the open parlor door. Her steps were always heavy, but seemed heavier when she pulled her usual balancing act by piling too much on an already heavy silver tray.

"Rosa Moon's bringing our gingerbread and coffee, Doctor. Thank you, Rosa Moon. Just put the tray on the table. I'll serve."

"Yes'm. It take me a long time to fix this, 'cause I done whip up a little warm brandy sauce fo' de doctah's gingahbread."

They both thanked her profusely and were silent for an awkward length of time after she left. At least, awkward for two friends always so comfortable together.

"I never smelled brandy sauce to compare with this," Dr. Bullie said, keeping his voice calm.

"Rosa Moon is a genius in her way, the same as Mrs. Kemble is in hers. I'll be sure to tell Rosa Moon you said that. She's already one of your greatest admirers, you know."

"Must we resort to small talk, Abby? You need not be careful with me."

"Whatever you say, Dr. Bullie."

"Abby, you haven't mentioned freeing your slaves to me since our time on the boat, so I hoped you had changed your mind. You know, of course, you can't possibly free them, no matter what you've decided. The community would make life unbearable for you. Your people cannot

eat or wear or sleep on freedom alone, and since Old Osawatomie Brown committed his criminal act up in Virginia, the lives of any slaves freed by you or anyone else
can't be worth a pittance! The whole South is in a panic.
It is now a known fact that when Colonel Lee captured
Brown he had maps of our Darien area in his possession
and plans for future violence. My prediction is that as panic
and dread and fear spread over the South, no decent, slave-
owning white Southerner will wait for an act of God to do
away with *any* free person of color, but will take the matter
into his own hands on sight. There is going to be such a
crackdown on Negroes found assembling or perhaps even
walking the streets not under the direct supervision of the
owner that the population will decrease in no time at all."

"You sound more like Obadiah by the minute," she said
sharply.

"Running off at the mouth, eh?"

"That's right. Spouting, pontificating! At least, that's
how I'm interpreting it."

"You are?"

"Yes, Dr. Bullie. So, can we clear our throats, eat our
gingerbread, drink our coffee, and then try talking to each
other again?"

Holmes gobbled his gingerbread, gulped down his coffee—both much faster than his manners ever allowed. He
dabbed at his mouth with the damask napkin. "Now, back
to Abraham Lincoln of Illinois."

"Please."

"Please? You sound truly solemn, Abby, as though this
had some deep—uh—intense meaning for you."

"Intense? I don't know about that, but I know I'm going
to do everything possible to free all my people. Of course,
I won't separate Rosa Moon and Obadiah and I intend to
keep them on salary as house servants. But please talk more
about Mr. Lincoln. My mother seems to be hoping—believing actually—that should he become President, he
would do something to find a way out of bondage for black
and white."

"White?"

"I'm in bondage too. Slave owners, if they'd only admit it, are in bondage to the ugly system."

"I see. Well, maybe you haven't noticed, but Lincoln does not seem to allow himself to speak often on the subject of slavery. Nor does he give much detail, if any, as to how or when slavery might come to an end. Certainly he says nothing about what might happen to free people of color. I even read that he declared freeing them might be as much as a hundred years in the future. I've also heard that he believes the white race to be superior. Your mother's good mind has been bent out of shape, my dear. Probably by Mrs. Kemble herself."

"Not only Mrs. Kemble. My mother is an ardent admirer of the late Dr. Channing, and of the authors Emerson, Hawthorne, and Thoreau."

Holmes made a scoffing sound. "Henry Thoreau is touched in the head. Did you know that early this month when Old Brown was on trial and put on a show of dignity and calm all the way to the scaffold, Thoreau was not only one of the abolitionists who made him a martyr; he likened him to Jesus Christ himself?"

"We were discussing Mr. Lincoln, Dr. Bullie. Not John Brown."

"Yes. Yes, so we were. Well, I don't know anything about the true politics of that homely, backwoods, half-baked lawyer from Illinois! And I feel it best to prove my friendship for you, Abigail, by insisting that we not discuss him any longer. I value our friendship far too much."

For a long time, Abby sat looking at him, her eyes brimming with tears, because as the minutes ticked by she realized more and more how much she had depended upon James Holmes's ready humor and always kind heart. Was he really so strongly in favor of slavery? Could a man of his intelligence, his spirituality, his tender ministrations to his patients, really be in favor of owning the very heartbeats of the slaves he looked after?

Even with Thad in complete agreement with her on

freeing her own people, she felt abruptly more alone than she remembered feeling since Eli went away. The pain in her this minute was not because she missed Eli, though, but because it frightened her to feel so alone.

Finally, she asked, her voice unsteady, "There's nothing I can say that will soften your wonderful heart even a little bit where the evil system is concerned, is there?"

He took his time answering. "My dear girl, you and I may just have to admit that we define a softened heart differently. Someday when I stand before my Maker, I may come to understand that you've been right all along. My heart is every bit as sympathetic toward the slaves I attend when they're ill as toward their white masters. I am a doctor first of all. But, face it, a doctor might just as well not be a doctor if he goes about the business of destroying the very system on which his practice depends. Without the white slavemasters who hire me to attend their people, as well as themselves, Susan and I, along with our beloved children, would be without a livelihood. I will do everything within the bounds of my beliefs to keep you as my dear friend. I need your friendship. Susan needs it. But, Abigail, there is no way you can just say the word and free the slaves you own legally. I'll pray to God that you will find a way to accept that. Do you understand at all?"

"No."

"Well, to keep my own slate clear with you, this seems the right time, regardless of the consequences, for me to let you know that I am well aware of your intention to marry Thad Greene."

"What?"

"Not many in Darien are unaware of it, Abby, dear girl. And perhaps in addition to trying to dissuade you from attempting such a self-destructive course, I should make at least an effort to dissuade him too. I imagine all this about freeing Negroes is his idea anyway. And even though I've always respected the man's expertise as an overseer, it's clear he would stand to gain a lot from marrying you. After all, you are a fairly wealthy and quite beautiful young widow. I'm glad you now know your secret is no longer a secret and that I will try to dissuade Greene from influencing you to do anything so foolish as freeing slaves—or marrying him."

Abby got slowly to her feet, stood very straight in the clutter of cedar branches, holly, and red ribbon on her carpet. "Before I say something for which I could be eternally sorry, Dr. Holmes, I am going to ask you to leave my house. Not in anger, but in heartbreak and—sorrow."

"You're—you're telling me to go, Abby?" he asked brokenly as he pulled himself up out of his chair. "So—so near Christmas, you're—asking me to leave your home?"

"Yes, if you please. I know I risk losing one of the best friends I've ever had, but—I do ask you to do me the courtesy of—leaving. Now."

Chapter 40

J ust after first light the next day, Obadiah, still in bed, could hear Rosa Moon bustling around the kitchen of their cabin behind Miss Abby's house. She was humming "Silent Night," the only white Christmas carol she knew. And for the few cherished minutes she allowed him, Obadiah nestled under the covers, still warm from her body.

"She be callin' me anytime now," he mumbled to himself from the pure luxury of the moment's indulgence, remembering the good feel of her beside him. Then, as naturally as breathing, he turned his mumbling talk heavenward. "Dat woman be callin', 'Obadiah, git up!' any minute now, Lord. But, Lord, I pray you give me a li'l more time—just a few seconds more in this good, warm bed. She leave such joy between these sheets, I vow to you I can't let it go quite so quick!"

But when he heard Rosa Moon's low, mellow voice stop in the middle of her carol, he knew she was heading his way.

"Happy Birf'day to de Lord," Rosa Moon said as she sank down on the side of their bed. "Ain' no use tryin' to let on you sleepin', Ob'diah. Come eat yo' breakfus'. I got plenty ob bakin' an' fixin' to do today. It be nigh Christmas an' Miss Abby's spectin' comp'ny to come callin' if fo' no other reason than to poke into her poor life. If dey don' all git here today, you know dey be here before Christmas

Day. Git up, man, it purty near de Lawd's Birf'day an' you got work to do."

He finally released the covers he'd been holding up over his head, knowing full well she'd grab them off anyway. "Ain' no use me tryin' to keep warm wif you pullin' on de covers," he grumbled, reaching for her. "Come here, 'oman. I needs kissin'.'"

"Ain' got time for no foolishness," she snapped. "But lemme git a good look at you."

"What wrong wif de way I look?"

Trying to give her normal chuckle, she said, "Ain' nothin' wrong I sees. But try to tell some ob de white women comin' to call dat you ain' hatchin' up some bloody deed to do."

"Oh, Rosa Moon, why you got to bring dat up firs' thing? Reckon dey don' know how bad dey make us niggers feel bein' scared ob us like we done all turn into devils 'cause a crazy white slavery-hater like Ol' Brown done try to git the black folks up in Virginny to kill their white people. It make me feel shame an' I ain' done nothin'. I ain' eben had one thought dat way!"

"Yo' skin's dark, Ob'diah. Us havin' dark skin make white folks 'fraid ob us on sight even way down here in Gawgia. They think some of Ol' Brown's mens is headin' dis way. It got me jumpy all ober jus' knowin' dey's scared ob us. My hands shakes so bad when I tries to pour some ob Miss Abby's visitors a cup of coffee, I gonna scald somebody one day. Come outa there—*now!*" She leaned to give him a perfunctory kiss, but couldn't move fast enough to get up from the bed until he'd made the most of it.

Rosa Moon managed to ask, "What kind of doin's is that?"

"Love doin's," he said, climbing out of the warm bed to sit beside her. "It'd be good, Rosa Moon, if dem white womens could see down inside all ob us—past our dark skin."

"Oh, yes, sweet man." On her feet, looking down at him,

she added, "Maybe someday we all see—us all down inside."

"I'll be gone a little longer than usual," Abby told Rosa Moon when they met in Abby's front hall sometime later. "I'm going to ask Obadiah to take me out to the Ridge to Dr. Bullie's house for a few minutes before we go to Abbyfield today."

"You ain' feelin' bad, is you, Miss Abby?"

"No. I feel fine, except I need to have a talk with my friend the doctor. We—didn't part on such good terms yesterday. Do you think Obadiah can go right away?"

"Oh, yes'm. I'll send him right out to the stable. He be ready with the buggy hitched in no time. Sure you don't want no more breakfus'?"

"My appetite may return if I can have some time with Dr. Bullie. I'm too nervous to eat now."

Abby was not surprised when Susan Holmes excused herself rather quickly after Abby was seated in the parlor with her friend the doctor. It was clear to Abby that Dr. Holmes had told his wife about their unusual parting the day before.

"I had to come," Abby said when she and Holmes were alone.

"I know. I had to see you too. If you hadn't reached the Ridge first, I'd be on my way to your house now—welcome or not."

"You're welcome! You're always welcome, Dr. Bullie. It's just that there's so much turmoil in my heart these days I speak before I give myself time to think. I also know you don't agree with me in my new decision to free my slaves."

"That's right, Abigail. I don't agree, because I see nothing practical about turning your people away with no means of earning a living. The new statute forbidding any free person of color from walking our streets alone without being arrested, possibly even jailed or put on the block for sale to someone else, creates a real danger. Aren't they all better off with you? Do you really want any of them arrested as vagrants?"

"You know me better than that."

"That's the point, my dear girl. I do know you better than that, which makes this whole decision of yours so troublesome."

"Can you forgive me for asking you to leave my home?"

"Yes, of course I can. But I thought Mr. Bentley would have made it clear to you by now why it's impossible for you to free your slaves and expect them to survive. And now the legal proceedings against freed blacks are so strict, so confusing, there's no possible way they could manage to keep it straight. Why, there are even new rules that forbid free persons of color from doing any work to earn a living. Also—"

"I don't want to hear any more. I've already taken your point."

"Does that mean you've decided at least to allow matters to develop for a time before doing anything so foolhardy?"

"No. It only means I grasp your meaning. That I've understood your side of this ridiculous argument. But right now, I need to know who else besides you is gossiping about Thad Greene and me. In a short time my late husband will have been gone long enough for me to marry again. Isn't that my personal decision to make? And I thought you liked Thad. You act as though you do when the two of you are together."

"I like the man fine, but not as your husband."

"We must not hurt each other again, Dr. Holmes. I already have enough pain in my heart, but isn't the choice of the man I marry up to me?"

"Of course it is, but Susan and I are so genuinely fond of you, Abby, we don't want you to do something rash that might well bring you still more heartache."

For a long moment, she studied the pattern in the parlor carpet. "I don't think I've ever known a man and wife who love each other more—as completely—as you and Susan."

"And that's the kind of love Susan and I want for you when—if—you marry again, Abby."

She stood up. Holmes stood too.

"I have to go, but before I do, I must tell you, dear friend, that the kind of love you and Susan have is what I have with Thad."

"God above knows I understand why you're romantically attracted to him. He's one of the most appealing gentlemen in the county. But how much do you really know about Thad Greene, Abby?"

"Enough. So much, in fact, that it makes me want to know him more and more and more. Freeing my slaves was not his idea. It was, and is, mine. Waiting until it's an acceptable time to marry Thad is the most difficult thing I've ever had to do. *Ever.* I'm going to him now, and I beg you not to say anything more to me other than—good day."

Chapter 41

When Obadiah reined the horse and buggy by the front path at the overseer's house, Thad was waiting. She'd seen him walking impatiently up and down as they neared the cottage and wondered why he appeared so agitated.

Both had stopped long ago trying to fool Obadiah, so, certain that no one else was around, Abby fell eagerly into Thad's outstretched arms.

"Abby," he breathed, "thank God you're here! I was worried."

"Good."

"Shame on you, ma'am."

"I said 'good' because I know you missed me or you wouldn't have been worried that I'm later than usual. But I had to see Dr. Holmes first thing today." Then she told him about having asked the doctor to leave her house yesterday. And about her relief that, for the most part, they had made up during her visit to him at the Ridge earlier this morning. She also told him that Dr. Bullie had sworn that everyone in town knew they were in love and planning to marry as soon as a decent time had passed after Eli's death. She did not mention the doctor's disapproval of their marriage.

"I already knew they were talking," he said, leading her toward his house.

"Why didn't you tell me?"

"Because our world was perfect as long as you thought it was only *our* world. I love you so much, Abby, I cherish every happy hour you have."

"Then give me *all* happy hours, Thad. It's fine with me that people already know about us, so why can't we get married as soon as possible? I'm sure the Reverend Goulding at my Presbyterian church will perform a simple, quick ceremony almost any time we ask. There's so much wild talk about the danger every white person is in—even though poor old John Brown is in his grave—it might do them good to have us to talk about for a change. And, dearest, if there is trouble up ahead for the country, we need to be together all the time. I'm tired of making this buggy trip out here every day. I need to go to bed at night with you . . . wake up each morning with you. Am I being brazenly forward?"

He gave her the tender, half-mischievous smile she loved. "Well, keep talking, Little One. I think I need to hear just a bit more in order to answer that question."

"Thad! Do you smell smoke?"

He sniffed the quiet, chilly late December air. "I smell something. It might be smoke."

They had reached his house, but still stood at the bottom of the wooden steps that led to the front porch. The smell of wood smoke was plain now and Thad stood listening intently.

"What are you listening for?" she asked. "Are you expecting to hear Thomas Jefferson's 'fire bell in the night'?"

"Don't make jokes, Abby. I'm listening in case someone might blow our conch shell to signal fire or trouble."

They heard nothing but a wren calling from the big oak tree in front of Thad's house.

"I know years and years ago old Tom Jefferson called our slavery problem a 'fire bell in the night' and I fear his prediction may be coming true. That 'bell' could still ring. Being out here at Abbyfield so much of the time, I think the panic that's spreading like a dark cloud over the county sometimes escapes me. But no one who spends an hour in Darien, as I did yesterday, can miss it," Thad said, frowning.

"Well, I guess nothing's burning at Abbyfield," she offered.

"Evidently not, but even our frequent accidental fires, like the ones that happen almost every late fall during ginning time, are being called 'Kansas work' by our highly imaginative citizens."

"Kansas work?"

"After John Brown and his sons. Have you forgotten that they were in Kansas long enough to murder five or six slave owners?"

"Of course I haven't forgotten. Dear heart, how could two people be so in love, so happy, so full of dreams for the future, while the rest of the country is sliding toward God knows what? I don't tell you everything people tell me in town because there are so many wonderful things for us to talk about during the few hours we can be together. But I've heard all the ugly rumors. I know there's treasonous talk all over the South about secession. That can't happen, Thad! It just *can't* happen."

"Who tells you these things, Abby?"

"Laura Mabry, Susan Holmes . . . and depending on how each person happens to feel about hating the North, almost everyone who calls at my house in town talks of the need for the South to secede from the rest of the country. I hate it. I hate that word! And don't tell me it's only woman talk, because lawyer Bentley thinks there's real danger too. I'm sure Dr. Holmes agrees. He's just such a diplomat, he doesn't come right out with it."

"Do you ever wonder what the man really thinks deep down?"

"Of course I wonder," she sighed. "And I'd guess he's mainly a peacemaker. Nothing makes Dr. Bullie happier than for everyone around him to be happy too."

A primitive blast from the big plantation conch shell broke the pre-noon silence.

"Thad!"

"Yes, dearest. I heard it. And I have to go—*now*. Wait for me on the porch, please."

From the direction of the Abbyfield barn, Obadiah came galloping up with Thad's horse, which Thad mounted bareback, racing off in the direction of the neighboring rice plantation.

"Wait, Abby," he called back. "I want you here when I get through helping. I think there's got to be a fire at old Uncle Bubba's place—maybe a big one."

"Be careful, please," she called after him, then turned to Obadiah. "Shouldn't you follow him to help? Obadiah! I—I love him. He's my life now. I know how you felt about Eli, but for my sake, please go help Thad!"

When Thad galloped within sight of old foul-mouthed Bubba Mins's ancient cottage, the once sturdy cottage seemed to be burning wildly inside, its appearance reminding Thad of a slab of pork left too long on hot coals. The walls were not yet falling, but bulging outward, almost rounded by the inner pressure of the roaring flames.

And then it happened. The cottage reached the bursting point and above the exploding roar of the fire, Thad saw the old house literally blow apart.

Spurring the horse with his heels, he reached the red-hot falling timbers just in time to see Bubba Mins's last motion. The hot-tempered, slave-beating old man, as burned and blackened as his house, his clothes and hair afire, crawled over the crackling doorstep, jerked twice, then collapsed in death on the burning grass.

There was no question in Thad's mind but that the old planter was dead. He had turned blacker than his darkest slave, proving even himself not tough or thick-skinned enough to withstand such a roasting.

By late afternoon, gossip was racing around Darien and the entire county that abolitionists from the North had, following Brown's maps of the county, invaded the peaceful

Georgia coast, enlisting slaves, probably arming them, and surely inciting them to burn, burn, burn.

From all directions, people rushed into the town shouting "Kansas work!" One would say, "Plain and simple, this is Kansas work!" Another would reply, "Right here in peaceful Darien, Georgia, Old Brown's Kansas work is still goin' on—the niggers are burnin' old Bubba Mins's place out adjoining Abbyfield an' only God knows what they'll do next!"

"It's Republicans," still another screamed, "maybe that infernal Abraham Lincoln himself causing it all! At least there's a Republican behind it, and if it goes on, the South's going to rise up an' fight back!"

Abby returned to town with Obadiah, the faithful, kind man plainly scared to show his dark face, but willing, as always, to take her wherever she wanted to go. Today she asked him to drop her off at Laura Mabry's house and return for her in time to eat the meal Rosa Moon would have ready as always for supper.

"I'm so glad you came by, Abby," Laura said, embracing her. "If you hadn't come soon, I was going to your house at least to find out from Rosa Moon whether or not you were still at Abbyfield. Were you there when old man Mins's house burned?"

"Yes, but Thad left me at Abbyfield while he went to the Mins place hoping to help. I didn't see the old man, but Thad told me the poor fellow rolled out of the place completely afire, burning to a crisp. Laura, I've heard the most awful things being said just in the few minutes I've been back in town! People are actually blaming poor old John Brown for inciting our slaves!"

"I know, and they're even blaming Abraham Lincoln, that fine man from Illinois. Abby, the Republican convention won't be held until May, so we won't know until then if he will be nominated to be President! Sometimes I wonder how normally quiet, well-mannered people can act so crazy. What do you suppose is going to happen to the

South? The North, for that matter? The whole country?"

"I don't have an answer to that, but, Laura, I need you to know that Dr. Bullie told me this morning everyone in town knows about my feelings for Thad. And I know the proper ladies of Darien must think I'm a loose woman because I see him every day. But I *am* the owner of Abbyfield, so there's a plausible reason for me to go out there. Eli went every day. Now I go."

"Good Eli is still looking after you in a way, isn't he?"

"Yes. Oh, Laura, you know I tried to—to love him, don't you? The truth is, I didn't even know back in those days what real love was all about."

"You know now, though. And I don't think some married women ever come to know that, Abby."

"How much longer do you think I'll have to—wait? How long is long enough in people's busy minds?"

"I honestly don't know," Laura said, thinking hard. "I try to imagine what they're saying among themselves. I'm sure you know the gossipy ones are very, very careful of what they say in front of me. But I'm truly, truly glad you now know that everyone in town already expects you and Thad will marry someday. Or does that make it worse?"

"No. It's better. Waiting is bad enough. Wondering what people know is even worse. But, Laura, I'm not the only one waiting. And neither is Thad. In a very real way, the whole country is waiting to find out what horror the future might hold for everyone. Oh, what must God think of us all? I know He loves us beyond our comprehension, but what must He *think* of us scrapping and gossiping and owning slaves and, heaven forbid, warring among ourselves?"

"Oh, Abby, you relieve me by wondering about such things!"

"Do you wonder about them too?"

"Every day! This morning I begged God to let us know somehow which man to pray for as President!"

Laughing a little, Abby said, "But, Laura, dear, as you said, we have to wait until spring even to find out who will be chosen to run."

"What does Thad Greene think about Lincoln and the mess we're in? Do you two really discuss such things or does he abide by the Southern gentleman's notion that women shouldn't trouble themselves with weighty matters?"

"We talk about—everything. That's one of the many, many reasons I love him so much. Thad talks to me—listens when I talk. Respects my opinion. He's even started reading Henry David Thoreau, and you know that man's one of the strongest abolitionists in the North. Oh, Laura, Thad is full of the most wonderful surprises. He vows the only hope for the country is the election of Abraham Lincoln. Thad told me just yesterday that he's sure Lincoln eventually could find a way to free all the slaves! Can you imagine that?"

"You've met your match in Thad, haven't you?"

Abby's smile was all relief. "Yes! Oh, yes. And I love you for knowing it! He'll always take care of me, but he actually believes I'm on the earth for more than mere pampering."

"And it doesn't bother you that he seems to hold basic abolitionist beliefs while earning his own living as a plantation overseer?"

After an easy silence, Abby asked, "Do you know anyone—anyone who always lives up to his or her own highest standards, Laura? Do you? Do I? Does your fine husband, Woodford? Thad is totally human and, best of all, he allows me my humanity too."

Chapter 42

On a late afternoon early in the new year, 1860, Thad rode away from his house in search of some time alone to sort out his thoughts about his own future with Abby. He had never asked, but Bentley intimated that Eli Edward Allyn had left her a relatively rich woman. Thad was grateful that Abbyfield, laid out in squares and canals and dikes for rice—now brown with stubble after harvest—also held a stand of pine and hickory and live oak. He had grown up in the woods of a Pennsylvania countryside and had learned to think there in the silence, hearing the wind music in the trees around him. Here in Georgia, when his overseer duties allowed, he had formed a habit of riding off into the Abbyfield woods as a sort of gift to himself. The gift of a little time alone from a busy day, time to be thankful that he had been given the gift of Abby's love, the strong woman-love he had never shared until he found her.

Was this awareness his own way of praying—thanking God for her? He couldn't have been sure enough to tell anyone such a thing without sounding pious, but he did believe there was a good God somewhere and that the same good God was mysteriously in charge of human affairs. Thad had just never formed his thoughts into words during his silent times. He read from the Bible often, mainly because he loved its literature, the music of its glorious phrasing, the cadence of the certainties he somehow knew were always there for him.

Abby prayed. She told him so months ago. He could count on her prayers because, with an almost childlike confidence, he knew her prayers included him.

Too good to be true? Perhaps. But true, just the same.

His new resolve was to make another effort to convince her to wait still longer to marry him. She would disagree as she had so often recently. But with the politics of the country in such chaos, with the problems of freeing her slaves too dangerous even for Abby's determination to overcome, and with the gossip about a slave uprising putting their financial future in limbo, he knew they should wait a few months longer. Undoubtedly, she would argue. She might even be angry, but he knew she would not pout or make use of any usual woman tricks with him. Abby would not beg or even weep. He had watched her turn into a mature, steady, usually balanced woman, as the two of them had endured their waiting time together for months and months. He trusted her, he knew she didn't think he wanted her money, but he also knew how his decision to wait still longer would trouble her. So the time alone today to steady himself seemed essential. He would tell her tomorrow, but he had no idea exactly how.

By now, he had ridden into the densest part of the woods, where even in winter the smilax crept thick over fallen trees and under his horse's hoofs the ground was still covered with autumn leaves. A fading winter sun shot rays across the deep brown carpet of pine needles and he smiled because, as with so many Northerners, he had fallen in love with the rich, evergreen wonder of Georgia's coast where nature was free to create its own sun-and-shadow-streaked beauty. Thad reined his horse and sat listening to the silence. It was the kind of silence in which he seemed sometimes to find music—even to imagine he heard singing or felt the throb of a great orchestra as though it coursed through his own blood. He had attended only two concerts as a university student years ago in Philadelphia, but the exaltation of the music had somehow stayed with him. Oh, weeks could pass when he gave no thought to it, but when he rode into a dense stand of trees as now, he could hear it—feel it, thrill to it.

Soon after he came South to take on the still surprising and, to him, unbecoming work of overseeing slaves, he had even wept at times in the blessed aloneness where no one could hear or see.

He had not wept since there had been Abby, though. Abby, natural as spattering sunlight, cooling his brow with her hand as would a spring shower, washing away the years of loneliness. Today, as he sat his horse in the deep woods, the silence was filled with music and with Abby.

Abruptly, his attention was caught by what sounded like a squirrel rustling the dried leaves. He took a deep breath and grinned at himself because for no reason he felt almost—afraid. Dismounting quickly, quietly, he walked toward the sound. There wasn't a squirrel anywhere to be seen. But he heard the leaves rustle again and then what was unmistakably a man's sneeze.

"Hello!" he called. "Who's there?"

And then he saw the slightly built figure of a young man lying face down in the dried autumn leaves, motionless. Beside him was a large square leather case with one handle, behind which the man had obviously hoped to hide.

"Good day," Thad said. "I—I thought I heard someone sneeze. Are you ill?"

"Oh, no, sir. Just tired. And there must be dust on the ground." He sat up slowly, his wavy dark hair tousled.

"What's a young fellow like you doing out here in the woods with that large case?" Thad asked pleasantly. "It must be quite heavy."

"As heavy as a case of bricks, sir. And I'm sorry if I'm trespassing, but I just—"

"You're not trespassing." Thad lifted the bag. "How in the name of common sense did you get this thing way out here in the woods, son?"

"I—I carried it. I've carried it all the way from Darien."

"Couldn't you find a ride of some kind? Where are you heading?"

"I guess to your house, sir, if you're the overseer of this land. I—I hope to sell you a book or two. They told me in town you might want one. Anyway, I—I'm scared to stay in Darien again tonight."

"Scared?"

"They seem like nice enough people, but I look and sound like a Yankee to them and, well, sir, I guess you could say they all but ran me out of town."

"Too bad," Thad said, putting the pieces of the puzzle together. "You must be a—peddler. There are slave owners here in Georgia who would swear on their mother's life that every Yankee peddler was somehow sent down here by John Brown—or at least the ghost of John Brown."

His anxiety a little eased, the young man smiled for the first time. "One old fellow accused me of being sent by some Republican."

"Did he say which Republican?" Thad asked, grinning.

"No. I was really taken aback by the people of Darien. I had no idea they'd treat a Bible salesman the way they treated me. Oh, I don't mean I was physically harmed, but—"

"Just not made particularly welcome, eh?"

"Right, sir. Anything but." The young man studied Thad's face. "You—you don't seem at all like the others. May I ask where you're from? You don't even have a Southern accent."

"And there are times when I almost wish I had." Thad laughed. "I'm a Pennsylvanian. Philadelphia. I came South out of curiosity at first, but the place captured me."

"Captured you, sir?"

"Its beauty. Oh, I admit if you haven't traveled far from Darien, charming as I find the little town, you might not understand. But there's a real natural beauty down here. You noticed those giant, gnarled live oak trees in Darien, didn't you?"

"Oh, yes, sir! And maybe because it's one of the books

I'm trying to sell, I couldn't help thinking how Mr. Henry David Thoreau would admire those trees. Did you ever notice that a kind of fern grows right on their wide branches?"

"I have indeed. The coastal natives seem to take them for granted, but I've never stopped looking for them. They're called resurrection ferns because they appear dried up until we have a good rain. Then they spring to life. But look here, Mr.—"

"Farrow," the boy said. "Robert Farrow. Hartford, Connecticut."

"I'm Thad Greene, and not treating you too well, I fear. Do you have a place to rest tonight? You're welcome to stay with me at my overseer's cottage. I'd like to see your Thoreau books too."

"Oh, I'm most grateful! Lugging these heavy books slows me down, but I'll follow you on foot."

"Fine. And I don't mean to insult you, but would you mind if I take a look at the contents of your trunk? I'm not suspicious of you, but a man can't be too careful these days."

"I don't mind at all. It's unlocked. Help yourself. You'll find mostly Bibles and I have an especially good offer if you're at all interested in owning a handsome family Bible."

"A Bible? Well, I might be—someday. But right now, I'll just have a quick look." He laughed a little. "I assure you, though, that I'm not a member of the Darien Vigilante Committee like the others you've come up against."

"You'll find in my trunk Bibles bound in a fine quality of leather and the real gold stamping is beautiful. I also hope you'll take note of the excellent quality of the paper containing the biblical text."

Thad laughed again softly. "I must say you're a born salesman."

"I believe you when you tell me you're not one of those vigilantes."

Thad took a quick look at the carefully packed Bibles and one or two other volumes in the case, which seemed impossibly heavy for one man to carry alone. "Did these self-appointed vigilantes accuse you of dirty work among our slaves in the county?"

"Oh, yes, sir! They got the idea somewhere that I would round up the Negroes and incite them to murder their white owners."

"Darienites are scared out of their wits, living day and night under the dark specter of John Brown, who's been in his grave almost a month. My guess is that people down here think Old Brown's men are still scouring coastal Georgia making their bloody mischief. I know one old lady not far from my house who can't sleep because she's so sure her own slaves will cut her throat."

Thad saw what seemed to be a genuine look of pity on the young face. "Poor old thing," Robert Farrow said, getting slowly to his feet. "What's your opinion, sir? Do you think Northern abolitionists are really trying to stir up slaves down here against their owners? I was under the impression that even though Old Brown did try to free slaves and turn them against their owners up there at Harper's Ferry, not one slave responded to his call."

"That's the way I heard it too," Thad said. "How about riding back to my house behind me on my horse? I'll send someone to bring your heavy case. And I'll help arrange a buggy ride back to Darien for you tomorrow. You can get a steamer from there to Savannah. And I'd go as soon as possible if I were you, Robert. These are weird, dangerous times and wagging tongues can be as cutting as knives. So many whites are downright afraid these days and fear breeds violence at the drop of a hat."

Much more persuasion might have been needed if young Robert Farrow had not been so exhausted. He was exhausted, though, and so hungry, Thad, who did his own cooking, longed for a good woman to take over his kitchen when he saw the gusto with which the boy attacked the bread, ham, and eggs he put before this unexpected, plainly guileless visitor as soon as they reached the cottage.

Thad found Black Mary, who worked in the Abbyfield

garden, and asked her if she would please make up a bed for Robert Farrow and see to his needs. He smiled, remembering that Obadiah and his driver, Baldy, teased Thad for continuing to say 'please' to the people. Suddenly thinking of Abby, he realized that he would need every minute possible with her tomorrow in order to try to explain his deepening conviction that they should wait still longer to be married. And certainly she should wait until some of the furor of fear died down in Darien before she even thought of letting it be known to any but her closest friends that she planned to try to free a hundred slaves.

"She simply can't do it anytime soon," he said aloud to himself as he waited. "There is just too much risk. There are laws against it now. I can't allow her to hunt for more trouble." He had never thought of himself as *allowing* Abby to do or not do anything, but they had grown so close lately, he felt the necessity this time. He had become convinced that she returned his love with the same wholeheartedness with which he gave it.

Without doubt, if word got around Darien of her intentions, the Vigilante Committee would be sent to Abbyfield to keep watch. And for what reason? Thad would swear that all the Abbyfield slaves held only benign intentions toward her and toward him as their overseer. He scoffed audibly at the ludicrous actions of the white slave owners in Darien who had frightened poor young Robert so that he took refuge in the dense woods at Abbyfield. "Maybe he did intend to sell me a Bible," Thad said aloud, "but found the woods tempting for hiding. The boy was terrified."

"You mighty quiet, Miss Abby," Obadiah said the next morning as the buggy neared Abbyfield and he slowed to turn in at the long lane that led past several acres of harvested rice fields toward Thad's house.

"Quiet? I was thinking the same about you, Obadiah. Is something weighing on your mind?"

"No, ma'am, no more'n usual, but it seem to me dey is

somepin' on the heavy side weighin' on yo' min' today."

"There is, but I intend to talk to Mr. Thad about it first."

"Oh, yes, ma'am," he said, slowing the buggy the minute they saw Thad waiting. "I know you jump right out to Mr. Thad," he chuckled, "so I ain' takin' no chances of this ol' pony trottin' too fast when you jump."

"I suppose you think I act like a schoolgirl."

"No'm. I don' think dat"—he chuckled again—" 'cause I ain't never knowed no schoolgirl!" After a moment, Obadiah asked, "You not feelin' good today, Miss Abby?"

"Oh, I'm not sure how I feel. Why?"

"Rosa Moon she give me a special warnin' not to upset you none 'bout nothin'. Sometime it look to me like dat woman know more dan she ought to know."

"She accused me of acting nervous at breakfast today."

"Den you mus' be. Rosa Moon know. She know. Could be Mr. Thad he help some."

Abby grabbed for Thad's outstretched hand almost desperately and felt cheated when he didn't hold her as long or as eagerly as usual.

"What's wrong, darling?"

"Why, nothing, dearest Abby. I just need a word with Obadiah before he drives off to the stable." He turned and gestured. "Wait, Obadiah!" Over his shoulder as he loped toward the buggy Thad called back, "Go on up to the porch, Abby, I'll be right there. Oh, and don't worry about the strange leather case by the front door. I'll explain in a minute."

Alone, she climbed the front steps and stood looking down at the battered, worn leather case. Almost idly and for no apparent reason, she pushed at it with her foot. It wouldn't budge. Something was different. Thad seemed different. Concerned, she waited while he exchanged a few words with Obadiah, who, curiously, did not drive on toward the Abbyfield stables.

"Sorry to keep you waiting, Abby," Thad said, bounding up the steps to take her in his arms—again for only a quick hug. "I'm sending Obadiah back into town with a young man who spent the night here. He's finishing his breakfast now. The boy's scared half out of his wits by the way he's been treated in Darien since he got off the boat from Savannah two days ago. This is his case. Heavy as it is, I couldn't bear to see him stagger off down the road lugging it. Obadiah can take him to the boat in Darien. The quicker he gets out of town, the better."

"Who is he? Where did he come from?"

"He's from Connecticut. And, as far as I can tell, an intelligent, clean-cut, but rumpled and travel-worn young man—a gentleman in all ways. You don't mind that I offered him a bed last night, do you?"

"Thad! Why on earth would you even ask a question like that? We're not strangers, you and I. But do I have to wait long to find out why he had such a bad experience in Darien? I'm already fidgety today. And for a reason even I don't know about—exactly."

"We'll fix your fidgets, whatever the reason, Little One. The lad will be through his breakfast soon and you can meet him."

"Is he out of money?"

"I don't think so. He's a Bible salesman, but money wasn't the reason he couldn't find anything to eat in Darien. He vows he has funds for a steamer ticket back up North."

"Oh, that's good. I suppose they were sure in Darien that he's an abolitionist?"

"That's right. Just hold on for a few more minutes and you'll learn everything he told me when I found him out in that stand of dense trees where we go for firewood."

She shivered. "I hope you have a good fire going in your parlor. I'm half frozen. Thad? Did Obadiah seem surprised the young man was here? And does he know why?"

"There's very little Obadiah doesn't know, my dear. And this may seem a strange time to tell you, but in case some of your worry is because you imagine that good man doesn't like me for being so quick to take Eli's place, you can forget it. He and I had a good talk last week. Obadiah swears he no longer resents my being on the scene."

"That's good of him," she said, "but I haven't worried much about that. I trust Obadiah's wisdom and I knew he'd realize sooner or later that what always mattered to Eli was my happiness. Eli was a fine and honorable man, Thad, but it's you I need now."

Chapter 43

Abby listened intently while both Thad and young Robert Farrow told her the story of his threatening Darien experiences with two members of the Vigilante Committee who were sure that he was an abolitionist come South to stir up trouble among the slaves in McIntosh County.

"But couldn't they see by your papers and that enormous case of Bibles and books that you represent a publishing house?" Abby asked.

"A publishing house in the North, ma'am. Evidently for them that's enough to prove I meant them harm down here."

"I still don't understand. What did they think you were planning to do, Mr. Farrow? How would you get in touch with key slaves on the large number of plantations in coastal Georgia?"

"Abby, they aren't thinking," Thad said. "Woodford Mabry told me the names of some of the Darien vigilantes not long ago and they're all normally intelligent men. They can all think. But now they're simply acting on their fears, their anger—twisting plain hearsay all out of shape."

"Especially in the area immediately surrounding your rice fields, Mrs. Allyn," Robert said.

"But why? Why here? Did you know that, Thad?"

"Only since Robert told me last night. I should have

suspected it. After all, I got there minutes before old Bubba rolled in flames out of his burning house and died. I'm sure they wondered what I was doing there."

An incredulous look on her face, Abby demanded, "Old Uncle Bubba? Don't tell me they think Northern abolitionists were behind the burning of that cruel old man's rickety house!"

"I could have told you that when it happened, Abby, my dear," Thad said, his voice calm.

"Then why didn't you?"

"Is there one good reason why you need any more to worry about?"

"But you've told me over and over again that you can trust me not to act up, or weep and fume at all that's going on. That you know in your heart I'm not the kind of woman who needs extra pampering. You'll give Mr. Farrow the wrong impression of me. I—I'm a Northern woman, sir, and I hate owning slaves with every fiber of my being. Mr. Greene just tends to overprotect me now and then."

With an open smile, the boy said, "I certainly understand why he might, ma'am. And I wonder if I dare ask a personal question."

"Of course," Abby said.

"Is it brash of me to wonder how you're accepted in the town of Darien if you don't approve of being a slave owner?"

"I not only don't approve—I just came to be a slave owner by—by chance. My late husband left all his funds and property to me, slaves included. I get along in Darien because only two or three close, trusted friends know how I feel about the ugly institution. I'd give almost anything if I owned no one!"

"I see. Uh—there are those in the North who believe sincerely that if a certain gentleman from Illinois named Lincoln could by some means be elected President this fall, there might be a way found someday to—free the slaves."

Abby sat bolt upright in her porch chair. "Young man, if I may offer a strong word of warning, I suggest that you keep as quiet as possible about him. Don't even mention

Mr. Lincoln's name down here to anyone. You're safe with both of us, but in the name of heaven, wait until you're back up North before you speak his name again!"

"Oh, thank you, Mrs. Allyn. I wouldn't think of it with anyone else. I hope you both know how grateful I'll be for the rest of my life that I found the two of you. I don't suppose you would consider selling your slaves."

"Never! How could I be sure they'd be well treated?"

"You couldn't, of course. But without mentioning his name even in the safe sanctuary of this cottage, does either of you believe the man I mentioned might find a way to emancipate the slaves?"

"With all my heart," Thad said, his voice solemn, "I hope that might happen, Robert, but only a very young man would ask a question like that. Only God could possibly know the answer." Then, before either Robert Farrow or Abby could say a word, Thad went on, his solemnity giving way to a growing, boyish excitement. "But I do believe I've just this instant had a wonderful idea!"

"Darling, I want to hear all your wonderful ideas, but could I ask Mr. Farrow a question first?"

Grinning now, Thad said, "Please do, my dear Abby."

"Are you—are you afraid to go back to Darien alone, young man? I know you're anything but a coward, but from what you've told me, I can't help hoping you'll be all right. You will likely have to spend the night in town before you can get a Savannah steamer."

"I guess I hadn't thought that far, ma'am, but I'm sure I'll be all right."

"Oh, I hope you won't judge coastal Georgia by what's going on down here now, Robert Farrow! There are parts of it where there is such beauty it takes your breath away. Thad and I are in a real quandary for more reasons than one. We both love the coast so much. There's not only the beauty of the trees and marshes and sunsets, there's a— kindness in the land itself and in its hospitable people. I know that might surprise you after the way you were treated in Darien, but these are frightening times. Don't blame the land. Someday I hope you can see some of our coastal islands, the way a winter sunset turns the live oak tree bark pure rose—I hope someday you can watch the bullis grape leaves turn yellow in the autumn, marvel at a stand of red-purple French mulberries. And normally the people are wonderfully warm. Thad and I both really want to spend the remainder of our lives down here. Together, of course. I suppose you gathered that."

"Yes, ma'am, I did. And I hope you can. Such trouble can't last forever in a great country like the United States—can it?"

"The answer to that is no," Thad said firmly, once he finally had the chance to get in a word edgewise. "And I'm not giving up the floor until I've told the two of you my splendid idea, because it concerns you both. Me too, of course."

"Oh, dear heart, forgive me," Abby said, grinning now. "Robert and I are practically on our knees apologizing."

"Don't apologize. Just tell me you agree that my idea is indeed wonderful."

"I trust you, sir," she said cheerfully, "but I do need to know what you're hatching up before I agree."

"Robert, Miss Abby and I plan to marry, true, and you may not believe this, but we've already waited almost a year and with such caution that I've never even had a meal at her house in Darien. But, Abby, with all my heart, I believe you and I should go to Darien with Robert and Obadiah. In your buggy if there's room for Robert's case of books, or in the plantation wagon if not."

"Thad, you're—"

"Now, wait. I'm not finished. Robert and I can sleep in your spare room in town tonight, and first thing tomorrow morning the three of us will boldly walk out onto the pier at the Darien waterfront and board a steamer for Savannah together! I don't think either of us is suspected of being a Northern abolitionist, which should protect Robert from harm. His very presence sanctifies our steamer trip to Savannah and, best of all, Abby, you can spend time with the lady you value so highly—"

"Miss Eliza Mackay!" Abby was glowing.

"While you and Miss Eliza talk to your heart's content, I'll see her longtime friend Mr. Mark Browning about the possibility of going to work for him someday when the country's troubles are somehow at an end. Browning owns no slaves, so he may help us find a way to—free yours."

Surprising herself, Abby began to weep.

"Thad! Oh, Thad. . . . Why did you wait so long to think of the perfect idea? It's perfect—perfect. Except Miss Eliza could be ill or still too grief-stricken for unexpected company. Remember, her only remaining son died back in August."

"You must mean Mr. William Mackay," Robert said. "Someone in Savannah told me how the gentleman always loved owning beautiful family Bibles and that I'd surely have a sale if he were still alive."

"Abby, don't you think Miss Eliza needs the comfort of a visit with you?" Thad wanted to know.

"I'm no good at comforting, I'm sure," she said. "All I'd know to do would be just sit there in her parlor with her and—love her. I do love her, you know, and I love you for your perfect idea, Thad. Let's go back to town now! Rosa Moon will have dinner ready and I must let her know. I'll need her to help me pack." She turned to the young man. "Has it occurred to you, Mr. Robert Farrow, that God must have sent you to us—now?" To Thad, she added, "Maybe the most important part of your wonderful idea is that I'll have the chance to get Miss Eliza's opinion about our—wedding date. Who knows the quirks of coastal custom better than that dear lady?"

After the hours spent inside the small but warm steamer cabin en route to Savannah, Abby, Thad, and Robert Farrow were glad to dock at the old waterfront below Factor's Walk even though the cold winter wind seemed to cut right through their warmest clothing.

A rented carriage took them to the Pulaski House, where

Thad rented three rooms for the night. If all went well, Abby and Thad would board the *St. John's* the next day to return to Darien and Mr. Farrow would be free to make his own plans. It was not yet noon and after walking Abby to East Broughton Street for her anticipated visit with Miss Eliza Mackay, Thad would head straight for Mark Browning's office on Commerce Row.

Clinging to Thad's arm as they walked toward the old Mackay house, excitement seemed to push Abby along even against the strong wind off the river. "We're behaving like idiots, Abby," Thad said, "but Robert doesn't seem to mind our foolishness. You know, I'll find it hard to tell him goodbye tomorrow. I wonder if we'll ever see him again."

"Who knows? I certainly hope we do, but I'm so happy to be taking our first trip together, I really can't think straight!"

"I don't even want to think straight," he said, tightening his arm on hers. "I hope Browning's free to see me at least for a few minutes."

"And I'll be so grateful if Miss Eliza has time for me. Don't make any promises to Mark Browning, Thad. You and I have to talk first. Somehow I'm almost positive that Miss Eliza Mackay will help me think through all our problems. I'm so, so tired of—waiting to belong wholly to you, my one love."

"Are you sure you can find your way back to the Pulaski House?" he asked.

"Of course! I might just as well learn Savannah, because who knows? We might be living here one day!"

"Abby, Abby, I do love you," he whispered before they started up Miss Eliza's front walk. "You truly know how to live, don't you?"

"With you, Thad. Only with you."

Faithful, white-haired old Hannah seemed especially happy to show Abby into the Mackay parlor, where Eliza Mackay, still pretty, her hair growing gray, sat smiling a warm, delighted welcome.

"Come in, Abby Allyn. Please come right on in! Somehow when I first woke up today I felt something wonderful was about to happen, but I didn't imagine anything so nice as a visit from you!"

Her arms lifted to Abby, who leaned down to give her a kiss on her forehead. "You're so gracious to receive me like this and, before we say anything else, I must tell you how sorry I am that your son William is—gone. I know he was your rock, that you truly depended upon him."

"I did depend on William, but when a mother loves a son as I loved that boy, she can only be glad that his long, lonely years separated from his adored wife and little children are over at last. They were all three drowned when the steamer *Pulaski* wrecked back in 1838, you know. But they're all four together again now."

"Yes. William's with his brother Jack too. Wasn't your son Jack the close friend of Colonel Robert E. Lee? I suppose you still hear from the Colonel and know of his success in capturing John Brown up in Harper's Ferry, Virginia."

Abby saw a look of sadness cross her friend's face. "He wrote to my daughter Eliza Anne about his rescue of the U.S. Arsenal and the capture and—hanging—of John Brown. Poor John Brown."

"Is that the way you feel about Old Brown?"

"I pitied him. The man was certainly not right in his head. God never, never tells anyone to—kill. But if we peel away the madness in John Brown's mind, he was obsessed with a—kindly cause. His one goal in life seemed to have been freeing slaves. With all my heart, Abby, I believe God wants them free too." She smiled slightly. "I don't know what my old Hannah or her helper, Emphie, would do without me, but neither do I know what I'd do without them. I suppose there are different kinds of freedom *and* bondage, don't you think so?"

"According to my Rosa Moon, yes. I want to free her and her husband, but the mere mention of it seems to frighten her."

"That's because she feels at home with you. And—" Eliza Mackay smiled. "You're good to her in the right way. You recognize her as a separate human being put on this earth for more than to serve you."

"Miss Eliza, one of the two main reasons I came to find help from you today is—this. I'm still determined to free my slaves. I hesitate to bother you again with my problems, but I need to know if you've thought of any way at all that I can stop being a slave owner short of selling everyone. That's out of the question. I want them all to be—free. I've spoken of this to a very few trusted friends—I find I'm actually almost afraid of most Darien people these days. Afraid, at least, to bring up the word 'slavery.' No one gives me any hope. Is there any hope that you know of?"

Eliza Mackay sighed deeply. "I don't know of any way to free your people now, Abby, but as long as there is God, we must have hope. There is God and we must hope. He's even laid out small signs for us if we look closely."

"Signs? What signs?"

"I'm only a couple of years younger than our country. I was born in 1778 into a family of strong patriots. My father moved us from South Carolina to Savannah because he thought those who believed in the future of a new nation would have more freedom to work and speak down here. I was reared on the tenets of the freedoms we cherish in the United States of America. It's sad, but we could not have formed our country to include the South if freedom had been put first—for colored too. Our forefathers had to compromise, but the years have slipped by and a quick glance at the state of our nation now looks anything but bright. I truly fear dreadful trouble ahead. But I also see the signs from God. I know you and I can't vote because we're women, but we can influence our men who can vote."

"But the signs, Miss Eliza. What are they?"

"I started to ask you not to mention that I said this, but I sometimes forget how old I am and how unimportant my opinions are."

"Not to me!"

"Thank you, my dear. We have to study the character of the man elected to be our next President. I may not live to know who he is, but there is one man whose name won't even be on the ballot down here in the Southern states."

"Abraham Lincoln."

"Yes. He bases his political beliefs on the Scriptures. 'A house divided against itself cannot stand.' "

"You think all the secession talk is true, don't you?"

"I wish I didn't, but I do. I'm very afraid the South, probably led by the firebrands in South Carolina, will break away from the Union if Mr. Lincoln is elected. I know he isn't even nominated yet, but it's time for us to begin to pray for him. Until someone of his caliber is in office, I know of no way you can free your people. No way you can stop being a slave owner, Abby, short of selling them."

"I can't do that!"

"I'm sure you can't. And God not only knows that, He'll do His best to find another way—somehow, someday." The older lady waited, then said with sorrow, "The people of Darien are among our best coastal folk, but they'd give you a hard, hard time if they even had the idea that you wanted to free your people."

"I know that. There are Vigilante Committee members everywhere in town these days still living in terror that John Brown's men are being sent by Northerners to incite slaves to murder their owners in their sleep—to burn their houses."

"God forgive us all."

"A rickety little house burned on a plantation near mine not long ago—burned to the ground, killing the old man who owned it. Everyone is sure some abolitionist is behind the fire."

"Oh, my dear! That was old Bubba Mins's place, wasn't it?"

"Yes. My—my overseer, Thad Greene, saw him literally tumble out of the burning house—afire himself all over!"

"And you know for a fact that no abolitionist arsonist set it afire."

"We know that. My overseer found the still smoldering live oak log on the far side of the old man's parlor. The log had simply rolled off the fire and everything caught and was destroyed."

"And your overseer is trustworthy?"

"What? Oh, yes! In fact, he's with me today in Savannah. He's on Commerce Row right now talking, I hope, to your longtime friend Mark Browning."

"How very interesting, Abby! Does he know Mark?"

"Slightly. The two, according to Thad, seemed to have a lot in common. They're both Northerners. Thad holds a degree in business from the University of Pennsylvania—and I know you're wondering, then, why he's a mere overseer. Well, he isn't a mere overseer. I'm going to marry him and that's the other reason I'm here to get your advice."

"Why me, Abby?"

"Because during our first visit, you convinced me that you, maybe more than any other woman I've ever known, loved your husband. You may not remember the things you told me, but I do and I need one other bit of counsel. My late husband, Eli Allyn, was drowned in a storm in November of 1858. I loved him, but I now know that love was more respect than romance. I held a childhood dream of being the mistress of a lavish Southern plantation. I know that sounds silly coming from someone born in Boston, but it must have been the romance in the novels I read after hours as a schoolgirl. At any rate, I convinced myself that I loved Eli because he had just bought a coastal rice plantation. After we married and moved to Darien, I discovered that he never discussed anything—was in no way a communicator—but he *was* good to me. He left me everything he owned. I have more than enough to live on for the rest of my days, but I knew even before I met his overseer, Thad Greene, that I did not love the man I married. Not as a woman can love a man. I knew almost the instant I met Thad that I could—that I probably did already love him. And, Miss Eliza, he loves me the same way. I have no doubt whatever that if God picks out marriage partners, he picked Thad for me. What I need to know from you is how long we should wait to avoid being slandered by the good folk of Darien."

Eliza Mackay thought a minute. " 'Slandered' is a strong word. I take it you mean that you need me to tell you the customary length of time down here."

"Please."

"Normally, the appropriate length of time varies with the stiffness of each person's neck—or upbringing. But listen, Abby, if you're sure you want to spend the remainder of your life with this man, marry him at once! If I let myself, I can still grieve for every hour my Robert and I were not together once we knew of our love. You and Thad must know too. Don't wait any longer, Abby. You've both come to the end of your waiting time."

"How did you know we've been calling this endless period our—waiting time?"

"I didn't, but I know that after forty-four years there are days when I believe with all my heart that I can't wait another hour to see my Robert again. Go to Thad, Abby! Mark Browning's offices are easy to find on Commerce Row. And don't bother being polite . . . just go. Now."

Standing abruptly, Abby could hear her own heart pound. Then, on impulse, she gave Miss Eliza Mackay another hard hug and a kiss. "Do you have any idea what you've done for me, beautiful lady? Maybe I can't free my people right now, but you've set me free. Do you know that?"

Laughing the happiest laugh Abby could remember, Miss Eliza said, "Go, child! Mark will tell me about his visit with Thad. Don't bother with amenities. Grab your cloak, run to my front door, down the steps, and hurry straight to hunt until you find Thad—then marry the man at the earliest possible minute!"

On her way to the front door, Abby could hear the still lovely voice call out, "Take my word for it, your waiting time is over!"

Afterword

Until I am faced with the actual numbers, I find it hard to believe that by the time you have this book to read more than thirty-five years will have passed since my best friend, Joyce Blackburn, and I began the extensive research for my first novel, *The Beloved Invader*. With Joyce's expert help and that of many others through the years, I have spent countless hours, days, weeks, and months attempting to *learn* a little something of what it must have been like to live in the nineteenth century. A fascinating search for me and, of course, I feel I have only scratched the surface, so I long foolishly for thirty-five more years to work.

Many of you have written that you like my work because it is about the lives of real people with real names and real joys and heartbreaks whose graves can still be found and visited along the Georgia-Florida coast. But love scenes and family confidences are not recorded in any courthouse or archive, so many of the stories about these families have to come from my own novelist's imagination.

And if you have read my Savannah Quartet, for example, you could also be one of those loyal readers who write that Mark Browning and his family are favorites of yours. Well, they are all straight out of my head. And one dear lady even vows she still prays for Mark Browning as though he had been an actual person. To me, he was and is real.

Well, as with Mark Browning, Abby and Thad in this book are also "mine"—based on extensive reading of old letters from their nineteenth-century period.

The *real* people whom I've made Abby's friends are Dr. James Holmes, his wife, Susan, their children, and his cousin, Oliver Wendell Holmes; Port Collector Woodford Mabry and his wife, Laura; the irresistible world-famous British actress Fanny Kemble; and Miss Eliza Mackay of Savannah.

This eighty-year-old novelist has again tried her wings with sheer fiction, something I have wanted to do since I wrote the Savannah Quartet. However, there was no need to fictionize about the picturesque little town of Darien, Georgia, because shortly after Joyce Blackburn and I built our home on St. Simons Island—Darien is a mere eighteen miles north on Route 17—one of our favorite relaxations was taking a picnic outing to the Ridge beyond Darien and roaming the country roads and the old town's interesting streets. We still love the old Scottish city (once named New Inverness) and find its people warm and welcoming.

I certainly could not have written *The Waiting Time* nor could my dear friend and principal researcher, Nancy Goshorn, have oriented me in the area and its history without the expertise and ready helpfulness of an informed, appealing young man named Buddy Sullivan. Buddy, for years the editor of the *Darien News*, has spent much of his adult life learning the colorful history of McIntosh County, Georgia, of which Darien is the county seat. Of course, Buddy has had access to all courthouse records, those of the excellent Darien library and the *News*'s files. With remarkable skill and readability, he wrote a definitive book titled *Early Days on the Georgia Tidewater* (Darien, Georgia: McIntosh Board of Commissioners, 1990). I used the book extensively and wish I knew its riches as well as does Nancy, who with me spent a memorable day with Buddy learning the feel and ambiance of the old city. We relied on Buddy during this book and will make even more use of his familiarity with the Georgia Tidewater in the sequel to *The Waiting Time*. The "waiting time" ends for Abby and Thad—two of my favorite lovers—but not for the land they both cherished. In 1860, the United States was still waiting.

My longtime friend Mr. Malcolm Bell, whose knowledge I revere, once more came to my rescue and enlightened me on the often dark, shadowy truths surrounding the thoughts and actions of slaves by referencing exact pages from his captivating and scholarly book *Major Butler's Legacy* (Athens: University of Georgia Press, 1987). I owe this gentleman so much and I hope my novel partially satisfies this debt.

Perhaps a good-natured sense of humor is one of God's finest gifts to anyone and He was generous with Fred Bentley, prominent Marietta, Georgia, attorney and his lovable wife, Sara, who tolerates Fred and me with remarkable grace. Probably no one is better respected than Fred for his knowledge of the history of Georgia's up-country. And I trust no one will be confused by my use of his name once again in this book for one of my fictional characters. From the Savannah Quartet to *Beauty from Ashes*, the third book of the Georgia Trilogy, "Lawyer Bentley" moved from Cassville to Marietta, and in *The Waiting Time* we find him in Darien, Georgia, serving as Abigail Allyn's lawyer! Thanks, Fred, for your willingness to move from pillar to post to serve my plot.

For their excellent help in research for still another book, Nancy Goshorn joins me in thanking Frances Kane, director of the St. Simons Public Library, and her fine staff; at the Brunswick-Glynn Regional Library, director Jim Darby, Marcia Hodges, Dorothy Houseal, and Diane Jackson; at the Georgia Historical Society in Savannah, we thank the director and our friend Anne Smith, Eileen Ielmini, and Frank Wheeler; at the Clara Gould Library of Brunswick College, director Al Spivey, Ginny Boyd, and Jamie Merwin; and in the archives of St. Simons's own Coastal Georgia Historical Society, of which I am a charter member, we thank director Linda King, curator Pat Morris, and Robert Wyllie. In their excellent display of rice fields at Hofwyl-Broadfield Plantation, under Superintendent William Rivers, we were greatly helped by Jackie Edwards, Singleton Butler, and Faye Cowart. I must also thank Charlene Tribble, Gene Greneker, Jimmie and Ben Harnsberger, and Burnette Vanstory for their singular encouragement and belief in me book after book. And I give special thanks to my great-hearted doctor, Bill Hitt, whose idea it was to include one of his favorite nineteenth-century "medical colleagues," James Holmes (nicknamed Dr. Bullie) of Darien, Georgia.

A big, happy welcome to Doubleday's new president, Arlene Friedman, who has generously continued the policy of engaging my dear friend and favorite editor Carolyn Blakemore for me. Having Carolyn with me to edit this book means far more than even she knows. And Arlene's presence completes a creative circle, since she, Carolyn, and my absolutely indispensable agent–literary manager, Lila Karpf, have known and respected one another for many years.

With special pleasure, I thank Whitney Cookman, Marysarah Quinn, and Rob Wood for their artistic sensitivity in the designing of my books. They bring type and book jackets alive! Jack Lynch carefully handled the always tedious, difficult work of copy-editing. The directors and staff of all Doubleday departments are still with me for my hardcover editions and all are still my professionally talented friends. I must add the name of Frances Jones, my in-house editor, who came aboard when Arlene Friedman took on the duties of president and publisher of Doubleday. Frances makes me believe she truly likes my work and I hope she believes how much I like her.

Another development in the ever changing world of New York publishing pleases me greatly and has turned out to be one key to my having fun again in the work I love so much: St. Martin's Press will be, so far as I know, my paperback publisher from now on, and if my contacts with president Sally Richardson, vice president Matthew Shear,

THE WAITING TIME · 339

in-house editor Jennifer Enderlin, and her assistant, Amy Kolonik, tell me anything, it is that this is one of the best moves my beloved agent, Lila Karpf, has made in my behalf. This may all sound confusing but it's the publishing world today and I anticipate fun and good things to come because I plan at least one more book about Abby and Thad.

I know that each person whose name would normally appear here in a paragraph of thanks will understand the limitations of time and space at this writing and continue their daily encouragement and love. You are each special to me in a way that only you know.

Over and over again in these Afterwords, I have tried to express my gratitude for the gift of one of the most outstanding agents in the publishing business, Lila Karpf. My respect for her, my trust in her, my dependence on her excellent judgment in making my book decisions, know no bounds. Aside from that, I love her as my real friend and enjoy her almost magical way of understanding the "feel" of my life on St. Simons Island. It was Lila who gave the name "Genie's Support Group" to the superior corps of people who keep me going day to day. Joyce Blackburn, who has been my best friend as long as I've known that God knows me as I really am, again, in the midst of her own busy writing schedule, went over *The Waiting Time* line by line. And as usual she made me sound better than I am. There is also Nancy Goshorn, who truly makes the books possible now by skillfully doing all my research, and, out of regard for my impaired vision, she copies entire chapters in large print—spaced so that I can make sense of her knowledge of what I do and do not need to know. And, of course, I am still much blessed to have Eileen Humphlett as my "Overqualified Keeper" and full-time assistant. She has learned the publishing world in far more perceptive detail than I'll ever know it and has been involved in the editing of this book from the rough draft through the final manuscript. Eileen, like Nancy and Joyce, is my wholly trusted and loving friend without whom there would be no more novels from me.

With all my heart, I hope you've noticed the dedication page for *The Waiting Time*. I have never dedicated a book to anyone with more joy and gratitude than this one, which I give wholly, and with all the love and admiration there is, to Sarah Bell Edmond. She not only knows every nook and cranny of my beloved house in the St. Simons woods, but definitely understands me as I am. Aside from the above-mentioned members of my Support Group, I consider Sarah Bell one of my most perceptive and test-worthy readers because after all these years, I know that if she is absorbed in one of my manuscripts, you will be. She not only reads with critical intelligence; she seems (happily for me) not to forget that we "talked" it while she was doing her own good work around me in my office. God gave me the shining gift of sharing thoughts and feelings with this wise, sensitive, humor-filled person. He gave me Sarah Bell and with a heart full of love, I give her this book.

(Everything I've written about Sarah Bell is true, but one of her most attractive features is her total loyalty to *our* Atlanta Braves baseball team. I certainly couldn't function as I do without her and, whether the Braves know it or not, neither could they.)

I would also write in a state of futility without my prized and true friends in the nation's bookstores, without my Doubleday and St. Martin's sales reps, and certainly without each and every one of you, my readers.

There are a few graves to find for those of you who enjoy searching. Darien, Georgia, has, to me at least, a special charm of its own, certainly when one ventures off overbuilt, busy Route 17 onto the old town streets. If you inquire of the pleasant folk at the Welcome Center on Fort King George Drive, you will be directed to picturesque St. Andrew's Cemetery, where you will find the gravestones of Dr. Bullie (James Holmes), his wife, Susan, their little daughter, Susan Florida, who died in her father's arms as a child, and that of her brother, James Edward Holmes. Pierce Butler Holmes, the eldest son, was killed during the Civil War in Virginia and is buried at Thornrose Cemetery in Staunton, Virginia. Dr. Bullie's home on the Ridge has been lovingly restored, and the Mabrys, so far as we could learn, left Darien during the upheaval of the war and we have no trace of their burial place, but their Darien house still stands (saved evidently because they were Unionists) on the corner of Adams and Rittenhouse streets.

After taking a few weeks for what my dear late friend Easter Straker used to call "maintenance," I will begin the sequel to the love story I have come to care about deeply—that of Abby and Thad. One thing is certain: As long as my writing energy lasts, you can know it is devoted to you, my valued readers, uppermost in my mind and always in my heart.

Eugenia Price
St. Simons Island, Georgia

AFTER
The Waiting Time

Joyce Knight Blackburn

By the time Genie began writing this book, the threat of blindness and waning vitality became more and more a battle. She banged her faithful old Olympia mercilessly and in the next room, listening, I "felt" her fury. Then I would hear her laugh at herself as her mind raced ahead imagining the next scene. She would begin again. Her raw courage awed me.

If ever an author was devoted to her craft and to her readers, Eugenia Price was. Her reputation for that quality of devotion is legendary.

Her publishers praised her professionalism: "Never temperamental." "Fulfilled contracts on time." In fact, the manuscript of this novel arrived at Doubleday ahead of her deadline. It is almost impossible to imagine the discipline which that required.

Whether speaking to an audience or writing her books, clarity and communication were Genie's vivid gifts. She shared her creative thoughts, her "humble dogmatic opinions," her human failings, her faith, her exuberant joy of living. Many of you knew her charm and compassion firsthand. Many more of you have written, "I haven't met you,

Genie, but you are my dear friend." The paradox is, she was a distinctly private person.

Those of us who worked intimately with her valued her complex, agile mind, her wit, her optimism (sometimes unrealistic), her generosity of spirit. She could be childlike and sophisticated, sensitive and tough, natural and eccentric. "One benefit of getting old is to be as eccentric as I please," she said. And she was!

One of the worst tragedies a writer can suffer is loss of sight. During our thirty-six years together, reading was our favorite pastime and writing was Genie's bliss, her consuming passion. I'll never forget the moment she complained of a sharp pain in her left eye and it was determined by specialists that a minute stroke had caused a vision field defect. That was three years ago. Nothing was ever the same after that. At first, the deterioration was gradual and, though it was frustrating, Genie refused to slow down. She completed *Beauty from Ashes* despite her vision problem and while undergoing radiation treatment for lung cancer. She was grateful when remission was pronounced later that year but it was the enormous effort of trying to *see* that plagued her most and depleted her energies.

By March of 1996, Genie could no longer come downstairs to invent her matchless vermicelli sauce. Our longtime breakfast ritual upstairs reversed. Instead of making the coffee and serving me in bed—such luxury—I now opened the shutters, made the "instant," and served her at her desk. It took a valiant effort for her to move from her desk to the comfortable chair in my room.

The chronic "writers' back pain" intense, her vision a blur, she worked. Fortitude wrote *The Waiting Time* and once the Afterword was put down, Genie started a second novel about Abby and Thad. "It has no tempo, no life!" she protested. But she tried. One afternoon, after completing a rewrite on Chapter Two, she asked me to sit with her. "I can't see," she said. "I can't work. Oh, God, let me die." Her prayer was answered a few days later, May 28, 1996, when she died of congestive heart failure—as had her mother. She would have been eighty on June 22.

On that day, we celebrated her life among us. And her On-Going Life, her venture into infinite Joy. The following words are carved on her stone in Christ Churchyard, Frederica:

> *EUGENIA PRICE*
> *JUNE 22, 1916—MAY 28, 1996*
>
> *AFTER HER CONVERSION TO JESUS CHRIST,*
> *OCTOBER 2, 1949, SHE WROTE*
> *"LIGHT . . .*
> *AND ETERNITY*
> *AND LOVE*
> *AND ALL*
> *ARE MINE*
> *AT LAST."*